FIVE CROWS
SILVER

VERNON OICKLE

MacIntyre Purcell Publishing Inc.

MacIntyre Purcell Publishing Inc.
194 Hospital Rd.
Lunenburg, Nova Scotia
B0J 2C0
(902) 640-3350

www.macintyrepurcell.com
info@macintyrepurcell.com

Printed and bound in Canada by Marquis.

Design and layout by Alex Hickey
Cover by Adam Murray
Author photo by Kenny Veinot
Edited by Cynthia McMurray

Library and Archives Canada Cataloguing in Publication

Oickle, Vernon, 1961-, author
        Five crows silver / Vernon Oickle.

Issued in print and electronic formats.
ISBN 978-1-77276-058-3 (softcover).--ISBN 978-1-77276-059-0
(ebook).--ISBN 978-1-77276-060-6 (digital)

        I. Title.

PS8579.I37F58 2017   C813'.6   C2016-908056-0
                                             C2016-908057-9

MacIntyre Purcell Publishing Inc. recognizes
the support of the Province of Nova Scotia
through the Department of Communities,
Culture & Heritage.

Funded by the Government of Canada

NOVA SCOTIA

Canadä

This one is for Gail, my number one fan!

One crow sorrow, two crows joy;
three crows a letter, four crows a boy;
five crows silver, six crows gold;
seven crows a secret, yet to be told;
eight crows for a wish;
nine crows for a kiss;
ten crows for a time of joyous bliss.

— A common Maritime saying

Prologue

They watch silently from their perch high atop the towering pine tree. The branches sway in the biting January wind, dancing softly with each icy gust. They would warn the small girl if they could, but they know she doesn't see them. Their pellet-like eyes follow his every move as he stalks his prey and then pounces, like a wolf cornering its next meal. The five black sentinels watch as the man quickly subdues the small child, his powerful arms too strong for her to break free.

As he carries her, kicking and screaming, to the van, they sound the alarm, their long, black beaks uttering a frantic call for help. Their raucous caws slice through the stillness of the frigid air. And they suddenly spring from their roost as they watch the van speed away from the secluded schoolyard, vanishing into the waning light of the late afternoon.

To some, the sight of their ebony wings beating in tandem is beautiful, almost spiritual. But for the birds, as the cool winter current catches their powerful wings, their only agenda is to ride the breeze to their next destination.

Something most foul is afoot here in this small Nova Scotian town and they must get help. And they know exactly where to find it.

Chapter 1

February 12

The sun peeks over the horizon, stretching slender fingers of light across the frozen landscape. A lone jogger makes his way along the abandoned trail still spotted with the remnants of light cast by the full moon. A few stars flicker in the crisp, clear sky, as though protesting the arrival of dawn.

With only the thud-thud-thud of his sneakers pounding on the frost-covered ground, he pushes on through the waning darkness, his lungs burning from the intense cold air he sucks between his gritted teeth. Clouds of white hang in the air like misshapen cotton balls with each breath he exhales. Always alert, his eyes scan the path in front of him, watching for anything that looks out of the ordinary. It's early, not even six yet, and most of the residents of this small seaside town are snug in their warm beds. The veteran RCMP officer hangs his head in a futile effort to fight the biting wind that has quickly turned his exposed skin blotchy red. He jogs at least ten kilometres every morning and today, two days before his fifty-fifth birthday, is no exception.

"Half way there," Sergeant Greg Paris pants, sucking in another lungful of the salty, cold air. He likes the sound of the crusted snow as it crunches under his size thirteen Nikes. It makes him feel powerful somehow.

He treads carefully over the slippery patches, purposefully planting his feet into the frozen ground. He takes another deep breath and cringes as the minuscule ice crystals scratch their way into his aching lungs, reminding him of how much he hates running in the winter. Greg Paris is no slouch though and running has been a daily routine for twenty-five years. And he is committed—weather be damn.

Following the winding trail along the former CN rail bed that twists along the banks of the frozen Mersey River, Greg finds himself contemplating his future. A lot can change in twelve months, he thinks, looking back at the events that led one of the country's foremost experts in forensic psychology to command a small detachment in rural Nova Scotia.

While Greg doesn't believe in 'chance,' he has to admit that winding up in 'the sticks' as he used to call Liverpool, was definitely not on his agenda. He originally approached his superiors in Ottawa with the intention of transferring to Halifax, a much smaller city, but one that still had an actual Starbucks. After spending most of his career investigating deranged serial killers, sadistic rapists, perverts, arsonists and murderers, Greg had decided it was time for a break. He hoped that by relocating to Nova Scotia with his second wife, Andrea, and her four-year-old daughter, Lucy, they could settle down and establish a routine that would allow them to spend quality time together. Things didn't go according to plan, however—they never seem to—and he ended up assuming control of the thirteen-member Liverpool detachment while his best friend, Cliff Graham, recovered from a heart attack.

Life in Liverpool got off to a rocky start when Greg and his new family of two years moved into a small cottage next to a lake in the nearby village of Greenfield. Originally, it was to be their vacation getaway, but the cabin brought nothing but pain and bad memories—Lucy almost died, not once, but twice there.

Greg picks up the pace as he thinks about how close his daughter came to death's door. *Thud, thud, thud.* His feet seem heavy as he moves across the frost-covered planks of the wooden bridge that crosses the Mersey River. The old bridge is a landmark in the small town. In the once thriving community it served as a pathway for freight and passenger trains. Today, it plays a subtler role and is used for recreational purposes. Mist rises from the water below, caressing his skin and embracing him in a dampness that permeates his insulated running suit.

He shivers. It's freaking cold, he thinks, as the water trickles from his eyes and freezes on his cheeks. Wiping at the tiny frozen hairs in his nose with his gloved right hand, he wonders why he pushes himself to do this everyday when it would be more tempting to stay in bed, snuggled up to his beautiful wife.

When the superintendent at the RCMP's central headquarters in Halifax asked him to stand in for Cliff, Greg didn't know what to do. Cliff Graham has been his best friend for 25 years. They went through basic training together. His first reaction was to reject the offer—he didn't want to step on Cliff's toes—but he eventually took the temporary post, urged to do so by his best friend. He assumed command at the beginning of January and now, more than a month later, he's settled into the daily routine, which he's decided he likes. But there are definitely challenges.

Greg speeds across the bridge. The wind licks at his eyes, causing them to water again. He raises his hand to wipe them, but the water has already frozen, leaving tiny icicles on his eyelashes.

He enjoys the steady pace and regular routine of the small detachment and will take it over the fast-paced, erratic work at HQ in Ottawa. He never knew when a heinous crime would require him to jump on a plane and fly thousands of miles to investigate the mutilation of a child or the abduction of a young woman. Greg Paris is known throughout North America as one of the best forensic investigators on the RCMP force and his expertise has even been sought by other police forces, including the FBI. But fame has a cost, and lately Greg fears all the gore he has seen over the years is taking its toll. He is beginning to feel the repercussions—'burn out' as the professionals call it. He just calls it bone-tired. He's always thrown himself into his work, but after more than two decades of studying such depravity, he knows he has to step back in order to preserve his sanity. Someday he may go back, but not now. For now, this small town is his 'break' from that dark world.

He reaches the midway point of the wooden bridge. He sucks in another breath of icy air through his nose and immediately regrets it as it burns his nostrils. He tries to exhale through his mouth and a visible puff of condensation escapes his lips. He tries to wipe his eyes again with the back of his hand, but quickly stops as the tiny icicles bite into his tender skin. This is just insane, he thinks, kicking himself for leaving the warmth of his house.

He tries to take his mind off the cold and thinks back to when he first arrived in the small town of roughly four thousand people. It took him a while to adjust, but now he admittedly likes it here. Everyone has welcomed him and his family into the fold, making them feel like they've lived here for years. Despite a rough start, Andrea seems to have finally settled in and now even works two mornings a week at one of the local daycare centres. He's glad she's making new friends. And then, last night, she surprised him with an early birthday present — she is pregnant.

Although he's excited at the prospect of having a child at fifty-five, he thought that part of his life was long behind him. He is content helping Andrea raise her daughter, Lucy, the sweet little girl he has embraced as his own. However, after the news sunk in last night, he realized just how excited he is at the thought of having a baby. He's actually finding it hard to contain his happiness.

He knows he's been lucky to find true love, not once, but twice in his lifetime. He also knows some people never find it at all. When his first wife, Jen, died of breast cancer five years ago, he withdrew, throwing himself completely into his work. He never dreamed he would ever find another woman he wanted to spend his life with. But after a mutual friend introduced him to Andrea, an elementary school teacher raising a small child on her own, he knew good fortune had smiled on him and he had found happiness yet again. It didn't matter to him that she was 20 years younger. He was impressed with her right away. She is smart, funny, and affectionate and a good mother, all qualities he admires. And, he admits, it doesn't hurt that she is one of the two most beautiful women he has ever seen.

Glancing down as he nears the end of the bridge, he notices the lace on his right runner has come untied. He stops and slips his gloves off then raises his long leg to the railing. He's just finishing the loop when he hears an all too familiar sound. Dropping his leg with a loud thud, he spins around. He instinctively jumps back, startled to see five large, black crows have taken up positions on the opposite railing.

"Shit," he says, backing up against the railing, the frost-covered wood feeling slippery to his bare hands.

Eyeing the birds that are now staring at him from their perch, Greg breathes deeply, unsure of what he should do. He's heard too many stories about the weird crow behaviour that's become synonymous with this town and he's witnessed some of their antics first hand.

"Where in the hell did you guys come from?" he finally whispers, another white cloud hanging in the air as he speaks.

The crows remain silent. Greg eyes the birds that look statuesque, as though frozen in the icy, morning air. He's not afraid, although good sense tells him he should be. He can't shake the feeling they are trying to reach out to him. Over the past several years, the crows have wreaked havoc on the residents of Liverpool. They have left people shaken to the core. They have even left many of the local residents questioning the world around them, or worse—left some of them dead.

Unable to think of something else to say, Greg whispers, keeping his voice steady. "You guys are up and about early this morning." He keeps his eyes glued to the dark-feathered creatures that have him backed up against the bridge railing. He wishes he could slip his gloves back on as the cold wind bites at his exposed skin, but he hesitates to make any sudden movement for fear of startling the ebony visitors. "What do you want?" He can't believe he's actually talking to the birds.

The crows remain silent. Their beady eyes blink in perfect unison and Greg shudders.

Seconds later, one of the crows—maybe the leader, Greg wonders—emits a low-pitched caw and the officer pulls his tall, lean body even closer to the railing. Unsure of the birds' intentions, his instincts tell him to become a small target or at least as small as a six-foot-three, two-hundred-and-ten pound man can make himself.

"I don't understand," he whispers, honing in on the majestic bird that seems larger than its brethren.

As the other birds in the group suddenly become still again, the leader begins to prance along the railing.

Greg shakes his head. "I don't get it," he tells the larger bird, its black feathers now glistening a purplish-green as the sun's early rays begin to caress its sleek, muscular body.

The crow stops. It stares at the man and then, in a surprise move, springs from the railing and swoops to the bridge deck where it moves closer to him. Greg can't shake the feeling that the bird is frustrated with him.

"I'm sorry," he says, forcing himself to remain still for fear of startling the bird further as it prances along the frost-covered wood. "I wish I knew what you wanted."

Almost as if in a last futile attempt to connect with the human, the crow springs from the bridge and lands immediately next to him on the railing.

"Hey," Greg says, quickly pulling back his frozen hands and bringing them up to his face. "Don't get mad at me. I just don't understand what you want."

Greg slowly lowers his hands. His eyes lock with the bird and he feels a cold chill suddenly run up his spine. He knows this isn't natural behaviour for a wild bird, although he also accepts that in this town, anything is possible when it comes to the crows. Then, as suddenly as they appeared, the four remaining crows spring from their roost and, catching an early morning current, soar upward, swooping and gliding in the cold air. They call out, as if beckoning their comrade to join them. As the fifth crow blinks to break the stare down, it springs from the railing and climbs into the breeze as it follows the others.

Watching the five crows disappear amid a growth of spruce and fir trees that tower over the riverbank, Greg shivers again. He finally brings his hands to his mouth and blows warm air into them. Then, pulling his gloves back over his hands, he resumes his jog, but he maintains a close watch on the clump of trees. If the crows return he wants to see them.

Leaving the bridge, his Nikes pound the frozen ground, which is more like concrete than a dirt trail. He heads up a small hill toward the home that he and Andrea are renting while he fulfills his commitment at the detachment. Thinking about what his day will bring, Greg decides he will have to make time to visit with his friend, Cliff. He knows that if there is one person in this town who will want to hear about his encounter with the crows, it will be his buddy.

Hopefully, he can shed some light on what it means when five crows come to roost.

Chapter 2

"It's seventeen minutes after six on this twelfth day of February," the muffled voice drones from the radio on the kitchen counter next to the fridge. "If you're venturing outside this morning, you'd better bundle up good and tight. It's cold. Minus thirteen cold. But with the wind chill, it's going to feel more like minus twenty-eight and we don't expect things to warm up much."

"God dammed winter." Greg groans. "Who in their right mind prays for this crap?" he says under his breath.

"Are you already complaining?" Andrea says, emerging from the hallway. "You know there's nothing you can do about the weather. What happened to you? There was a time when winter didn't bother you so much." She smirks. "Besides, it's early and it's almost your birthday. Can't you just try to accept it?" she teases him as she wraps her arms around his tight waist, accentuated by the running pants and T-shirt he had worn on his earlier jog around the river.

He shrugs but says nothing, staring at the coffee pot as if his steely glare will make the machine brew faster.

"Did you have a good run?" she asks.

"I did," he nods and then adds, "I know there's nothing I can do about the weather." He smiles at his wife of two years and pulls her close and kisses her forehead. "But that doesn't mean I have to like it." She chuckles and squeezes him again. "What are you doing up at this hour?"

"I have things to do today," she answers, snuggling her head into his broad, muscular chest. "You know I don't sleep late."

Holding her close, he lifts her face to his and then kisses her gently on the lips.

"And if you like the cold, folks," the annoying voice of the DJ quips, obviously amused by his feeble attempt to make a joke of the bad weather, "then you'll really like this. We now have a heavy snowfall warning for later this afternoon and overnight as a Nor'easter blows in from New England. The snow will begin sometime after lunch but is expected to be falling heavy by this evening. Looks like we could get anywhere from twenty to twenty-five centimeters over the next twenty-four hours."

"Jesus Christ," Greg blurts out, pulling away from his wife. "That's just great. That's all we need today. Can it get any worse?"

The DJ's perky, youthful voice grates on the seasoned police officer's nerves. "We can expect the storm to hit the province up Yarmouth way by early afternoon then make its way up the coast where it will stall over much of southern Nova Scotia. It's going to leave a mess before it moves off toward Newfoundland by early to-morrow morning. So, if you have plans to travel later today, you may want to put them on hold, or leave right now. Guess that's winter in Nova Scotia, folks," he adds.

Another useless attempt at humour, Greg thinks, an exaggerated pout crossing his face.

"Yeah, winter in Nova Scotia. Isn't it great?" Greg sighs, reaching for the off switch on the radio. "That'll be enough of that crap." He smacks the button and then reaches for a coffee cup in the cupboard.

"This is not going to be a good day," he whispers, pouring a cup of black coffee for himself. "Want one," he asks his wife who has been studying her husband's reaction for the past few minutes.

"Sure," she nods, heading toward the main level bathroom of their three-bedroom, two-storey house. Since they are renting, most of their belongings are still in storage, so the house is modestly furnished. Until he is assigned a more permanent position, Greg feels there is no reason to set roots by buying a home.

Andrea can tell something other than the crappy weather is bothering her husband, but she decides not to press him on it. "That would be great, thanks, but I've got to pee first. Go ahead and make it and I'll be right back," she calls over her shoulder as she darts into the washroom.

"That's good stuff," he sighs, reveling in the warm sensation as the first gulp of the intense liquid rushes down his throat. Coffee is his one guilty pleasure—and the stronger the better as far as he is concerned. *Don't know how I could ever give it up. Now that would kill me for sure*, he muses, thinking about his friend, Cliff, who has to follow a strict dietary regiment since his heart surgery in December.

He savours another gulp as he watches the toaster, waiting for his whole-wheat bread to brown. Greg knows he takes better care of himself than Cliff ever did, so he quickly dismisses any guilt about the coffee. He becomes lost in the glow of the red-hot element as it toasts the bread, his thoughts returning to the crows on the trail bridge earlier this morning. The phone rings and he instinctively knows the call isn't good news. Calls at this hour seldom are.

Quickly picking up the phone before it can ring a second time he says, "Greg Paris here."

"Good morning, Sir." It's Constable Emily Murphy, a five-year veteran of the RCMP who transferred to Liverpool from Fredericton three years ago. "Sorry to bother you at this hour, Sir. Hope I didn't wake you, but I know you go for your run early, so I just took a chance on catching you."

"No problem, Constable. I just got back and poured myself a cup of coffee," he reassures the young officer. He takes another sip of the hot liquid—ambrosia to his lips.

"What's up?"

"Well, Sir, I hate to tell you this." She forces herself to sound calm and collected—professional, but her urgent tone quickly betrays her. "We have a body."

"Where?" Unlike the young officer, Greg remains calm, calling upon his years of experience and training to help him assimilate the news. "Male or female?"

"Young female, Sir," the officer answers. "Beach Meadows . . . near the water's edge."

"Any doubt it's a homicide?"

"No doubt, Sir."

"Okay . . ." He pauses and thinks about his next command. "You stay put. I'll be there in about half an hour. Don't let anyone near the body . . . And don't touch a thing," Greg orders the officer. "And Emily," he adds. "Do me and yourself a favour. Don't look at it, okay?"

"But I've already seen it, Sir," she replies, her voice cracking slightly.

"I know, but don't dwell on it, all right? Just sit tight in your cruiser until I get there, but keep a keen eye out. We don't need anyone messing things up, not that anyone should be around at this time of day."

"Sure . . . Okay." She pushed the End Call button on her cell.

"Shit." Greg sighs, exhaling forcefully as he swishes the coffee around in his cup before taking another gulp of the hot, black liquid that will no doubt be his lifeline today.

Greg knows the young constable is trained to deal with these types of incidents, but he also knows it's difficult to witness such gruesome sights first-hand, especially if it involves a young victim. He remembers his first murder scene and he knows how difficult it is to get something like that out of your head. It's like they become permanently etched in your mind—and once there, they tend to stay with you for the rest of your life, lingering, sometimes revealing their ugliness when you least expect it. It's inevitable, that's just the way it is, and eventually all police officers must face death straight in the face, but he regrets Constable Murphy had to take the call. After reviewing her personnel file, as he does with all the officers in his command, he knows, that despite her years of service, this is her first homicide investigation. He is concerned for her, as he would be for any officer dispatched to such a scene.

Mechanically spreading a generous helping of margarine onto his toast, he feels a slight pang of remorse rise in the pit of his stomach as he stuffs half the slice in his mouth, quickly chewing before following it with a coffee chaser. Stuffing the other half into his mouth and then draining the coffee mug, he wonders why people have to be so cruel and why there is so much violence in the world.

"What's up?" Andrea asks as she returns to the kitchen and finds him staring out the small window over the sink. She's lived with Greg long enough to know when something is going on with him. "You have that look," she says. "Who was that on the phone?"

"That look?" He raises his eyebrows and grins. "What look?"

"That look that tells me something's going on."

"You know me too well," he nods and winks. "That was Constable Murphy. I have to go. They've found a body."

"Oh my God." Her breath catches in her throat. "Can you tell me anything?"

"Not yet," he says as he places the empty cup into the stainless steel sink, turns on the tap and watches as it fills with warm water. "I've got to grab a quick shower and then head out."

"Are you okay?"

"I am," he says, giving her a quick kiss on the cheek as he passes her on his way to the bathroom. "I don't know any details. All I know is the victim is a young female."

*****

Greg pulls the heavy leather belt—with its force issued Smith & Wesson revolver secured in its holster, handcuffs and other necessary gear—around his trim waist. He then slips his mandatory bulletproof vest over his khaki uniform shirt and breathes deeply. He wishes such gear wasn't necessary, but he knows these weapons could be his only line of defense in a life-threatening situation. It's been a while since he's had to use his weapon, but if he had to he'd never hesitate to squeeze the trigger.

Sliding into his down-filled RCMP overcoat and placing his brown fur cap neatly on top his thick, black hair, Greg braces to greet the cold air as he pushes open the back door of his rental home and steps out into the early, winter morning. Thick bursts of warm air flow from his nose, forming small white puffs that float motionless, as though stranded in the frigid air. The stark, white snow crunches under his black, insulated boots, a sure sign it is far too cold to be outside, at least in Greg's thinking. He heads toward the cruiser he parked in his driveway not less than eight hours earlier after returning from a local budget meeting with town council. He can certainly empathize with Cliff's grumpy outburst each time he has to meet with the local government.

"Goddamn winter," Greg sputters as he scrapes the thick blanket of frost from the windshield, wishing there was someone with him this morning to share his misery—*because misery loves company*. He thinks it feels colder now than it did just half an hour ago when he was out for his run. Who in their right mind would wish for something like this?

Time to move south, he thinks, knowing that's about as likely as him winning the lottery—nice to dream, but not realistic.

After waiting several minutes for the heater to kick in as it struggles to warm up the car's interior, Greg backs out of the driveway and then heads along the town's main street, still quiet at this early hour. He guides the car over the town bridge along historic Bristol Avenue with its stately homes built in an earlier seafaring era. He then passes through the village of Brooklyn, a small settlement on the outskirts of Liverpool, with a heritage steeped in forestry and the pulp industry. As he passes over a small bridge, he shudders as the cold, morning mist rises eerily from the water's still surface, reminding him of some horror movie he's seen. The title eludes him, which is unusual for him—his memory is usually sharp—but he's distracted this morning, so that may explain it, he reasons.

Navigating the twisting and curving Shore Road, he notices many of the homes are in complete darkness as most everyone is still warmly snuggled into their beds, oblivious to the events unfolding in their neighbourhood. Travelling southeast along the road that's part of Nova Scotia's famed Lighthouse Route, Greg heads toward a picturesque coastal hamlet known as Beach Meadows where he is to meet with Constable Emily Murphy—a pretty woman, but he knows she is not to be underestimated because of her looks. As a trained RCMP officer he is sure she is more than qualified to handle most perpetrators, regardless of size and strength. In fact, he knows she is as capable as any other officer at the detachment and he would trust her for backup without hesitation.

"Dispatch, do you copy? Sergeant Greg Paris here from the Liverpool detachment," he says. "I am in transit."

"Yes, Sir," the woman's voice responds, her shrill tone slicing through the quiet within the police cruiser. And Greg wonders how anyone with such a voice could get a job on coms at dispatch. He has spent years studying people and he can tell a lot about people, even without seeing them. He's already decided this woman hates being on duty at this early hour.

"I'm on my way to the scene to meet Constable Murphy. If you haven't done so already, please notify H Division what's happening down here," Greg says into the mic. "Please inform them we need some assistance from Major Crimes and then notify the dog unit in Bedford. We'll want them down here ASAP. We need them fast, understand? We've got a lot to do today before the snow flies."

"Yes, Sir. . . . Out."

"Out," he answers, clicking off the mic and placing it back in its holder on the dash.

Ten minutes later, Sergeant Paris makes a right-hand turn off the Shore Road and follows a narrow gravel, unplowed road that leads him to the secluded dunes of Beach Meadows beach. In the middle of summer this place is a paradise with a sandy beach and crystal-clear water. In the middle of winter, however, it's a frozen, barren waste-land, a place he'd rather avoid at this time of day—or any time in the winter for that matter.

Over the tops of a cluster of spruce trees, their growth stunted from the salt water spray and sand, he sees the distinctive red and blue flashing lights from Constable Murphy's cruiser as they signal her location. As he approaches, he notices the vehicle is empty. His stomach immediately tightens.

"Shit, Emily. I thought I told you stay with the car," Greg says from concern, not anger.

Pulling alongside Constable Murphy's cruiser, he parks and turns off the engine, leaving the red and blue overhead lights flashing—like a beacon in a storm alerting anyone who sees them that something is seriously awry in this quaint seaside community. Exiting the car, he's immediately taken aback as the intense cold slaps his face like a two-by-four, causing his breath to catch in his throat and flash-freeze the tiny hairs in his nose. Gaining his footing on the ice-covered sand, he walks over to where he sees the young officer has stationed herself along the edge of the dunes at a place where the grass and beach collide. He grabs his collar tightly around his chin in a vain attempt to keep out the biting salt sea spray.

Damn cold, he whines to himself.

He reaches Constable Murphy's location on the dunes and im-mediately raises his voice over the blowing ocean wind—admittedly a little louder than he wished. "I thought I told you to stay in the cruiser?"

"I couldn't just sit there," the constable responds, hoping she hasn't angered her superior by disobeying the order.

"I didn't want you getting too close." He shows genuine concern for the young officer in his command. In the eerie pre-storm light of the early morning, Greg can see the tears in the constable's eyes. "Are you sure you're all right, Emily?"

"I'm fine, Sir."

"How do you stand the cold?" Greg tries to lighten the mood.

"I thought you Upper Canadians were used to the cold," Constable Murphy replies, hoping the sergeant will forgive her impertinence in disobeying a direct order.

"Not on your life," Greg responds, relieved the officer seems to be okay, for now at least. "I've hated the cold for as long as I can remember and I don't have plans to change my ways now."

"I never would have guessed," she says with a wry smile, a feeble attempt to avoid the horror that lies at their feet in the frozen sand.

"Are you really okay, Emily?" The seasoned officer asks again.

"Yes, Sir." He sees her nod in the dawn's early light. "As I said, I'm fine. Just felt drawn here, almost compelled."

"You sure? This isn't easy stuff we're dealing with."

"Yes, Sir," she insists. "I'm okay . . . really. Now, maybe we should get this done."

While Constable Murphy appreciates the concern from her superior officer, she doesn't like being treated like a rookie. Emily Murphy takes great pride in her natural abilities and resents anyone thinking otherwise, even if she knows that concern is well intentioned. She graduated from depot, second in her class, and she knows she can hold her own against any of the other officers at the detachment.

Sensing he may have pushed her too hard, he nods. "Okay, Constable. I didn't mean to offend you. You're a fine officer and I just don't want to lose you in the middle of this mess."

"You don't have to worry about me, Sir. And I'm sorry if I sounded sharp." Constable Murphy feels sheepish for raising her voice to her commanding officer. "I promise I will tell you if it gets to the point where I can't handle something."

"Point taken," he smiles back at her as a way of saying everything is okay between them. Knowing it's time to drop the subject, Greg asks, "Where is she, Constable?"

"Over there, between the two highest dunes." Constable Murphy points with her gloved left hand.

"Who found her?"

"A jogger who lives not too far from the beach," she explains. "He says he runs here every morning after coming home from work. That's when he stumbled over her. At first, he said he thought it was a piece of large driftwood or a clump of seaweed."

"What time was that?" Greg asks as he and Emily Murphy move toward the dunes, the frigid, icy wind from the Atlantic Ocean biting at their exposed faces, turning their cheeks bright red as the waves continue their incessant dance, crashing on the shore, one after the other in a never-ending game of tag.

"He called in the report just before five-twenty," she says, lighting their way with a flashlight and carefully placing her feet to avoid the areas where there are already footprints, and possible evidence. "He says that was about ten minutes after he got home from work. By the time I got here, talked with him, checked out the scene and called you, it took me almost forty minutes."

"Why didn't you call for backup sooner?"

"Didn't think I'd have to," she quickly answers, knowing the question is routine. "Based on the jogger's report, I knew whoever did this was long gone by the time I got here."

"That doesn't matter Constable," Greg says, following closely behind her and placing his feet in her footprints. "You never assume anything. I expect better from you just as I do all my officers. We don't know what we've got here. For all you knew, the killer could have still been here when you arrived. That's the first thing they teach you at depot—never go in alone. You know that, Emily."

"Yes, Sir. I know, but I was comfortable with my decision," she answers. "I assessed the situation and I am confident I made the right call. It was late and cold and I didn't want to bother you until I knew exactly what I had. I made a judgment call." She pauses and then adds, "As soon as I got here and saw this, I called you immediately."

"Next time, Constable, don't wait. Call as soon as you get a report of something like this."

"Yes, Sir." The officer understands she has breached protocol and Sergeant Paris is known to be a stickler for following the game plan as set out in the official rulebook. "I wonder how long she's been out here?"

"It will be hard to tell, but it's cold enough here that just about everything would have been frozen so our scene should be fairly well preserved. The only thing we need to be concerned about right now is the wind—and the freaking snow," he adds. "We're going to have to get a tent over the scene as fast as we can. I've already notified Division. They should have the ident team rolling by now. It's calling for heavy snow this afternoon, so we'll have to move quickly and get this place locked down before we lose potential evidence."

Following Constable Murphy to the dunes, Greg notes the length of time it takes for them to arrive. "Seven and a half minutes," he says, observing the digital display on the new watch Andrea and Lucy gave him for Christmas. "And we're not carrying anything heavy . . . like a body. It would have taken our guy a lot longer while transporting dead weight, even the weight of a child." He pauses and then says, "Unless he has super human strength, I'd guess it would have taken him at least another five minutes—maybe more—to get a body to this location from the parking lot."

"Maybe," she nods, "unless there was more than one of them."

"Good point," Greg concedes, pleased the officer has kept her wits about her. "We can't rule anything out and with this wind wiping around, it's likely all the footprints are long gone by now, or at least pushed around enough that we won't be able to tell how many there were."

"There," Constable Murphy says, coming to a standstill and pointing to a clump of dune grass, the brown strands covered in ice. "She's in there."

From where he stands next to the constable, Sergeant Paris can see the faint outline of a body dumped on the sand and grass.

"You stay here," he says. "By the way, what did you do with our witness?"

"His house is just five minutes down the road," she says. "Because it was so cold, I took an initial statement in my cruiser and then told him to go directly home. I instructed him to stay there until someone comes to talk to him. I figured we'd go by later and see him."

"Smart move. No need for three of us to freeze to death out

here," Greg smirks, instinctively rubbing his gloved hands together, as if hoping for warmth. "Man, it's cold," he sighs. "Have I ever told you how much I hate the cold?"

"No, I don't think you have, Sir," Constable Murphy replies, smirking. She knows the commander is trying to lighten the mood for her benefit. "I don't believe you did."

Leaving the young officer on the edge of the grass, Greg moves carefully toward the large, dark lump clearly evident in the light of the early sun. He stops and yells back to Emily, "Is our witness sure this wasn't here yesterday?"

"He says not," she replies, hoping her voice can be heard over the howling wind and crashing waves. "He runs every day along this same route and says he would have seen it if it had been there."

Approaching the form, Greg can now distinguish the outline of a tiny body. Getting closer, he sees it's the nude body of a white female—a child less than ten years old. Shining his flashlight on her face, he instantly recognizes the body as young Holly Conrad. She is the five-year-old, blonde-haired girl reported missing from her Windsor home more than a month ago. The Liverpool detachment, like all police forces in the province, had received a missing person's bulletin and Amber Alert, including a photo, so he's sure it's her. Realistically though, the Liverpool officer never expected to find the missing girl in his jurisdiction and he surely never thought they'd find her under these circumstances.

The missing girl was placed in the frozen sand with her arms folded across her chest, as if resting in a coffin. Greg wonders how such a young child goes from being reported snatched right out from under her parents' noses four weeks ago, to being found naked and dead on a deserted beach near Liverpool in the middle of winter?

"What is it, Sir?" the constable calls to him, her words barely audible over the howling wind whistling around his ears.

"It's not good," he answers. "I need you to go back to the cruiser and call for more officers. We need backup out here as quickly as possible. I want this place locked down within the half hour."

Chapter 3

Sergeant Greg Paris fights the urge to scream. His stomach tightens as he looks at the lifeless child lying face up in the frozen sand, her skin barely distinguishable from the stark snow that's gathered around her tiny body. Her long, blonde hair is pulled back neatly into a tight ponytail. Greg stares at her silky hair, knowing it was once lovingly brushed by her mother, as he often does with his own daughter. Now, the pieces of the long ponytail are frozen into thin strands, like bits of dry spaghetti. It's a gruesome picture by any comparison.

The image makes him think of his own four-year-old daughter who is still asleep in her bed, and he quickly crosses his chest, although he does not known why—he's not an outwardly religious man—but something about this scene makes him hope there is a higher justice of some sort.

No one should be treated like this, least of all a child, he thinks, wiping his eyes with his leather gloves. He can't help but compare the small discarded body to a bag of garbage, illegally dumped at the beach like he's often seen when he's taken Lucy to play in the sand.

"Hope you didn't suffer much," Greg whispers, knowing his words are wasted on the ears of this young victim. "I hope whoever did this to you showed you some mercy," he says to the corpse as he scans the body and realizes it appears the skin has been scrubbed clean, most likely in an effort to remove any trace evidence like hair and fibers. That tells him he's dealing with a cold and calculating killer, someone who knows some- thing about forensics—and he shudders.

Bending to get a closer look, he uses the butt end of his flashlight to poke the girl's leg. It's frozen solid. He doesn't need an autopsy to know the child has been dead for at least a day.

Scanning the naked body, Greg begins at her head and moves to her feet. His heart breaks for the child whose life was stolen before she even had a chance to begin living it. He tries to shake the thought from his head. He turns his attention back to the dead girl. Her lifeless body shows clear signs of rope burns around her wrists and ankles—she was obviously kept tied up by her abductor. He can also tell by the protrusion of her ribs that she was fed very little, if anything, during her captivity. There is no question this little girl was tortured before death rescued her from her captor.

"You poor baby," he says, struggling to keep his emotions under control.

Greg Paris bristles at the prospect of what this means. He knows the press will be all over this story when news breaks that the missing Windsor girl has been found dead and discarded on the beach. He also knows there will be a landslide of rumours and speculation and lots of questions. But there will be few answers—at this point, at least. He's worked on similar cases during his career as a forensic investigator and he knows there are always more questions than answers. Based on his cursory visual examination, however, he can say the perpetrator exerted complete and absolute control over this child and whoever has done this is a sociopath. Because sociopaths can easily disconnect from reality, essentially shutting off any emotions or reasoning of right and wrong, he knows they are dangerous and aren't likely to stop killing on their own. Like most sociopaths, this monster gets his thrill from the kill—like an addiction.

Sucking a deep breath of cold air into his lungs, he feels the toast and coffee churning in the pit of his stomach. Gulping in the air, he swallows hard to keep the mixture down as he hears Constable Emily Murphy approaching from behind, her boots crunching in the frozen sand and snow.

"This is the missing girl, isn't it?" she asks. He can barely hear Constable Murphy's voice over the rush of wind wiping around his head.

"Yes," he finally replies. "It's her."

"Goddamn it." Her voice is now much clearer as she inches toward the dunes and her commanding officer. "What kind of sick bastard would do something like this to a child?"

"Someone pretty twisted," Greg says, as Emily reaches the body and stands beside him. Her small body shields him slightly from the biting winds. "This is going to be big and it's going to attract a lot of attention."

"I'm sure," the constable agrees. "Any idea why someone would go to this much trouble to dispose of a body?"

"I've got lots of ideas," he says, the theories already forming. "But it's clear that whoever has done this has some remorse."

"Why would you say that?"

"Well, clearly the perp's first instinct was self-preservation and that's why the body was dumped here, a remote area with plenty of seclusion, especially this time of year," Greg says, continuing to study the girl's remains. The wind blows sand and snow around her body, as though oblivious to the poor child frozen to the ground. "But the fact that she was dumped in a place where she would eventually be found, and the way in which the body is posed, also tells me the person, or persons, responsible did have some remorse for what they've done."

"They should have," she says. "Anyone who would do something like this to a child has to be a perverted son of a bitch."

"Indeed," Greg agrees. Scanning the area around the body, he looks for clues he knows aren't there. He's hoping that perhaps the killer may have gotten careless and left something behind that might help them solve the crime, but based on the body's position, he doesn't think it's very likely. He can see the killer was meticulous in the way he placed the body. Studying the body once again, he suddenly pauses at the girl's tiny neck. "What's this?" he says, inching closer to get a better look.

"What'cha got?" the constable asks, moving closer as well.

"Not sure," Greg answers, examining a thin silver chain secured around the dead girl's neck and following it to a tiny silver cross that's attached at the bottom. It rests on the girl's chest, which at first glance, seems oddly cruel to him. Obviously, the cross didn't protect her from the evil she's endured. "It was so tiny I missed it the first time I scanned the body. It's hardly noticeable in the darkness and blowing snow, but I believe what we have here may be our first clue."

"I see that," she says.

"We'll have to double check the file to see if there was any reference to this in the report, but I've looked at that file many times and I don't recall seeing anything about her wearing a silver chain and cross when she went missing," Greg says.

"Neither do I," Emily nods, "and I can tell you, that as a woman, there's no way I would be going to bed with a fragile chain like that around my neck, and I'm pretty sure there's no way a mother would put her five-year-old to bed with something like that either. For one thing, it's likely to get broken—the chain looks pretty thin."

"Paper thin," Greg adds, "from the looks of it. We should double check with the parents though, just to be certain, but there's no way the investigators would have missed an important detail like this."

"So, if she didn't have the chain and cross with her when she was abducted, what does that tell us?"

"It could be our perpetrator's signature," Greg answers, eyeing the tiny cross he estimates to be no more than a half-inch in length. "We've got to make sure we document every detail of it. It's a priority because it could be a link to whoever did this."

"Yes, Sir," the constable agrees. "I will make sure the ident team takes lots of photos of it before anything is moved."

"Let's hope the team gets here sooner than later," Greg says, standing up and straightening his legs. "We've got a lot of work to do before the storm hits and we have to secure this area, and I mean I want it air tight. I don't want anyone or any vehicle in or out of this beach road unless they get clearance from me. If they're not working on this investigation, then I don't want them on the beach. They have no business here. . . . that includes the press. I want a wide radius around this place and I mean wide. I want it all locked down. Understand?"

"I understand," Constable Murphy responds to the order. "I will see to it, Sir."

"And I want officers scouring this neighbourhood as quickly as possible. I know it's early, but I want them to knock on every door in a five-kilometre radius of this beach," Greg continues as the wind blows his breath away. "If we're lucky, maybe someone heard or saw something last night that might give us a lead on what the hell's going on around here. I'm skeptical anyone will have seen anything though—our guy's too good to be seen. This is a game to him and somehow, although this is the first body we've found, I have a feeling this isn't the first time he's done this. My guess is that he carefully chose his dumpsite for good reason. He knows the body would be found, but he also knows that he wouldn't be noticed, that he'd have plenty of time to get in, make the dump and then leave without being discovered. I'm sure he's scouted the location well in advance. He knows this place well. As to evidence at the scene, Major Crimes and the dog team should already be well on their way and they'll handle most of the forensics."

"Very well, Sir," the constable nods.

"Emily, I want you to talk to the witness again," Greg continues as they begin to retrace their steps and head back toward their vehicles. "He may have seen or heard something that seems unimportant to him. Press him for every detail, no matter how minute it seems. We don't have any idea what we're dealing with here, so we can't take anything for granted. Even the most insignificant thing can be a clue."

"I'm on it. I'll go see him right away," the officer replies, turning back to look at the body again.

"You sure you're okay? I'll understand if you find this hard to stomach," Greg says, worried the officer may be struggling to keep her focus. "Truthfully, I find it hard to take. And I've been around a long time. It's always hard, but it's especially difficult when the victim is a child. There's no shame in being sick over this. It makes my stomach churn, too."

"I'm okay, Sir. It's just that it's hard to imagine why anyone would want to do this to another human being, especially a child," she says, closely following her commander. She's aware of his reputation and she knows he's likely seen more than his share of horrific things over the course of his career. "I just can't stop wondering what kind of monster would do this."

"An evil one," Greg answers. "We're talking pure evil—a sick, twisted individual with no conscience. Now, you go talk with the jogger while his memory is still fresh and I'll stay here with the body until help arrives."

Sergeant Paris likes the young constable. He thinks someday

Emily Murphy will be a good investigator, not that she isn't already doing well on the job, but he sees early potential in her. Greg believes, however, that there are certain things that can't be taught. He knows there are skills that make an exceptional investigator and those must be learned from experience. Instincts need time to be honed. Emily has potential. She's smart, inquisitive and she thinks she can make a difference through the RCMP, all benchmarks of a good investigator. But today, the young officer needs to be kept at arm's length from this case . . . for her own good, he decides. His experience has taught him that, in the beginning, it's best to take these things in small doses, even for someone so enthusiastic.

Turning back to the corpse as Constable Murphy makes her way toward the cruisers, their flashing red and blue lights still filling the early morning sky, Greg can't help but empathize with the victim and wonder about the circumstances that brought them together on this cold, winter morning.

"What are you doing here?" he whispers, his words lost on the icy wind, floating off to some unknown destination. "Who did this to you? Why did he treat you like this? With such indignity? . . . Why not just kill you and be done with it and hide you some place where no one would ever find you?"

He wonders, *what's this guy trying to tell us?*

*****

Glancing at his watch again for what he is sure is the twentieth time, Greg is growing increasingly frustrated at having to wait for the ident and dog teams to arrive. He understands it's still early in the day and it takes time to mobilize resources. He also knows the teams have to commute from Halifax, but considering the urgency of the matter, he had hoped the investigators would have arrived by now. It's been almost three hours since the jogger who discovered the body of young Holly Conrad called the detachment and Greg knows that time is of the essence. With each passing minute, there's greater risk of evidence degradation. The elements are fierce today and he fears that with only a small window of opportunity to gather evidence before the snow hits, there may not be sufficient time to secure the dumpsite.

"Come on guys," he whispers to the inside of his empty cruiser.

The digital clock says 7:47. He expected the teams to have been here at least half an hour ago.

He pulls himself upright behind the steering wheel, where he's been sitting for the past hour with the heat cranked to high in an effort to stay warm. Greg glances around the deserted beach. It always amazes him how time just goes on, regardless of the circumstances. But for today at least, this small patch of prime oceanfront property will remain locked in time. After Constable Murphy completed her interview with the jogger, Greg sent her back to the detachment to decipher her notes and complete her reports. He ordered officers stationed at all access points, so no one will disrupt the scene.

Feeling the cruiser shake with the force of the cold Atlantic wind, he shivers at the thought of soon having to get out of the warm vehicle. That is if the teams ever arrive. Finally, pulling the mic from its stand, he's had enough.

"Dispatch?" he says, his tone conveying his discontent with having to wait. "Paris here."

"Go ahead, Sergeant," another, more pleasant voice replies. Clearly, there's been a shift change at headquarters as this woman immediately impresses him as being much friendlier than the previous dispatcher working the com earlier this morning.

"Wondering if you can provide me with an ETA for the ident and dog teams," he responds. "It's getting late."

"Certainly, Sergeant," the friendly woman replies. "Just a moment, please."

"Ten-four," Greg answers. Glancing around the dunes, his attention is drawn to a sparsely limbed fir tree—obviously dead for many years.

"What the hell," he whispers, staring out through the cruiser's salt and snow-covered windshield where he sees five crows swoop in and land. They calmly perch on the rotting tree branches and return his glare. He can feel their eyes studying him through the dirty glass.

"Holy crap." He sighs, a quick puff of condensation escaping his warm body. He watches the large, ebony birds bob their heads in unison—something he's seen too many times for his liking.

"You guys again?" he says. "What the hell is up with you damn birds?"

"Sergeant?" The woman says, her friendly voice jumping

from the radio speaker, breaking the silence within the vehicle like shattering glass.

Pressing the transmitter, he replies, "Go ahead dispatch. Paris here."

"Yes, Sergeant. Both teams estimate time of arrival at your location in approximately ten minutes, Sir," the woman says, but Greg hardly hears her as his attention is drawn back to the crows.

When he doesn't respond, the woman asks, "Sergeant? Can you please confirm?"

Snapping to his senses, Greg quickly answers, "Sorry, dispatch. Can you repeat please?"

"Less than ten minutes to your location, Sir," she says again, "for both teams."

"Very good, dispatch," he answers. "Thank you for the update."

"Sir," the dispatcher asks over the secured channel. "May I ask if everything is okay?"

"Ah, yes, dispatch," he immediately replies. "Everything is locked down here and fully secured. Just waiting on ident and the dogs."

"Very well, Sir," the woman says. "Ten-four."

"Ten-four," he answers, keeping his eyes glued to the black birds. Their new perch looks as if it could topple over any minute in the fierce wind. "Paris out."

Returning the mic to its stand, Greg pulls on his leather gloves and places his fur hat on top of his thick, black hair. He grabs the door handle and pauses. He dreads exiting the vehicle but he feels compelled to get out.

Slowly pushing on the heavy, reinforced door, he throws his left foot out into the sand and snow and then follows with his right— almost forcing himself into the cold wind. Pulling his tall, but trim, frame from the cruiser, he stands next to the open door and studies the avian visitors.

"What do you want?" he finally whispers and immediately, as if on cue, the five crows spring from the rotting tree branch, catch the cold wind and soar directly toward the car, forcing the officer to duck.

"Jesus," he says, keeping his eyes on the crows as the black birds swoop over the dunes where the body of young Holly Conrad lies exposed to the brutal elements and then disappear into the gathering storm clouds. "What are you guys up to?"

Now he's more convinced than ever that he must talk with Cliff because if there is one person in this town who can relate with his experiences this morning, it will be his long-time friend who has had his own run-ins with the crows over the years.

"Okay," he says to no one as he slams the car door. "That was more than a little weird."

Leaning against the car, Greg scans the sky for any sign of the black birds, but he sees none. They've gone.

"What the hell do you want?"

He can only hope it's not a sign of something worse to come. This town's track record with crows is not good.

Hearing the indisputable sound of vehicles clunking down the dirt road that leads to the beach, Greg spins around to see the dog transport truck coming into view.

"Finally," he says, glancing once more toward the sky and waving to the driver to pull in and park beside his cruiser. The crows, he thinks, will have to wait until later.

Chapter 4

It is nearly nine-thirty by the time Sergeant Greg Paris arrives at the Liverpool RCMP detachment. The building, at the north end of town, near the hospital, may be small in comparison to other detachments, but its officers cover a lot of territory and serve almost 12,000 citizens. And today, this RCMP detachment is anything but small. In fact, by the time Greg enters the chalet-style building, word that the missing young girl's body has been found on a local beach has already spread, even more quickly than he expected. And her murder has put Liverpool on the map—yet again.

Marvels of an electronic world—where everyone is plugged in, he thinks. The phones are ringing nonstop as reporters from across the province and beyond press for details. He cringes as he enters the reception area. He knows it will be difficult to contain this story.

"Look, I don't care who you are. You could be with CNN for all I care," the fiery, forty-something receptionist says to whoever she is talking to on the phone. She is less than cordial as she shoots back at the caller. "I'm telling you for the last time that the investigating officer is not available to take any calls right now. He's somewhat busy," she continues, her voice dripping in sarcasm. "Yes, I understand you're on a deadline . . . I know you need more details for your story, but do you understand what's going on here? I don't have time for any more of your crap . . . Goodbye."

Slamming down the phone, she notices Greg's attempt to sneak by her desk, hoping to go unnoticed.

"No you don't," she barks, glaring at him. "Stop right there, mister."

"Rough morning, Donna?" He is sincere. He knows this is not the time to make light of her predicament—it's abundantly clear she's already had more to deal with this morning than she would see in an entire normal workday. Even though he's only worked with her for a few weeks, Greg has the utmost respect for the sixteen-year employee. He's sure that in that time she's seen a lot of messy stuff go down, but she's impressed him as being the picture of professionalism. However, today, none of the staff is handling the news well. How could they? An abducted little girl was found murdered in their jurisdiction. So, he understands her emotions are running high. He also knows such stress would put anyone on edge.

"You don't know the half of it, Sergeant," she responds, motioning toward the ringing phone on her desk—three little red lights blinking continuously. "Just a minute," she sighs, quickly picking up the receiver and pressing one of the red lights to connect her to the next caller. "RCMP Liverpool. Hold, please." She turns back toward Greg. He smiles but says nothing, silently marveling at her abilities. It's clear she's done this before.

"It's worse than a zoo," Donna continues. "What am I supposed to tell these guys? Some of them can be pretty nasty, especially the ones from outside the province. It's like they think that just because they work for some big newspaper or some national television station, they own the world or something. Don't they understand what's going on around here?"

"They know." Greg has always tried to respect the press. He appreciates the reality that while some reporters can be nuisances, others are professional and courteous. That being said, he also knows many of them can be obnoxious at times. "They've got deadlines and this is a big story. That's all they care about, right or wrong. And sometimes they lose sight of the reality we face in doing our jobs."

"Does that give them a license to be rude?" she waves the phone at him. "So," she continues, "what do I tell them?"

"Don't tell them anything," Greg suggests, slowly inching his way toward his cubical-like office. "No, wait. Tell them we'll make a statement at two o'clock this afternoon and ask them please not to phone back before then. We won't have anything to tell them until then so they're just wasting their time and ours."

"Yes, Sir," Donna responds, knowing that while such an offer may appease some reporters, others won't be put off so easily and they will demand information. "I'll try that, but some of these guys are like mad dogs after a bone and they'll want more."

"Okay, do the best you can and I will check with the media relations officer to see when he's expected to arrive. That should relieve some of your stress. When he gets here, you can pass all the calls over to him. That's his job, so let him handle it." Greg likes the feisty receptionist and he feels bad she's stuck in the middle between reporters and those who might know something—although he really doesn't know anything, himself at this point. "By the way," he continues, his voice mellow as he heads toward his office in the back of the building, hoping it will provide him a brief escape from the confusion. "If you manage to get a few minutes, can you please see if you can reach Corporal Cliff Graham at home. I really need to speak with him today, if he's going to be around."

"No problem."

"Thanks. And one more thing," he says feeling sheepish for asking her to do something else for him considering how much pressure she's under right now. "When you see Constable Murphy, could you please tell her I want to see her right away."

"She was here a few minutes ago," Donna says, glancing around the detachment's crowded administrative area. "I just saw her."

"Well please tell her I need to see her in my office when she has a minute."

"Right," the receptionist says. "She's been trying to work on her report despite the distractions, but I will tell her you want her ASAP."

"Thanks, Donna."

"No problem," she smiles and glances back to the phone receiver in her hand. "Guess I should take this call, shouldn't I?"

"Probably."

"Sorry to keep you waiting," she says into the phone, putting on the best fake-sincere attitude she can find. "What can I do for you?"

Greg pauses just outside his door as if to say something to Donna, but he thinks better of it when he hears the exchange.

"Look, I said I was sorry. . . . No, there's no one who can answer your questions at this time. There will be a press conference at two o'clock here at the detachment. If that's not good enough for you, then the best I can do is put your name on the list and have someone call you as soon as they're available. . . . But I have no idea how long that will be. . . . Goodbye."

This is a not a good time to bother her with anything else, he decides.

Inside his office, Greg sits in Cliff's green swivel chair that, after years of use, has been permanently molded to fit his friend's form. He begins to review the morning's events and wonders what's happening in this small, seaside town; this quaint community that's known as one of the friendliest places in the province. It sickens him to think of the pain the young victim may have endured before death released her from whatever horrors she faced. He's so deep in thought that he doesn't hear the knock on his door.

"Sorry to barge in, Sir, but you didn't answer when I knocked," Constable Emily Murphy says, opening the door just wide enough to be seen through the crack. "Donna said you wanted to see me but I can come back later if you're busy."

"No, Constable. Come in, and please close the door," Greg responds, realizing he has momentarily lost track of his surroundings with thoughts of the monster that took the little girl's life. He believed his family would be safer in this small, close-knit community than the large city they left behind. The cruel murder, however, has shattered this fantasy and it sends a cold shiver racing up his spine as he tries to regain his focus. "Let's compare notes from this morning," he says, motioning for her to enter. "In these cases, I've found it's important to look at everything we've got while it's still fresh in our minds. My experience has shown me that we lose details the longer we wait to discuss them and we know that even the most minute detail can sometimes be the clue that can help solve the case."

Joining Sergeant Paris in the nondescript, windowless office that in essence is no larger than a broom closet, Constable Murphy hands her superior officer the cup of black coffee she brought him. She remains quiet while Greg shuffles some papers spread across his desk.

The commanding officer then smiles at her over the files he's stacked on the right side of the desk next to the picture of his young daughter and wife and a coffee mug that proudly proclaims "World's Greatest Dad." It was a Father's Day gift from Lucy last year. He doesn't use it every day, simply because he's afraid he might break it. Instead, he uses it to hold pens. Also on the desk is a small plastic plaque adorned with the image of a monkey clinging to one end of a rope with a knot in it and a slogan in red that reads: "When you get to the end of your rope, tie a knot and hang on." It was a gift from his long-time friend, Cliff, when he assumed command of the detachment last month, a nice gesture, Greg thinks, considering he was taking over the man's job, temporarily at least.

Greg sighs deeply while eyeing the slender constable sitting across from him, as if trying to get his thoughts in order. Then he speaks in a professional tone, "Are you okay, Emily?" He smiles. "That was a pretty nasty scene out there this morning. It's a lot for any officer to handle. Truthfully, even us old farts have a hard time dealing with something like this, especially when a child is involved. If you need anything I want you to tell me right away. No one will hold it against you if you feel the need to talk—I promise that."

"I'm doing fine, really. Thanks for your concern, Sergeant." She returns his smile and Greg realizes how pretty she is, but he would never say anything like that to her. He's much too professional to make such a personal and inappropriate comment to an officer in his command, or to any woman for that matter, except his wife, of course. "But I can handle this," Emily insists. "I'm a big girl and I'm well trained. This is not my first day on the job and I'm ready for whatever you need me to do."

"Okay, then," Greg nods, fearing he may have inadvertently insulted her with his outward show of concern, but he would be asking the same question of any officer in his command. He drops the matter and moves on. "Let's get on with it then. Let's look at what we've got."

"Very well, Sir," she begins and he notices she's become very professional with her tone and mannerisms. He likes her and thinks she's a great cop. "The call came in shortly after five this morning. I was on duty and after receiving the 911 page, I immediately responded to the scene at Beach Meadows. Once there, I met the man—the jogger—who made the call. He said he stumbled upon the body while out for an early-morning run and he's positive the body wasn't there yesterday when he went for his daily run. He's sure he would have seen it, if it had been there . . . and I believe him."

"And," Greg jumps in. "We know the body is the remains of young Holly Conrad who was kidnapped from her Windsor home sometime in the middle of the night early last month."

"Correct," Constable Murphy nods.

"The question that keeps nagging me though is how she ended up here?" Greg adds.

The constable shrugs. "There's not much to go on, Sir."

"Not really," he agrees, shaking his head. "I think our best clues are the silver chain and cross that were around the girl's neck. We need to make absolutely sure the little girl did not have any jewelry in her possession when she was abducted." He pauses. "Have the parents been notified that her remains have been found?"

"Yes, Sir," Emily answers and he can detect an inflection of emotion in her words. "Two officers from the Windsor detachment notified them earlier this morning before the news broke in the media. I can't imagine what that would have been like for those officers."

"Trust me," Greg says, recalling the many times he's had to deal with bereaved parents during his career. "It's never easy, no matter how many times you've done it. I just remember that however hard it is for me, it is a thousand times worse for the parents." He looks at the coffee mug and sighs, knowing his daughter is safe. Shaking off the image of any possible harm coming to Lucy, he says, "I will have to call the parents to talk to them about this cross, but first, I will give them some time to deal with their grief."

"Would you like for me to call them, Sir?" the constable asks.

"Thanks," Greg smiles. "But I think I want to talk to them, not that I don't think you can't handle it."

"Fine by me," she shrugs. "I was just offering because I know how busy you are."

"And I appreciate the offer, but this is something I've got to do myself," he nods and then pauses as his mind wanders back to his daughter.

"Are you okay, Sir," the constable asks after several minutes of silence.

"Sorry," he finally says, pulling himself up in his chair and running his right hand through his thick, black hair, something he does when he's distracted. "I was just thinking."

"About the case?"

"Yes," he says, hoping the constable doesn't detect the small white lie. He forces himself to focus. "There's something we're missing here. I want to talk about the jogger again. What did he see? What did he hear? Did he elaborate when you talked to him again?"

"Honestly," Constable Murphy begins while referring to the notes she made during the second interview with the jogger after she left Greg Paris at the beach earlier this morning. "Not much. I don't think he's going to be of any help to us. Like I reported earlier, our witness says he was running along the beach when he spotted a large mound in the grass between two sand dunes. It caught his attention because he had not recalled previously seeing it and he says he's on the beach everyday, even in this cold. At first, he said he thought maybe it was a seal as they sometimes wash up on shore. But when he approached it and saw that it was a human body, he said he used his cell phone and called 911 right away. They sent me down, I called you and here we are."

"Did he say if he saw a car or anyone else around?" Greg asks after considering her report. "Maybe he passed another vehicle while he was driving home from work. Would that be unusual if he did?"

"No, Sir. He said he had not seen any vehicles in the area either before or during his run. It was late and he's sure he would have noticed the lights if there had been a vehicle down on the beach. Likewise with people. He said there was no one else on the beach except him. . . . He's sure of that."

"I don't get it," Greg says, leaning back in the old swivel chair he thinks should have been thrown in the trash years ago, but he admits it's still pretty damn comfortable. "There are all kinds of houses around that beach. Someone must have seen something."

"You'd think so, wouldn't you?" she nods. "But I guess it was just too dark last night."

"I guess," he pauses. "Major Crimes is still there talking to people, but my guess is they won't find anything. And they're still collecting evidence at the beach. They're hoping to move the body to Halifax for the autopsy by around two this afternoon—before too much snow falls. They'll put a rush on it, but it will be a day or two before we start to see the paperwork on their efforts. There's lots to do and a limited number of officers to go around."

The phone rings. Greg answers.

"Sorry to interrupt, Sir," Donna's voice booms through the phone's intercom system. ". . . but I've got Corporal Graham on the phone like you asked."

"No problem. I'll take it, thanks. I need to speak with him," he tells the receptionist. Turning to the young officer, he adds, "Excuse me, Constable. That's all I need right now. You can finish your report and we'll talk again later this afternoon. Maybe we'll have something more to look at."

"Yes, Sir," Constable Murphy pauses on her way out the door and looks at him. "Are we going to catch this creep before he has a chance to do this again?" she asks. For the first time, Greg sees she's let her guard down.

"I hope so, Emily," Greg smiles and then sighs heavily. "I certainly hope so."

*****

She wasn't supposed to die, but she wouldn't stop crying.

He hates the sound of children crying. It makes every nerve in his body burn.

"Why wouldn't she stop crying?" he asks even though there's no one there to answer him.

Pacing the small, window-less room with the dirt floor, he screams, "Why? . . . Why? . . . Why wouldn't she just stop when I told her to?"

For weeks, he told her to stop crying and asking for her mommy and daddy. He told her she'd never see them again, but she wouldn't listen to him and she wouldn't obey his orders. They were simple, but very strict orders—no crying, no screaming, only one meal a day, only water to drink, speak only when he told her to speak, no trying to get free of the ropes that held her secured to the bed, and no clothes, only the diapers he provided her. This, he knew, made her more vulnerable.

Even when he brought her a friend, he could see she wasn't happy. He could see it in her terrified eyes and he hated how she looked at him. Why couldn't he make her happy, he wonders, pacing the dirt floor.

"Goddamn it," he screams while staring at the empty bed in the dark, damp room where she had been held captive for more than a month. Addressing the stained mattress, void of any blankets, he screams again. "You weren't supposed to die and leave me. Now what I am going to do? You've left me and it wasn't time."

Moving about the small dungeon-like room, as if searching for answers, he's hoping to find any inspiration that might tell him what to do next.

"Fuck. Fuck. Fuck," he yells, picking up a plastic tray resting on the floor. It contains the spoiled remains of the food—a bowl of tomato soup, one slice of buttered bread, now stale, and a glass of water—he brought her the day she died, the day he found her dead on the bed when he came to spend time with her.

He remembers she was cold when he touched her and her eyes were empty when he looked into them, like endless dark pools. He closed them immediately—he didn't want them staring at him, like he was some depraved monster. Her lips were blue and her skin was pale. Her blonde hair was all matted and knotted, but she had been his and he wasn't ready to let her go.

"What am I going to do, now?" He screams again, heaving the tray against the cement wall. It crashes to the floor but not before the soup splashes across the crack-filled wall, mixing with the water damage caused by a century of wear and tear. He becomes fixated on the spoiled tomato soup that has left an obscene stain on the wall—the thick, dark-red droplets suddenly looking like congealed blood.

He falls to his knees. The loose dirt covers his torn jeans and he begins to sob. The warm tears streak his face and he suddenly switches gears—his grief turning into pure rage.

"Bitch," he seethes, the spit frothing from his mouth as he speaks. "Useless, selfish little bitch." He bolts to his feet. "I gave you every-thing you needed but you were never happy. No," he says, sarcasm spewing from his lips. "You wanted your mommy and daddy," his voice seethes with hate as he mocks the small girl's words. "What did that get you?" he continues, every word increasing the intensity of his anger. Well, they can have you. I've put you where they can find you and I hope you're happy, now. You brought this on yourself."

He begins pacing the small room that contains only the bed

where she had been confined. He stops when he spots the girl's pink pajamas she'd been wearing when he rescued her from that other man and woman—her mommy and daddy—just after Christmas. She peed in them the first night here, in her new home, and he made her take them off. That's when he got her the diapers. If she couldn't control herself and wanted to be treated like a baby, then that's how he would treat her. The pajamas have been in the corner ever since and he decides it's time to finally get rid of them.

Grabbing the soiled clothes from the dirt floor, he balls them up and puts them in the black garbage bag he's brought with him. Scanning the room for anything else that may have been hers, he decides it's time to get rid of anything that might remind him of Holly Conrad. She's gone now. He has to accept that. He doesn't have to like it, but he has to accept it.

Besides, he thinks, turning to leave the prison-like room . . . *it won't be long before I have another companion . . . and this time, I won't be so easy on her.*

Chapter 5

Greg Paris and Cliff Graham go way back. They've been best friends since the first day of basic training at the depot in Regina. Even when their career paths deviated, they maintained contact, often calling each for help when times got tough, and for fellowship when they had something to celebrate. They were best men at each other's weddings and Greg was there for Cliff when a drunk driver killed his friend's first child. Cliff became Greg's source of strength when his first wife, Jen, died of breast cancer five years ago. Despite their history, though, Greg still finds it difficult to face his buddy after he effectively took over the man's job. Logically, he knows Cliff understands and holds no ill will toward him. After suffering a major heart attack in December, which required by-pass surgery, there was no way Cliff could continue working. But Greg still feels uneasy about coming face-to-face with his friend—the man he replaced as commander of the detachment.

Steering the police cruiser through downtown Liverpool, Greg can feel the intense energy of the commercial district, as though it is suddenly alive. People are buzzing about with the usual pre-storm panic that inevitably hits as they scurry to grab supplies before the major blizzard lands, now only a few hours offshore. As he waits for the town's single set of traffic lights to turn green, he can see small snowflakes already starting to fall. If all the weather forecasters are accurate, then they should brace for a real dumping by this evening.

Damn stuff, Greg thinks. He flicks on his wipers to clear the light dusting that has already covered the windshield and then accelerates, as the light turns green. There was a time when he wouldn't care about things like a snowstorm because he understood it did no good to complain about things he couldn't change. But lately, he's developed a real nasty streak when it comes to anything 'winter.'

He eases the cruiser into the slick intersection and smirks, thinking he should probably blame his newfound disdain for anything winter-related on Cliff. Everyone who knows the man also knows his long-standing contempt for winter is legendary. The cruiser is almost through the intersection when Greg sees a white van skidding directly into his path.

"Jesus!" He instinctively yanks the steering wheel to the left and swerves to avoid the collision.

The van, which Greg notices is covered in a layer of thick mud, continues on, not even bothering to slow down to make sure everything is okay. Greg quickly switches on the red and blue roof lights and straightens the cruiser as he pursues the other vehicle still making its way along the street. As the siren roars to life, the driver finally looks in his rear view mirror and then finds a place to safely pull over.

Greg pulls in behind the van and jams the car in park, admittedly a little perturbed at the driver. He grabs his brown fur cap and places it on his head. He pulls it down snugly and then opens the heavy door and steps out into the steadily falling snow, which he notices, much to his displeasure, seems to be accumulating rather quickly. The street is already white with a growing layer of snow, an early indication a lot more of the white stuff is on the way. Slamming the door, he stands beside the cruiser and studies the van with Manitoba plates for several seconds before approaching the driver's side window, which is already rolled down.

"Mr. McCarthy," he says, recognizing the slightly built, bald man sitting behind the steering wheel.

Murdock McCarthy is the owner of the historic Haddon House, which until last fall was operated by its previous owners as a bed and breakfast. Murdock purchased the stately mansion from Viola Toole who sold the property following her husband's death to move to Ottawa to be with her family.

"Officer," the man answers, his tone low and steady. He glances over his left shoulder and out the door window. "How are you today, Sir?"

"Fine," Greg says, standing beside the van. "Or at least I was until it started snowing."

"I know what you mean," the driver chuckles. "Sounds like we're in for a few nasty hours."

"It sure does," Greg nods, scanning the inside of the van and noticing a young girl sitting in the passenger seat.

"Everything okay, officer?" Murdock asks.

"Not sure," Greg quickly replies. "Just curious why you ran the red light back there and then didn't bother to stop when you almost hit me."

"Did I?" The man answers, smiling at the police officer. "I'm totally sorry about that but I didn't think I was all that close to your vehicle. I hope everything is okay."

"Well, you were very close," Greg says. "So why didn't you stop at the red light?"

"I tried stopping," he explains, "but when I hit the brakes, I just kept right on going and slid through the light. After I managed to get the van under control, I just thought it best if I kept on going so I could get out of the intersection before someone else came along and plowed into me."

"Just a second," Greg says, walking away from the window and making his way to the front of the van. He then walks to the back of the vehicle and finally returns to the window several minutes later. "You need new tires, Mr. McCarthy, that's your problem."

"Really. These tires are only two years old."

"You can't count on all-weathers in these conditions," Greg says, "and these ones look pretty worn, so if I were you I'd invest in some snow tires and I wouldn't wait until next fall to do it. It's only February and we could still have a lot of snow this year."

"That's good advice and I'll look into it right away," Murdock nods. He smiles. "So are you giving me a ticket?"

"Not this time, but I would urge you to think not only about your safety and the safety of your family, but also about the safety of everyone else on the road as well," Greg says, smiling into the van at the young girl. "Hi, Emma. Remember me?" he asks. "We've never managed to get you and Lucy together for a play date, have we?"

The girl says nothing but shakes her head.

"We should do that soon," he continues. "Would you like that?"

She shrugs, glances at her father and then slowly nods.

"Okay, then," Greg nods back. "I will talk with Lucy's mom tonight and we'll see what we can do to make that happen as soon as we can."

"That would be nice," Murdock speaks up. "I am sure Emma will really enjoy that. She still doesn't have any friends even though we've been here since November. She could use a playmate."

"Well," Greg says, "we can't have that, can we? We'll have to make sure the girls get together real soon." Pausing and scanning the van's interior once again, he adds, "Where are you heading, anyway?"

"Home," Murdock quickly answers. "We're just on our way back from Bridgewater. Had to go in and get some parts for my old snow blower. It's seen better days, as you can well imagine after surviving those Winnipeg winters. I figure I might need it if we get the amount of snow they're calling for."

"Based on the way it's coming down right now, I'd say there's a pretty good chance we're going to get everything they're calling for and then some," Greg says, smiling once more at the little girl. Finally, he adds, "Okay, then, Mr. McCarthy, you can be going now, but please get those tires changed as soon as possible."

"Yes, Sir," the driver says as he begins to roll up the window. "And thank you for understanding. I promise I will take care of it right way."

Watching the van pull away, Greg stands near the police cruiser and makes a mental note to remember to ask Andrea to make arrangements to bring the little girl over to play with Lucy. Greg opens the car door, removes his hat and shakes off the snow that has accumulated in the brown fur, but he can't shake the feeling that the little girl seems really unhappy. Maybe having a friend like Lucy, who is an out-going gregarious girl if there ever was one, will be a great thing for her. Thinking about how fortunate he was to meet Lucy and her mother two years ago, he slides his tall frame back into the cruiser and puts the car in drive.

Time to see what Cliff has to say about what's happening in his town, Greg thinks as he carefully drives along the snow-covered street.

"Nasty," he says to no one, peering through the windshield as the wipers work overtime to keep the glass cleared.

*****

"Carly," Greg says as the fifteen-year-old brunette opens the front door and beams at him. Quickly brushing the snow from his bulky RCMP overcoat and stepping inside the modest bungalow, he bends down and gives the petite girl a quick kiss on the cheek. "How's my favourite goddaughter today?"

"Don't you mean, your only goddaughter?" She giggles, turns and heads down the hallway that leads into the living room. "I'm fine," she adds. "Daddy," she yells. "Uncle Greg's here."

"How's school going, young lady?" he asks, pulling off the heavy coat and then slipping out of his heavy military-like uniform boots. "Still making straight 'As'?"

"I wish," she laughs. "Not quite straight 'As,' but I'm holding my own."

"I'm sure you're doing great," he says, following the small featured girl into the living room that's been rearranged since his last visit about a week ago. "I have no doubt that someday you'll be a rocket scientist or something impressive like that."

"A rocket scientist? Really?" she laughs, flopping into the large, brown easy chair she's pulled over to the bay window so she can watch the snow, which is now coming down in droves. He knows the roads will be treacherous. Cringing at the prospect of the inevitable onslaught of car accidents that come with such storms, typically because drivers refuse to slow down, he listens as the girl continues. "Maybe not a scientist or anything that requires math," Carly grins. "That's my worst subject. A dancer, I hope. That's what I want to be, or at least something that allows me to work in theatre."

"It will happen," Greg says, sitting on the matching brown sofa and facing his goddaughter. "When it comes to your future, you control your destiny. If that's what you want then chase your dreams young lady and don't let anyone knock you off course. If you see something you want, don't be afraid to go after it."

"Not a chance," she nods, gazing out the window. "Isn't it lovely?" she says with the enthusiasm of a young child. "I like it when the snow falls so hard you can't see out the window. I think it makes the whole house feel warm and cozy."

"If you like it." Greg shrugs. He had forgotten how much Carly likes the snow. "Me? Not so much."

"Oh, Uncle Greg," she laughs, throwing him a broad grin that makes her green eyes sparkle. He can see her spirit come to life when she smiles. "You're just like Daddy. You've been hanging around him way too long. What is it with you old guys and the snow? Why do you hate it so much?" she says with an impish grin.

"Just one of the few things we agree on," he answers with a wink. "There aren't many," he chuckles. Pausing, he then adds, "So how is he doing?"

"Surprisingly, he's doing very well," Carly says, glancing down the hallway to make sure her father isn't approaching. "Honestly," she continues, assured he's not within earshot, "I thought he'd be a bear after missing all this time from work and being stuck in the house most of the time, but he seems to have adjusted really, really well. And he's working hard at his diet and exercising every day like the doctors told him to."

"That's great news." Greg sighs. "I'm glad to hear it."

"What's great news?" Cliff asks entering the living room. Carly is amazed at how he just seems to have appeared out of thin air. "You're glad to hear what?"

"I'm glad to hear you've finally gotten over your hate for winter," Greg says without cracking a smile.

"Not in this lifetime, friend," Cliff laughs, sitting in another plush chair next to his daughter. "Not in this lifetime."

"Seriously?" Greg laughs. "I never would have guessed. He grins, "And you seem to have passed it on to me; must be contagious or something."

"Don't blame me." Cliff smiles. "I had nothing to do with that."

"Sure you did. After hearing you bitch and complain about it for all those years, I figure it's easier just to go along with you than try to argue about it," Greg counters with a smirk. "But seriously, it's good to see you looking so well. You gave us all quite a scare a few months ago and now you look great, much healthier than you did last fall."

"Thanks," Cliff says, beaming with pride. "I've dropped twenty-three and a half pounds since the surgery. I'm even going to start jogging once the doctor gives me the go ahead."

"That's fantastic," Greg answers. "Let me know if there's anything I can do to help you with the diet or exercise, even if it's just someone to run with. I'm there for you, pal."

"Will do," Cliff nods and then stares at his friend. Finally, he adds, "But that's not really what you want to talk about, is it?"

"Wait a minute," Carly speaks up, glancing at the men who are sitting on opposite sides of the room. "Are you guys going to get heavy?"

"Sorry, honey," Cliff smiles. "But I'm afraid so. I think Uncle Greg is here to talk business."

"Well then," she says, getting out of her chair and gathering her books, which Greg assumes must be her homework, "I'm going to my room so you guys can talk without worrying about me." Heading out of the room, she adds, "Daddy, we've got to think about dinner soon. I don't mind making something, but you've got to give me a little clue as to what you want."

"That's fine, honey," Cliff says. "You do your homework and I'll make supper. How does chicken sound? I've got some in the fridge. I'll just throw it in the oven."

"Sounds good, Daddy," she says as she disappears down the hallway. "Let me know if I can help," she calls back, adding, "See you later, Uncle Greg."

"See you soon, kiddo," he yells. "And don't forget you're going to babysit Lucy on Saturday night. Andrea is taking me out for my birthday, right? I'll pick you up around five. Is that still good?"

"I'll be ready." He hears her bedroom door close.

"Lovely girl," Greg says to Cliff. "You've done a great job with her."

"She is great, isn't she?" He beams with a father's pride. "And it's wonderful having her around here with me. She's a big help. We've become really close over the past few months."

"I can see that," Greg says. "I think she worships the ground you walk on."

"Let's not get carried away," Cliff chuckles. "So, pal, what can I do for you? How's life going in my job?"

"Come on, Cliff. You know how I feel about that."

"I'm only kidding." Cliff grins. "And you're right. After what dropped into your lap this morning, I shouldn't be kidding around, should I?"

"It's been a rough day, for sure." Greg sighs deeply—as though finally letting out the mounting tension from the morning's horrible discovery. "I'd forgotten about the daily pressures of working in a detachment, but this was an especially rough one."

"So," Cliff says, shifting in his chair and getting comfortable, preparing for a long story. "Fill me in."

Pausing for several minutes, Greg finally begins. "I'm assuming you've heard the remains of the missing girl from Windsor were found this morning out at Beach Meadows?"

"I have," Cliff nods. "Who would have ever expected that?"

"I forgot how strong those lines of communication are in small towns," Greg laughs. "What do you know?"

"Everything, I suspect," Cliff winks. "Or at least as much as you know at this point. . . . Sounds nasty. Who in their freaking mind would do something like that to a child, the poor little thing?"

"That's the question, isn't it?"

"It always is," Cliff nods. "What can I do to help you catch the bastard?"

"Not sure," Greg shrugs. "I think I just needed someone to talk to who isn't close to the investigation—so of course, I thought of you."

"Naturally."

"Yes." Greg laughs. "Naturally, but seriously, here's the thing. We don't have much to go on and we're still waiting on the autopsy. We're expecting a preliminary report from the ME later today, but it's clear that whoever did this was really careful about it. They knew what they were doing. They were methodical and everything was planned out like they've done this before. They've pretty much wiped out any forensic evidence and without that, I'm afraid we don't have much to go on—we don't have any witnesses—the dump site is in such a secluded area."

"What's your worst fear?" Cliff asks.

"That this is just the first one." Greg sighs and then glances out the window at the accumulating snow. Speaking again in a softer tone, he adds, "I just can't shake this feeling that we've only begun our dance with this pervert."

"That's a pretty ominous thing to say," Cliff observes. "Do you really think it's that bad?"

"I do," Greg nods.

"Bastard," Cliff sighs. "What is it with these sick perverts that they have to prey on children?"

"They're vulnerable. They're easy targets. They can't fight back," Greg says. "But . . ." He pauses.

"But?" Cliff picks up on his friend's sudden and obvious change of demeanour. "But what?"

"As much as I appreciate your insights on the case," Greg says, looking into his friend's eyes, "I need your help with something else that's been bothering me all day. Truthfully, I really want your thoughts on another matter and I don't know who else to ask."

"What?" Cliff asks, his eyebrows rising as he speaks. Greg hesitates. "What?" Cliff asks again, trying to keep the frustration out of his tone. "We've been friends a long time and you know you can talk to me about anything. I know you didn't come over here in a freaking blizzard just to sit and smile at me, so tell me how I can help."

Finally, his friend blurts it out. "Crows," Greg says. "I want to talk to you about crows."

"Jesus Christ!" Cliff snaps back in his chair like he's suddenly been hit in the face with a two-by-four. "What the hell are they up to, now?"

"I'm not sure," Greg answers. "And maybe I'm being paranoid, but whatever it is, I fear it's probably not good."

"Of course not," Cliff nods, studying the one man in the world he would never accuse of being paranoid—over anything. Greg always remains cool and calm even through some of the worst cases even he can imagine, but he can see his friend is clearly bothered by whatever has happened with the crows. "It hardly ever is with those winged, black devils. Even when they're trying to help they're a problem because you never know how to react around them and you never know what they're really up to, or more to the point, whose side they're on."

"That's a problem," Greg agrees. "That and the fact that I don't know a whole lot about them. That's precisely the reason I wanted to talk to you. I know you've been immersed in this stuff for years now and I am hoping you can tell me what five crows mean."

Cliff stares at his friend for a few minutes then says, "You're kidding, right?"

"No," Greg says and Cliff can see his friend is sincere. "I'm very serious. Ever since this morning when I was out for my run, I've had this feeling the crows are following me, and there are five of them. I'd like to know what it means."

Cliff smiles and he suddenly seems surprisingly smug to Greg, but he doesn't react negatively when Cliff says, "You used to think I was crazy when I'd talk about this stuff."

"I know," Greg nods. "But I've slowly come around to your way of thinking." "Really?"

"Yes. . . . Really," he says. "So, what can you tell me?"

Pausing and scratching his balding head, Cliff finally sighs, "Okay, friend. If that's what you want, I'll tell you what I know or at least what I've experienced and witnessed over the years, if you think it will help somehow."

"I really have no idea if it will help," Greg answers, relieved his friend will help him. "But it certainly can't hurt at this point."

Chapter 6

Checking his gear one more time, like an experienced hunter checks his supplies before heading out for the kill, he goes through his black vinyl kit bag to make sure he has everything he needs. He makes a mental note of every item, checking and then double-checking.

Rope? Check.

Duct tape? Check.

Gloves? Check.

Plastic? Check.

Lock pick? Check.

Kitchen catcher garbage bags? Check.

String? Check.

Cigarettes? Check.

Knife, in case he needs it? Check.

Flashlight for emergencies? Check.

Everything is in order, he thinks.

He's ready for the hunt. Tonight, he will bring home his next prize. He's had his eyes on this one for the past two weeks, staking out her home and following her every move. She'll make a nice addition to his collection.

Glancing out the window at the steadily falling snow, he knows it will be a challenge driving in the storm, but he can't wait any longer. He needs to do this tonight. He's ready and he's sure she's ready, too. He's watched her and he can tell she wants to be with him.

He glances at the clock and sees that it's only four-seventeen in the afternoon. Although he's happy the heavy snow will cover his tracks and provide him with the cover he needs, he still falters slightly as he sees the density of the snow that is continuing to fall.

No. No more waiting. This will happen tonight and nothing will stop me. Nothing will get in my way, not even the snow. She will be mine. She will come home with me tonight and we will be happy together.

He's positive of that.

*****

"Do you want something before we start?" Cliff asks his friend as he gets out of the easy chair. His clothes hang easily from his body, and for the first time, Greg can see just how much weight the man has really lost. Heading toward the kitchen, Cliff adds, "I need some tea. I drink a lot of tea these days." As if he feels the need to explain himself. "Would you like some? It might calm your nerves."

"No thanks," Greg answers, getting off the sofa and following Cliff into the kitchen. "Honestly, I'd like something a little stronger, but I never drink alcohol while working a case. Besides, I'm driving."

"Yes," Cliff smirks while filling the kettle with water and plugging the cord into the outlet over the kitchen counter. "I always thought you were a wuss."

"Beats being an overstuffed coach potato," Greg answers, smiling broadly. "But to your credit, friend, it's really good to see you're taking better care of yourself. I wasn't ready to attend your funeral just yet."

"That's good," Cliff says, shrugging as he removes a large, blue ceramic cup from the cupboard, "because I wasn't ready to have one just yet." He pauses as he takes a tea bag from the Red Rose box on the counter and tosses it in the cup. He then turns to his friend and says, "So here's the thing, Greg. When it comes to these freaking crows, you never really know what to expect from them."

"What do you mean?" Greg asks, finding a chair next to the wooden kitchen table and taking a seat.

"I mean," Cliff says, while leaning against the counter as he waits for the kettle to boil, "you never know if they're friend or foe."

"Again . . ." Greg sighs and squints in his friend's direction, a sure sign he's growing impatient. "You're talking in riddles and I'm really not following you."

"That's because the damn crows and their involvement with this town is one big riddle," Cliff continues, folding his arms over his chest and looking at his friend. "Let me take you back five years to the first time the crows started acting up—or at least the first time we noticed anything unusual."

"That's the Maggie Collins' case, right?"

"Right," Cliff nods. "It will be five years next month, the end of March, when all hell broke loose around here . . . and when I say hell broke loose, that's exactly what I mean. That's when the crows first arrived in Liverpool, and from all accounts, they seemed to come in with that girl. No one believed me when I told them she and those birds were connected somehow, but I was right. Everyone thought I was crazy or at the very least, paranoid. Everyone was ready to write it off as one big coincidence, but to me, the arrival of thousands of crows at the same time a stranger arrives and then four members of the same family end up dead, it all seemed like too much of a coincidence for me."

"It does sound suspicious when you put it like that," Greg says. "But we're talking crows, here. Wild creatures with a mind of their own."

"There's more," Cliff says as the teakettle clicks off. He pours the steaming hot water into the cup. "Are you sure you wouldn't like one?" he asks, raising his right eyebrow. "A nice cup of hot tea on a day like this might do you good."

"No, thanks. I'm fine," Greg says, shifting in his chair. "But you said there was more to the story so keep going, please." He can feel his patience waning—it's been a long day and he has a sinking feeling things are not going to improve anytime soon.

Retrieving a carton of two-percent milk from the fridge and pouring several drops into the tea, Cliff continues. "It didn't stop with that first incident. Later that same year in November, that young reporter, Hannah Simms, who worked for the *The Daily Post*, arrived in town on a mission to investigate the Collins' story, and you know how that ended."

"I do." Greg nods. "She ends up getting shot and killed by Constable Mike Cahill."

"Correct," Cliff says, grabbing his cup and making his way to the kitchen table where his friend is sitting. "And you know what was at the centre of all that, don't you?"

"Crows." Greg sighs, sitting up in his chair and hanging on every word his friend speaks.

"Crows." Cliff nods, sitting in a chair across from him. "Mike insisted he accidentally shot the reporter when he meant to shoot at a crow that was attacking him. Again, kind of a coincidence, don't you think?"

"I guess," Greg says.

"No guessing, my friend," Cliff says with a reassuring smile. "Every time something big happens in this town, lately, those bloody crows are right there in the middle of it."

"Okay. I know what you're going to say next," Greg replies.

"Yes. Amy Bishop," Cliff says. "You remember her? You were there. You were part of that mess. She's the one who flipped out and brutally murdered Mike Cahill and Matt Miller, the local DJ. And that twisted revenge plot almost ended up killing Kate Webster as well. If I remember correctly, Amy almost succeeded except . . ."

"Except the crows stopped her," Greg jumps in. "I see what you mean about this being weird."

"That's one word for it," Cliff says, taking a sip of tea. "I think it's more than that."

"I don't follow."

"I believe there's some kind of malevolent force at work in this town that compels the crows to do its work. It's like something or someone controls them, somehow," Cliff explains, his eyebrows contorting as he speaks. "Don't ask me to explain what I mean, but that's just what I feel. I've got nothing to back up those feelings, but I've been thinking about this for a while, now."

"So, then," Greg asks, "what happened next?"

"I'm not too sure," Cliff admits. "The last report of strange crow activity around town was actually just last year, but since it didn't involve any kind of crime, it's hard to know what really happened—but

I've heard rumours."

"Rumours?" Greg asks. "I've lived here since last fall when we bought the cottage, but I'm not sure I know what you mean."

"Come on, Greg. Some people may still consider you an outsider because you're a 'Come-From-Away,' as they say, but I know you're not naïve," Cliff says, taking another drink of tea. "Look at all the strange things that happened last year around the holidays. Lucy almost died—twice—but miraculously survived both incidents. I almost died but I somehow managed to escape death's door. We both should have been dead—and you know it. Oliver Lewis had terminal cancer, yet he fully recovered. Lily Pittmann has twins, only one is born dead, but the second one is perfectly healthy and from what I hear, is showing signs of extraordinary growth and development well beyond his age. You see? The rumour mill has been working overtime these past few years." He pauses, studies his friend and then adds, "doesn't it all seem just a little strange to you that all of that happened all at once?"

"Yes . . . maybe." Greg nods. "I see what you mean. I guess it does seem strange when you lump all those events together but I don't recall seeing too many crows around here last year."

"Don't you?" Cliff asks, his eyebrows rising again as they always do whenever he's being sarcastic. "That doesn't mean they weren't around. Just because you didn't see them, doesn't mean someone else didn't and it doesn't mean they weren't behind all of it, somehow. And," he pauses, "what about that mysterious woman? You know, that Tessa Williams who blew into town with her son and then suddenly disappeared? He was a strange little boy. You knew them. Weren't they a bit weird?"

"I wouldn't necessarily say *weird*," Greg answers. "I prefer to describe them as being *different* or *unusual* and yes, I did have a lot of dealings with them."

"Weird. Different. It doesn't matter what you call it," Cliff says. "I say it was all another big coincidence and again, I don't buy it and," he pauses, "neither do you, my friend, or you wouldn't be here today looking for information about crows."

Greg doesn't answer.

"Look, Greg," Cliff continues, placing his hands on the table, palms down as if making a point. "You came to me looking for answers and I'm telling you what I know." Leaning back in his chair, he adds,

"And this is what I know. . . . If you're seeing crows and you think there's some kind of connection to the murder of that little girl, then chances are there is a connection. Don't ask me how, but there must be. You just have to figure out what it is. That's the tricky part because it's not always easy to know what they're trying to tell you, and worse, it's not always clear if they're on your side."

"I understand that, but I've tried to avoid getting into all that superstition stuff," Greg says and then pauses. "But maybe it's not all superstition. Maybe what you're saying makes sense, somehow."

"Maybe," Cliff says. "So then, tell me. What have you experienced with these crows?"

Greg hesitates.

"Come on, Greg," Cliff prods. "You wanted me to help and I can't help if you don't tell me what's going on."

"Okay, okay," Greg says, leaning forward over the table as if he wants to make sure no one else hears what he's about to say. Lowering his voice, he says, "I've seen five of them several times today and each time I got the strange sensation they were trying to reach out to me . . . I swear, it's like they're trying to tell me something."

"And they probably are." Cliff takes another drink of tea. "I've had that sensation many times myself over the past few years."

"So what do I do about it?"

"Wait," Cliff says matter-of-factly. "Wait for them to connect with you, but watch for clues. They will try to tell you what they can. They will attempt to reach out to you." He takes another sip and then continues, "Watch them. Watch their behaviour. Try to draw lines between what they're doing and what's happening around you. Make note of their actions. There are clues there somewhere. . . . There always are."

"So, then, I'm wondering what you know about the old Maritime rhyme about crows?" Greg asks. "Does it have anything to do with what the crows do?"

"Maybe," Cliff answers, nodding. "I've wondered about that myself and I've thought that maybe it's possible that rhyme is more than just an old wives tale. Maybe we shouldn't be so quick to dismiss it."

Greg studies his friend then asks, "Do you know all the lines?"

Cliff nods.

"Well?"

Cliff stares at his friend and then begins, his voice low, emotionless. "One crow sorrow; two crows joy; three crows a letter; four crows a boy; five crows silver; six crows . . ."

"Silver," Greg suddenly proclaims. "That's it. Five crows silver."

"You've lost me." Cliff shrugs.

"At the murder scene this morning, we found a thin silver chain with a tiny silver cross attached to it and it was hanging around the girl's neck," Greg explains. "Five crows . . ."

"Silver," Cliff finishes his friend's sentence as the two men stare at each other, a heavy silence suddenly filling the kitchen.

*****

Minutes pass without the two RCMP officers exchanging a word, each lost in their own thoughts about the meaning of the silver cross and the crows' involvement in the latest mystery to embrace the small community, but neither is prepared to offer a theory on what it all means. Greg's just about to speak when his cell phone rings.

"Yes," he says, pressing the tiny red talk button on the face of the phone and bringing it to his ear. "Greg Paris, here."

"Sergeant." It's Constable Emily Murphy. "Sorry to bother you, Sir, but I need to speak with you right away."

"No problem, Constable," Greg says, nodding to Cliff. "Got some news on the Conrad case?"

"No, Sir," the constable answers. "Nothing yet except that the Ident team reported they were able to secure the tents before the heavy snow started."

"That's a good thing because it's coming down pretty hard right now," Greg says. "So what's up then?"

"We've just received another Amber Alert over the wires," Constable Murphy answers.

"What? Shit," Greg reacts. "Just a minute, Constable. I'm here with Corporal Graham. Let me put you on speaker. I want him to hear this as well." Pulling his cell away from his ear, he presses another button and then places the phone on the centre of the kitchen table. "Hey, there, Constable," Cliff immediately says. "Can you hear me?"

"Yes, Sir," she replies. "Loud and clear. How are you?"

"Fine," Cliff answers.

"Good," Greg jumps in. "Okay, Constable. Tell us what you know."

"Not much," she begins. "The Yarmouth detachment is reporting that a seven-year-old girl was abducted yesterday afternoon from the playground of an elementary school in the middle of town."

"We're just hearing about this, now?" Cliff asks.

"Afraid so, Sir," Constable Murphy says. "Once the word got out about the missing Windsor girl being found, here, Yarmouth members felt this might be connected."

"Why didn't they release this earlier?" Greg asks.

"They were just informed the girl was missing," the constable explains. "Apparently, there was some kind of communication break-down between the parents who are separated and not speaking. One parent thought the other had picked up the girl, and the other one thought the same. As it turns out, neither of them picked her up so she's been missing for more than twenty-four hours, and neither parent has heard from her."

"Now that's a shit-storm of a mess," Cliff observes.

"Indeed," Greg agrees. "Let's just hope their screw-up didn't cost another young girl her life."

"What are they releasing about the girl?" Cliff asks.

"The basics, Sir," Constable Murphy answers. "Just a second, please. Let me check the bulletin again. . . . Okay," she says, "here's what they've released. She's seven years old. Average build and weight. She's got light-coloured hair and dark eyes. There was an early dismissal at school yesterday, which may account for some of the parental mix-up, but she was last seen on the playground and was reported wearing jeans, black boots, a red bomber-style coat with a hood, black mittens and carrying a green backpack with her school-books in it, which was recovered near the school, like someone tossed it. Other than that, they've got nothing. She just vanished from the playground. Her name is Hillary Lawrence."

"Anyone see anything?" Greg asks, fearing he already knows the answer.

"The Yarmouth members have not been able to locate any wit-nesses, yet," the constable informs them. "But they're still canvassing the neighbourhood, so maybe they'll get lucky."

"Damn." Cliff releases an exaggerated sigh. "This isn't good."

"How do they know she was on the playground if no one saw her?" Greg asks.

"They're assuming that's where she was because both the mom and dad say they thought that's where the other one was picking her up," she explains.

"Any chance that either of the parents may have done something?" Greg asks. "Maybe, because of what's happened, here, they see this as an opportunity to cover their tracks."

"The Yarmouth members are looking into that," she says, "but I'm guessing they've decided to issue the alert instead of waiting just in case."

"Smart move." Cliff nods. "And they've already lost valuable time."

"Okay, Constable," Greg says. "Thanks. I'm just finishing up here with the Corporal then I'll be in."

Chapter 7

Murdock McCarthy is still fuming that the police officer had the balls to pull him over when he hadn't done anything wrong. *The audacity. Why the hell don't the police spend more time chasing real criminals instead of harassing an innocent civilian like me?*

He and his family may be new to Liverpool but he doesn't believe that gives police the right to single him out. Murdock has felt like an outcast all his life and that's one of the reasons he's moved so many times over the years, never staying put long enough to make friends or to consider any place home.

Based on everything he heard about Liverpool being such a friendly and welcoming place, he hoped this town would be different, but he knows now that isn't the case. It was all lies, false advertising, he thinks, as he pulls into the driveway next to his house and turns off the vehicle. He believes he and his family will never be welcome here and wonders if maybe it isn't time to start looking for another place.

"Prick," he fumes and hits the steering wheel with his right fist as his young daughter ducks for cover, cowering like a frightened dog. She knows that in his current frame of mind he will not hesitate to lash out at her to release his frustration.

Pulling her small body into a ball on the seat and turning away from him, she says nothing. Instead, she keeps her eyes glued on her father, fearing he will strike her even though she has done nothing to deserve his wrath. But that hasn't stopped him in the past and it may not stop him now, either. In fact, he's done it many times—more times than she can or cares to remember.

She doesn't know how long they've been sitting in the van, but she knows it's been awhile because the snow has totally blanketed the windshield and has almost covered all the side windows, too—it's almost impossible to see through them. It's like they are hiding in a cave, but even though she's freezing, the little girl knows she can't open the door and leave until her father tells her it's okay to do so.

He is a very strict disciplinarian, just like his parents before him, or at least that's how he explains it. And his children obey his every command. Although only eight, his youngest daughter is also the most compliant of his three children and she will not budge without his consent. But that doesn't mean she doesn't want to jump out and get away from him. She'd probably like nothing better than to open the van door, jump out and run into their big, old house. She'd like to be able to run up the large, oak staircase in the foyer of the historic struc-ture and hide in the safety of her bedroom with the door closed—and locked. She would like nothing more than to never see him again, but she also knows that if she opens the door, even a crack, without his permission, she'll feel the stinging blow of the back of his hand and she doesn't want that today. Memories of the last time he hit her are still fresh in her young mind and she will do nothing to bring that upon herself this time.

So, instead of running away from him, she pulls herself up against the passenger side door and waits for him to speak. Eventually, he will grow tired of sitting in the cold van, but until then, she is his prisoner.

"Emma," he finally barks, the spit flying from his thin lips, which are drawn so tight they look as though the skin might crack. Spittle hits the windshield, dotting it in a thick, white slime. "Go inside and tell your no-good, lazy brother to get his sorry ass out here right now and help me carry in the package." His face becomes redder with each word he spews at the small child.

The little girl obediently reaches down with her small right hand, grabs the handle and opens the door without saying a word. Jumping out into the snow, her boots immediately being swallowed by the mounds of white powder, she turns and slams the door shut behind her. Despite the blast of cold, she is relieved to be out his sight.

*****

"Constable Murphy," Greg says, brushing the snow from his overcoat and entering the detachment's command centre. A row of computers runs down one wall of the large room, while radio and other communications equipment take up the other side. "Any word from Yarmouth? Have they found their missing girl, yet?"

"No, Sir," the slender brunette says, spinning around in the padded, brown, vinyl chair where she's been sitting in front of the communications centre for the past hour. "Not a whimper since they issued the Amber Alert."

"This isn't good," Greg says, pulling another brown chair over beside the constable and sitting down next to her. Glancing at the computer screen where an image of the second child is displayed, he asks, "Can you please pull up the photo of Holly Conrad and put the two girls together?"

"No problem." She complies, pressing a button on the keyboard. Instantly, a photo of the first missing girl, who was taken from her Windsor home while her parents were sleeping, flashes on the screen.

"Jesus." Greg sighs, studying the two photos side by side. "They look like they could be sisters."

"I noticed that, too," she says.

"They're so young . . . so innocent," he observes. "Who would do something like this?"

"You would know more about that than I would, Sir," Constable Murphy replies.

"Yes." He sighs again. "You would think so, wouldn't you? But no matter how many of these cases I work on, I can never truly figure these guys out. It's always more complicated when they target children because it's difficult to determine what motivates them."

"It makes me sick to my stomach to think about what those poor little girls may have gone through," the constable says, studying the photos on the computer. "I think about how frightened they must be, how much they must want their mommies and daddies, and how alone they must feel. What were they thinking about when the creep took them? What would they be thinking about when they were being held captive? How afraid must they be?"

"I know it's our tendency to think about the victims in these cases and we have to sympathize with them," Greg says, "but in order to catch this guy, we've got to try to concentrate all our efforts on thinking about the perpetrator. He or she is a monster. The odds are it's a 'he,' but either way, they don't think like you and I think . . . like normal people think. They're crafty and they're self-preservationists." He pauses, squinting at the computer screen. "We've got to get inside his head. What's he like? Where does he live? What pushes him to the point where he takes these little girls? What does he get from them? Is it for a sexual purpose? Is he trying to fill some sort of gap in his own life? Is he living a fantasy and if so, what role do the girls play in that fantasy? Why does he keep them prisoner before killing them?"

"Okay, then." She sighs without looking at her commanding officer. "What you're saying is that we basically don't know squat about this guy."

"I wouldn't say that," Greg answers. "We know he's careful and meticulous. He's a thinker and a planner. He also knows something about forensics and police work because he's good enough at what he does that he doesn't leave any clues."

"That's something," the constable says, "but it's not a lot."

"We also know he targets victims with light-coloured hair," Greg continues. "That's a clue, but the question is whether it is a coincidence that both of his victims have light hair or is it part of his fantasy? And their ages. Is that important? And let's not forget about the silver chain and cross. That's the best clue of all."

"Hmmmm," the constable responds. "But how do we connect all that?"

"Not sure, yet," Greg admits, leaning back in the chair and adding, "The other question we have to look at is the locations. The girls were abducted miles apart, one in Windsor and one in Yarmouth, yet the body of Holly Conrad was dumped near Liverpool. What's the significance of the locations? Why choose Liverpool as his dumping ground?"

"Maybe it's central to him," Constable Murphy suggests.

"Excellent thought, Constable," Greg says. "Perhaps it's his base of operation or does this area hold some other meaning to him? Was he born here but doesn't live here, now? Did something significant in his life happen in Liverpool? Did his family vacation here when he was young? Does he have family in the area? Or maybe," he pauses, rubs his chin, then continues, ". . . the beach was just a convenient location, a place he picked because he thought it would throw us off his scent and maybe Liverpool has no meaning whatsoever to him . . . but I don't think so."

"Shit," she says and sighs. "When you start asking all of these questions, you find you have more questions than answers."

"That's a fact." Greg nods again. "And it's always like this when it comes to these cases. The sad reality is that even if we catch this guy we'll still have more questions than answers and in the end, many of those questions may never be answered. Sometimes, you just never learn what makes these guys tick."

"What would push someone to do something like this?"

"Lots of reasons," Greg says, turning to face the young officer who is soaking up all his knowledge like an eager child wanting to learn. "He could have been abused as a child or maybe he grew up in a home where there was violence. It could be that something traumatic happened in his life, like a serious accident or a major crime that changed his perspective, something that triggered this reaction. Or," he pauses and then continues, "it could simply be that this pervert was born this way and it's part of his DNA. It's just who he is and he's compelled to do these horrific things."

"Are you saying he can't control himself?" she asks.

"I am," Greg answers, his face becoming stern and his eyes narrowing, as if he's carefully considering his next thought. "And the worst part about that is that these guys are the most difficult predators to apprehend because they've spent a lifetime honing their skills, living with their fantasies and planning their moves. They plot and lay in wait for years until they can no longer resist the urges and then," he snaps his fingers, "they snap just like that. These are the most difficult guys to catch. It's like they are always one step ahead of you."

"So, then," she wonders aloud, "what do we do?"

"At this point, we wait and we learn. We study what we know," Greg explains. "We go over every scrap of evidence and every piece of information we have so far, no matter how big or how small, and when we've done that, we go over all of it again and again. . . . But for now, I think it's time for you to go home and get some rest, Constable. You've been at this all day and it's time you had a break."

"I'm fine, Sir."

"Don't try to be a hero, Emily," he says. "This is a long way from being over and we're looking at some long hours in the next few days—maybe weeks, so it's important that you learn to pace yourself. Part of being a good police officer is knowing when to push forward and when to step back and catch your breath. This is one of those times to take a breather. "So," he lowers his voice, "please, go home. The roads are a mess and you've got to be tired because I know I am. Get some rest and when you come back in the morning, you'll be able to look at things with a fresh perspective. By that time, we should have the first reports to look at. I know the labs are working overtime tonight and maybe that will give us something to go on."

"Very well," she sighs, rising from her chair. "And you? What about you, Sir? Are you leaving as well?"

"Soon. I've got a few reports to file that I don't want to let go because I may not get a chance to do them tomorrow and then I'll shut things down and go home," he says. "See you in the morning."

Heading toward the officers' locker room, Constable Murphy stops and turns. "Sir," she says. "Thank you for trusting me to work on this with you."

"Don't thank me just yet, Constable," he smiles. "Before this is over, you may wish I had pulled in someone else to help with this."

*****

It has been almost an hour since Constable Emily Murphy left the detachment and Sergeant Greg Paris has spent the time completing the necessary paper work. He told his wife, Andrea, he would be home by six and glancing at his watch, he sees it's almost that time. Switching off his computer and pushing himself away from his desk, he knows it's time to head out. He doesn't like to keep her waiting, even if he isn't finished his work. Once he's told her a time of arrival, he likes to stick to it and he knows there will likely be many days in the coming weeks that he'll be home late, so tonight he plans to make it on time. Before exiting his office, he turns off the lights and pulls the door almost closed, but he leaves it open just a crack. He sees no need to keep the door locked. If he can't trust a bunch of cops, he laughs to himself, then who in the hell can he trust?

Moving through the administration area, empty now following a day of hurried activity, Greg turns off the florescent overhead lights as he goes, plunging the offices into almost complete darkness. His mind is already in overdrive, thinking about what the next few days will bring. He understands the situation is going to become increasingly hectic as this case moves forward, especially now since it appears there may be a serial abductor on the prowl, preying on young children. He stops momentarily at the reception counter when his eyes are drawn to several posters hanging there. His gaze moves to several wanted posters advising of outstanding Canada-wide warrants for an assortment of criminals being sought for a variety of offences including murder and armed robbery. There are also several posters telling sad stories of missing children and these capture Greg's attention, probably, he thinks, because of the current case.

These posters relate information about missing boys and girls who were reported abducted from all across Canada, some dating back decades, but one poster in particular piques his interest for some reason. It's one of a four-year-old boy who was abducted from his home in Lethbridge, Alberta almost twenty years ago and has never been found. A computerized rendition of what he would look like today presents a haunting image of a lost child. He finds the child's eyes captivating. *He seems so innocent*, Greg thinks. He finds himself speculating on the boy's current whereabouts and wonders if, in fact, he is still alive at all after all this time. He shudders at the possibilities, as he is fully aware of the statistics that say most abducted children are never found alive. He knows full well that Holly Conrad and possibly Hillary Lawrence are now part of those statistics.

Caught up in his thoughts, he doesn't notice the figure approaching him from behind until it's too late.

"Excuse me, Constable," the voice says, interrupting his thoughts and snapping him out his trance-like state.

"Jesus," Greg reacts, instinctively spinning around and seeing a short, plump woman dressed in jeans and a navy blouse standing behind him. "Doris? You just about gave me a heart attack."

"Sorry," she whispers. Greg can tell he's embarrassed the older woman who wears her grey-streaked black hair back in a tight bun at the top of her head. "Didn't mean to frighten you. . . . I've already found one of you here on the floor with a heart attack and I don't want to do that again anytime, soon. Once was bad enough," she says, referring to when she found his best friend, Cliff Graham, on the floor only a few months earlier, fighting for his life.

"It's fine," he says, smiling at her in hopes of conveying his sincerity. "I was just so caught up in my thoughts that I didn't hear you come in and honestly, I'm surprised to even see you here, especially in this mess. The roads aren't fit to be driving on. We've already issued an advisory telling all motorists to stay off the roads. What are you doing here?"

"Cleaning," she says with a smile that reveals the dimples in her fat cheeks.

"You didn't drive here, did you?"

"Heaven's no. I don't like driving at the best of times," she answers. "I would never drive in these conditions. "My husband drove me over in the truck. It's really good in the snow. He's waiting for me outside."

"How are the roads?"

"They're a mess," she answers, bending to retrieve a blue wastebasket from under a desk close to where she's standing and then dumping the paper into a tall recycling bin on wheels. "It's not fit for anyone to be on them."

"So then you should have stayed home, Doris," he says, not missing the irony of her comment. "The garbage could have waited."

"It wasn't a problem, Constable."

He overlooks the fact that she's called him constable twice now, as he knows she doesn't mean any disrespect. "I just wouldn't want to see you have an accident."

"We've got four-wheel drive," she quickly answers. "We're good."

"Okay then," he shrugs. "I guess maybe I should be heading home. I think dinner's waiting and I don't like to keep my wife waiting."

"If you don't mind me saying, Constable," the impish woman continues, "it seems to me as though something is bothering you. Is everything okay?"

"I don't mind at all. It's just this case we're working on," he says, finding himself drawn to this woman's down-home personality. "It's really gotten inside my head."

"Heard about that this morning. It's a terrible thing," the cleaning woman says, retrieving another wastebasket from under another desk. "Anyone doing something like that to a child is heartbreakin' and now they say there's another gone missing up Yarmouth way. What's the world coming to?"

"There are a lot of sick people out there," he sighs. "A lot of sick people."

"There sure are," she agrees, dumping the paper into the recycling bin. "But it seems to me that something else is bothering you."

"Well," he pauses, studying the woman's face. Then he says, "It's nothing, really."

"Go on, Constable. Don't be afraid to talk about it," she urges him. "You're a lot like that other nice man who used to run this place."

"You mean Corporal Graham?"

"Yes," she nods. "Nice man, but he gave us a real good scare."

"He sure did," Greg nods.

"Hope he's feeling better these days."

"He is doing much better now, as a matter of fact."

"Well," the woman continues, "like I always told him, and now I'll tell you, it's not good to keep anything bottled up inside. Unless it's something too private to talk about or something to do with your cases, then just let it out. I've been around here long enough to know not to ask any of the constables any questions about anything they're working on."

"It's not really anything connected with the case," Greg says, suddenly feeling comfortable enough to talk to this woman, something he very seldom does with people outside the force. "It's just that I've had the weirdest experience today with some . . . crows."

"Crows, you say?" Her eyebrows rise as she stops what she's doing with the trash and studies him.

"Yes," he nods. "Crows."

"And how many are we talking about?"

He hesitates, not sure if he should continue the conversation, but finally he sighs, "Five."

"Five crows silver," she nods. "I see."

"You see what?"

"The crows are trying to tell you that silver is going to play a prominent role in your life in the near future."

"That's just an old wives tale."

"Is it?"

"Isn't it?"

"Some people dismiss these old sayings as superstitions, but not me. I've seen too much in my lifetime to know better than to do that. When the crows have something to say, I believe we should listen to them. Sometimes, ignoring them makes it worse and whatever they're trying to tell you simply won't go away just because you don't want to accept their warnings." She winks at him. "Take heed, Constable. If the crows are reaching out to you, then they have a message for you and you should listen to them."

"What kind of message?"

"Now that, I can't say."

"So then, who might know what they're trying to tell me?"

"The best person to talk to about that would be Clara Underwood, providing she'll talk to you," Doris replies, all of a sudden playing coy. "She knows everything there is to know about the crows. You should go see her."

"I should?"

"Yes, Constable," she nods. "You should."

"Where do I find this Clara Underwood? I've never heard of her . . . mind you I haven't been here that long."

"Not many people have seen her in recent years," Doris admits. "She keeps to herself mostly and people from these parts leave her alone. They say she's a witch."

"A witch?" Greg shrugs, thinking he's wasting his time here and he should really be getting home. "Come on, Doris. Really? This is the 21st Century. No one believes in witches these days."

"You're just like that other officer," she scoffs. "But like I told him and I'll tell you—you should not make light of things you don't understand, Constable. Just because you don't believe in them, doesn't mean they aren't real."

"So now I'm supposed to go talk to a witch about an old superstition?" he replies. "First crows, now witches. This just gets weirder and weirder. So, for argument's sake, Doris, what can you tell me about this Clara Underwood?"

The cleaning woman studies him and then finally says, "There's a local legend about an old woman who used to live around these parts. Her name was Alexandria Gorham. The story goes that she lived here more than two hundred years ago. Her family was one of the first to settle in these parts and they were important people back then, rich and powerful, but for whatever reason, Alexandria became an outcast and the early people shunned her."

"Why?"

"I don't know, Constable," Doris answers. "I'm not really sure if the truth about that ever came out, but the legend goes that at first Alexandria was considered a saint by some of the locals. They said she could work miracles and did all kinds of impressive things to help people when they faced hardships."

"That doesn't sound like any reason to make her an outcast."

"That's not the whole story," the woman quickly replies. "Even though some thought she was a saint and supposedly she did many good things, a lot of the other people thought she was a witch and it appears they had more control over the early settlement than those who thought the other way . . . and they are the ones who made her an outcast."

"So what happened to her?"

"The story goes that something tragic happened and she was to blame. Eventually, the townspeople drove her away. They say she went into the woods one day and just disappeared, never to be heard of again." The woman pauses and then adds, "That's all I know about it."

"That's supposed to help me with the crows?"

"I didn't say I could help you," the woman smiles coyly. "I said Clara Underwood could help you."

"What's her connection to this?"

"Well," Doris sighs, "You see, according to legend, Clara Underwood is a direct descendant of Alexandria Gorham and that's all I can tell you about that."

Chapter 8

It's already after 6 p.m. by the time Greg finishes talking with Doris. The elderly woman has been cleaning the detachment office for the past fourteen years and he hasn't paid that much attention to her since he's been there, but today, she has kept him longer than he intended. While he definitely finds the chat both amusing and enlightening, he isn't sure he should take her seriously. His logical mind tells him to chalk up her story to old folktales, but his analytical mind tells him not to be so quick to dismiss things—not even information that seems obscure and bizarre. Over the past few years, many things have happened in this town that defy logic and sometimes it's necessary to look beyond the realm of reality to find answers.

By the time Greg leaves the Liverpool RCMP detachment it's close to 6:15 p.m. and the blizzard's full force has now moved up the coast. Hitting Nova Scotia's South Shore with a vengeance, the Nor'easter has already deposited almost twenty centimetres of wind-driven snow over the region, blanketing everything in a stark pure white. Making his way along the town's deserted main street, he watches as the gale-force wind whips the snow into a frenzy and deposits it in drifts, the depths of which this region hasn't experienced in years—the past three winters were relatively mild, according to Cliff, at least. The latest radio reports predict another ten-to-fifteen centimetres overnight before the storm moves off and that, mixed with the senseless murder of a young child and his run-in with the crows, leaves the tired police officer in a foul mood.

Casting an ominous pall over the town, the late winter darkness has fully settled in, enveloping everything in its sinister embrace. The entire town seems eerily quiet as the wind forces the large flakes to fall in a horizontal pattern, as if defying gravity. He knows this will not be a good night for the officers holding down the late shift, but at least they are secure in their homes, waiting for whatever emergency calls might come—and Greg is sure they will definitely come. Such weather usually brings a rash of car accidents, house fires and other tragedies. He expects he'll be called for assistance before the morning's light. The seasoned officer has seen many winter storms and although he feels for his colleagues, he also knows such demands come with the territory. Before the winter storm is over, he's sure he'll also have his share of headaches.

Skilfully guiding his cruiser through the empty streets of downtown Liverpool, Greg marvels at how empty the town seems. Scanning the sidewalks for movement, it's clear the town is entirely deserted. It's as though it's been abandoned, like some of those old ghost towns he's seen in the movies. Not a living soul is in sight and, except for the occasional security light in some buildings, all the stores and offices are in virtual darkness, a testament to the severity of this February storm.

Navigating the car around and through the large drifts blocking his path, he watches the snowplow operators as they fight a losing battle to keep a clear passage for emergency crews. It's a futile task and Greg expects it won't be long before the plows are called back to wait until the heavy snowfall abates. Ten minutes later, after navigating the slick roads, he pulls into his driveway and parks. Sitting inside the cruiser, surrounded by the radio, force-issued shotgun and other police paraphernalia, he listens to some chatter on the airwaves, just in case he's needed somewhere else and has to turn around.

"Good." Turning the car off. It's nothing important, he concludes, much to his relief.

He sits for a moment mesmerized by the snowflakes as they meet their demise the moment they land on the heated windshield, the melted water then running toward the engine hood. Greg's mind is overtaken by the tragedy unfolding in this small town. Even though he's alone, he still tries to maintain his composure as images of young Holly Conrad lying naked on the frozen sand invade his thoughts. *Ironic*, he thinks, rubbing the tears from his eyes, that a place that provides so much enjoyment in the summer could become a place of such sorrow. Greg knows her death is an act perpetrated by someone full of hatred and evil—someone with complete disdain for human life.

"What a mess," he says and then sighs loudly, as though trying to expel the horrifying thoughts from his mind. But it doesn't work and his mind quickly races over the events of the past thirteen hours. *How can something like this be happening here? Why in Liverpool. ... Why not?* he answers his own question. He knows no place, big or small, is immune to such perversion. These days, small-town living is really just a façade of safety.

Finally sliding his large, six-foot, three-inch frame from behind the steering wheel and stepping out into the wind-driven snow, his mind continues to race. He speaks aloud, as if an unseen companion is standing beside him, intent to hang on his every word.

"We're missing something in all of this. I just can't see it," he says, hoping someone will agree with his observation, but he's alone. In fact, he thinks as he looks up and down the vacant street, the snow blowing past his eyes making it difficult to see, he's not sure if he's ever felt so alone in a long time.

There has to be a reason this is happening, he thinks while pushing through the knee-deep drifts already piling up at the front door of his rented 130-year-old clapboard home located in an unassuming neighbourhood on Mersey Avenue. Stomping up the front steps to shake the snow from his boots, he pauses before grabbing the doorknob. He spins around as if expecting to find someone following behind, as he can't shake the uneasiness that's suddenly taken hold of him.

Ever since the first incident with the crows this morning, he's had a nagging feeling in the pit of his stomach that something beyond the scope of reality is at play here and even though he considers himself to be a rational and intelligent man, he's slowly beginning to accept there are things that defy a simple explanation. Glancing up and down the street one more time, the snow falling so heavy it looks like one continuous sheet, he recalls the story that Doris just passed onto him and he shudders when he thinks of the implications.

"Come on Gregory Paris," he finally says to himself. "You're a smart man. You don't really believe in old wives' tales and superstitions and witches."

Still, he thinks, finally taking hold of the doorknob with his gloved hand, *something weird is definitely going on around this town.*

He slowly turns the knob. *I'll have to track down this Clara Underwood and see what she has to say about these crows and what they could be up to.*

What do I have to lose? he thinks. He opens the door to the warmth that awaits him inside the house. *I'll see if Cliff wants to tag along. This will be right up his alley.*

"Honey," Greg yells. "I'm home. Sorry I'm late."

*****

"I really am sorry. I got delayed," Greg says as he helps his wife load the dishwasher. "I promised I'd be home by six and I know I kept you waiting. I don't like to do that."

"No harm done," Andrea smiles, stacking the plates in the washing tray. "It's hard to ruin stew."

"That's not the point," he replies, his tone apologetic. "I promised you I wouldn't be late."

"It's police work, Greg." She shrugs. "I know you had a rough day and there's lots going on, so honestly, I really didn't expect you home this early. I know you have a demanding job and that's just part of who you are." Smiling, she adds, "It's part of the man I love."

"Yes, well," he explains. "The storm has pretty well brought everything to a standstill. Nothing's moving on those roads and I mean nothing."

"I'm just glad you're home," Andrea smiles again. "Why don't you go read to Lucy and I'll finish up here. Then I'll fix us some coffee. I think we could both use a little pick-me-up."

"What did I ever do to deserve you?" He grins, pulling her close and kissing her firmly on her soft lips. Breaking the seal, he whispers, "I needed that."

"Keep that up, Mister and you might end up with more than a hot cup of coffee." She winks, kissing him again and then pulls away.

"Now, go spend some time with your daughter and when you come back, we'll talk."

"Fine." Greg shrugs, letting go of his wife. "But don't forget what you promised."

"What?" she laughs. He loves how her eyes sparkle when she grins at him. "I didn't promise anything."

"You're such a tease," he says, heading to the living room. "Oh," he adds, "I almost forgot. I ran into that Murdock McCarthy earlier today and I promised his youngest daughter, Emma, that maybe you'd call and invite her over to have a play-date with Lucy. Think we could do that soon? She looks so lonely. I really think she could use a friend. There's just something about her that really gets to me."

"I think we can do that," Andrea says. "What's up with them anyway? They are a strange bunch, aren't they?"

"How do you mean?" Greg asks, stopping in the doorway to look at his wife who is just switching on the dishwasher.

"I don't know," she answers. "They just seem to keep to themselves. It's like they don't want to get to know the local people."

"What do you mean? Didn't they host that News Year's Eve party?" Greg asks. "That doesn't sound like someone who doesn't want to meet people. . . . The whole town was there."

"Honestly, I'm not really sure what that was all about," Andrea says. "But I will call and invite the little one over to play with Lucy if you want."

"I think that would be nice and I think Lucy would like it, too."

"I'll do it in a day or two," she promises. "Once things settle down some."

"Don't you mean, if they settle down?" Greg replies, turning and heading for his daughter's room.

*****

"She fought it, but she's finally gone to sleep," Greg says as he joins his wife in the living room where she's curled up in a sea-foam love seat reading a magazine article about middle-aged women becoming new mothers. "I ended up reading her three books before she finally dozed off," he adds. "She's pretty excited about the snow. That's all she could talk about."

"She's a child, Greg, and children love snow," Andrea smiles up at him and pats the cushion beside her, her soft features illuminated by the lamp on the table next to her. *She really is a natural beauty*, he thinks. "Come and sit down beside me. Have your coffee and try to relax. You've had a rough day."

"You have no idea," he says, plopping onto the cushion beside his wife of two years and wrapping his left arm around her. Placing his right hand on her belly, he whispers, "How's the little guy doing?"

"What makes you think it's a little guy?" Andrea smirks and gives him a wink. "Maybe it's a little gal."

"Maybe," he nods, the thought brightening his mood.

"And if it is," she smiles back, "would you be okay with that?"

"I'd be ecstatic," he beams, grinning from ear to ear. "It doesn't matter to me if it's a boy or girl just as long as he or she is healthy and takes after his or her mom."

"I don't know," she laughs. "If it's a boy, I'd kind of like to see him take after his dad."

"Well, okay then," he smirks. "If it's a girl, she can take after you. If it's a boy, he can take after me, just as long as he has your brains."

"Oh, I don't know about that. I think his dad's pretty smart," Andrea says, cocking her head in his direction and studying his face. "What's up with you?" she finally asks. "You seem a little off this evening. You're not usually this self-deprecating."

"It's just this case," Greg sighs, throwing his head back against the cushion and closing his eyes. "It's really getting to me. The idea that there's someone out there abducting children and doing God knows what to them before killing them, is really playing on my nerves, especially with Lucy in the house."

"We'll keep her close," Andrea assures him. "You don't think that whoever is doing this would come looking around here do you? I mean, this town?"

"I don't know," he admits. "But why wouldn't he? All I know is that whenever one of these guys is out trolling for victims, you can't take anything for granted and you can't let your guard down, not for one minute. So we've got to be careful because honestly, we have no idea where he'll strike next. After all, we know he was in Windsor and now maybe Yarmouth and he's been to Liverpool at least once since he dumped his first victim here."

Andrea sighs and pulls him closer. "I can't stop thinking about those poor little girls and their parents. How can they cope with such a loss? It's such a terrible thing to have to live with. If something like that happened to Lucy—God willing it doesn't— I don't know what I'd do, but I'm sure I'd go crazy. . . . I just can't imagine it."

"It's a terrible thing, that's for sure." He nods and finally grabs his cup from the table in front of the love seat. He likes the feel of the warm, smooth ceramic glass in his hands. Pausing, he takes a sip and then says, "That's a great cup of coffee. I really need this." Smiling at her, he adds, "Thank you." And she can tell he means it.

"No problem," she returns his smile and studies his rugged, but handsome face with the sharp features that remind her of an actor in one of those old Hollywood movies that she likes so much—like Jimmy Stewart, Cary Grant or Clark Gable. Finally, she says, "So what else is going on, Greg? I know you and I've seen you work some pretty tough cases in the past, but I'm not sure I've ever seen you act like this. You seem rattled, so I know something else is bothering you."

He sighs. "Honestly," he begins, "I'm not really sure about this place. This whole town is starting to freak me out. And before you say anything," he pauses then nods in her direction, "I know you had reservations right from the beginning about staying here and you only agreed to it because of me. Trust me, I've been thinking about that all day and wondering if maybe I was wrong to force the issue."

"You didn't force me to do anything," she replies, smiling gently at him and placing her hand on his lap. "I made up my own mind."

"I certainly didn't give you many choices, though."

"I don't know about that." She pauses and watches him closely. "So what's got you thinking about this today, after all these months?" She asks. "I mean, it's not that you didn't have other things on your mind today. And for the record, honey," she smirks, "you didn't force me to stay here. I'm a big girl and you know I wouldn't do anything that I didn't want to do."

"True," he concedes. "I know that. . . . It was just something that Cliff said when I talked to him today."

"You saw Cliff today?"

"I did," he nods. "I needed to run something past him."

"How's he doing?"

"Really well," Greg says. "He looks good. Better than he's

looked in a long time. I'm really proud of him because of how he's turned his life around. He was heading for trouble, but that heart attack put a real scare in him. . . . And I reminded Carly that we're still counting on her for Saturday night. Hope you still want to go out. I may need a break by then."

"I'd like to, but do you think we should go out with everything that's going on?"

"Carly's a good kid," he says. "We can trust her and we won't be going that far."

"So then, what did Cliff say that's got you all worked up?"

"I don't know," Greg hesitates. "We were just talking about the strange events that seem to happen around here and it got me thinking."

"Thinking?" she asks, her eyebrows rising with curiosity. "Thinking about what?"

"Like I said, I really don't know," he shrugs and hesitates again. Then he says, "Like the people, for one thing. Remember all the strange events that happened around our involvement with Oliver Lewis when we arrived last fall? You have to admit, it was all pretty weird. I mean, first of all, the guy's got terminal cancer and then he's miraculously cured. How can that happen? Cancer just doesn't go away and as far as I know, they still haven't found a cure for it."

"Miracles do sometimes happen, Greg."

"Seems to me, they happen a lot around here." Greg shrugs. "I wonder whatever happened to him."

"According to Samantha Henderson, who I see once and awhile when she drops off her son at the daycare centre, he's doing very well. Apparently, he's in Europe or someplace like that."

"See, that's what I mean. One minute this guy's on his death bed with one foot in the grave and the next he's gallivanting all over the world doing God knows what," he takes another sip of coffee. "I just don't get it."

"I'm sure it wasn't that simple," Andrea says. "And honestly, honey, I'm not really sure why this has gotten you all worked up after all this time. You knew all of this when you took the job, so why now? Why today?"

He says nothing but takes another drink of coffee, casting his eyes to the floor and staring at the braided mat under the table.

"Come on, Greg," she probes. "If something is bothering you

then please tell me what it is. I know this case has you on edge and I get that, but this thing with Oliver Lewis is old news and I can't understand why you would be thinking about that today. So what's up? Remember your promise to me when we got married? You told me that you would never keep anything from me and now I'd appreciate it if you would honour that promise."

"I want to," he says. "But you are going to think I'm crazy."

"Please give me more credit than that," she answers, rubbing his shoulder. "I live with a cop whose job over the past twenty years has been chasing crazed perverts all across the country, so I know to expect anything. I won't think you're crazy and you know that. In fact, you're the sanest person I know."

"Okay, then." He sighs and glances at her. Leaning forward and placing his coffee cup back on the table, he says, "Well then maybe *I* think I'm going crazy."

"You're being cryptic, Greg. I don't like it when you do that," squeezing him tighter, she adds, "in fact, I hate it when you do that and you know it."

"Sorry. You're right." He sighs again, trying to just let the words flow. He leans back into the plush cushion again. "Okay. Okay. . . . So here's the thing. I think a bunch of crows are trying to talk to me and the worst thing about it all, is that I think they're actually trying to tell me something about this case."

"The case of the missing girls?" she asks, her voice steady, trying not to seem surprised by his statement.

"Yes."

"And how are they trying to talk to you?"

"It's not through words, if that's what you're think . . . I'm not that crazy yet," he says. "It's in their actions and how they've been hanging around me all day. I just can't shake the feeling that they are trying to make contact with me." Turning to her, he adds, "I know. Weird, huh?"

"Truthfully," she answers. "A little, but that doesn't mean I don't believe you or that I think you're crazy. It just means it's a little outside the realm of our reality."

"Just a little," he says and gives her a coy grin. "Really?"

"So what are you going to do?"

"Seriously," he answers, "I have no idea. That's one of the things

I was talking to Cliff about today. I knew he's had some dealings with crows in the past so I wanted to pick his brains."

"Did it help?"

"Not much. He commiserated with me, but he couldn't offer me anything concrete, so I'm back to square one," Greg says. He sighs heavily. "My fear is that I'm going to become so distracted by the crows that I will lose focus on this case."

"You won't," she assures him, running her hands over his back and shoulders. "I know you. You're too good at what you do to lose focus on an important case like this. You would never let those little girls down."

"You give me too much credit."

"It's well deserved," she answers. "Now, I think you just need to relax. Finish your coffee and we'll turn in for the night."

"That's the best thing I've heard all day," he says, picking up his coffee again and bringing it to his mouth. Hesitating, he thinks about telling his wife the story that Doris shared with him earlier, but he changes his mind. "I am a little tired," he sighs, taking a sip of the hot, black liquid.

Chapter 9

February 13

The chimes clang in the wind, their lilting song lost within the howling blizzard, but he can still hear them from where he's standing. He's very close to where the beautiful sea-glass now sings, polished smooth to perfection by years of tumbling through the wild ocean waves. The chimes hang in the leafless branch of the dying birch tree, its fragile and rotting wood threatening to break under the excessive weight of the falling snow. He purposely avoids jarring the tree and dislodging the snow. He'd like to see the branch snap right now, the potential cracking excites him. He wishes he could watch it fall to the ground, revel in the randomness of its death as it becomes collateral damage of the now raging storm, but the bare branch clings to the tree trunk, as if holding on for dear life in one last desperate attempt to save itself.

Pitiful, he thinks.

The gale-force winds continue to push the snow into deep drifts, as the biting cold chews at the bare skin on his cheeks. But he refuses to leave. It's been three hours since he arrived. He's watched as the snow has slowly transformed the modest century-old home into a winter wonderland, painted by some invisible artist who has been working diligently to cover up the dirty white, vinyl siding and green trim. The snow has inched past his ankles and is quickly working its way up his legs, as though it is alive, secretly devouring him. His hood, normally grey, is awash in a thick layer of heavy white snow. In fact, his entire coat is white. To an unsuspecting passerby, he could simply blend into the background. He watched from the shadows as the lights went out, plunging the home into utter darkness. And then, as if oblivious to the natural elements, he remained frozen in his hidden spot, until he was sure everyone inside had gone to sleep.

He's actually been watching this house for several weeks now so he knows the occupants' routines—right down to the last second. He knows when the mother and father get up and when the little girl first opens her eyes every morning, like clockwork. He knows when they eat breakfast and when they leave the house each day—the mother and father heading to their jobs, the little girl going off to school, dropped there by her mother. He knows when the family returns each afternoon, what time they have supper, when the girl does her homework at the little desk in front of the room's single window. He knows the small child goes to bed at eight and that her father is always the last one to turn in. That's usually around midnight, except on Saturday nights, when it's a bit later. But this is Friday and the lights click off just before twelve. Right on schedule.

It's almost 3 a.m. now and he's confident everyone is sleeping. *It's time.*

It's time to claim his prize. He pushes his way through a clump of alders and dense brier bushes growing on the northern edge of the neglected property. He stops for a minute and then flicks his cigarette into the snow. He stares at it, almost mesmerized as the bright-red cinders let out an almost inaudible hiss as they die out and then turn black in the pristinely white snow. The sounds and sight of the now extinguished cigarette excite him. He can feel that his senses are heightened. He is like a lion, silently sneaking up on his unsuspecting prey. He doesn't care that the half smoked cigarette could be evidence because he knows by the time the police arrive, it will be well buried and any trace of him will be long gone, obliterated by the storm. That, and the fact that he knows he is smarter than any of the wannabe-small-town cops that pretend to be in control of their domain. Tonight, this is his town.

He has been honing his skills for years. He chose this location because the shrubs provided perfect protection. There are no street-lights. Even the lights from the nearest homes don't reach this far. He knew he could watch the house undetected—like a ghost. Trudging through the deep snow, the black ski mask under his hood is now white, covered in a layer of wet snow that clings easily to the wool. Everything is perfect. By morning, his tracks will be mere indentations in the drifts, leaving behind nothing for the incompetent police. They have no idea who he is.

He is a genius. A master of manipulation and right now, he has everyone spinning in circles. There is a method to his madness though. He's always careful to choose families with only one child—always a little girl. Fewer people in the household means less chance someone will hear him.

Reaching the bottom of the back steps, he looks up at the sec-ond-floor windows. He knows where her bedroom is and he knows he must be extremely quiet because her parents' room is right next to hers. Before climbing the first rotting step, he pulls two white kitchen catcher garbage bags from his black vinyl kit bag and pulls one over his right boot, then secures it in place with string. Then he repeats the process with the left boot. He will leave no footprints inside the house.

Snaking his way up the rickety steps to avoid the creaking spots, he knows there is no need to rush. He has practiced this many times now and he knows every inch of this house. It will be four hours before the mom and dad awake and by that time, he'll be long gone with his prized possession—one he's coveted from afar. He saw her several weeks ago while he was scouting the playground near the school and he's kept close watch on her ever since. The instant he saw her, he knew she was the one—that she was special and that she belonged with him. He's certain if he asked her to go with him, she'd come freely, but he doesn't have time for such things. Time is too important. But it doesn't matter because he's certain she'll be happy with him. He knows it. . . . They always are.

It's six steps from the bottom to the top. He's been inside the house twice now while the family was gone and he remembers all the corners and obstacles. He's planned this night right down to the last detail. He has imagined this every waking moment for weeks now.

Reaching the back door, he shakes the snow from his gloves and pulls the lock pick from the kit bag. He knows there is no alarm system. People in this neighbourhood don't have such luxuries. Besides, even if they could afford one, they don't have anything valuable worth stealing . . . or so they think. But he knows better. Seconds later, he's opened the door and is standing inside the cluttered kitchen, its early 1970s appliances looking like someone had vomited putrid avocado green all over their chipped and cracked enamel. The snow drips onto the bulging vinyl floor, but he doesn't care. He has more important things to do than worry about some cheap, thirty-year-old flooring.

He cautiously glances around the room, wiping the dripping snow from his eyes. Good. No one has gotten up to use the downstairs bathroom. A small, shell-shaped night light flickers in the tiny room, as though it, like the rest of the house, has seen better days. Everything is quiet. He's confident he has free access to the house. He moves quickly through the kitchen, down a dark hallway that leads past the living room and to the stairs. He takes them one at a time just to be cautious—although he wants to fly up the stairs now that he can sense she is so close, he wills himself to go slowly. He glances at the pictures hanging on the wall to his right; the aging pictures of the happy bride and groom cutting the cake, of the couple in some warm and sunny locale, a baby in a christening gown, a little girl in various stages of growth, both before and after she started school. There's even one with the little girl hugging a dog, a beagle, but there's no dog in this house, so he thinks it's either dead or belonged to someone else. He hates the pictures because he hates the happiness they represent. He's never been in any such pictures of his own.

He hesitates briefly at the top of the stairs and studies the hallway that leads to her bedroom, but first he must pass the parents' room. He steps gingerly, stealth-like. Outside their door, he pauses and listens for any sign of movement. Hearing nothing, he moves on until he reaches her door, which is still open a crack. As he stands there, longing to put his arms around her, his breath comes in short spurts. His excitement rises. This is the moment he's been dreaming about for weeks.

Struggling to stifle his anticipation, he reaches into the black bag and removes the duct tape. He then pushes the door open just a bit and slips inside her room, carefully closing the door behind him. It creaks slightly, and he freezes. . . . Nothing. He's good to go.

It's dark inside, but he's not worried. He's been here before so he knows the layout of the room. He's done his homework and he knows it's only nine steps from the door to the head of the bed where her head, covered in beautiful blonde curls, will be resting on her pillow. He knows there is a tiny desk near the window, a dresser in the far corner of the room where she keeps her small jewellery box, a toy chest next to the dresser filled with Barbie dolls, a small table beside the bed and a closet behind the bedroom door where she hangs all her pretty clothes.

Forcing himself to slow his breathing, he counts the steps as he goes.

One. Two. Three. He thinks, making sure not to miscount.

Four. Five. Six. Seven. He pauses. Breathes. Holds his breath, then steps again. *Eight. Nine.*

He knows he's at the head of the bed now because he can hear her softly breathing. Closing his eyes for a second, he listens. She sounds like an angel and as he envisions her long blonde hair spread out over the pink pillowcase, he imagines she also looks like an angel. He can't wait to touch her, feel her, to hold her.

Soon, he thinks, pulling a strip of duct tape from the roll and, peering down at her tiny face in the darkness, he quickly pushes the silver tape over her mouth. Her eyes snap open, the whites clearly visible in the darkness, the fear contained there as her worst nightmare has suddenly become real. *At least she can't scream*, he thinks.

"Shhhh," he whispers, suddenly angry she is not happy to see him. Throwing the bag on the bed and reaching inside with his left hand as he pushes down on her chest with the other hand, applying just enough weight to hold her tiny body in place while her arms and legs flail about. He doesn't want to crush his little angel just yet.

"Stop moving," he commands, still trying to whisper, as he pulls a sheet of plastic from the kit bag and unfolds it. Then he pulls out several pieces of rope.

As the girl continues to struggle under his weight, he decides it's time to show her who's in charge. Quickly pulling off his glove, he hits her tiny face with the back of his right hand then pulls his glove back on.

"Quiet," he barks, his tone muted. "Or I will hit you again."

The girl immediately stops struggling, becoming still and making only a muffled whimpering sound under the duct tape, but he images if he could see her clearly, her beautiful blue eyes would be filled with tears.

"Don't cry," he whispers, his harsh tone clearly evident in his words. "I don't like it when kids cry."

Starting at her feet, he pulls the sheet of plastic up to her chin and then rolls her onto her stomach and then onto her back again, in the process, wrapping her in the plastic and trapping her within the cocoon. He knows she cannot move now.

Taking the first piece of rope, he pulls it around her ankles and ties it. Tight. The next piece goes around her waist with her arms at her sides, and the third piece is secured around her shoulders. *Now*, he thinks, there is no way she can move. *She's mine*. He finally smiles.

Tossing the roll of duct tape back inside the bag and closing the zipper, he slips the kit on this back. Moving like he's done this before, he bends and picks up the plastic-wrapped girl—her head and feet sticking out of either end—and holds her under his left arm as he would a bundle of wood. He then makes his way back to her bedroom door, slowly turns the doorknob and opens the door just wide enough to peek outside. The hallway is empty, so he slips through the crack and then, ever so gently, closes the door behind him.

Slowly moving past the parents' bedroom door, he feels her struggling to get free, but he squeezes her tighter and reaches the stairway. Descending the steps he glances at the wall of photos to his left, the many happy faces smiling out from under the glass in the various size frames and, for a second, he becomes angry that he's never had any of those experiences. But the little girl squirming under his arm reminds him that he has just brought balance to his existence.

Reaching the bottom of the staircase, he moves stealthily back down the hallway, past the living room and into the kitchen. At the back door, he switches his package to the other arm, grabs the door handle with his right hand and eases it open. Lowering his head as he braces for the cold wind, he steps out onto the rotting back doorstep, his boots immediately disappearing in the deep snow.

Turning to close the kitchen door behind him, he purposefully steps slowly as he makes his way down the steps, across the back yard and into the alders and brier bushes, their branches hanging heavy with the burden of snow. Glancing back to scout out the house, he smiles with pride as he sees it's cloaked in darkness.

A foghorn sounds in the distance, its mournful sound muffled by the heavily falling snow, as it attempts to echo along the coast. *All is well*, he thinks. And he now feels complete.

He's done it again, he thinks, pushing through the snow and following a small trail, now buried under inches of snow that will lead him out to a side street where the van is parked. Once there, he will disappear. Feeling the tiny girl struggling to break free of his grip, he squeezes hard again and she becomes still.

She belongs to him now. *She will learn to listen*, he thinks. *If not, she will suffer the consequences.*

*****

He tried to sleep, but every time he closed his eyes, visions of the girl's tiny naked body splayed on the frozen sand, her arms folded on her chest like some hideous trophy, kept invading his thoughts. The images caused him to toss and turn and four times he got out of bed and made his way to Lucy's room down the hallway to check on her. He needed to make sure his four-year-old daughter was still safe in her bed.

But it wasn't only thoughts of the child abductor prowling his community and trolling for little girls that made him restless. The crows—all five of them—have also infiltrated his every thought, making him edgy. Dealing with a real threat, like a kidnapper is bad enough, but facing something that might be from beyond what he considers normal, is something completely different and he doesn't know if he's prepared to accept the possibilities they may bring, let alone deal with them.

Greg Paris is a well-educated man and he's had more experience in dealing with cases of the sick and perverted persuasion than he cares to admit, but he's never had to deal with anything quite like what he's seen in Liverpool over the past four or five years. Throwing the covers back once again, he now understands why Cliff has become so paranoid anytime he sees crows. He, too, is beginning to feel anxious and out of sorts whenever he thinks of the powerful black birds.

What does he really know about crows? He slides over to the

edge of the bed and plants his feet in the plush fur mat covering the cold, hardwood floor.

What, indeed, he thinks, grabbing a navy sweatshirt dangling over the arm of a white wicker chair near the bed and pulling it on over his head. He grabs his grey jogging pants and slips them up over his long, muscular legs. If he can't sleep, he may as well go down stairs and do some work.

Glancing at the digital clock on his night table, he sees it's almost 4:30 a.m. and still pitch black outside. Based on the wind howling outside the bedroom window, he also knows the storms is still raging.

Too early to go to work, he decides, watching his wife as she sleeps, snuggled under the covers like a child, her form slowly rising and falling as she breathes. She's the most beautiful woman he's seen in a very long time. He considers himself lucky to have met her and now, she's going to have his baby. That's more happiness than he thought he'd ever find after the death of his first wife. *How lucky can one man get,* he thinks. He found not one, but two true loves in his lifetime, when some people never find it once.

Slowly making his way out of the bedroom, he pulls the door closed with a gentle click and moves to Lucy's door, which is still slightly ajar. Pushing it in just a few inches he sticks his head inside and glances around so he can reassure himself one more time that everything is in order.

All is good, he thinks, seeing that the little blonde-haired girl is sleeping soundly with Mr. Ted, her stuffed brown Teddy bear pulled in closely to her face.

Sweet, he thinks, wondering what he would do if something ever happened to her, and for a minute, his mind wanders to the Conrads and the Lawrences, the parents of the two missing girls, and he wonders how they're coping. He knows it can't be easy and, pulling Lucy's door almost closed, he thinks if it were him, he'd hunt the pervert to the depths of hell and then kill the bastard.

Actually, that's pretty much what he's doing with his investigation, although he's sure he'd never kill the bastard. He steps lightly as he goes down the stairs. *Not intentionally at least,* he thinks, knowing that as a police officer, he's sworn to uphold the law — no matter what.

Making his way through the kitchen, he stops at the back door and checks the locks. He needs to remove the chains and install deadbolts—real locks—chains are for wimps. *Real men use dead-bolts*, he thinks, grinning at his own humour. But for tonight at least, everything appears to be in order.

All secure. He slips the chain out of the block and presses the lock in the doorknob. Opening the door, he's immediately met by a blast of blowing snow, and by the looks of it, he's sure the storm has already dumped at least thirty centimetres on the area, for more than the original forecast had called for.

Freaking snow. Holding the door open, he leans out, sticking his head into the raging snow squall and looking around the backyard, his eyes scanning every corner and crevasse of the property as he peers through the shadows looking for anything that appears out of the ordinary.

"Nothing," he sighs, relieved the backyard is still and unbroken, like an oil painting, but he knows such beauty can be deceiving.

Closing the door and securing the locks once again, he wipes the snow from his black hair and makes his way into the dining room where he's left his laptop on the large and expensive oak table where they dine with guests, although there have been no dinner parties since they moved into this house. There hasn't been time.

Snapping on the three-pronged light that hangs over the table, its fake crystal teardrops catching the light and throwing it around the room, he sits in one of the six chairs and flips open the cover of his Mac. Clicking on the Firefox icon, he waits for the search engine to open, then he types in the words, "crow superstitions" and waits for the worldwide web to do its work. Seconds later, he's reading a web page that tells him about various crow superstitions and beliefs. He's surprised at how many there are.

"Crows have been used for the purpose of divination since the time of ancient Rome," he reads, keeping his voice at a whisper.

He pauses and listens as the wind howls around the trees in the backyard. He keeps reading.

Finding a dead crow on the road is good luck. Well, certainly not for the crow, he thinks, grinning to himself.

He listens as the wind throws the snow against the windows, the frozen pellets clunking against the glass. He turns to look at the windows and suddenly hopes they can withstand the barrage of ice pellets. He shudders and keeps reading.

Crows in a churchyard are bad luck.

He pauses and thinks about the missing girl from Yarmouth. He wonders if she's still alive and if she is, what hell she is enduring.

A single crow over a house means bad news and often foretells a death within.

It was unlucky in Wales to have a crow cross your path. However, if two crows crossed your path, the luck was reversed.

He shrugs, that doesn't mean much to him.

In New England, however, to see two crows flying together from the left was bad luck.

Interesting, he thinks, but of little consequence to him.

In Chinese mythology, a three-legged crow was used to represent the sun because three was the number for light and goodness.

Nothing there, he thinks, shaking his head. *Haven't seen any three-legged crows lately*, he shrugs.

In Somerset, England, locals used to carry an onion with them for protection from crows. He keeps scrolling down the page.

Where do they get this stuff? he wonders.

In Yorkshire, children were threatened with the Great Black Bird, which would carry them off if they were bad.

Hmmmm, Greg thinks. *Now that's interesting.*

He continues reading.

It has been said that a baby will die if a crow's eggs are stolen.

He pauses and scratches his head as he listens to the wind blustering outside. *What a brutal night to be out there*, he thinks—*but no one would be that stupid.*

Crows and ravens are considered royal birds. Legend has it that King Arthur turned into one. Alexander the Great was supposedly guided across the desert by two ravens sent from heaven, another site states.

Recalling the silver cross they found around the little girl's neck, Greg wonders if that is significant.

Probably not, he decides with a shrug, answering his own question. He reads further.

The French had a saying—evil priests became crows and bad nuns became magpies.

Really? Greg thinks. *Bizarre.*

The Greeks said 'Go to the Crows' the same way we would say

'Go to Hell.'

Well, aren't we all in hell of some sort? Greg thinks.

The Romans used the expression 'To pierce a crow's eye' in relation to something that was almost impossible to do.

This is getting me nowhere, he thinks, but he keeps reading.

The expression, 'I have a bone to pick with you' used to be 'I have a crow to pick with you.'

Who the hell keeps track of this stuff, Greg scoffs, deciding this is a waste of time.

Returning to the main search engine page, he types in the words *Maritime crow rhyme* and his interest is immediately piqued when the results pop up on his screen.

He reads aloud, but in a muted tone. "One crow sorrow, two crows joy; three crows a letter, four crows a boy; five crows silver, six crows gold; seven crows a secret yet to be told; eight crows for a wish; nine crows for a kiss; ten crows for a time of joyous bliss."

"What are you doing, Greg?"

The voice startles him. He hasn't heard anyone enter the room. Spinning around in his chair he's surprised to see his wife standing in the doorway.

"Jesus, Andrea," he says, releasing a loud sigh. "You scared the shit out of me."

"Sorry, honey," she whispers, stepping up to him, wrapping her arms around his broad shoulders and kissing the back of his head. "When I woke up to pee and found you weren't in bed, I figured you'd be down here. Can't sleep?"

"Not a wink," he answers, retuning his focus to the computer.

"Crows?" she asks, following his field of attention.

He nods.

"Find anything interesting?"

"Not much."

"Would you like some tea or something?" she asks, kissing his head again. "I can make you something."

"No thanks, hon," he whispers. "Why don't you go back to bed and try to get some sleep. It's still early. I'll be up in a few minutes."

"Are you okay, Greg?" She glances at the computer screen. "It isn't like you to be so consumed like this—and by silly superstitions, of all things."

He nods and forces a smile. "I'm fine. Just restless. It happens sometimes when I'm working a case like this, and the wind isn't helping."

"I don't know," she says. "I don't ever remember a case affecting you like this before."

"I think it's because the victims are young girls," he replies. "But I'm okay. I promise. Go back to bed where it's warm and I'll be right up."

"Okay," she says, kissing him one more time on the top of his head. "But five minutes and if you're not there, I'll be back down to get you."

"Right," he nods. "Five minutes."

Listening as his wife makes her way back up the stairs, Greg refocuses on the computer screen and the words in front of him, zeroing in on one line in particular—*Five crows silver*.

"Five crows silver," he whispers. "Five crows silver," he repeats it again.

The words intrigue him and he wonders about their meaning or what connection they might possibly have to this case. He's just about to search the phrase when there is a sudden loud thump at the back door.

"Fuck," he says, jumping from the chair, his mind immediately flashes to the gun secured in the lock box high on a shelf in a closet near the front entrance—which he also keeps locked. *Wish I had that sucker right now*, he thinks.

"What the hell is going on around here tonight?" he whispers, glancing around the dining room and kitchen as if checking out his surroundings.

Quickly moving to the back door, he pulls the blind back from the small glass window and peeks out into the darkness. He glances around the backyard and sees nothing except the steadily falling snow—but he's sure he heard a bang.

Reaching for the switch beside the door, he flicks on the outside light. Sliding the chain loose and then pushing the lock in the doorknob, he slowly turns the knob until he hears it click. He then pushes the door open, slowly, until he can see outside.

"Jesus," he says, relieved to see a branch is lying on the doorstep. He couldn't see it when he looked out the window because it was out of his field of vision. "The wind," he says to no one. "Just a fucking tree branch," he shrugs, forcing his heart to slow down.

Pausing to scan the backyard again, he sighs heavily, his breath turning white, is immediately carried away by the wind. The stark whiteness causes him to shiver.

"What a night," he says, swallowing hard and stepping back inside the kitchen, closing the door and securing both locks again. Flicking the switch, the outside light blinks out, flooding the backyard in complete darkness once again.

Pulling the blind aside a crack, he peeks out into the darkness one more time just to reassure himself. He sees nothing.

Returning to the dining room table and studying the computer screen again, he forgets about his promise to his wife. There will be no sleep tonight for Greg Paris.

Chapter 10

It's almost 7:30 by the time Andrea makes her way back down-stairs. Even at this early hour, the snowplow has already made two runs down their street, carving out a narrow path in the deep drifts. Greg pours his second cup of coffee, already thinking about the havoc the storm will have caused for early commuters.

"You didn't come back to bed last night," the slender, dark haired woman says to her husband, who is now fully dressed in his RCMP uniform and standing in the middle of the kitchen sipping his coffee.

"Sorry," he whispers, without looking up at her, his thoughts venturing to what lies in front of him today. "I had too much on my mind and I knew I'd never get to sleep if I came back to bed." He finally looks up at her and smiles. "I didn't want to wake you, so I just stayed down here and worked."

"On crows?"

"Sort of," he says, a small sigh escaping.

"Find anything interesting?"

"Not really." He shrugs. "But if you want to know anything about crows—anything at all—I'm your man." He smirks.

"Is it still snowing?" she asks, wrapping her arms around his trim waist and hugging him tight.

"It finally stopped about an hour and a half ago," he says, holding the cup in his right hand and rubbing her back with his left, his large palm sliding up and down her slender frame. "But it's one hell of a mess out there. It's going to take them days to get everything cleaned up and moving again."

"I'm sure," she whispers, snuggling her face into his chest. "I missed you last night. Every time I rolled over to get warm, your side of the bed was empty and cold. I'm worried about you. You must be tired."

"I'm okay," he says. "I don't need much sleep."

"Right," she replies. "Because you're Superman."

"That's me," he chuckles. "Just call me Clark." Changing the subject, he asks, "Would you like coffee now or later?"

"I think I'll have a shower and get dressed first," she says, recognizing his attempt to deflect the conversation. She knows her husband hates talking about himself so she gives him that concession. "You're not heading into the office yet, are you? We must be snowed in."

"Actually," he says. "We're in pretty good shape. When I heard the plow coming down the street about an hour ago, I went out and asked the operator to clear off the driveway for me."

"They don't do that for private properties," she replies.

"No, they don't. Not usually." He nods. "But when the driver found out I'm the commanding officer at the detachment and I told him I needed to get to the office right away, he did it for me." He grins. "All I had to do was clean off and around the cars and then the doorsteps. That took me about thirty minutes and now it's done, but there are some whopping piles out there. It's going to be a challenge navigating around some of those corners, so if you go out today, drive carefully."

"I guess it pays to have some clout," she smiles. "But I have to admit I didn't hear a thing. I dozed off as soon as I got back into bed. I guess I was tired."

"Are you okay?"

"I'm fine," she smiles. "It's a hormonal thing and it's perfectly normal for pregnant women to be tired. It comes with the territory."

"You're sure?"

"Yes, honey," she laughs, rubbing his chest. "I'm sure. Don't forget. I've done this before and it's much too early into this process for you to start worrying about things. We've got a long way to go so you've got to pace yourself. Promise me, you'll remain calm over the next seven months."

"I'll try," he says and smiles broadly. "But this is all new to me, so you'll have to bear with me. I promise I'll try not to get on your nerves, but it's not going to be easy for me."

"That's one of the things I love so much about you," she giggles. "I appreciate that you care so much." Bending her face up to meet his, she adds, "Now give us a quick kiss so I can go to the bathroom. Bladder control is another issue for hormonal pregnant women."

"I love you," he whispers as he lets her go.

"I know," she answers before leaving the kitchen. "I love you, too. ... Now, I've really got to go." She scampers off to the bathroom and he can hear the door close behind her.

Leaning back against the kitchen counter, he's just about to bring the cup to his mouth again when the phone rings, causing him to jump.

"Shit," he says as the coffee sloshes over the side of the cup and lands on the front of his clean uniform shirt. *Who the hell is calling at this hour*, he wonders, but he knows it's not good news. No one calls before 8 a.m. for good news, he decides.

Snatching the cordless phone from its base on the counter before it can ring a second time, he says, "Greg Paris."

"Hi, Greg," the deep male voice immediately responds. "It's Sergeant Blake Brown calling from the Bridgewater detachment. Remember me?"

"Of course, Blake," Greg answers, setting the coffee cup on the counter and, while resting the phone under his chin and against his right shoulder, he grabs a piece of paper towel from a roll hanging under the cupboard, quickly runs it under the cold water and then dabs his shirt, hoping to remove the stain before it sets in. "If you're calling me at this hour, I know it's not with good news so I won't ask you how you're doing. What's up?"

"Can you talk?" Blake asks. "Is this line secure?"

"We can," Greg answers still wiping at his shirt. "This isn't good, is it?"

"No." Blake is the officer in charge of the detachment just down the coast from Liverpool. "It's not good at all."

"Wait a second," Greg says, giving his shirt one last rub and then tossing the paper towel into the sink. He then returns the phone snuggly to his ear. "Sorry about that. Please go on."

"Considering what's been going on around this end of the province for the past few days, you're the first person I've called this morning after the Ident teams," Blake begins as Greg feels the knot in his gut tightening.

"Please don't tell me we have another missing girl," Greg says, dreading the response he's pretty sure is coming.

"I'm afraid so," Blake answers, his voice conveying no emotion other than desperation. "We've got a report of a missing eight year old from one of the neighbourhoods on the outskirts of town. It appears she was taken from her home sometime through the night while her parents were sleeping in the room next door."

"Jesus Christ," Greg says, leaning his tall, trim body against the counter for support—he feels his knees are about to give out. "How does the bastard do that? It's like he's a freaking ghost."

"We got the report about half an hour ago and we're in the process of issuing an Amber Alert, but we have no idea how long she's been missing," Blake says. "Because the first missing girl from Windsor was found in your jurisdiction, I'm giving you this courtesy call as a heads-up in case something falls in your lap again."

"Thanks, Blake. I appreciate that," Greg answers. "Can you tell me if this girl meets the profile of the other missing children?"

"She does," the Bridgewater commanding officer tells him. "Blonde hair. Under ten years of age. Light complexion. The only difference I can see from looking at the other case files is the colour of her eyes. They are blue, but I'm not sure if that means anything."

"Damn it," Greg says. "It means the hair colour is the key." He pauses and then asks, "Her name?"

"Ruby Smith," Blake tells him. "She's from a modest family. Both parents work and they're just getting by. I know of them and they're good people. I'm sure this will kill them."

"Money isn't a factor in these cases." Greg is matter of fact. "Can you tell me if there are any other children in the house?"

"No," his colleague answers. "Ruby is an only child."

"As was Holly Conrad," Greg observes.

"Think that's important?" Blake asks.

"Oh, yes," Greg says. "Without a doubt. Hillary Lawrence was not an only child, but her sibling is a teenager and he lives with the father so whenever she's at home with her mother, she's the only child there. The only difference here is that she was taken at a schoolyard and not the house, which tells me he had been stalking the child and her abduction was a matter of convenience. He saw an opening and he took it. It breaks the profile, but it also tells us he can be spontaneous and isn't afraid to step outside his comfort zone when the moment and circumstances serve his purposes."

"Sounds like he targets specific victims," the Bridgewater commander says, "and maybe the location isn't all that important."

"He does, but we don't know why," Greg says. "My guess is that he chooses the homes with only one child because he's a coward and he knows there is less chance of getting caught if there are no other children in the house. It could also mean that he was an only child himself, or that he was from a large group of siblings and felt neglected or ostracized. He may feel he was pushed aside in favour of a sister, which may have contributed to his targeting young girls. There are still too many unknown variables that it remains difficult to get an accurate handle on this guy."

"Well, that's all I have for you, I'm afraid," Blake says. "I've got to go—the shit's about to hit the fan here. The Amber Alert has just been issued so it's about to break wide open."

"Listen," Greg says. "If there is anything I can do to help, just give me a shout. I'm only half an hour away. We've got to get our heads together if we're going to get this guy."

"For sure," Blake answers. "I'll be in touch as soon as I hear anything."

"I'll do the same," Greg says. "Let's compare notes later this afternoon."

"Sounds like a plan."

"Good luck," Greg adds, fully understanding the hell his colleague is about to walk into.

"Thanks," Blake says. "I'm sure I'll need it."

*****

News of the abducted Bridgewater girl has already broken by the time Greg arrives at the detachment. The office is abuzz with the early-arriving constables talking about the latest missing child. As he makes his way through the communication centre, he notes that images of Holly Conrad, Hillary Lawrence and Ruby Smith, are flashing across the computer screens. Seeing their images together like that causes him to stop in his tracks.

"Damn." *Cute kids*, he thinks as Constable Emily Murphy spots him and moves in his direction.

"Good morning, Sir," she says, joining him as he heads toward his office. "Something, huh? Another one and this one being taken so soon after the second girl and so close to home."

"Yes," Greg answers. "These types of escalations tell me he's devolving but at the same time, he's becoming more comfortable with what he's doing. It's like he's daring us to catch him."

"That doesn't sound good."

"It's not," Greg says. "We've got to find this guy and we've got to find him fast because he's not going to stop. Clearly, he's lost control and he thinks he's invincible. . . . He really doesn't believe he will get caught and that makes him even more dangerous."

"So what do we do?"

"We'll start by pulling up all the files we have on these three cases. I want us to go over every detail, no matter how minor it may seem. I want everything verified and double checked," Greg says. "I also want to go back over the past five years to see if there are any cases anywhere else in the province that may have similar patterns. We also need to follow up on any leads that may have been reported about attempted abductions or stalking of children in these communities. If there are any, they could be his earlier attempts while perfecting his routine."

"Good idea, Sergeant," Constable Murphy nods.

"We have to start somewhere," he says. "Have any of the reports we've been expecting come in overnight?"

"Yes, Sir," she nods, following him into his office. "Early autopsy results are in and the very preliminary forensic report, but they don't give us much to go on. The ME says the cause of death of the Conrad girl was asphyxiation."

"Strangled?"

"No, Sir. The Medical Examiner says she was smothered. There were signs of significant bruising around her mouth and nose, but nothing on the throat or neck."

"Any idea what he may have used?" Greg asks.

"The ME says it was most likely the perp's hand."

"Damn," Greg reacts. "What a miserable way to go, the poor child. Clearly, this son of a bitch gets off on making his victims suffer—he likes to watch them as they die. . . . This is very personal for him."

"Pervert."

"Exactly," Greg says, reaching inside his office door and snapping on the lights. "Anything from forensics?"

"Not much," Constable Murphy says. "They are confirming the body was scrubbed clean with water and some kind of ammonia, most likely something simple like bleach but it would wipe out any evidence that may have been on the body."

"I suspected as much." Pausing before he enters his office, he says to the constable, "This guy is good. He knows what he's doing."

"How do we catch him?"

"We have to hope he makes a mistake," Greg says, pulling off his overcoat. "Now, if you'll give me a few minutes, I've got to make a very difficult call."

*****

Listening as the phone on the other end rings, Greg wonders how he'll begin the conversation. He's sure that whoever answers won't feel like talking to him this morning, but he needs information and he has no choice but to ask the questions. If it hadn't snowed so much, and if things weren't so crazy around here, he would drive to Windsor to speak with the girl's parents face-to-face, but as things are right now, that's not practical. He hopes they will understand.

"Hello." It's a man's voice and Greg assumes it's Holly Conrad's father.

"Mr. Conrad?"

"Yes." The man is short, but not curt. "Who is this? We're not talking to reporters."

"Hi, Mr. Conrad. I'm not a reporter. It's Sergeant Greg Paris with the Liverpool RCMP," Greg pauses, as if to let the information settle in. "First of all, please accept my deepest sympathies for your loss."

"Thank you, Sergeant."

"How are you and Mrs. Conrad holding up?" Greg asks, knowing it's a question that can't be easily answered and he wishes there was something he could say to make the man feel better.

"About as well as you would expect."

"I'm sorry, Mr. Conrad," Greg replies, pausing and then taking a deep breath. "So am I Sergeant . . . So am I." The man in Windsor becomes silent and Greg can visualize him struggling to speak again. He allows the girl's father to pull himself together. Finally, the man continues. "How can I help you?" he asks.

"I really hate to bother you at this difficult time. I know you have a lot to deal with right now," Greg begins. "But I really do have to ask you an important question."

"Will it help find the bastard who did this to my baby?"

"That's my hope," Greg says, feeling the tears welling in his eyes. He fights to hold them back. "It's my only objective right now."

"I'll do anything I can to help find that son of a bitch." Greg can tell the man is crying. "What do you need?"

"First of all, Mr. Conrad," Greg says. "I must ask that you please not tell anyone what I am about to tell you as it could be an important piece of evidence and it could jeopardize our case if it got out."

"If it's important to solving this, then yes, Sergeant, I promise. You have my word."

"Very well," Greg pauses, gathering his thoughts. "Can you tell me if Holly had a silver chain and cross and was it with her when she went missing?"

"Not that I am aware of, but just hold on a minute, please, I'll be right back."

Greg hears the man place the phone on a table or some other surface and he stares at the phone as if he's expecting the man to suddenly emerge. Minutes later, he hears him return.

"Sergeant?"

"I'm here, Mr. Conrad."

"No, Sir," he says, his tone softer and mellower than it had been. "Holly didn't have any such thing. Why?"

"Again, Mr. Conrad, you must keep this to yourself and please ask Mrs. Conrad not to repeat it, not even to family or friends." Greg pauses and then explains the significance of his question. "When we found Holly, she was wearing a silver chain around her neck with a little silver cross attached."

"What does that mean?"

"At this point," Greg sighs and then says, "we're really not sure, but clearly, someone put it there."

"Was it the killer?"

"I don't know," Greg answers. "Maybe. . . . Probably. But it's a good piece of evidence since we know it means something."

"What?"

"I'd only be guessing at this point and I prefer not to do that," Greg says. "Listen, Mr. Conrad, again please accept my sympathies for your loss. I wish there was something I could say to make you feel better."

"Are you a father, Sergeant?"

Greg hesitates, but finally answers. "I am," he says. "A little girl."

"Well, then. Please get this guy for your daughter and for all the other little girls out there. Get the bastard before he does it again."

Obviously, Greg thinks, this man isn't listening to the news this morning and that's a good thing. "We're doing everything we can, Mr. Conrad. I promise."

"I trust you, Sergeant. You sound like a good man."

"I must be going," Greg responds, fighting hard to keep his tears damned up. "I will keep you posted every step of the way and please contact me if you need anything from me or if you think of anything that might help in our investigation."

"Thank you."

"Goodbye, Mr. Conrad."

Hanging up, Greg can fight it no longer. "We're trying, Mr. Conrad," he whispers as the tears roll down his cheeks. "We're trying."

*****

It's a long shot, he knows, but Greg dials the number anyway.

"Hello," his friend Cliff Graham answers on the third ring.

"Hey, Cliff," Greg says. "How are you?"

"Better than you, I bet," Cliff says. "I just heard the news. What a freakin' shame. He got another one, the bastard."

"He did and that's why I'm calling," Greg pauses. "I need your help."

"I'll do whatever I can, Buddy. You know that," Cliff says. "But you do remember that I'm not on active duty, don't you? The brass will be pissed if they find out that I'm helping you."

"I do. But this is unofficial police work and I need someone I can trust and someone who can be discrete. You fit the bill, my friend. What da ya say? Up for a little excitement today?"

"What's cooking?"

"I'm taking a little field trip this afternoon," Greg explains. "I'd like you to tag along and be my second set of eyes and ears."

"Where are we going?"

Greg hesitates, but finally says, "To see an old woman about some crows."

"Who?"

"Clara Underwood."

"Seriously? That senile old bat?" Cliff huffs. "Or maybe I should say old crow."

"Seriously," Greg says. "Do you want to come or not?"

Cliff hesitates then finally says, "Okay. I'm in. What time are you picking me up?"

"Around two."

"I'll be ready."

Chapter 11

It feels like he's been shovelling for hours—and making little progress for his efforts. He can't stop until he's dug out the family van though, cleared the long driveway that runs to the back of the house and removed the snow from all the walkways that wrap around the large, sprawling property. *A little help wouldn't be too much to ask for!* he thinks as he tosses a heavy load onto a growing mountain at the end of the driveway. But like always, he doesn't ask for help and he certainly doesn't expect to receive any—he knows his father is preoccupied with other things.

Standing at the edge of the driveway, he looks at the long line of thick, heavy snow that seems to go on forever and he sighs, leaning on the shovel to catch his breath. At twenty-three, the sandy-haired young man could easily pass for sixteen, something that has often worked in his father's favour. In fact, most things are pretty one-sided when it comes to Murdock McCarthy. He can't remember the last time his father helped him with anything, much less his chores, so he certainly won't be helping him today, no matter how much snow has fallen or how tired he becomes.

"That's your job and your responsibility," his father practically spat at Lucas earlier this morning when the subject came up during breakfast, if you can call his father's can of beer breakfast. Lucas had his usual bowl of Fruit Loops, his favourite cereal.

He remembers thinking he should be used to this treatment by now. After all, he's suffered under his father's tyranny for years. He knows the abuse will continue as long as he stays under the man's roof. The thought angers him as he plunges the blue, heavy plastic shovel into the clumps of snow pushed into the driveway by the plow, but he also knows he has no other choice but to remain here until his two younger sisters are either capable of defending themselves against the old man's assaults or running away. Emma, who is still only eight, and Sophie, ten, are not yet capable of fending for themselves, so he stays and suffers the brunt of the abuse because he believes his mother would have wanted him to. She would expect him to look after his sisters. He just hopes he can survive long enough to see the day when they can walk away from the monster—and never look back.

Murdoch McCarthy wasn't always an abusive, alcohol-guzzling bastard. In fact, there was a time when he was a loving, supportive father with all the nurturing instincts one would expect to find in a man with three children. But that all changed a few years ago when Lucas' mother was suddenly killed in a car crash that left him to raise the children on his own. It's a responsibility he's failed miserably. Lucas whips the snow from his shovel onto the towering mountain at the corner of the driveway. His muscles are aching. He thrusts the shovel into the large, heavy clumps and lifts yet another load. With each new shovel-load, his muscles scream from the weight.

At first, the drinking was gradual, and then Lucas remembers his father would be fine for a couple of days between benders. But, like most aspiring drunks, the drinking became a regular thing—and along with it, came the abuse. It started with verbal attacks. The constant ridicule and the insults, but it soon escalated to regular physical altercations. The beatings included slapping, punching, kicking and even the occasional smack upside the head or crack over the back with whatever weapon Murdoch had in his hand at the time. Over the years, Lucas remembers being hit by flying shoes, belts, a piece of fire wood, a broom handle, cutlery, a tire iron and an extension cord, all of which left permanent scars on his fragile, skinny body. If he thought about it hard enough, he's sure he could easily add about a dozen other objects to the list of items used as "weapons" to beat him into submission, but he's chosen to block out as much of the abuse as he can. *It's better to push the pain to the far recess of my mind and simply bury it*, he reasons. At least there, he can ignore the suffering he's had to endure.

Still, he wonders as he tosses another heavy load from his shovel, what would push a man—a father—to turn on his children as Murdoch has done? The young man has no answers but he knows he's not the only one suffering at the hands of this maniac.

Lucas has already lost track of all the places they've had to move in recent years. This latest move being from Winnipeg to Nova Scotia last November. This was supposed to be a new beginning for the family. Here, in Liverpool, Murdoch promised it would be different. He said they would have an exciting life filled with fun, happiness and plenty of new friends, but they've had none of that in the three months they've been here. *It's just more of the same*, he thinks. His father sequesters the three children in this big, old house while he disappears at all hours of the night, sometimes staying away for several days at a time without explanation. But while nothing has changed for them in this new town, the McCarthy children look forward to those times when their father is away. It gives them a break from the abuse. They dread his return.

The only reprieve Lucas gets from the responsibility of taking care of the house and his sisters comes on those days he has to work. He considers himself fortunate to have found a casual job in the current depressed economy. Jobs are scarce. Most of what he earns goes to his father though—the older man demands it. He does manage to skim a few dollars, which he uses for personal things like cigarettes and the occasional case of beer that he keeps hidden out back in one of the old sheds he discovered shortly after they moved to town. He's not sure if his father ever ventures to these buildings, but he's confident he's found a good hiding place for his stash.

Will the torture ever end, Lucas wonders, as he pauses, pulls off his mittens and wipes the snow and sweat from his face with the back of his left hand?

Not likely, he thinks, pulling his gloves back on his skinny hands. He sighs and grabs the shovel, thrusting it deeper into the snow again. He's tired, and he'd like to take a break, but he knows his father is likely watching from one of the windows. He always does whenever he gives Lucas a job.

The man-boy, as he thinks of himself, knows his father to be a mean-spirited taskmaster who will not tolerate him stopping until the job is done, no matter how tired he is. He'd also like a cigarette, but he doesn't have any of his own and his father refused to give him one this morning. So for now, he'll do without the nicotine that his body desperately craves. When he's finished, however, he'll have a smoke, even if he has to steal one from his father and risk another assault. He knows the old man counts them and whenever he's caught Lucas in the past taking his smokes, he's made him suffer dearly for having the balls to steal from his father.

But this is a risk worth taking because he needs one. His body aches for a long, slow draw of the addictive drug. It calms him. He tosses the latest load of snow atop the high mound at the corner of the driveway just as he hears the unmistakable heavy footsteps of his father approaching from behind. He wonders what he's done wrong now.

"What the hell are you doing?" Murdoch yells, grabbing his son by the right shoulder and spinning him around.

"What?" Lucas asks, trying hard to stifle his fear. He knows his father's first plan of attack is to always intimidate him. Showing his fear is a sign of weakness and he refuses to reveal any such emotion to his tormentor.

"What do you mean, 'what'?" Murdoch's voice rises even higher, his eyes bulge with anger and his complexion grows blood red. "You stupid son of a bitch. Can't you see you're creating a blind spot at the end of the driveway by building that mountain of snow? Why are you so stupid?"

"Sorry," Lucas stammers, glancing at the pile and deciding it's not as bad as his father claims, but he keeps that thought to himself. He knows it's best not to argue with the older man, even if he's wrong . . . especially if he's wrong. That just makes matters worse and leads to a harsher punishment. "I'll lower it."

"You bet your sweet ass you'll lower it," Murdoch snaps, the spit flying from his twisted mouth as he verbally launches his attack. "And don't even think about coming into the house until you're done with everything 'cause the doors will be locked. You stupid ass, why would you pile it so high in the first place? Can't you see how dangerous that is? Moron."

"I said I am sorry and I'll move it," Lucas says, his voice low and steady. "What more do you want me to do?"

With that, the man-boy feels the stinging blow as his father's hand connects with his cold right cheek. "What have I told you about talking back to me?" Murdoch yells as his son drops the snow shovel and backs up against the van like a mangy, old dog cowering from its master. "You know I don't tolerate backtalk, yet you've got to prove how big of a man you are."

Watching as his father bends and picks up the shovel, Lucas whispers, "All I said was that I was sorry." He spits fresh blood from his mouth, making a bright red splotch in the pristine snow. It looks like a splatter of paint on an artist's canvass. "What more can I do?"

"Nothing," Murdoch screams as he turns the shovel handle into a club and delivers the first blow to his son's head. "You can't do anything because you're a no-good-for-nothing idiot." Delivering another blow to the boy's shoulders, he screams again, "I don't expect anything from you. You *always* disappoint me, you worthless piece of shit."

"Stop," Lucas demands, raising his hands in self-defence as he tries to protect his face. He refuses to waste one tear on the twisted old man. "Just stop it."

"Stop it?" Murdock says, smirking because he is actually happy the boy has foolishly decided to continue the issue—it gives him more reason to beat him like a dog. He quickly delivers a third blow to his son's arms. "I'll stop it when I'm goddamn good and ready to stop it, you freaking idiot. I'm the boss here. Don't tell me to stop. Don't you *ever* tell me to 'stop it.' *I'll decide* when it's time for me to stop." He lifts the shovel to send another blow adding, "You got it?"

"Whatever," Lucas fires back in a useless show of defiance as he falls to his knees, resigned to take whatever punishment his father decides to dish out. Turning his back to his abuser, he has no more will to resist. But he will *not* cry.

"Why are you so stupid? Can you answer that for me? Why?" Murdock screams and strikes his son three more times on the back with the wooden shovel handle. "What did I do to deserve this?" Standing over the young man who is now slumped on the ground in a quivering heap, Murdock glances skyward. "Why did I have to have such stupid kids?" he asks, his voice becoming cold and distant, void of any sense of feeling for his offspring.

Throwing the shovel to the ground, the tall, lanky man walks away, heading toward the house where he sees his two young daughters have been watching the attack against their older brother from the open front door.

"Get back inside," he commands, and the two little girls scurry inside the large historic house and disappear without a word.

Turning back to his son, who is still sprawled in the snow like a defeated and bludgeoned foe, he barks, "Get back to work, dummy, and don't come inside until you've cleaned up everything. I don't care how long it takes." He pauses and then says, "Do you hear me? I want every Goddamn piece of snow out of this driveway, do you understand?"

"Yes." Lucas forces the word through gritted teeth. He knows his father expects an answer. "Yes, Sir," he says again, refusing to show him how much pain he is in right now. "I hear you."

"Fine." Murdock stomps up the front steps. "And don't make me come out here after you again or the next time you'll be *really* sorry."

But the young man is already sorry—sorry he was ever born and sorry he ended up with Murdock as his father.

"Prick," Lucas whispers, knowing his tormentor is not within earshot. Slowly pulling himself up to his feet, his back, head and shoulders throbbing from the brutal assault, he refuses to look at the man who should be giving him comfort and safety but instead, is handing out pain and suffering as if they were Halloween treats.

Picking up the shovel and returning to the snow pile at the end of the driveway, forcing the pain out of his mind, he begins the task of relocating the snow he had already deposited there. *Someday*, he thinks, *that old bastard will pay for what he's done. Someday, he'll get what's coming to him*, Lucas promises.

*****

Glancing at his watch, he sees it's almost 2 p.m. and that means he's late. He promised Cliff he'd pick him up by now, but he's lost track of the time, which is something he never does. He prides himself on always being punctual, but he'll admit he's a little off his game today. He also tells himself that he should take time to eat something, but he has no appetite right now.

With visions of the young Conrad girl continuing to force their way into his thoughts, especially after speaking with the girl's father this morning, Greg Paris fears that anything he puts into his stomach would only find its way back up. He's dealt with difficult cases in the past, but he's never run into anything that has impacted him in such a profound way as this one. Somehow, he feels as though he's letting down these young victims, even though he's sure he's doing all he can to help them.

"Excuse me, Sergeant," Constable Emily Murphy says after knocking and poking her head inside his office door. "We've just received another forensics report over the wire. This one deals with the chain and cross. You asked to be notified when we got anything."

"Let's see it," he says, glancing at the officer and running his right hand through his thick, black hair as he does whenever he's stressed. "Anything useful?"

"Honestly, Sir?" the constable replies, stepping inside his office and handing him the two-page report she's printed off for him. She shrugs and says, "Not much I'm afraid. There's nothing special about it. Just your normal cheap jewellery you can buy anywhere. So I doubt that will help much."

"Shit," he sighs, taking the papers from her and scanning the first sheet and then flipping to the second. "I was hoping there would be something useful here, like a partial print or maybe even a hair trapped in the chain, but this guy's obviously too good for that. He knows what he's doing. He's either studied forensics or he's done his research, which would be easy these days with everything on the freaking Internet for every goddamn pervert to find—especially if he knows where to look."

"If I might, Sir," the constable replies. "I was thinking about that and I'm wondering why, if he's so careful about not leaving behind any trace of himself on the body, would he leave the chain and cross in the first place?"

"Well, that's the question, isn't it?" Greg says, pausing and placing the report on his desk. Even though he knows he's running late, he motions for the constable to sit in the chair across from him. "I believe it's his way of communicating with us," he says, explaining his theory to the young cop. "He's reaching out to us."

"Why?"

"Maybe he's remorseful or feels guilty for what he's done to these little girls," Greg suggests as he sees the young officer is hanging on his every word.

"Is he religious?"

"Because of the cross? I don't believe that's necessarily the case. He could be, but the cross could also be symbolic of a major event in his life or perhaps it's a representation of someone who was important to him, either now or in the past," Greg explains. "But we may never know the truth about this until we get him."

She sighs but says nothing.

"Are you okay, Constable? You look upset," Greg says. "I know this is a tough case. Cases that deal with children are especially difficult."

"It's hard, Sir," Constable Murphy nods, wiping a few wayward tears from her eyes. She's been working hard to maintain her tough façade and regrets that she's revealed even this slightest of emotion.

"Do you want to talk about it?" He pauses and studies her reaction. He won't push her if he thinks she's not willing to open up to him. He adds, "I'm not trying to pry or anything like that, but it does help to talk things out with someone and as I cautioned yesterday, you've got to pace yourself when dealing with these types of cases."

She hesitates and Greg sees she's deciding. He says nothing further but gives her time to consider her options. Several minutes later, she begins.

"It's just that when I see these little girls, it brings back memories of my sister." She pauses, her words quivering slightly as she adds, "She died when I seven."

"What was her name?"

"Molly," the constable says as the tears now trickle down both cheeks. "She was two years older than me but even though I was only young when she died, I still have such vivid memories of her and the day she was killed."

"How did she die?"

"She was hit by a car while we were riding our bikes," she says, glancing away from her superior officer, as if she's ashamed to think he may see her cry.

"It's okay," he says, his tone soothing. "Do you feel like telling me what happened? If not, I understand, but it usually helps to talk about these things."

She swallows and says, her voice soft and low, "It was August. There were three of us riding our bikes that day along the highway. Me, Molly and a friend who lived in our neighbourhood. We didn't see the car coming up behind us. Molly was the last one in the row and before we could react, he hit Molly. We heard tires squealing and before we could even turn around, she was down on the ground and the car was speeding away. I can still see her lying on the hot pavement, crying and saying her head hurt. I was just so happy to see she was alive. But she died later that day in the hospital. I still can't get those images out of my head, even after all these years. It's horrible growing up with something like that, something that stays in your head, as though it's engraved there or something."

"Do you have any other siblings?"

"No, Sir," she shakes her head. "And my parents were never the same after Molly died. How could they be? They tried to be there for me, but it was hard on them."

"Did they ever get the driver?"

"I'm not sure they ever really tried to find him," the constable answers, her response matter of fact.

"What do you mean?"

"They took all the information my friend and I could remember, like the colour of the car, and that it only had two doors, but we didn't know the make and model and we didn't know enough about that sort of thing to even think about getting the license plate number, so the guy got away with murder."

"You know it was a man?"

"I'm pretty sure it was a man," she nods. "He was big, like a man would look behind the steering wheel, but I was only small, so it really is difficult to say for certain because everyone looked big to me back then."

"I didn't know any of this," Greg says. "It isn't in your personnel file. It says you had a sibling who was deceased but that's it. There are no details about how she died."

"Guess they didn't think it was important enough to include, but I can tell you for a fact that it was that incident that convinced me that I wanted to be a police officer. And I promised myself that if I ever made it, I would never do what the police did back then. I promised I would work every case until it was solved. I'd give it everything I had and I'd do it for the victims."

"That's a tall order," Greg suggests. "Honourable, but not always easy to accomplish. Sometimes, despite our best efforts, these things are never solved."

"I know that now, but I didn't know it when I was seven," she says, again wiping her eyes. Sighing, she adds, "Well that's enough of that. You don't want to talk about me anymore. You've got enough on your mind."

"Yes I do, Constable," he nods. "But I'll talk to you any time you need to get something off your chest. My door is always open. That's such a terrible tragedy that I can only imagine what you went through. You can't keep it bottled up. Even after all these years, something like that can eat you up if you keep it to yourself."

"It was hard, I'll admit that," she says, rising from the chair. "If you'll excuse me, Sir, I've got more phone calls to make. I'm still looking to see if we can connect this guy to any past cases."

"Very well, Constable," Greg nods, "but I want you to promise me that if you ever need someone to talk to, you'll come and find me."

"I promise," she says, slipping out his office door.

Funny, Greg thinks as he pulls on his heavy force-issued overcoat. *The things you don't know about the people you work with.*

*****

He knows for certain he had told Cliff he'd be over around 2 p.m. to pick him up, but the house looks empty. He's a few minutes later than he planned, but he would have expected Cliff to wait for him.

That's not like him, Greg thinks. He pushes open the reinforced door of the police cruiser and slowly puts his steel-toed boots into the snow and slush. The air feels heavy. It's as if a dense shroud has suddenly fallen over the town. He's surprised at how warm it actually feels today, considering the area has just been dumped on by one of the worst storms to hit the region in a long time, or so he's heard. He wouldn't know for sure since this is his first winter in Nova Scotia.

Slamming the car door and glancing around the yard, he spots Cliff's truck parked near the house and notes the driveway and all the walkways have been cleared. He immediately panics thinking that maybe his friend shovelled the heavy snow and had another heart attack. Stepping quickly, he makes his way up the walk to the front door and knocks.

"Come on, Cliff," he whispers as beads of perspiration emerge on his forehead. "Open the goddamn door."

Hearing no movement from the other side, he presses closer to the door and knocks again.

"Where the hell are you?" he says. He's suddenly surprised by an unusual cackle-like sound coming from behind him.

"What the hell?" He spins around to see a crow has landed in the front yard. It's prancing atop the deep snowdrifts as though it's wearing snowshoes.

"What the hell do you want?" he asks, watching the black bird's reaction.

Seconds later, he's startled as a second crow lands beside the first one and the two birds exchange several glances.

"Another one?" Greg sighs. "Listen guys," he addresses the black birds. "I have no idea what you want, but I wish you would leave me alone." He pauses and then adds, "Just go away—please. We've got enough to worry about right now. We sure as hell don't need you guys hanging around."

The two avian visitors go about their business, ignoring him.

"Come on, guys," Greg says again when he's startled as two more land in the front yard. "What the hell?" he says again, stepping backwards and pressing against the front of his friend's house. He suddenly feels cornered by the crows.

Thinking that maybe he should go around to the back door where he hopes he will find his friend and be able to get away from the freaking black birds, Greg begins to slowly inch off the front steps. He's about to take another step down when yet another crow suddenly drops onto the walkway where he's about to place his feet. It appears to be larger than the others.

"Five," Greg says, carefully studying the bird now blocking his path. "I wondered where you were."

The ebony bird, its black feathers reflecting a purplish-green in the mid-afternoon sun, looks up at him and Greg has the distinct feeling it wants to tell him something.

"What?" Greg asks, inching down the step. "What do you want from me?"

"What does who want from you?" asks a voice from behind.

"Shit," Greg says, spinning around to see Cliff standing in the doorway staring at him. "How long have you been there?"

"Just got here," Cliff says, stepping out onto the doorstep and pulling the front door closed behind him.

"Where were you?" Greg asks. "I knocked several times, but you didn't answer. Why didn't you answer?"

"Hey, Greg. Calm down. I was just putting on my boots and getting my coat," Cliff explains. "I figured you would wait. Are we in a rush?"

"Not so much," Greg says as he heads down the walkway and then back down the driveway toward the cruiser. "But I was worried when you didn't answer. Why didn't you yell to me or something to let me know you were okay?"

"Sorry," Cliff says as he follows behind his friend. "Didn't mean to frighten you."

"Just concerned, that's all."

"Thanks. I appreciate that," Cliff says. "But really, I'm okay. I can take care of myself so you can stop worrying about me."

"Glad to hear it."

"Just a second," Cliff says, catching up to Greg.

"What?"

"Who were you talking to when I came out the door?"

Reaching the driver's side door of the RCMP cruiser, Greg stops and looks at his friend over the car. "You are kidding, right?"

"What do you mean?"

"I mean," Greg pauses. "You saw them. . . . Please tell me you saw them."

"Who?" Cliff asks, opening the passenger side door and slipping inside.

Also sliding inside the car, Greg places his hands on the steering wheel and then turns, slowly to look at his friend.

"The crows," he whispers. "Please tell me you saw the freaking crows in your front yard."

Chapter 12

Sergeant Greg Paris and Cliff Graham have been best friends for twenty-five years. They've shared many experiences together over the years—some great, some even memorable. And some upsetting, like this case. Right now, the veteran officers are silent. Since leaving Cliff's driveway the two men are both lost in thought, as the cruiser pushes its way past the mounds of snow, some up to six feet high in places.

Greg turns to look at his friend and finally breaks the silence. "You are kidding, aren't you?" he asks, turning his gaze back to the snow-covered roads. Some roads are still nearly impassable even though the storm moved northeast toward Newfoundland earlier this morning. It could be several hours or perhaps even as late as tomorrow, before snow removal crews reach the secondary roads. Major routes are the first priority for emergency purposes and so traffic in this area of the county is moving slowly this afternoon.

"About what?" Cliff asks. He instinctively moves his hand to brace himself as his buddy swerves to avoid major drifts that have banked across the road, the blustering wind pushing and swirling the snow effortlessly.

"You know," Greg answers, keeping a tight grip on the steering wheel as the cruiser is pulled into the ruts created by other vehicles.

"No," Cliff quips. "Actually, I don't."

Greg pauses then says, "The crows." He glances to his friend who remains stoned-faced. "The fucking crows," he says again. "Tell me you saw the fucking crows in your goddamn front yard just now, or I'll jump out of my freaking skin because if you didn't see them, then it means I'm losing my fucking mind."

"Calm down, Greg," Cliff smiles. "I saw them. Okay? . . . I saw them."

"Why would you do that?" Greg demands, his words exploding.

"Wow. Slow down," Cliff says, grinning like a schoolboy who just pulled off the prank of the year. "I was just busting your chops." He pauses and then takes a softer tone. "Honestly, friend." He shakes his head. "I don't know how to tell you this, but I have no idea what you're talking about."

"So, you didn't see the crows?" Greg sighs, feeling his heart sink and a numb feeling fill his body. "There were five of them. You didn't see them."

"Sorry, pal," Cliff shakes his head. "I didn't notice them, but honestly, we left in such a rush that they may have been there and they just didn't register with me. I've seen so many goddamn crows in the past few years that I've learned to block them out, especially if they're trying to get to me."

"I don't see how you could have missed them," Greg says, looking straight ahead, his mind reeling, trying to figure out if he actually is losing his mind. "They were right there . . . in front of you. You had to have seen them when you came out the front door."

"Maybe I just wasn't looking for them." Cliff shrugs. "But seriously, Greg, are these crows still hounding you?"

"Lately, that's all I can think about," he admits. "They're in my thoughts every goddamn minute of every goddamn day."

"Been there, done that, so I know what that's like," Cliff confesses. "I feel for you, buddy, and I wish I could tell you they'll go away, but it's not that simple. They'll stick with you until their mission is done . . . that's been my experience anyway. And by the way," he adds, "sorry for kidding with you back there. I had no idea how badly this is affecting you."

"You really are an asshole sometimes." Greg smirks and then the two men fall silent again, each thinking about their experiences with the crows.

Finally, Cliff asks, "So how do you really like being in charge?"

"It's not so bad." Greg shrugs and looks at his friend. "Other than the fact that there's a crazed child abductor running around this end of the province, dumping the bodies of dead young girls in my jurisdiction, it's great. . . . I'm really not sure how I got here and it's certainly not what I bargained for."

"Sorry," Cliff says. He really feels for his friend. No cop wants to experience the death of a child under their watch, a watch that should have been his.

"Sorry for what? It's not your fault."

"In a way, it is," Cliff says. "If I hadn't had a heart attack and had been forced to take time off, I'd be the one dealing with this mess, not you."

"Would you want to be the one dealing with this?"

Cliff pauses, glances out the side window and marvels at the snowdrifts. He then says, "Honestly, buddy? Not a chance. I'd end up calling you for help anyway. So I guess, at least this way, you're involved from the ground floor up."

"But you miss being in the thick of things, don't you?" Greg says. "I know you and I bet it's driving you crazy, isn't it?"

"I'd be lying if I said it didn't," Cliff says, thinking about the question. "Of course I do . . . miss it, working that is. I'm a police officer—fighting crime and protecting people are in my blood. But this is a tough one, and, honestly, part of me is actually grateful I'm not the one who has to deal with the shit storm that's coming your way."

"It's definitely a tough one," Greg admits. "Any idea when the doctors will give the go-ahead for your return? You can have your chair back anytime you want it," Greg smirks.

"Actually, I have a check up next week with the heart specialist in Halifax and I'm hoping he'll give me the green light so I can be back by early next month, but it will still have to be approved by division."

"They'll be okay with it," Greg assures him. "Why wouldn't they be? I think you're in better shape now than I've seen you in a long time and if the doctor says you're fit to return, then I can't see why division would stand in your way. It's your job and you can have it back anytime you want it."

"I do feel good," Cliff admits. "I feel better right now than I've felt in a really long time. I know it was a close call," he pauses. "I know I was lucky. . . . I almost died." The words catch in his throat.

"Yes, you did and if you had died I would have been so pissed at you that I'd kick your sorry ass all the way to hell and back again," Greg smirks, slowing the car to make a left-hand turn from Route 3 onto a narrow gravel road that hasn't seen a snowplow in a long time.

Gull Island, about ten minutes west of Liverpool near the resort area of White Point, got its name many years ago from the locals. Once a thriving fishing village, the seagulls were attracted to the area in large flocks to feast on the fish offal. Today, however, the fishing wharves are rotting, sliding off their pillars and ready to tumble into the unforgiving Atlantic Ocean. Along the road, the occasional fishing shack still stands, but they are boarded over and their roofs caving in, a reminder of a long ago era when the sea provided a rich bounty.

The modest houses here are separated by acres of woods and they are inhabited by an assortment of kindly people who put the wellbeing of their neighbour ahead of their own. They are a close-knit collection of people, whose roots go way back to the early years of settlement. Closer to the coast, wealthy come-from-aways (CFAs), mostly Upper Canadians, Americans and Europeans are quickly snatching up the ocean-front properties for bargain-basement prices and converting the pristine coastline into summer getaways to be used for two or three weeks out of the year. For the remainder of the time, the rich homes are kept locked up and managed by local caretakers who see the land more often than its owners.

For the duration of the trip, the two RCMP officers remain silent—each thankful for the other's friendship but not caring to discuss their personal situations any further. Greg carefully navigates the cruiser over the snow-covered road, breaking tracks as he goes. With so much snow, it's nearly impossible to tell where the road's shoulders meet the ditch, and one wrong turn of the wheel could mean a long wait for a tow truck, not to mention the litany of jokes at his expense back at the detachment.

"I sure hope this woman has something worthwhile to say," Cliff says, finally breaking the tense silence within the cruiser. "I won't be happy if we drove all the way out here in this shit only to find we've been led on a fool's errand."

Greg says nothing. Instead, he eases the car right and plows down a driveway flagged with a rusting mailbox on a rotting post leaning drastically to the right. The mailbox is emblazoned with the name "Underwood" in fluorescent orange paint.

"You never know about these things, Cliff," Greg finally responds as he inches the police car through the deep snow. "I'm just finding it hard to concentrate on this case with these freaking crows hanging around. It's like they are in my head and I just can't get the damn things out. It's distracting and that scares the hell out of me because I'm not used to that. If this old woman can tell me anything that might help, then I have to try. What harm will it do to talk to her? Besides, what if she really knows something and I didn't listen to her?"

"I suppose you have a point and if it can give you peace of mind then I'm with you, bud," Cliff says. He gently slaps his friend on the shoulder.

"Have you had any dealings with this woman in the past?" Greg asks, watching as the wind whips the snow into mountainous drifts.

"Never. I've only laid eyes on her a few times over the years and she pretty much keeps to herself," Cliff answers, focusing his attention on the snow swirling in front of the vehicle as it dances across the driveway with the strong wind. "She's a bit eccentric and somewhat of a recluse."

*****

The cruiser finally makes it to the end of the narrow driveway where snow-laden pine and fir trees make a fairy-tale like passageway, their branches bending to the ground under the added weight. Greg inches the car forward, thinking it's a miracle the branches haven't snapped yet, considering many of them are almost scraping the surface of the snow.

He parks the cruiser as close to the house as possible, knowing they will have to tread through the deep snow before they reach the old woman's house. He sighs, wondering what she is doing living alone, so far removed from even the nearest neighbour. He peers out through the foggy windshield as a large clump of snow falls from one of the trees, landing on the heated glass where it instantly melts. He notices the woman's weather-worn house is in desperate need of a fresh coat of paint, the whitewash having almost disappeared from years of neglect.

"Looks like this is it," he says, stating the obvious. Turning off the ignition he stuffs the keys into a pocket on his bulky navy overcoat. He opens the car door and steps out into the winter weather, a gust of wind slapping his face as the drifting snow quickly rushes over the tops of his insulated boots then creeps its way down to his feet as it warms. "Come on partner," he glances back at Cliff. "Let's go see if this woman can give us any answers. I need to know what the hell these crows want from me."

Cliff chuckles as he pulls himself out of the car and follows close behind, both men plowing through knee-deep snowdrifts. "You really surprise me, friend," he says. "I didn't know you were the superstitious kind."

"Usually, I'm not," Greg answers, climbing three snow-covered steps that lead up to the wooden door, its black paint blistered and peeling, exposing the old wood underneath.

Reaching the entrance to the Underwood house, the officers are startled when the door quickly swings open and the light from inside the humble home rushes out into the grayness of the late afternoon to greet them. There to usher them inside is a short, grey-haired woman in a flowered housedress that resembles a frock. She looks tired and worn, Greg thinks, wondering how old the woman really is, but deciding it would not be polite to ask her such a thing.

"I heard the car," she utters and beckons for the two men to enter the house, the warm air from the roaring fire in the airtight woodstove quickly embracing them. "Get in here outta the cold 'fore you catch your death," she says in a local drawl that resembles Scottish or Irish, Greg thinks—the words coming from her mouth are too twisted to know which it is.

"Come on in," she tells them again. "Don't worry 'bout your boots. It's only a bit a water," the woman says, instructing them to come directly into the small, but cozy room. "It'll dry."

Upon entering the house, the two officers are immediately standing in the kitchen, their large frames towering over the stout woman, her wrinkled face glowing in the soft light of the bare light bulb in the ceiling fixture. Since there is no porch or entryway, both men stand on an old braided mat just inside the door.

Glancing about the interior, Greg notes that it appears the woman's entire life is plastered over the walls. There are pictures of men and woman of various ages, and babies and children in a variety of situations and at a variety of ages. The pictures span many decades — some are coloured, others are black and white.

"Ya like my pictures?" she asks, noticing him scanning her walls, any paint there barely visible, although he thinks he sees glimpses of pale yellow around the photos.

"Sure," Greg quickly replies. "They're very nice."

"They keep me company. . . . They're all I got," she explains, smiling a toothy smile at the two officers. "I live here all by myself. Just me an' the cats."

"Cats?" Cliff responds, looking about but failing to see any.

"Five of 'em. They're my babies," she says. "I put 'em in the bedroom when I knew you were comin.' Some folks don't like cats crawlin' over 'em, so I always put 'em in the room. It's better for talkin'."

"Well, thanks for doing that and thanks for seeing us," Cliff responds. "Most people don't like to talk to cops. I'm Cliff Graham."

"Yes, of course you are," the diminutive woman says. In the soft glow of the lone light in the kitchen, her age is plainly visible. She looks worn and haggard, as if she's been carrying a burden on her shoulders for many years. "I seen you 'round town many times. I know you're the head boss."

"Well," Cliff shrugs, as if embarrassed by her comment, "not right at the moment."

"Oh, that's right," she looks at him and smiles. "My old memory ain't what it used to be. I heard you were sick, but you're feelin' better now, aren't you?"

"As a matter of fact, I am." Cliff nods, his pride bursting through. "And I hope to be back to work very soon, but in the meantime, my friend here, Sergeant Greg Paris, is looking out for things while I'm gone."

"I see," the woman responds, smiling at Greg. "You're the one in charge now?"

"Yes, ma'am. I suppose I am," Greg replies and he returns her smile. "For awhile at least, until Corporal Graham is able to come to back to work."

"And what a time you're havin,'" she says matter-of-factly. "I heard you got a big case on your hands and it's a bad one. . . . Those poor little dears."

"I'm afraid so," Greg nods.

"So then, how can I help you?" the woman asks. Motioning to four wooden chairs with stuffed seat pads surrounding a small wooden table cluttered with pieces of cloth in various colours, each cut in perfect six-inch-by-six inch squares. There is also a collection of darning needles and other sewing paraphernalia cluttered on the table. "Come an' sit," she tells the two hulking RCMP officers who look desperately out of place in her kitchen. "Don't pay no mind to this mess. I like to make quilts and I'm cuttin' up the material to start a new one. One of the girls down the road had a baby last week. . . . She's only fifteen, can you believe that? I ain't one to judge, but it ain't right that kids these days are havin' kids. . . . It just ain't right."

"Maybe we should stand right here on the mat," Cliff interrupts. "Our boots really are a mess from the snow and we don't want to get water all over your floor."

"Won't hear of it," she insists, sharply raising her voice. "An' like I already said, don't worry 'bout them boots. Ya can't hurt this floor none. It's seen more than its fair share of water over the years." Making her way to the table, she motions for the two officers to join her. "These are pictures of my children and grandchildren," she points out, nodding toward a neat stack of pictures on one corner of the table as she sits in a chair at the end of the table. "They all live far away from here, but they send me lots of pictures. I like pictures. They keep me in touch. It's like they've sent me a piece of themselves."

"I understand," Cliff says, taking a chair at the opposite end of the table from the aged woman while Greg sits to the right of her. "My daughter lives with me now, but my son lives in Vancouver with his mother, so it's nice to have pictures of him. Sometimes, pictures are all we have."

"I know," the woman replies. "And you miss him dearly, don't you? He misses you, too, but you should not worry so much about him. Your boy will be all right. He's a fine young man but he wants you to call him tonight."

"Chesley wants me to call him?" Cliff asks. "Why?" The woman's sudden proclamation catches Cliff off guard as he opens his outer coat to keep from overheating. "Is something wrong with my son?" he asks, not even thinking that it's unusual for the woman to have even said such a thing.

"There ain't nothin' wrong," she smiles. "He just needs to talk to his father. It's man stuff."

Cliff wants to ask another question, but he's interrupted by his colleague.

"Who's the fine looking older gentleman," Greg asks, showing a keen interest in the many pictures. He estimates there must be hundreds of them strategically placed on shelves, cupboards and covering just about every inch of wall space in the small, cluttered room, which is barely large enough to hold the table and chairs, fridge and the stove.

"That's my Henry," she answers, flashing a shy smile. "He's been dead now for almost thirty years. We were married for fifty-seven years. We met when we was only young. Life ain't been the same without him, but you know what that's like, don't you, Sergeant?"

Shooting Cliff a bewildered look, Greg slowly answers the woman, sympathy emanating from nearly every part of his body. "Yes, I do understand how you feel," he stutters.

"But it's good that you found someone else," she says.

"How do you know about me?" Greg asks.

She pauses, as if trying to remain coy. Finally, her impish-like face becomes serious and she adds, "I know a lot of things, Sergeant."

"Such as?"

"Heart attack took Henry, just like that," the woman says, snapping her twisted, arthritic index finger and thumb on her left hand. "But the cancer's terrible stuff. Kills too many people and it don't matter how old you are with that stuff. Hopefully, they'll find a cure for it someday. My Henry was old, but your misses was only young when she died," staring into Greg's eyes, she says, her voice soft, "and that's so sad. Broke your heart, didn't it?"

Greg's body tenses in reaction to her comments, but he says nothing.

"I recognize that woman," Cliff quickly jumps in, seeing that his friend is suddenly squirming in his seat. Pointing to a picture of a young, pretty red head woman sitting on a chair with three children standing around her. "That's Lily Pittmann and her children. Why would you have a picture of Lily?"

"Lily is my great-granddaughter," the old woman replies. "Her children are a lot older now from when that picture was taken and I don't have one of her new baby. I'd like one though. I hear he's a special little boy."

"I didn't know Lily was an Underwood before she married Tom Pittmann," Cliff says.

"Technically, she wasn't because she's my daughter's granddaughter, but the family bloodline flows through her just as sure as it does her children," she explains. "Lily's had a rough couple a months, what with everything that happened with the twins. I hope I can get to see her soon while there's still time."

"I don't understand, Mrs. Underwood," Cliff says. "Time for what?"

"Call me Clara," the old woman insists. "And that ain't important. You men didn't come all this way out here to talk about my pictures. . . . How can I help you with your case?"

"Okay, Clara," Cliff says. "You're right. My friend and I did come out here to talk to you about something, but it isn't the case that we're working on."

"Oh?" she stares directly into Cliff's eyes. "Then what can I do for you, Corporal?"

"Well," Cliff begins, finally pulling his eyes away and casting his gaze toward the floor, as if the old woman intimidates him. "We want to talk to you about crows."

"Crows?" she says and lets out a long, slow sigh. "Well, for heaven's sake. "What are they up to now?"

"We're really not sure," Cliff answers. "Can you help us understand what they're doing?"

"Perhaps," she smiles. "First, though, before we talk about them black birds, you must have a cup a tea. It's already on the stove and after bein' out in the cold, it will do 'ya a world of good."

Despite repeated protests from the two officers, the plump woman, whom Cliff estimates to be somewhere over ninety years old, rises from the table and moves to the stove where the tea is brewing.

"Please don't go to any bother for us," Greg tells her as she nimbly moves about the kitchen, filling two ceramic cups—one blue and the other red—with tea.

"It's no bother. I like havin' company. I don't get many visitors these days." Placing the tea in front of them, she then says, "You must drink this. It will warm you up. It's my own special blend. I'm sure you'll really like it and you'll feel a lot better afterward."

Without further protests, both officers slowly lift their cups and sip the tea. Feeling the warm liquid rush to their stomachs as it begins thawing their insides, the men become relaxed.

Finally, Cliff asks, "So, now, Clara, what can you tell us about the crows?"

In an instant, the officers observe the woman's face become sullen and drawn, her lips tensing and her eyes narrowing to slits, the wrinkles on her face becoming more defined. And when she speaks, the tone of her voice is stern, with an air of urgency.

"It's a warnin'," she quickly proclaims, her rouge drawl becoming more profound, as if she slipped back in time. "They're warnin' 'ya 'bout somethin.'"

"What kind of warning?" Greg asks.

"They're tryin' to tell 'ya this ain't over," she says, her voice monotone. "This is far from over."

"What do you mean?" Cliff probes. "Do you mean the case of the missing children?"

"Ey," she whispers and the men watch as tears trickle from the old woman's eyes and tumble down her aged cheeks.

"I'm sorry, Clara, but I don't understand," Greg replies. "What would they know about the missing children?"

"A lot," the old woman insists and her mood swings to one of determination. "Them black birds know a lot."

"How?" Greg asks as Cliff watches closely, studying the woman's facial expressions.

"They know everythin' that happens 'round here," she says. "They've been watchin' this place for a long time."

"Are you telling us the crows are intelligent?" Cliff jumps in.

"Oh, yes," she chuckles, but neither officer detects any humour in her laugh. She pulls a deep breath of air between her decaying teeth and adds, "They are smart . . . smarter than a lot of people. . . . Don't ever underestimate them."

"So how can they know what's happening with the children?" Greg asks.

"From where they roost, they can see everythin'," she explains, "and if they're tryin' to reach out to you, Sergeant, then they're tryin' to tell 'ya what they've seen."

"Okay," Greg sighs. "So let's say that's true."

"It is true, Sergeant," she interrupts. "You can believe me about that."

"Very well." He nods. "It's true. They see everything and know everything, but why are they trying to reach out to me?"

"'Cause they sense you are a good man," she explains. "They know you have a good heart. They sense this case is a heavy burden for you and they're tryin' to lighten the load. They're tryin' to help you."

"What do they know?" Greg wonders aloud.

She looks at the two men and then asks, "How many crows are there?"

"Five," Greg says. "Why? Are the numbers important?"

"Ey," she nods. "Each number in the flock is a specific message. So then, if they're coming to you in a group of five, then that means somethin' silver plays an important role in their message."

"Silver?" Cliff says. "Silver what? Like something made of silver, like maybe jewellery?"

"Could be," she says and nods. "But it's not always the obvious." Turning to Greg, she adds, "Don't look for the obvious, it's not always that simple. And sometimes, there can be double meanin' in their messages."

"How do you know so much about the crows?" Greg asks.

"I just seem to have a connection with 'em," she says. "I get visions about 'em."

"Visions?" Cliff asks. "What do you mean?"

"Pictures," she explains. "In my head. They just come to me."

"How long has this been happening, Clara?" Cliff asks. "How do you get them?"

"A very long time," she says and then hesitates as if wondering if she can tell them her story. It's obvious to the officers that she has encountered skeptics in the past. But she begins, "I can't tell 'ya how it happens 'cause I don't know how it happens. It just happens. The pictures come to me. Don't know why but all of a sudden, there they are."

"So when you say it's happened for a long time," Greg adds, "what exactly do you mean?"

"I mean a long time." She smiles at him. "It even happened when I was a little girl and that was a lot of years ago, but I know I was maybe four or five years old when it started. It could have even been earlier, but that's as far back as I can remember."

"So what's it like then, when you get these pictures?" Greg inquires, wondering if he's really buying what she's selling, but telling himself to keep an open mind.

"It just hits me," she says. "When I'm awake. When I'm sewin' or eatin.' Even when I'm sleepin.' Sometimes the pictures are so strong, they wake me up and then I can't get back to sleep again."

"So have you been having pictures about this investigation?" Greg probes.

"Ey." She pauses and studies the two officers. "A lot of 'em and they scare me. I don't like 'em," she adds. "Not all the pictures I see are about bad things, but these ones are very bad. . . . They're evil and black and they scare me."

"Can you tell us what you see, Clara?" Greg asks, reaching out and touching her arm, as if to offer her comfort or moral support. "Unless it's too painful for you."

"I can see there will be another one 'fore the winter sun sits in tomorrow's sky," she whispers, rubbing her eyes with her short, pudgy fingers.

"Another what?" Cliff asks.

"Another killin,' that's what," she quickly answers, tears streaming down her flushed cheeks.

"How do you know that?" Greg asks.

"I just know it," she answers in a faint whisper that's nearly impossible for the officers to hear.

"You know it?" Greg replies.

"I seen it."

"When?" Greg asks. "When did you see it?"

"The picture started about a week ago, maybe a little longer." The officers can sense the alarm in the woman's changing demeanour. Her voice trembles as she tells them more. "And I've seen it four or five times since then, if not six. There will be more killin's, I'm tellin' 'ya, and the next one will be very soon."

"Okay, Clara. We understand that," Cliff jumps in. "Did you see anything else in your pictures? Maybe something that will help us figure out who's doing this or maybe where he's doing it?"

"I can see that another little girl is goin' to die soon," she says, the tears still falling from her face. "That's bad enough."

The officers share a glance.

"Yes, Clara, that is bad enough," Greg says, his voice comforting. "Can you see her face?"

"No," the woman shakes her head. "But she has light-coloured hair and she is seven years old."

The officers exchange another glance. They don't say anything, but they immediately think of the second abducted girl, seven-year-old Hillary Lawrence from Yarmouth.

Finally, Cliff asks, "Can you tell us anything else?"

She hesitates and then says, "He leaves the silver crosses 'cause he's tryin' to tell 'ya he's sorry for what he's done."

Again, the men fall silent. There is no way this woman should know that detail as it has not been released publicly.

Greg then asks, "Can you tell us anything about the man who's doing this? Can you see his face?"

"No," she answers quickly and forcibly. "I don't want to see him. . . . but he wears a black mask over his face so I can't see him anyway. And most times, when I see these things, I only get a glimpse . . . like a fast movin' picture in my head. Sometimes it's fuzzy and very blurry. He's always hazy to me. I just see his outline."

"Do you know what he drives?" Cliff asks.

"Ain't never seen it," she says.

"About the crosses, Clara," Greg adds. "Do you think that's the silver the crows are trying to tell me about?"

"Could be," she nods. "But there could be another meanin,' too." She pauses and then adds, "Remember what I said, Sergeant, don't look for the obvious."

"Yes," he nods. "You said that, but I'm not sure what you mean."

"You'll figure it out, Sergeant," she smiles. "You're a smart man and they've chosen you, so they trust you to get it."

"About this guy," Cliff adds, "can you tell us where he lives or where he takes his victims once he has them?"

"I see little girls being locked in a dark room where there is only dirt on the floor, like a cellar or somethin' like that," she says, the tears continuing to fall. "It's like a dungeon in there. It's dark and wet and cold and they're very scared, the poor dears. I hear 'em cryin' for their mommies. It breaks my heart."

"Do you know where it is?" Cliff asks

"No." She shakes her head.

"That's not going to help us much," Cliff says, not meaning to sound discouraged.

"It's all I see," she whispers. "I'm sorry."

"No, Clara, don't be sorry," Greg whispers. "It's all very helpful, but are you sure there isn't anything else. Maybe even a tiny detail that seems like it's not important."

"I'm sorry I can't be more helpful," the woman answers, wiping her eyes with her now shaking hands. "I hope I've given 'ya somethin' that will lead 'ya to the killer."

Greg pauses and studies the old woman. He thinks she looks tired. "Well," he says. "I think we should be going. We do want to thank you for talking to us. If you think of anything else will you please call?"

"Of course," she nods and straightens herself. "I will," she assures them.

Standing, both men extend their hands to her.

"Thank you again," Cliff says.

"Sure," she says, taking Cliff's hand. Smiling at him, she adds, "Don't worry, Corporal. Your heart's strong and healthy now. You'll be good for a while."

Taking Greg's hand she says, "Sergeant. Listen to your heart and listen to the crows. They trust 'ya. You're a good man. They're tryin' to help 'ya."

Greg nods, but says nothing.

"And," she adds, "congratulations on the baby." She pauses. "Don't worry 'bout bein' too old to be a good father, you can handle it. You will be a good father, I know it. . . . By the way, happy birthday."

"How?" he whispers.

She doesn't answer but moves to the door.

"Bye, now. Watch the roads. They're a mess," the woman warns as the men leave the warmth of the small, modest house and enter the cold winter afternoon. She closes the door behind them as the police officers make their way back down the steps. They hear her secure the locks.

Stopping near the car, Greg turns to his companion, as if to say something, but pauses. He looks at him, then shrugs. He can't find the right words to say what's on his mind.

"I hear you, friend," Cliff says, sliding into the passenger side of the police cruiser, its windshield once again covered with inches of heavy snow that has fallen from the trees. "That was pretty freaking weird. I'm not sure what that was all about, but I think our puzzle just got a whole lot more complicated, and I think you better work fast."

"Real fast," Greg agrees, slipping behind the steering wheel.

"Is she for real?" Cliff asks.

"I guess," Greg answers, switching on the windshield wipers and throwing the transmission into reverse. He backs the car around and heads down the narrow driveway, their tracks from less than an hour earlier now nearly impossible to see as the wind has blown the snow off the trees and onto the ground. "You know, I was skeptical when we first got here, but now, I really don't know what to think," he says.

"It's difficult to dismiss what she said," Cliff suggests, wiping the side window with the back of his large, right hand. "It's just uncanny how she knew so much about us. Certainly adds credence to what she told us about the investigation."

"What do you make of this place that she claims to have seen?" Greg asks. "Does it sound like any place you might recognize around here?"

"Nothing that comes to mind," Cliff says shaking his head.

"Well, if she's right, we don't have much time to waste." Greg sighs. "She says we can expect another child to die before tomorrow evening. That doesn't give us much time."

"Let's hope she's not right then," Cliff says.

The men remain quite as Greg retraces his snow-filled tracks back out of the road and then heads into town. As the sun is setting over the small coastal hamlet, they know that time is not on their side.

Chapter 13

Greg pulls into Cliff's driveway and puts the cruiser in park, turns off the ignition and then slumps back in the vinyl seat. He takes a long, deep breath and sighs, turning his head to stare out the side window. "So," he says, his breath fogging the glass. "What do you think?"

"About what," Cliff asks, unsnapping his seat belt and letting it slid back over his right shoulder. "About the old woman? The crows? The case?"

"Yes," Greg nods, turning to look at his friend. "All of the above. . . . Everything. What do you think?"

"Honestly," Cliff shrugs. "I have no idea, pal, but the old woman seems to know a lot about you and me and everything else that's going on around here. And," he pauses, "I have to admit, it's more than a little freaky. Truthfully, it all makes me a little uneasy."

"Me, too," Greg agrees, sighing again, this time more forcefully. "It's really uncanny how she knew some of the details about the case, like the silver cross. That information wasn't released to the media. How could she know that? And then all the stuff she knew about us." He looks out the windshield and stares into the grey sky. "How could she possibly know all those personal details about our lives, like today is my birthday? How could she know Andrea is pregnant? We haven't told anyone."

"I have no idea." Cliff shrugs again. "Lucky guess, maybe?"

"You think?"

"No," Cliff shakes his head. "Not likely."

"Well, here's something else that doesn't add up," Greg continues. "I'm confused by her age."

"How so?"

"By looking at her, you'd say she must be what?" Greg asks. "Eighty? Eighty-five maybe? Ninety at the most."

"I guess that would be about right," Cliff agrees. "Why?"

"Here's the thing," Greg explains. "Didn't she tell us her husband has been dead for almost thirty years?"

"She did."

"And didn't she say they had been married for fifty-seven years when he died?"

"She did."

"So that's the thing," Greg says. "That's something like eighty-seven years. Giving that she could have been around seventeen or eighteen when she got married, based on the wedding picture I saw her staring at when she was talking about her dead husband, that would make her what?"

"At least one hundred and five," Cliff answers and pauses. "I see what you mean. She certainly doesn't look anything like that."

"It's just another mystery that doesn't add up," Greg suggests. "I know people can live to be very old, but it's very rare and she doesn't look like she is anywhere near that age."

"I told you when you went out there that you should be prepared for the unusual," Cliff says, fidgeting with the door handle, but not opening it. "I told you I heard stories about her, but now you know for yourself what I was talking about."

"I do," Greg nods. "The question is, what do I do now?"

"Friend," Cliff answers, shaking his head. "I have no idea, but, if what she says turns out to be true, then it's clear there's a lot more shit coming down the pipe and you're going to be right in the middle of it."

"It would seem that way, wouldn't it?" Greg sighs again. "I'll just have to take it as it comes. But," he pauses and turns to face his friend, the man he would trust with his life. "What do you think she meant about the crows? That I should look beyond the obvious when it comes to trying to figure out the meaning of the five crows?"

Cliff shrugs. "I don't know, pal. Sounds like a bigger riddle than my little brain can handle. I'm not much good with puzzles."

"It really is a puzzle, isn't it?" Greg says.

"It is," Cliff says and nods. "But you know what? My advice to you is to try really hard not to let this get under your skin. The harder you think about this, the more difficult it will become to solve."

"It's not that easy for me to push things aside," Greg says. "I don't function that way. Maybe it's my job but my mind's always thinking."

"Sure it is, but you're going to have to make an effort," Cliff insists. "Try to step back from it. Put some distance between you, the case and the crows. I find that sometimes when you're not trying so hard, the answers just come to you. My experience has been that sometimes when you try too hard, you make things harder on yourself. Take a deep breath and relax."

"Relax?" Greg says. "Kind of an odd way to do police work, and for the record, Cliff, I've never known you to relax over anything."

"It's the new me," Cliff chuckles. "I've turned over a new leaf ever since I nearly died, and I'm trying really hard not to dwell on things. Doctor's orders. He says that worrying about things only builds stress and that stress contributed to my heart attack. I can't let that happen again."

"Well," Greg says. "I'm afraid the stress is all on me this time."

"Sorry about that," Cliff says, finally pulling up on the handle and opening the door just a crack. "I guess it's all my fault for having a heart attack."

"Yes," Greg chuckles. "It is your fault."

"Oh well." Cliff shrugs. "It is what it is. Tomorrow is Saturday so maybe you'll have an easier day."

"From your lips to God's ears," Greg replies and smiles at his friend. "In case I'm not talking to you before then, can you please tell Carly I'll pick her up around five? Andrea's still planning on taking me out for my birthday and we're going to leave around six, so we won't be out too late."

"Roger," Cliff answers, pushing the door all the way open. "And try not to let this eat away at you."

"I'll try," Greg promises, "but you know that's not going to happen."

"I know," Cliff says, as he closes the door. "I know all about it."

*****

"Hello?" the little blonde-haired girl yells, pounding the thick wooden door with her tiny hands, its rough surface causing splinters to puncture her soft skin. "Mommy? Daddy?" she sobs. "Can anyone hear me? I want to go home."

"No," the other girl whispers from the other side of the dark room, her voice hardly a whisper. "Don't do that. He don't like it when you make a lot of noise and if he hears you, he'll come back. . . . I don't want him to come back. He'll hurt us."

"Why?" The blonde girl cries, squinting her eyes in an effort to see the other girl through the blackness. "Why will he hurt us? . . . Who is he?"

"I don't know," the other girl answers, her voice barely audible. "But he don't like it if you make noise and he really don't like it if you cry."

"Did he hurt you?" the first girl asks, groping through the darkness, following the tiny voice, until she finds the bed without blankets, its mattress, dirty and stained with God knows what. Sitting on the edge of the mattress, she asks again, "Did he hurt you?"

"Yes," the other girl whispers, trying hard to suppress her tears. "He hurt me real bad."

"Why?" the first girl sobs.

"He says he likes me," the girl on the bed whispers. "But I don't like him."

"You're tied up," the first girl whispers, her eyes finally adjusting enough in the pitch-black room that she can see the other girl spread eagle on the mattress, her legs and arms tied down and secure with rope. "And you got no clothes on."

"He hurt me real bad," the girl cries, biting her bottom lip in an effort to stifle her tears. "And he's gonna hurt you, too."

"I wanna go home," she sobs. Fear churns in her stomach like an angry dragon, its claws ripping at her insides. "I want my mommy."

"I want my mommy, too," the girl on the bed says, "but don't make any noise or he'll come back. He hates the noise."

"But I'm scared," the blonde girl cries.

"I'm scared, too, but don't make him come back—please," the one on the bed whispers. "You *have* to stop crying," she pleads again.

"Okay," the first girl says. She nods and begins to wipe her eyes. "I'll try."

"What's your name?"

"Ruby," the girl sobs in shorts gasps as she tries to stifle her tears. "Ruby Smith."

The girl tied to the bed tries to force as weak smile, but she hurts too bad to make the effort. Finally, she whispers, "I'm Hillary."

"Can I untie you?" Ruby asks.

"No!" Hillary quickly answers. "That will make him madder. . . . You don't want to make him mad. . . . Ever."

Wiping tears from her eyes again, Ruby asks, "Who is he?"

"I don't know his name."

"Where are we?" she asks, forcing herself to keep her voice at a whisper.

"I don't know," Hillary answers.

"What's he going to do with us?" Ruby asks.

"I don't know."

"I want to go home." Ruby begins to cry again.

"Me, too," Hillary agrees, now sobbing herself. "But he won't let us go . . . and we have to be quiet or he will come back. . . . We don't want him to come back."

*****

"Are you okay, honey?" Andrea asks, smiling at him across the table. "You haven't touched your dinner. I thought you liked chicken Parmesan?"

"I do, but I'm not very hungry," he sighs and leans back in the wooden chair, forcing himself to return her smile. "Sorry, I know you worked really hard on it and it's great."

"Daddy," the little girl sitting next to him says, "will you play with me?"

"Sure." He nods and smiles. "After you eat your dinner. Okay, sweetie?" Getting up from the table he says to his wife, "Sorry, honey, I just can't eat right now. If you wouldn't mind putting it in the fridge,

I'll eat it later."

"Okay," Andrea says. "Are you okay, Greg?" She looks at him, concern etched into her face. "You're starting to worry me," she adds.

"Just got a lot on my mind," he says, turning and heading into the living room. "I'll be fine. I just gotta think. I have to get my head wrapped around a few things, that's all."

*****

The small, dank room is black and the little girls are cold, their tiny bodies shaking.

Lying beside Hillary, whose hands and feet are numb from the ropes biting into her small wrists and ankles, Ruby asks, "Why has he brought us here?"

"I don't know," she answers, her voice failing. Ruby moves to the small child.

"Are you okay, Hillary?" she asks.

"Just really tired, and I'm cold," Hillary answers. "My arms and legs hurt."

"What's he going to do to us?" Ruby asks, pulling her body even closer to the other girl, hoping to keep her warm.

Hillary doesn't answer.

Finally, Ruby asks again, "Are you okay?"

"I just want to sleep," Hillary responds, her words no more than a wisp in the icy air. "Remember," she adds, as her eyes close, "Don't make any noise or he'll come back. . . . Don't make him mad." She closes her innocent blue eyes.

*****

"Greg?" Andrea asks, gently touching his shoulder. "Are you sleeping?"

"What?" he responds, pulling himself up straight in the easy chair. He's been sitting, staring blankly at the ceiling for the past hour since leaving the dining room table.

"I asked if you were sleeping," she says, kneeling beside the chair and looking up into her husband's eyes. Pain and confusion fill his normally bright, blue eyes. "Are you okay?" she asks.

"Yes."

"You seemed like you were lost in another world, just now. Somewhere far away," she says.

"No," he whispers, forcing a smile. "Just thinking."

"About the case?"

"Yes," he says again. "I can't get those poor girls out of my mind. Their sweet little faces just keep popping into my head over and over, like they're screaming out for me to come and rescue them."

"That's natural," Andrea says, softly running her hand over his left arm. "You're a cop and you're a father so you're identifying with them on both levels. I understand you're worried. It's part of who you are, but you can't let this case get to you like this or you won't be able to help them. Those little girls need you and you can't help them if you're in such a state that you can't concentrate on what you're doing. You've got to keep it together for them—and for your own sake."

"I know you're right," he says. He leans his head back against the plush chair and closes his eyes. "I know you're right, but this one's really getting to me. I've worked some tough cases before and never lost my focus, but this one is killing me. I just need time to think. I've got to clear my head." He lets out an exhausted sigh.

"Okay, honey," she whispers, rising to her feet. "You rest a while longer. I'll give Lucy her bath and I'll let you know when she's ready for you. Remember, you promised her you'd play with her for a bit before she goes to bed."

"Yes, of course," he says. "Just give me a shout when she's ready and I'll come right up."

"I love you," she says, bending and kissing his forehead. "And I'm worried about you."

"I love you, too," he smiles. "I'm okay, I promise, so please don't worry."

*****

"Quiet," Ruby whispers, pulling her tiny body closer to Hillary. "I hear something."

As the door lock clunks open, Hillary instinctively jumps, causing the thick, rough ropes to cut deeper into her already raw skin.

She cries as she whispers, "It's him."

"No," Ruby sobs, wrapping her arms around the other girl. Her stomach clenches and her heart pounds as the door creaks open. She sees his form outlined in the darkness, like the monster she used to imagine was hiding in her bedroom closet. "What does he want?"

"I heard you two," he snaps. "I want you to be quiet." Stomping toward the bed, he grabs Ruby by the legs and tosses her to the floor with the ease of an impetuous child hurling an unwanted rag doll. "Get away from her. She's mine."

"Owww," Ruby cries as her tiny body scrapes across the rough ground.

Standing over her, he kicks the little girl in the side. As she lets out a small whimper he kicks her again, like she is nothing more than a mangy old mutt. A searing pain rushes through her body, every nerve in her tiny abdomen screaming in protest. "No crying!" he screams. "I don't like it when kids cry. Kids are not supposed to cry. They're supposed to be seen and not heard."

She quickly stifles her tears and pulls herself into the fetal position, hugging her knees up to her chest as tightly as she can—her instincts for self-preservation kicking in.

Turning back to the bed, he looks at the girl tied there, "You're coming with me."

"No," she pleads, her voice exploding with desperation as he roughly unties her wrists and then her ankles. "I want to stay," she cries. "I promise to be good."

"Don't worry," he says, taking a softer tone. Scooping her up in his arms, he says again, "I'm not going to hurt you. We're going to have some fun."

"No," she whispers. "Please leave me be."

"Enough," he snaps, turning to face the girl crumpled on the floor. "Don't you say anything and don't you get on that bed. It's not yours. I'll be back to deal with you later."

Clinging to her knees and pulling herself into a tight ball, Ruby watches helplessly as the man carries Hillary to the door and then he grabs it, slamming it closed behind him. She hears the lock click into place again. The loud thud echoing throughout the empty, dark room.

"Please," she whimpers. "Please bring her back. I'm so afraid. I don't want to be alone."

*****

Greg stares into the darkness at the ceiling. His head is pushed into the pile of pillows as he listens to the steady, gentle breathing of his wife lying next to him under the cozy quilts. His mind reels with horrifying thoughts of what the monster is doing to the helpless girls. And he can't help but think it will be his fault if this next child dies, just like the old woman predicted. He has to save them!

He glances at the digital clock on the small bedside table, the bright red numbers flashing 2:45 a.m. He knows he should be sleeping, but he can't bring himself to close his eyes. Instead, he reviews the case, repeatedly going over the details in his mind.

What do we know? he thinks.

Three missing girls, ages seven and eight.

Why that age?

Taken from Windsor, Yarmouth and Bridgewater.

Why those locations? What's so special about them?

All three had light-coloured hair.

Why light? Why not black or brown or red?

All were the only children in their families.

Why is that important? How does he know that?

The remains of one was found, naked, on the frozen sand of a beach not far from Liverpool.

Why dump the body here? Why is this place so important to him?

The only clue left behind was a silver chain and tiny cross that was hanging around the first victim's neck.

Why is that significant to him?

So many questions. . . . So few answers.

These must be clues, he believes, tossing in the bed and thinking that somehow he has to find answers. Somehow, he has to put all these details together to help solve these crimes. And, he's certain he must do it quickly before another child is stolen . . . and before another is killed.

*****

She hasn't moved from the spot where she landed on the hard, gravel floor when he threw her there. She's too afraid.

She doesn't know how long it's been since he came and took Hillary away from the dark room, but she wishes he would bring her back. She's scared and being alone in this windowless place makes it even worse. She's afraid and her side hurts where he kicked her. At least with the other little girl there, she didn't feel so alone.

"Mommy?" she whispers, as she hears the lock click and watches as the door opens just a crack. To her immediate horror, she realizes it's him.

"It's not your mommy," he barks and stomps into the room. "You're mine now. You will never see your mommy again."

"Mommy," she cries, wishing someone would come and rescue her.

Rushing up to her, he grabs her by the shoulders, shakes her roughly and yells, "Stop asking for her. I told you you're never going back there. You're staying here with me."

"No," she fires back in a sudden burst of defiance that she immediately regrets as she feels the stinging blow of the back of his right hand when it connects with her cheek.

"Shut the fuck up, you little bitch," he commands and she feels his spit hit the stinging skin on her face. "You will listen to me or you'll get another one."

Although she would like to say something to him, plead with him, Ruby resists, fearing he will hit her again if she speaks.

"Get on the bed," he tells her and she immediately complies, scampering across the damp gravel on her hands and knees and then climbing up on the thin, bare mattress.

"Where's Hillary?" she whispers, as he grabs her ankles and roughly wraps the rough, thick rope around them and secures it to the bed railing.

"Gone," he says, repeating the process with her wrists. "And she ain't never coming back. I don't need her now that I got you."

"Where?" Ruby cries.

"Gone. That's all you need to know," he snaps. "And I told you not to cry."

"Sorry," she whispers, quickly willing herself to stop her tears.

"You better be," he says, standing over her and glaring down at her, her arms and legs spread eagle, making her totally vulnerable to her captor. "There," he seethes. "Now, that's more like it."

"It hurts," she sobs.

"Shut the fuck up," he yells. "Did I say you could talk? Do you want me to cover your mouth?"

She shakes her head—and says nothing.

"Good," he says. "Maybe you're finally learning."

She stares up at him, her head resting on the bare mattress.

"Are you hungry?" he asks.

She says nothing.

"I bet you are," he says, his voice calmer, as he reaches out with his right hand and rubs it through her long, blonde hair. "You're so pretty," he says and sighs. He then quickly pulls his hand back. "I will get you something to eat and then we can play."

She doesn't answer, but watches quietly as he walks toward the door.

"You and me are going to have a lot of fun together," he says as he reaches the heavy wooden door. Exiting the dank room, he turns and adds, "Now you stay right where you are and don't say anything until I get back."

She wants to cry as the heavy door slams closed and the darkness floods the room, enveloping her, but she doesn't. She has learned the hard way that crying will only make the situation worse for her, but in her mind, she's crying . . . yelling . . . and screaming, hoping that someone—maybe even her mommy—will hear her. Maybe, she hopes, someone will come and save her soon. She just hopes it's real soon.

Chapter 14

February 14

Doctors Charlie Webster and Rebecca Brighton have known each other for several years, meeting when she came to town to set up a family practice after completing her internship in Ontario. He's a local boy, born in Liverpool. His father raised him and his twin sister, Kate, after their mother died when they were still young children. Without hesitation, he tells everyone he's always intended on remaining in his hometown despite the promise of better money elsewhere and the lure of more prestige in the larger metro hospitals. In fact, he's had many job offers over the years, but turned them down to stay where he believes he belongs. Despite their professional relationship and the occasional date, the two doctors have only gotten serious since Christmas—but the relationship is moving quickly and now they're even talking about marriage.

With all the freshly fallen snow over the past two days, she's convinced him, today is the perfect opportunity for him to try snowshoeing—something he's never wanted to do.

"But it's fun," she laughs as they enter the trail that follows the abandoned CN rail line and meanders along the banks of the historic Mersey River, its water frozen over this morning with a thick layer of ice and snow. "And," she teases, her warm breath clinging to the crisp air as she speaks, "It's really good exercise. . . . Good for the ole ticker," she laughs as she enters the trail.

"I don't need exercise," he huffs, haphazardly following her footsteps and struggling to maintain his balance against the laws of physics. To him, as he carefully places one snowshoe in front of the other, it feels like the snowdrifts want to swallow him up. "I'm in great shape," he says, struggling slightly for breath. "I could run a marathon."

"Sure," she laughs again, cautiously breaking tracks as she stays four steps in front of him. "Just because you're skinny, Charlie, doesn't mean you're in good shape."

"What?" He makes an exaggerated shrug. "You don't like the shape I'm in? It seems to me you didn't have any complaints last night about my shape." He smirks, recalling their night together. "Besides, when we started dating I thought you knew I was the local stud."

"I've heard the stories," she admits with a broad grin. "But I think the legend of Charlie Webster's exploits with members of the opposite sex are greatly exaggerated and mostly by you."

"Oh," he says, struggling to keep up with her. "You think so?"

"Yup," she laughs, glancing back at him over her right shoulder. Seeing her face light up when she grins, he likes how she teases him, but he would never admit it to her. It was her playful side that first attracted him to her, but it is only one of the many qualities he likes so much about her—*that*, he thinks, and the fact that she's smart, caring, beautiful and one of the sexiest women he's ever met. Together, all of these qualities combine to make a lethal package. "Now, can you keep up?" she teases, as she increases the distance between them. "So much for stamina."

"I'm coming," he puffs, struggling to lift one snowshoe and then the other. "I'm coming. Just hold up a second until I get my footing."

"A second?" she answers, coming to a standstill and watching him struggle in the deep snow to catch up to her, his long legs sinking up to his knees. "Honey, I think it's going to take you more than a second to get used to those things." Pausing, she adds, "I'll wait for you."

"I thought these things were supposed to help me stay on top of the snow," he says, slowly closing the distance between them.

"They're supposed to," she laughs, as he finally reaches her and grabs hold of her arms. "Charlie," she reacts to his added weight. "Don't grab me like that or you'll pull me over."

"That's the idea," he chuckles, falling on his back in the deep snow and pulling her with him.

"You're bad, Dr. Charlie Webster," she says and laughs as she lands on top of him, pinning his back to the snow. "You're so bad." She grins, leaning in and giving him a deep, passionate kiss.

"I am," he says grinning back and wrapping his arms around her, pulling her body into his. "You have no idea how bad I can be."

"So," she asks, breaking the embrace and staring into his dark eyes, "have you told Kate yet?"

"Told her what?" he teases adding a wink for good measure. "That you've taken me prisoner and you're holding me hostage, using me as nothing more than your sex slave?"

"Yeah, right," she replies. "In your dreams."

"You have no idea what I do to you in my dreams," he chuckles, pulling her close to him again and kissing her pert lips.

"I think I have some idea," she says, pulling away. "I mean, did you tell your sister that we're thinking about getting married?"

"Haven't had chance," he says, staring up at her well-chiselled face, the bright blue sky of the early morning in the background making her features sharp and crisp. "God . . ." He sighs and adds, "You're beautiful."

"Charlie," she smiles. "Stay on topic. I swear to God that you're ADHD. Why haven't you told your sister about us?"

"Well," he says, giving her an exaggerated shrug. "In case you haven't noticed, I've been kind of busy doing double shifts at the hospital because, as you know, we're shorthanded because of the doctor shortage and now Kate and Sam have taken Hunter on a trip to Florida. The child psychologist in Halifax suggested they need some away time with few distractions to bond with their son and I don't want to tell them the good news over the phone. Actually," he says and smiles, "I was thinking it would be nice if we could tell them together."

"Great idea," she says, "but let's not wait too long because I don't want them to hear about it from someone else. She should hear this from you. After all, she is the only family you have."

"Just as soon as they get back, we'll invite them out for dinner," he promises.

"Great," she says. "And after spending a week alone with that little rug-rat of theirs, I think they'll need some adult company."

"He is a precocious little tyke, isn't he?" Charlie adds.

"I'm not sure those two women had any idea what they were signing up for when they adopted him," Rebecca agrees. "But they are strong women and they are both good mothers. I'm sure they'll figure it out and they'll work through it with him. They're exactly what he needs right now."

"I hope so," Charlie says. "I've never seen Kate this stressed before. It's really not like her to lose control like she's been doing lately. I'm worried about her."

"She'll be fine," Rebecca assures him. "And speaking of people being fine, have you heard anymore from Oliver?"

"We had a Skype chat last Saturday when he was in Spain. He looks really good."

"What's he doing in Spain of all places?"

"Just passing through, I guess," Charlie says. "After his bout with cancer last year, he told me when he left after the holidays that he didn't know where he was going or when he'd be back. He said all he knew was that he had to get away for awhile . . . because of all the memories around here."

"He did go through a lot over the past few years," Rebecca says. "First, with Amy Bishop, then the death of your friend, Matt Miller. Then the cancer and this thing with Tessa Williams moving away on top of that. I have no idea what happened there, but I think he really liked her. It's a wonder he survived it all."

"Yeah, well," Charlie says, lifting his back off the snow-covered ground. "He seems to be fine now and my ass is getting cold lying here so let's get this over with so we can get back someplace warm."

"What's the rush?" She smiles, leaning in and preparing to give him another kiss when her eyes are drawn to a rustling in the trees further down the trail. "What's that?" she whispers, focusing her attention on the trail up ahead.

"What?" Charlie asks, following her gaze. He's surprised to see several crows have landed on the snow further along the trail where they were headed. "Fuck," he says. "Not them again."

"Who?"

"Not who," Charlie says. "What. . . . Crows to be exact . . . How many do you count?"

"One, two, three, four, five," she counts while pointing at each of the black birds to confirm the number. "There's five of them."

"Five crows silver," Charlie whispers. "What the hell does that mean?"

"I'm not really sure I know what you're talking about," she says, pushing herself off the man sprawled under her on the snow. "But it looks to me like the crows are huddled around something on the trail." Pulling herself up and then helping him regain his footing, she looks at the mound that's still too far away to distinguish. "What is that Charlie?"

"A dog maybe? Or some other animal . . . I don't know," Charlie answers, stepping out in front of her. "Let's have a look."

Making their way further along the trail in the direction of the crows that are now prancing around in the snow, Charlie wishes the large black birds would leave, but he doesn't say anything. He knows Rebecca has yet to experience the crows like he has.

Pausing and studying the crows' actions, Rebecca suggests, "You know Charlie, in an odd way, it looks like they want us to see whatever that is. I get the feeling they're trying to get our attention."

"It sure seems that way," he agrees, pushing forward with small steps, still wobbling as he goes. Finally, now within view of the object that's attracted the crows' attention, he stops and then falls to knees. "Oh my God," he whispers. "It's a child."

Dropping to her knees beside him, she can't help but look at the naked remains of the young blonde-haired girl resting on top of the snow. Rebecca begins to cry. "My God, Charlie. It's that little girl reported missing from Yarmouth. I saw her picture on the news just this morning while you were still sleeping. How did she end up here, like this?"

"I don't know," Charlie says. Quickly pulling off his gloves and thrusting his right hand inside the pocket of his blue parka, he retrieves his cell. Dialing 911, he pulls Rebecca to him and hugs her closely.

"She looks so sad," Rebecca says. She can't stop staring at the frozen child—like a horrible car accident you know you shouldn't look at but you can't help yourself. "She's so exposed. We should cover her up." She begins to undo her coat and Charlie grabs her arm, recognizing she is probably feeling the onset of shock.

"Just wait," he says, hugging her to him.

"911. What is your emergency?" the nameless woman answers as Charlie watches the five crows suddenly spring from the ground and soar into the cloudless morning sky. Clearly, he thinks, their work is done.

"My name is Dr. Charlie Webster," he says, forcing himself to remain focused on the conversation. "I need to report a body."

*****

Fifty-five, Greg thinks as he squeezes a healthy dollop of shampoo into the palm of his left hand. He doesn't feel fifty-five. In fact, if not for the occasional grey streak through his otherwise jet-black hair, it would be difficult to tell he's older than his mid-forties.

But over the past few days, he thinks, rubbing the shampoo through his thick hair, he's been feeling a lot older than he used to. He's been tired and generally worn down, most likely, he believes, because of the events that have rocked this once pristine town, a place where the residents usually feel safe, where people often leave their doors unlocked at night and their children play unattended in their yards.

Not anymore, he thinks, sticking his head under the steady stream of water pouring from the showerhead. Things are different now and people no longer feel safe in their homes and, he thinks, as the steaming hot water caresses his head and face, he feels responsible for that.

Maybe I shouldn't take this so personally. He reaches down and turns off both water taps and stands in the shower stall as the water runs down his taut body, dripping from his tall muscular frame. But for him, it is personal because he's in charge of the local detachment and he considers all crimes in his jurisdiction to be his responsibility.

He reaches out and retrieves a large blue towel hanging on a hook just outside the stall. He can't stop thinking about the crows and wondering what connection they have to this case.

Wrapping the towel around his waist and stepping out onto a large blue bath mat that sits on top of the grey, tile-like linoleum floor, he thinks about the black birds and wonders what message they're trying to send him. He also recalls the words of Clara Underwood and he's convinced there is more to that old woman than she reveals. Beyond that, he'll admit she's unlike any other person he has ever met.

Standing in front of the mirror and staring at the image looking back at him, Greg tries hard to convince himself that since today is Saturday, and it's his birthday, he should try to forget about the case for a few hours and relax. For one thing, he's promised Andrea he won't go into the office today. Instead, he's told her he plans to hang around the house where he can take it easy and maybe get caught up on some reading. He still hasn't had time to start that new Patricia Cornwell book Cliff bought him for Christmas, so maybe he'll crack that open. But, he sighs as he runs the comb through his hair—*that's not likely.* Even if he stays home today, he knows he's not likely to relax, let alone be able to concentrate enough to read a book.

How can he? He wonders.

He hangs the towel on the hook and pulls on his green, knee-length velour housecoat. The rate of these crimes against the young girls is escalating. This tells him the perpetrator is quickly becoming unglued—losing touch with reality. He's clearly devolving. The thought sends an icy chill up his spine. He shivers. Greg knows when a scenario reaches this point the pervert won't stop until he's fulfilled whatever fantasy he's concocted in his screwed-up brain, or until the police stop him. And in this case, that has to be him. He just hopes he can do it before any more children are hurt.

Sergeant Greg Paris has worked twenty-five years of cases, many of them dealing with missing and murdered children across the country and into the United States. He knows the statistics by heart. He knows that every year, more than 50,000 reports of missing children are made to police in Canada alone. He also knows that children go missing for many reasons, and they come from every walk of life and from every corner of this country. While some cases are solved quickly, many of these missing children are never recovered. In fact, if the child is not found within the first twelve hours, the likelihood they will be found alive diminishes with each passing minute.

"What are you doing, you son of a bitch?" he whispers. "Where are you hiding? Why have you targeted little girls? How can you be so cruel? What happened to you in your life to turn you into such a monster? . . . What do the silver crosses mean?" The questions keep rolling off his tongue, as though asking them out loud might help reveal answers.

There are too many questions surrounding this case and they're consuming him. He knows if he can't find a way to cope with this, he will become ineffective as an investigator. His success over the years has been his uncanny ability to get inside the perpetrators' heads and see the world through their eyes. He's learned through experience that the best way to catch these creeps is to think like they think, but because his head is so clouded with his personal feelings, which he's sure stem from the fact that he has a young daughter of his own now— and with the damn crows—he's been unable to do that effectively in this case.

Too much static, he thinks, emerging from the bathroom and heading down the hallway toward the master bedroom. *Too much interference.*

If he's going to crack this case, he thinks, entering the bedroom and pulling on a pair of boxers and then a pair of jeans over his underwear, he knows he's got to find a way to push aside all these distractions and focus on the facts in front of him.

I have to block out all the noise, he thinks.

He pulls his navy sweatshirt with a small yellow RCMP crest on the left side of the chest, down over his wet hair. *That's easier said than done.*

Sitting on the edge of the bed, he's just about to pull on his socks when the phone rings. He immediately cringes.

Shit, he thinks, glancing at the digital clock and seeing it's almost 9:30 a.m. Instinctively, he fears, this isn't good.

"Hello." He picks up the phone before the second ring. "Greg Paris here."

"Sergeant Paris," the female replies. He doesn't recognize the voice. "I'm calling from dispatch. We've just received a 911 call that a body has been discovered in your jurisdiction. Emergency personnel and several members have been dispatched to the location."

"Damn it." He sighs, immediately concluding it's one of the two missing girls even before hearing the details. "Where?"

"Along the recreational trail that runs through town," the female tells him. He cringes again. That's the same trail he uses when he runs . . . it's not far from his house. "Near the northern end, according to the caller."

"How long ago?"

"Less than ten minutes, Sir."

"Will you please notify the members that I am en route?"

"Yes, Sir."

"Have Major Crimes been notified?"

"Affirmative," the woman says. "I called them before I called you."

"Good decision." Greg nods even though the woman can't see him. "It's important to get that site secured as quickly as possible. What's the ETA for the Ident and dog teams?"

"Roughly an hour, Sir. Maybe an hour and fifteen minutes."

"Very well," he says. "We'll lock that place down until they get here."

"Is there anyone else you would like notified, Sir?"

"The Medical Examiner, please."

"Will do," the dispatcher confirms. "Anyone else?"

"Not right now, thanks."

"Okay," the woman says as she hangs up, leaving him standing in his bedroom, holding his phone and socks and feeling as though he has just been run over by a freight train. This isn't the kind of news he had hoped to hear today.

So much for a relaxing birthday, he thinks. He sits again and quickly pulls on the white athletic socks he's been clenching in his right hand.

Retrieving his watch and wallet from the top of his dresser, he's just about to exit the bedroom to head down stairs for his coat and boots, when a sudden and loud clunking noise at the window causes him to stop.

"What the hell?" he whispers, slowly making his way to the window and pulling back the dark brown curtains and lace white sheers. Peering out into the clear day, the sunshine reflecting off the snow immediately blinding him, he squints and scans the backyard.

"Damn." His eyes finally adjust to the bright light. Five crows are prancing around the yard, pecking and preening at each other. "Now what do you guys want?"

"What was that, honey?" Andrea says as she walks into the bedroom carrying a basket of neatly folded clothes, recently removed from the dryer.

"Huh? What was what?"

"What did you say? Were you talking to me?"

"No," Greg says, letting the curtains fall closed. "Just talking to myself."

"What's up?" she asks. "Who was that on the phone?"

"Dispatch."

"Don't tell me . . ."

"'Fraid so." He sighs heavily. "I've got to go out."

"But what about your day off? It's your birthday."

"Guess that will have to wait for another time," he says, stopping to kiss her on the forehead. "Duty calls."

"I know. I know, but Lucy was expecting to spend some time with you."

"Sorry," he whispers as he heads toward the door. "Believe me, I'd rather stay here all day with the two of you, but I really have no choice."

Chapter 15

At first, he thinks the pounding is in his head. It reverberates throughout his brain, each thud ricocheting like an out of control ping-pong ball, bouncing wildly in an empty room. But as his mind slowly finds its way back to reality, he realizes the hammering is coming from his bedroom door.

"Yes," he manages to stutter. He slowly pushes the blanket off his thin, fragile-looking body and glares at the wooden door, afraid that his father will somehow knock it down and burst into his room. "What do you want?" he says, weakly. He's not feeling well today.

He worked late last night. Now he's tired and the ping-pong in his head has graduated to a basketball careening across his skull. If he didn't know better, he'd say he has a hangover, but he wasn't drinking last night—so he's sure it isn't that. *Maybe I'm getting a cold*, he thinks, as the incessant pounding starts again. He drives his head back into the pillow and pulls it up tightly around his ears trying to block out the noise.

"Lucas," Murdock McCarthy yells through the closed door. "Are you awake, you little bastard? It's almost nine-thirty." He pounds again. "It's time for you to get your no-good-for-nothing, lazy ass out of bed and get some work done around here. The place is a pig pen."

"Please go away. I don't feel well," he answers back, the throbbing in his head intensifying as he speaks. "I've got a really bad headache."

"I don't give a Goddamn if your fucking head is falling off," the man says through gritted teeth so the words seem almost slurred. "I'm going out for awhile and you've got to get up. You should have been up long ago. Your sisters are hungry and they're waiting for breakfast. Now get the fuck out of that bed or I'll come in there and haul you out."

"Can't you give them some cereal?" Lucas calls back, forcing his eyes open. He immediately feels the sharp pain from the light spilling into his room through the window, which has no curtains or blinds. It rushes to the back of his skull where it explodes and sends ripples of pain pulsating throughout his exhausted body. Pushing his hands against his head, he adds, "I am really sick. I need to rest for a while longer."

"Not a fucking chance," the man yells and then pounds on the door again, only this time louder and harder. "You're lucky I let you sleep this long, you lazy bastard. Now, I'm leaving and I want to know you're up before I go or do I have to rip this fucking door off its hinges and pull your sorry ass down these stairs?"

"Where you going?" Lucas asks feebly, finally rolling to the edge of his bed. He readies himself before placing his feet on the cold hardwood floor, his skinny body bending at the waist so that his head continues to rest on the pillow. "Can't you wait for a while longer? What's so important that you have to leave right this minute?"

"It's none of your Goddamn business where I'm going or what I'm doing," Murdock screams, this time following his words with a kick that causes the door to rattle on its hinges. "I said to get the fuck up, you little creep, and I mean it. . . . Right now!" His words fill the house, echoing off the centuries old construction.

"Okay. Okay," Lucas says without conviction, forcing himself to sit up. The movement immediately causes him to feel a wave of nausea so he grits his teeth to avoid throwing up. "I'm up."

"Come over and unlock the door so I know you're really up," his father commands. "And hurry up. I ain't got all morning."

"Just a minute," Lucas whispers, the room spinning as he stands. A few minutes later he manages to make his way to the door and opens it to see his father standing in the hallway already dressed in his black winter coat and snow boots. "There," he whispers, squinting in an effort to keep the light out. "Are you happy? I'm up."

"It's about time," Murdock fires back as he unleashes a blow with his closed right fist and strikes the slender young man in the stomach. He seethes as he watches his son crumple to the floor in obvious pain. "What did I tell you about locking your door?"

"I'm sorry," Lucas manages to answer between gasps. He grabs his stomach and although he is in obvious agony, he refuses to cry. He is determined to never let this man see him cry. "I forgot," he adds through laboured breath as he gasps for air.

"What are you hiding in there?" Murdock demands.

"Nothing," Lucas snaps. "I'm not hiding anything."

"Then don't let it happen again," the older man yells, kicking his son in the legs as he's sprawled in the doorway. "Now, I'm going out and I don't know when I'll be back. Take care of your sisters and clean up this goddamn mess."

"Yes, sir," Lucas answers, his teeth clenched so tightly he's sure they may crack. "Where you going?"

"It don't matter where I'm going," Murdock answers, turning to head down the long, dimly lit corridor to the oak staircase. "It's not any of your fucking business."

"When will you back?"

"That's none of your business, either," Murdock says as he stomps down the staircase. "Just do what I told you to do and I'll be back when I get back."

"Prick," Lucas whispers under his breath.

"Did you say something?" The older man stops in his tracks and turns to face the young man. Glaring at his son, he says again, "Did you say something?"

"No, sir." Lucas answers. "Not a word."

"Good." Murdock continues down the steps. "Now get your ass up," he calls back up the stairs.

*****

It's a long, cold, walk from the entrance of the gated trail to where the naked body of seven-year-old Hillary Lawrence was found on a snow bank by two local doctors less than an hour ago. He curses that he had to park the cruiser and make the trek by foot through the knee-deep snow, but even more, he dreads the thought of reaching his destination. When he got up this morning, this was the furthest thing from his mind. He planned to relax and enjoy his birthday, as he promised his wife he would do. The last thing he thought he would be doing was visiting the disposal site of another dead child, discarded like yesterday's garbage.

Greg knows this trail well. It has become one of his favourite running routes since he moved to town a few months ago. He runs here several days of the week but with the recent snowfall, it's practically impassable to joggers so he wasn't thinking about coming this way until the path was beat down by cross-country skiers and snowshoers, something he's never tried. . . . But here he is.

Following the established footsteps, he notes the first impressions in the deep snow were those made by someone wearing snowshoes. Besides those tracks, he notes the footprints of two pairs of boots with distinctive tread marks — detachment-issued boots.

On the outer edge of the path, however, he notes a series of depressions that could have been made by someone else, possibly even the killer, but because the footprints are now mostly covered in by the blowing snow, these tracks will be of little use to the investigators. Still, he thinks, he'll have the forensic guys check them out just in case there is anything there.

But I doubt it, he shrugs, pushing onward, stepping carefully and placing each of his size thirteens in the previously established footprints.

Passing over the wooden bridge that traverses the frozen Mersey River and following the trail around a sharp bend, he sees the spot where a group of four is congregated, two of whom are the constables that were dispatched immediately after the 911 call and the witnesses, doctors Charlie Webster and Rebecca Brighton. They are all keeping a wide berth around the deranged madman's latest victim.

He finds the fact that the killer is leaving the victims fully exposed and at the mercy of the elements to be one of the most disturbing things he's ever encountered in his career—and he's discovered many disturbing things in that time

"Keep it under control, Greg," he whispers, recalling the

countless sick bastards he's helped put away, their faces and crimes still as vivid today as they were when he first encountered them. The images of each victim are forever ingrained in his memory, as if haunting him and are now part of who he is.

Jesus, he thinks. *Why is there so much depravity in the world?*

He's asked this question many times over the years, but he's never found an answer—probably because there is no answer. *Evil is just evil.*

Drawing closer to the scene and noting the unmistakable form of a tiny corpse resting on top of the snow in the centre of the trail, he feels his stomach tighten. He sucks back the urge to vomit, and says a silent thank you that he didn't take the time to eat breakfast before heading out. Approaching the foursome, he nods to Dr. Webster while waving to the constables.

"Sir," Constable Emily Murphy says, walking up to greet him.

"I figured I'd see you here," Greg nods. "Don't you ever take a day off?"

"I could ask you the same thing," she replies, her voice and expression exhibiting the raw grief that everyone is feeling. The air drips with sadness, making for an almost unbearable mixture with the stinging cold. Constable Murphy's face is stoic, almost as white as the virgin snow, but determination exudes from her tiny body. "I won't be able to take a day off until we get this sick son of a bitch."

"It's the second missing girl, correct?" Greg asks, scanning the body from a distance. "The one from Yarmouth?"

"Yes," the constable nods. Greg can tell she's fighting hard to hold back her tears. He knows it isn't easy because he's trying hard to do the same thing. "Yes, it is."

"So he's killing them in sequence," Greg says, running his eyes over the corpse, starting from the head, with her light hair, and running to her frozen toes. He cringes as he sees her skin is a light shade of purplish-blue as the frost invades her flesh. "The problem is, he appears to be escalating. There's now only two days between kills, which means we don't have much time to find the third victim and as much as I hate to say this, if his pattern holds, then he's already on the hunt for a fourth."

"Do you really think so, Sir?" she asks, as a sudden gust of cold air sweeps along the trail. She wraps her arms around herself, pulling her hands up under her underarms for warmth.

"I don't think there's much doubt about that," Greg suggests, the bright sunlight bouncing off the snow is blinding. "He's already trolling. It's what he does. He hunts. . . . It looks like he enjoys an overlap. It seems there's a period of time when he has two victims at the same time but then he tires of that routine and disposes of the one he's held the longest. This time, it's Hillary Lawrence. The next time it will be Ruby Smith."

"Why would he do that?" Constable Murphy asks.

"Because he's playing some kind of sick perverted game with these little girls. He's living out some sort of fantasy, but there is no doubt that he's getting his jollies from dominating his victims. . . . . This routine is part of it somehow. This guy's a sick son of a bitch," Greg says, turning to look at the doctors. "They found her?"

"Yes, Sir."

"I want to talk with them for a minute," Greg says. "Anyone get close to the body?"

"No, Sir," she shakes her head, "apart from the two that found her. They knelt beside her although they said they never touched her. Other than that, we maintained a parameter around her of several metres to preserve any evidence that might be here, although with the snow blowing around the way it is, anything that was there might already be gone."

"Good work, Constable," Greg says, making his way toward the doctors. "It's hard to tell what might be buried under there. Let's hope it's something that finally leads us to the bastard."

"Sergeant Paris," Charlie says, extending his right hand as Greg approaches.

"Greg, please," he says, grabbing the doctor's hand and then smiling at Dr. Rebecca Brighton.

"Right," Charlie nods. "I wish we were meeting under different circumstances." Hugging Rebecca close to him, he adds, "We certainly didn't expect to see anything like this when we headed out this morning."

"I'm sure," Greg agrees. "It's a pretty horrific sight."

"The worst," Rebecca says, rubbing her eyes with her bright yellow mittens that have tiny black stars on them. "Even as doctors, we can never be prepared for anything like this."

"You're still human," Greg says, trying to force a smile across his sullen face, but he knows he's failing miserably. "So," he says, "what can you tell me about what you saw?"

"Basically," Charlie answers, glancing toward the human remains in the middle of the trail. "We were making our way along the trail when we noticed this mound up ahead and when we got closer, we recognized it as a body."

"Did you touch the body?"

"No, Sir," Charlie shakes his head. "We knew the girl was dead. It was pretty obvious."

"When you started out this morning, did you see anyone else around? On the trail? Off the trail? Anyone in the vicinity at all?"

"No, Sir," Charlie shakes his head again. "No one. The place was deserted and very quiet."

"Actually," Rebecca jumps in, "There was an older woman walking a little dog—a toy poodle, I think—in front of a house just down the road, but other than that, there was no one else around that we could see."

"I've heard about her. That would be Mrs. Broome and her poodle, Stewart," Greg suggests. "I'm sure she didn't see anything. I've heard she pretty much stays close to her house as her eyesight's not very good these days. My guys keep a watch on her since she lives alone."

"Sorry, Greg." Charlie shrugs. "That was it. There wasn't anyone else that we noticed."

Greg pauses then asks, "Did you notice any footprints in the snow when you started out on the trail?"

"No," Rebecca answers. "We broke tracks as we went along and the snow was very deep so we would have seen them for sure."

"That's what I thought," Greg replies, and then asks, "Did you see anything at all that seemed out of the ordinary?"

"Nothing," Charlie sighs, a white cloud forming in front of his face and then quickly dissipating on the cool morning breeze. "Nothing unless you count the crows."

"Crows?" Greg asks, cocking his eyebrow toward the tall, lean doctor who he's gotten to know in recent years through other cases.

"Yes," Charlie answers without hesitation. "Crows."

"How many?" Greg probes.

"Five," Rebecca jumps in again. "We counted five of them."

"Damn," Greg says.

"Something wrong?" Charlie asks.

"Don't know." Greg shrugs and then says, "Just got this thing about crows lately."

"We've all got 'this thing' about crows," Charlie replies almost sheepishly. "It's hard to live in this town and not have 'a thing' about crows."

"Yes," Greg says and nods. "I've noticed that. What is it with this town and crows?"

"That," Charlie answers, "is a good question. It's like there's a curse or something hanging over the town and the crows are a big part of it."

"The word curse implies that it's something bad or evil," Greg says. "I'm not so sure this group of crows are up to something evil—at least this time."

"I wouldn't know," Charlie admits, his eyebrows knitting together as he speaks. "I gave up trying to figure out those freaking black birds years ago. My philosophy is to take whatever comes along and not to stress over the crows. I've seen what the presence of those birds can do to people, and if you're not careful, Sergeant, they *will* control your life."

"Makes them crazy, doesn't it?" Greg asks.

"That's not exactly the word I was going to use," Charlie suggests. "But yes, they can certainly play hell with one's mind if you let them."

"Indeed," Greg agrees. "Okay, doctors," he adds. "I think you can go home now, but we will want to talk to you again to get an official statement. We can do that someplace where it's warm. Is it okay if I send one of the constables by later today to get you on the record?"

"Sure," Charlie says. "Not a problem. I think after this, we'll be sticking close to home for the rest of the day—unless one of us gets called into the hospital."

"Of course," Greg says. "If something comes up today, we can do it another time but we should get your statement as quickly as possible while everything is still fresh in your mind."

"We'll be available whenever you need us," Rebecca promises.

"Very well," Greg says. "Can I ask you to please follow the same footprints on the way out?"

"Certainly," she adds, following Charlie as he begins to head back down the trail. "We'll be careful."

Watching for several minutes as the doctors slowly trudge along the trail, Greg then turns to face the body. He notes there are no footprints around the remains and the snow has started to mound up around the tiny form. Considering the height of the snowdrifts he wonders how long the body would have been lying here. He concludes it has to be several hours. He knows the timing was deliberate because the perp would have known that no one would use the trail before daylight. By that time, his tracks would be gone, effectively erasing what could have been a key piece of evidence.

"Smart," Greg says.

"Sorry, Sir?" Constable Murphy says, standing beside him. "I couldn't hear what you said."

"I said the guy was smart," Greg answers, bending to get a different angle of the tiny body. "He has his moves well planned. He's familiar with these places. He knew the wind would take care of his footprints. . . . . By the time forensics get here, I'm afraid the wind and snow will have taken care of any evidence he may have left behind, but," he pauses, his eyes lingering on the silver chain and tiny cross around the dead girl's neck, "I do see he's left his calling card."

"Yes, Sir," the constable says. "I noted that, too. Just like the first victim."

"So we know this is definitely a message," Greg says. "I just wish I could figure out what the hell he's trying to tell us."

"She's so tiny," Constable Murphy says, letting out a short sigh, despite trying to remain professional. Greg can detect the emotion in her words. "And she looks so innocent. God knows what the bastard put the poor little thing through before he killed her. I hope he didn't make her suffer much."

"Forensics and autopsy will rush their reports," he says, scanning the body again for anything that might lead them to the killer, "but I'm afraid it will be just like the last time. I don't expect we'll get anything. It seems he's scrubbed this body just like he did the other one."

"Who the hell could do something like this to a little girl?" the constable wonders.

"Oh," Greg says, standing up and stretching his legs. "Make no mistake about it. There are a lot of sickos in the world, people who can't control their impulses. They live in a fantasy world where laws and rules simply don't exist—except for theirs, of course."

"I'd like to have just five minutes alone with this guy," she says, her fists tightening. "I can guarantee you the son of bitch would never do it again."

"We've all had those thoughts at some time in our careers," Greg admits, "but we have the ability to control them. This guy can't control his urges and now he can't stop himself."

"You sound like you're defending him," the constable says and Greg detects a sudden change in her demeanour.

"No," he says. "Just trying to understand him. We can't stop him if we can't understand him. But I know this is hard for you. It's hard for all of us to be standing here looking at the senseless loss of such a young, innocent life, but we've got to focus on the challenge before us and solve this thing before we find another victim. Can you do that?"

"Yes, Sir." She straightens her body and nods.

"I think you can, too," he agrees. "You're a good police officer and part of what makes you good at the job, is your ability to empathize with the victim—but don't let those emotions consume you."

"No, Sir," she says.

"Very good." Greg sighs, glancing at the second officer who has remained stationed with his eyes glued to the body, as if expecting it to get up and walk away. He knows this case is taking its toll on all his officers. "You two remain here and keep this place locked down until Major Crimes arrive. I'm going back to the detachment and make some calls. I'll post constables at both ends of the trail and I'll release the paramedics who are standing by. Sadly, their services are not needed this morning."

Chapter 16

"But I don't want cereal," the little girl says, tears forming in the corners of her tiny blue eyes. She raises her hand to push the bowl away but it doesn't move far as the table is already cluttered with an array of papers, dirty dishes and ashtrays overflowing with cigarette butts and ashes. The entire kitchen is a mess, dirty pots, now encrusted with old food, and dishes stacked on the counter vying for space with a collection of empty boxes, cans and bottles containing the remnants of their former contents, long since spoiled. She watches as the young man removes a bright yellow box from a cupboard near the fridge and opens the lid. "Can't I have toast and peanut butter?"

"Not this morning, Emma," her older brother answers while dumping the Corn Pops into the plain white bowl and then pouring milk over the tiny round balls. "I've been up almost all last night working and I've got a wicked headache," he tells her. "I really don't feel like making toast. "

"But, Lucas," she protests, her voice beginning to grate on his nerves. "You always make me peanut butter toast. I like how you make it."

"I know." He sighs as he places the bowl in front of her. "Just please eat the cereal this morning and I promise I will make toast tomorrow."

"I don't like Corn Pops," she whines, curling up her tiny nose as if it disgusts her to even look at the cereal.

"Yes you do," he says, pushing the bowl toward her. "You've eaten them before and liked them."

"No, I haven't," she continues, crossing her tiny arms in front of her in an act of defiance.

"Listen," he snaps. "Please don't make me raise my voice." Glancing at Sophie, the other girl sitting at the table, he adds, "Your sister is eating them and she's not causing a fuss. Either eat the cereal or go without. I'm afraid that's all there is this morning, so it's your choice."

"Okay," she begins to cry as she picks up the spoon and scoops up several of the round, crunchy balls. "Okay, Lucas," she whispers between chews.

"I'm sorry, Emma," he says, turning away from the table. "But I really don't feel well and I've got to lie down before I throw up. Just eat your cereal and then play for a while." Heading to the living room, which is also filthy from several days of neglect, he adds, "I'm going to lie down on the couch. Don't touch anything and come get me if you need me. I just need to close my eyes for a little while."

*****

Since it's Saturday morning, the detachment is empty and dark when Greg arrives. Usually, he would embrace the solitude, but this morning he's longing for human contact. He often finds that talking to someone he trusts and respects usually clears his mind when something serious is bothering him and this morning, recalling the scene he just left behind on the trail, he decides he could use an understanding ear.

Stepping into his office and switching on the fluorescent lights, he pauses as the room fills with the stark, cold light. He's always hated fluorescent light, but they are standard in older detachments. The newer buildings use LED lights. He sighs, thinking the light matches his mood. Eventually, the force will also get around to retrofitting the older buildings and replacing the lights with the modern standard, but it certainly isn't going to happen today. And honestly, even if it did, even the warmer lights wouldn't affect his mood.

Pulling off his coat and hanging it on the stand in the corner behind the door, he sits at his desk and picks up the phone. He hesitates at first, thinking he shouldn't really bother his friend while he's on sick leave, but then he shrugs and dials Cliff Graham's number anyway. He *needs* to make the call. He hopes that talking to Cliff might ease his tension, which he realizes is reaching a critical point. He listens as the phone rings once, then twice and starts a third time.

"Hello," finally Cliff answers, sounding a little winded.

Recognizing the voice right away, Greg says, "Hey, bud." He pauses, wondering if he should have called. Then he asks, "What's up?"

"Greg?" Cliff answers. "I'm guessing this is not a social call if you're calling this time of day."

"You weren't sleeping were you?"

"Good God, no," Cliff laughs. "Just finally getting around to cleaning out my closet. Ever since I lost some weight, I can't find anything that fits me like it should and Carly's finally convinced me it's time to take some of this stuff to the Salvation Army."

"You sound like my wife," Greg laughs. "Only, she's always complaining about putting weight on and her clothes becoming too small."

"Wow," Cliff says. "That didn't sound very sincere. What's up?"

"You know me too well." Greg pauses.

"Come on, Greg," Cliff says. "I know you well enough to know you didn't call me this morning just so we can listen to each other breathe. What's on your mind?"

"No," he sighs. "You're right. I didn't call for idol chit-chat."

"So, then what's going on?"

"It's not good," Greg says.

"How so?"

"We've discovered another body."

"No," Cliff replies. "Shit. . . . Where?"

"The old CN trail . . . near the mid-way point, just past the bridge."

"Jesus." Cliff sighs and Greg can picture his friend's eyes exploding in anguish and disgust at the news. "Is it one of the missing girls?"

"Yes." Greg says and sighs, feeling a sense of helplessness overcome him. "I'm afraid it's the body of Hillary Lawrence, the little girl from Yarmouth."

"God."

"And, it's just like the first one," Greg continues. "The pose, the nudity, the silver chain and cross. Everything. The scene is nearly identical, except for the location."

"That low-life son of a bitch, piece of shit," Cliff fires back and Greg can feel his friend's anger boiling through the phone. "So what you're telling me is that you don't have anything to work with, right?"

"That's right," Greg admits. "The forensics team is on the way, but I'm sure they won't have any luck out there. This guy is too good to get caught that easily."

"What are you going to do? You gotta get this scumbag."

"Honestly," Greg answers, hanging his head and studying the stack of papers on the desk. "I really don't know, but I feel like I'm treading water here. This case feels different than all the others I've dealt with. I can't explain it, but I feel lost with this one."

"You sound like you need to talk," Cliff suggests. "Are you at the detachment?"

"I am?"

"Want me to come over?"

"You're busy."

"The clothes can wait," Cliff says. "This can't."

"Okay then," Greg says, secretly relived. "If you're up for it, I'd welcome the company. Besides, it might help to talk things out with someone other than the constables, not that they aren't good listeners."

"Give me about ten minutes to clean up and then I'm on way."

"Thanks," Greg says. "I'll see you in a bit."

"I'll be there, partner," Cliff says.

"Great." Greg hangs up the phone and stares at his black computer screen, thinking he should turn it on and do some work while waiting for Cliff, but his mind's not there, so he leans back in the old green swivel chair and closes his eyes. He needs to think, he decides.

*****

"Lucas," the young girl says, shaking her older brother who's sleeping on the sofa. "Come on, Lucas. Wake up."

"What is it Emma?" he says, slowly opening his eyes with the realization that the pounding in his head has eased somewhat, but he can sense the throbbing is still there, like a persistent nagging toothache that won't go away. "What's wrong? Why are you so upset?"

"It's Sophie," the eight year old whispers, tugging on her brother's left arm, trying to pull him off the couch. "You need to get up. You need to come right now. She's crying."

"Why?" he asks, glancing at the clock on the wall that hangs over the television, the old analog screen betraying its true age.

"I don't know," she answers.

"Did something happen while I was sleeping?" He's surprised to see that he slept for almost three hours.

"I don't know," the small-framed girl answers again, glancing away from him.

"Emma?" Lucas says, pulling himself into a sitting position and, grabbing her skinny young face, turns her so he can look into her eyes. "What happened?"

"He came back while you were sleeping," she finally answers, her voice so soft he can hardly hear it.

"Who?" he asks, quickly springing to his feet. "The old man?"

"Yes," she nods as tears drip from her eyes and trickle down her freckled checks, leaving behind a watery trail on her pale skin as they flow. "But he left again."

"What did he do?" Lucas asks, squatting and looking into the hollow, lifeless eyes of his youngest sister. "Did he hurt you?"

"No." She shakes her head.

"Did he hurt Sophie?"

"I don't know," she cries. "Maybe."

"Where is your sister?"

"In her room," the little girl whispers.

"Did he take her there?"

"Yes," she nods, as the tears continue to fall.

Picking her up in his arms, the young man hugs her and then places her on the couch.

"Emma," he whispers. "I want you to stay right here. Do not follow me upstairs. Do you understand?"

"Yes," she whispers.

"Remember what I told you," he says, leaving the room. "Stay right there."

"Okay, Lucas," she answers. "But please come right back. I'm scared."

*****

"Are you feeling better?" Cliff asks as he studies his friend from across the desk. It's the first time he's been in his office since Greg took over while he's been on sick leave—and he feels a little weird about being here. He feels even weirder sitting on the opposite side of his old desk, but he pretends it doesn't bother him.

"Some," Greg says, nodding at his friend.

"Do you mind if I'm honest with you?"

"Not at all," Greg answers, unsure of where this question is going. "You know you can tell me anything. If you don't know that after all these years, then you don't know me very well. What's on your mind?"

"Okay, then." Cliff sighs before he begins. "I don't like what this is doing to you. I've never seen you this rattled before and I'm getting worried the stress over this case might be too much for you. You're usually the guy who keeps it, and everyone else, together, but this time, you seem to be the one coming unglued and it's freaking me out."

"Honestly," Greg pauses, carefully choosing his words. He then adds, "It's freaking me out as well. I'm not used to feeling like this. It's like I've lost my way and don't know how to get back to reality."

"Why?" Cliff asks. "What is it about this case that's got you in such a state? I know this is bad but I've seen you work similar cases in the past, some even more disturbing—if that's possible—but you've managed them. What's with this one?"

"I'm not sure. Maybe it's because the victims are little girls and I have a young daughter now. Maybe it's because the crimes are happening right where I live," Greg says, resting his head back against the green swivel chair—a fixture of this small office. "Or," he continues, "maybe it's because I'm going to be a father again and I'm thinking about all those perverts out there in the world who prey on young children. . . . Maybe it's because I'm not used to running a detachment." He lets out a loud sigh. "Who the hell knows?"

Cliff remains quiet as he thinks about his friend's admission.

Then he says, "Yes, it could have something to do with the fact that Andrea is pregnant and even about being a father, but I don't buy your reservations about running the detachment. You're too good as a cop to be thinking like that." He smiles and adds, "I never did get around to asking you how she's doing and how far along she is?"

"She's fine. Very excited," Greg smiles, leaning forward. "And she figures she's about two months along, maybe two and a half."

"Wow," Cliff chuckles. "You old dog you. I didn't think you had it in you. . . . And at your age. Good for you."

"What does that mean? Good for me?"

"It means good for you," Cliff grins. "I'm happy for you."

"Are you really? You don't think I'm too old be the father of a new baby?"

"Well," Cliff chuckles again. "Maybe just a little."

"You asshole," Greg says, exposing a wide grin.

"That's me," Cliff nods. "But seriously, pal. I'm happy for you. Andrea is a wonderful woman and a terrific mother to Lucy. She'll be great with a baby. You deserve to be happy."

"Thanks, Cliff," Greg says. "That support means a lot to me."

"You know it. Anytime you need me, I'm here for you buddy, but I'm sure I'd be a little on edge, too, if I found out I was going to be a new father right in the middle of this horrific mess."

"That's got to be it," Greg says, pushing himself back from the desk and glancing at his watch. "And speaking of those horrific things, I think I should get back to the scene and see how the Major Crime guys are doing."

Rising and standing in front of the desk, Cliff asks, "I know I'm not on official duty, but would you mind if I tagged along? I promise I won't get in the way. I'll stand back and keep my mouth shut."

"You won't be in the way," Greg says, grabbing his coat from the stand behind the door. "Happy to have the company. Let's go."

Pausing at the reception counter while Greg goes about the office turning off lights and double-checking security doors, Cliff's eyes roam the walls, the desks, the computers and even the counter itself. He suddenly realizes how anxious he is about coming back to work.

"Man," he sighs. "I never realized how much I've missed this place."

"You never realize how much you'll miss something until it's gone," Greg answers, returning to the area where Cliff is waiting. "You spent a lot of time here, so it only stands to reason you'd miss it."

"I'd be lying if I didn't say I can't wait to get back," Cliff admits.

"I understand," Greg says, nodding in Cliff's direction as he pulls up his coat zipper. "I'm sure I'd feel the same if I were in your shoes. And don't worry about it, you'll be back soon enough."

"You do realize I'm not suggesting you aren't doing a good job, don't you?"

"Yes," Greg laughs as he pulls on his gloves. "I understand that. Ready?"

"I am," Cliff says, turning and glancing around the room once more. "In a strange way it's kind of like being home."

Heading toward the door, he suddenly stops next to the reception counter when his eyes are drawn to several posters. His gaze moves across the wanted posters, advising of outstanding Canada-wide warrants for an assortment of criminals being sought for a variety of offences, including murder and armed robbery. There's also several posters telling sad stories of missing children and these capture Cliff's attention.

"What's wrong?" Greg asks, noticing his friend's sudden reaction. "You've seen those posters a million times."

"I'm not sure," Cliff answers as his gaze roams the many posters plastered on the wall. His skin begins to crawl, as tiny goose bumps emerge with each poster he scans.

The posters tell stories about missing boys and girls who were reported abducted from all across Canada, some dating back decades, but one poster in particular piques his interest. It's one of a four-year-old boy named Robbie Finch. The poster says the boy was abducted from his home in Lethbridge, Alberta almost twenty years ago. The boy has never been found. A computerized rendition of what he might look like today presents a haunting image of a lost child. He finds the child's eyes captivating. *He seems so innocent*, Cliff thinks and he finds himself speculating on the boy's current whereabouts and wonders if, in fact, he is still alive after all this time.

"What's wrong?" Greg asks. "You aren't sick are you?"

"No," Cliff shakes his head. "I feel fine, but there's something about this poster," he says pointing to the picture of the young boy.

"What do you mean?"

"I don't know," Cliff answers, stepping up to the wall and bringing his face closer to the poster. "I've seen these posters many times over the years, but they look different to me now, probably because I haven't been staring at them every day and for some reason, this one feels familiar."

"Being away from something can give you a fresh perspective," Greg explains, also moving closer to the wall. "What is it about this particular poster that's caught your eye today though?"

"I'm not sure." Cliff sighs as he studies the image on the glossy paper. "But there's something about this kid's eyes that are speaking to me."

"What are they saying?" Greg now studies the poster of the missing Lethbridge boy.

"You're going to think I'm losing it," Cliff answers. "But I think I've seen this kid."

Chapter 17

Ruby Smith has no idea where she is. She has no idea who took her or what he plans to do with her. Only hours ago, she was sleeping in her bed, feeling safe and warm, snuggled under her Hello Kitty comforter, her favourite bear held tightly to her tiny chest—and then he was there. Now all she can think about is going home. She's hungry, cold and dirty and she wants to see her mom and dad. But above all, she's lonely, confused and very scared.

When the man took the other little girl away, she hoped he'd bring her back. But she never saw Hillary again and now she fears something bad has happened to her. She liked the other girl and she wishes they had more time together, but the bad man wouldn't let that happen.

Why, she wonders as she feels the warm tears trickle down her dirty face.

No! She tells herself, remembering Hillary's warning. '*Don't cry. . . . He don't like it when little kids cry.*'

Now, tied to the bed like Hillary had been, with her wrists and ankles bound so tight she can hardly move, she's afraid he will hurt her, too, and she will end up just like the other little girl—wherever she is.

Her mind reels with the endless possibilities of a child's imagination, horrible images of what has happened to Hillary, creeping into
her thoughts. She is terrified he will come back to get her. She cries
some more, despite her best attempt to stay strong, but the tears roll
down her face, falling onto the bare, dirty mattress where they saturate
the dirty, smelly material covered with stains caused by things a child
of Ruby's age could never even imagine.

Ruby wills herself to think of anything but the horrible man
and sweet Hillary, but the dark, dank room is filled with shadows and
an evil she can feel, crawling across her bare, cold skin. She doesn't
understand why someone would do this to her.

Maybe I am being punished for something, she thinks. Trying to
remember everything that happened to her in the past few days, she
trembles. She can't think of anything she'd done that would result in
such punishment. She's sure she's been good. She hasn't misbehaved
in school and she's done whatever her mommy and daddy have told
her to do. She's even been doing chores around the house without
being asked, like helping to clear the table after dinner, putting away
her own laundry and even making her own bed, something she's never
really liked doing, but she knows her mommy has been busy lately and
she wants to help out.

Like most children these days, Ruby was taught to avoid strangers, both by her parents and her teachers. She learned from an early
age that she should stay away from people offering to be her friend
or wanting to give her things, such as candy and gifts, and to never
walk alone or play alone in places where she can't be seen by an adult
she knows. She's done all that. She's followed the rules just like the
grownups told her to, yet somehow she's ended up here and she can't
understand how that could happen.

How could she be taken from the safety of her bed? Will she
ever go home again, she wonders? Why didn't her mommy and daddy
save her? Why haven't they come for her? The tears come freely now,
as she tries to stifle the sound of her sobs.

She always thought her daddy could do anything.

Maybe they don't want me anymore, she thinks. *Maybe they will
never come for me. Maybe I'll never see them again*, this time letting
out a loud sob as she tries to catch her breath.

"Mommy?" she whimpers. But no one answers. She is alone in the dark room. The smell makes her stomach churn and her tiny eyes burn. "Please help me."

"Daddy?" she says between sobs. "I want to go home."

Then she remembers the warning the bad man yelled before he left. Never cry, he told her.

"I hate it when kids cry," he said.

Quickly stifling her tears, she closes her eyes tight. Maybe when she opens them all of this will be gone and she will be home, she hopes. Maybe it's all just a bad dream, she prays.

*****

It was a bold move, he knows that.

Disposing of the bodies in such public places was risky, but somehow the chance of getting caught only added to the intensity of the rush he felt when he dumped them there. *It was exhilarating* he thinks as he moves about his room recalling his latest conquest—the feelings, the smells, the sights and the power he felt as he watched her die.

I'm in control of my destiny.

He knew they'd be found, but he never thought he'd get caught.

I'm too smart for them, he believes.

He's thought about this for a long time and he has carefully planned both the abduction and the disposal of the remains right down to the smallest detail. He's taken precautions and he's confident they will never find him.

No one suspects him, he's sure of that. Why would they? He's remained well hidden, he's confident of that.

As he reviews the photos of the house he took the other day with his digital camera and as he plans his next step, he knows he needs to up the ante. If he's going to prove to them that he's the master, that he's the one in control, that he's truly untouchable, then his next move will have to be even bolder and more extreme than the others.

He's up to the challenge. He wants to make them cower at the mere mention of his exploits. He wants them to fear him because fear is all he's ever known. It's the one constant that he clings to. It was part of his childhood and it's with him every minute of everyday.

The fear motivates him. And it's the fear that has driven him to this point. Fear that has turned him into the superior, dominate human being that he has become. And it is fear that will make him invincible.

He's positive about all of these things.

Reviewing the layout of the next house he plans to invade, he recalls the excitement he felt when he found the others. He knew immediately when he saw them that they were the chosen ones. They stood out from the rest. They called to him and he knew they wanted to be with him. They spoke to him in a language that no one else can understand, so he knew they were his and they were meant to be together.

He feels that excitement again when he sees her because he knows she will soon be his.

Of that, he is certain, just as he is certain that no one can stop him.

*****

Instinctively, they know they have to do something.

They've been witnessing the horrors around here and they are compelled to intervene, but as of right now, they aren't sure what to do next.

Huddled together to keep the cold at bay, the flock clings to the fir trees on the northern edge of town. The five black birds have tried to communicate with the one person who could help, but they aren't sure he's heard them, or that he even understands them.

Still, they know they must keep trying because they know who is bringing the evil down upon this town. They've seen him. They've watched him. And they are compelled to try and stop it . . . to stop him.

They must.

They understand that their best hope of doing that is to get through to the one person in their midst who understands how this entity thinks. But they are running out of time.

Cocking their heads toward the centre of town, as if listening for their queue, they know the evil one is about to strike again.

Collectively stretching their wings toward the cloudless sky, the five ebony feathered soldiers prepare for flight. They must act now.

Silently springing into the cold afternoon air, they understand their mission. They also know they must get through to the one man who can stop this simmering evil.

Flapping their ten, powerful wings in unison, the five crows head in a straight line. They know his destination and that's where they will rendezvous with their anointed champion. They will help him to understand . . . somehow.

They are determined. They are committed. He will get the message. He must. The five crows know they are running out of time.

Chapter 18

Greg stops alongside the curb in front of the historic bed and breakfast. He slides the cruiser in park and turns off the ignition and then just sits for a moment and stares out through the grime-covered windshield. The Victorian-style building has been a prominent part of the Liverpool social and economic landscape for more than two centuries. He's driven past the large, rambling house many times and he's heard all the stories about how it was supposedly haunted and how it has played prominently in many of the town's mysteries over the years. Even though he doesn't buy all those stories, he suddenly feels a tinge of uneasiness wash over him and he lets out a long, frustrated sigh.

"Are you absolutely sure about this?" he says, turning to look at Cliff Graham. Wearing street clothes with a black knitted hat pulled down over his balding head, Greg thinks his friend and colleague looks more like an undercover drug agent than a commander of the detachment. *It's a role that would fit him perfectly* Greg thinks and chuckles to himself. "As you know, once we go down this road, there's no turning back," he says.

"You don't trust me, pal?" Cliff replies coolly, his eyes scanning the large snow-covered yard where spectacular gardens bloom all spring and summer long. He wonders if the new owners will put as much loving care into the property as its previous owners, Ronald and Viola Toole. His thoughts then turn to Viola, and he wonders how she is doing in Ottawa. "You don't think I know what I'm talking about?" Cliff says, quickly dismissing Viola Toole and her beautiful gardens for the task at hand.

"Yes, of course," Greg say. "I trust you. I'd trust you with my life and you know that," he adds, glancing up and down the street searching for any sign of activity but the neighbourhood appears deserted this Saturday afternoon. "I'm just being cautious because if we're wrong, then we're screwed and we may start something we can't stop."

"I know," Cliff agrees with a heavy sigh. "Believe me, I've thought of all the possibilities while you were driving over here, but I'm confident about this."

"Why didn't you make this connection before?"

"I don't know. Just not very observant, I guess," Cliff answers with a shrug. "Honestly, I've never really taken the time to study those posters all that closely because I didn't think there was any chance any of them would ever turn up here. What are the chances of that?"

"Slim to none," Greg agrees. "But we know these things always go against the odds, which goes to show we should never assume anything."

"Seems that way," Cliff agrees. "You know what they say. When you assume, you make an ass out of you and me."

"So, this is just a basic information gathering visit?" Greg asks, preparing to open the car door. "And you're not going to go off half-cocked, are you?"

"I don't do that," Cliff scoffs then pauses. "Well," he continues with a screw-you grin. Then he shrugs. "Okay. I guess maybe I do go off, just a little."

"Yeah." Greg chuckles. "Just a little. That's like saying the earth is just a little round."

"Now who's being the asshole?" Cliff laughs.

"Okay, that really wasn't called for," Greg says. "But you're right. I was just kidding and we should be serious." Pulling up on the door handle, he's about to push the door opened when he stops. "Shit."

"What's wrong?"

"Cliff?" he whispers, his voice dry and morbid, as if he's just seen a ghost. "Please tell me you see them this time."

"See what?" Cliff asks, craning his neck to look out the driver's side window in an effort to see what has his friend so freaked out.

"Them," Greg answers, pointing toward the front yard of the bed and breakfast where some of the massive snowdrifts are so deep they cover the bottoms of the ground-floor windows. "Tell me you see the crows."

"I do," Cliff says and slowly nods, seeing the large black birds as they prance around the yard, their ebony feathers shimmering in stark contrast to the bright white that's blanketing everything in sight. "I see them," he says. "Five of them . . . right?"

"Yes," Greg whispers, his throat suddenly so dry he can hardly swallow. "Five of them."

"Are these the same ones that have been following you the past few days?"

"I don't know," Greg says, suddenly feeling powerless, as if something has drained his energy. "I can't say for certain—they're crows—they all look the same, but for some reason, I'm going to say, yes. I just feel they're the same birds."

"I've had those feelings before, friend, so I know exactly what you're going through," Cliff admits, keeping his eyes glued to the crows as they continue their ritual-like dance on top of the snow. "It's like they've chosen you for some reason and they won't let up until they make you understand what they want."

"So, what do they want?"

"You're asking the wrong person," Cliff admits. "If there's one thing I've learned over the years in dealing with the crows, it's that they never make this easy."

"I don't know what to do," Greg says, slouching back behind the steering wheel. "I feel so helpless. I've never felt this way before."

Cliff studies his friend before he speaks while at the same time keeping an eye on the crows as they continue to prance around the yard, picking at the occasional bush in search of food or playfully pulling at each other. Finally, he says, "You're trying too hard to figure this out."

"What do you mean?" Greg says. "I've never been accused of thinking too hard."

"I don't mean that literally, Greg," Cliff says. "I mean, that you're looking at this from your perspective. Try looking at the case and the crows as if you were an outsider and stop focusing on the things you know. What are the things you don't know? If you can figure that out, then maybe you'll understand what the crows are trying to tell you."

"You're talking in riddles," Greg says, exasperation evident in his words. "And you've lost me. How in the hell am I supposed to see what the crows see?"

"All I'm saying is that they know something and they are trying like hell to make you see it."

"Well then," Greg reacts, grabbing the handle and pushing the heavy door open. "Let's see if I can finally get it out of them," he adds, sliding out from behind the wheel and planting his large feet in the brown, salt-saturated slush near the roadside curb where the cruiser is parked.

"Shit," Cliff says, fearing his friend has finally lost it. Quickly pushing open the passenger's side door, he pulls himself out into the cool afternoon air. "What are you doing?" he asks.

"I'm going to talk to them," Greg says, taking large strides as he heads into the yard. "I'm going to ask those Goddamn birds what the fuck they want from me?"

"You're losing it, pal," Cliff says, sprinting around the front of the cruiser and following his friend down the front path that leads to the large wrap around veranda of Haddon House.

"Am I?" Greg says before plunging into the knee-deep snowdrifts. "Then so be it."

Standing in the path and watching as Greg pushes his way through the deep snow until he's standing right in front of the five crows, Cliff remains quiet and listens.

"Listen," Greg speaks in a soft, mellow tone as he addresses the crows. "I've had enough. I just don't understand and if you can't help me to understand then you've got to leave me alone. You're driving me fucking crazy. You're actually interfering with my ability to work on this case."

As the man speaks, the crows become still and Cliff thinks it looks as if they have suddenly been flash-frozen in their spots. The birds remain silent and Cliff feels a sudden coldness descend over him, as if someone or something has wrapped him in an icy grip. He shivers as he watches and listens to the exchange between his friend and the large black birds.

"I know you're trying to reach me," Greg says, suddenly dropping to his knees in front of the birds, almost as if praying to them. "And I think you are trying to help somehow, but you have got to give me more. Give me another clue. Something. Anything I can understand."

The birds watch him, their ten tiny, black, pellet-like eyes following his every move, as though searching for a way to reach his soul.

"What is it?" Greg asks, lowering his head and becoming still. "What do you want me to do?"

From where he stands, Cliff remains quiet. He's seen a lot of strange things in recent years involving the crows, but he's never seen anything like this before. He isn't sure what is happening, but it appears as though his friend and the crows have somehow connected on a different level, someplace that he can't see.

As the icy breeze bites at his ears, Cliff shudders. He struggles to understand what is happening before him. He's not sure what forces are currently at play in this town, but he has the uneasy feeling he is witnessing a union of sorts and he's a little more than freaked out about it. He knew his friend was going through a tough time lately, but he had no idea it was anything like this.

Finally, after watching for several minutes, he calls, "Greg? Are you okay?" He pauses and waits for his friend to respond. "Say something to me."

Without a word, Greg rises to his feet and then turns to face his friend. At the same time, almost as if in sync, the crows spring from the ground, catch a current and soar upward. Seconds later, they disappear behind the large house and out of sight.

"Let's go," Greg says, trudging back through the snow to the front pathway. "We've got a job to do."

Cliff thinks about asking his friend what the hell just happened, but instead follows Greg up the front steps and onto the wrap-around veranda. He watches as his friend knocks on the door. He's not sure what has just transpired in the front yard between the man he's known for more than a quarter of a century—the man he would trust with his life—and those five beady-eyed crows, but he's positive that whatever it was, it's not something that can be explained logically. Then again, he knows that logic is hardly ever a consideration when it comes to understanding the behaviour of the crows that hover around this town.

*****

When no one answers, Greg knocks again on the large wooden door of the stately manor again. The old house looks like it could fit well into the plot of some old black and white mystery movie, the kind Andrea likes so much.

"Maybe no one's home," Cliff suggests, closely observing his friend's actions and facial expressions. He's known this man for many years and he thought he knew everything there was to know about him, but after what he just witnessed between Greg and the crows, he isn't so sure. Now, he's worried that maybe the stress of this case has finally gotten to him and maybe he's gone off the deep end. It's happened to greater men than Greg Paris, but he always thought his friend was strong and could handle anything. He's seen Greg juggle many difficult issues in the past and keep it all together, but this time, he seems to be struggling, as if treading to keep his head above water, and that bothers him. "I don't see any movement inside and I don't hear anything," Cliff says, trying to peer through the windows but having little luck as the curtains are pulled tight. Thinking that in light of what he just witnessed, maybe they've made a mistake coming here, he adds, "Perhaps we should regroup and come back."

"They're home," Greg replies, his voice cold and distant. Knocking one more time, he adds, "Give them another minute."

Just as Cliff is about to say again that they should leave and come back another time, the door opens a crack and he sees the tiny face of a young girl peering out, her eyes glazed over and staring into the distance.

"Hi, Emma," Greg says, dropping to his right knee on the wet wood of the veranda, not caring that his pants will get soaked. "How are you today?" He smiles. "Do you like all the snow we've had? Have you been outside to play in it yet?"

She doesn't answer.

Greg continues. "So, listen, I've spoken to Mrs. Paris, my wife, about having you come over to play with Lucy someday soon and she thinks that's a great idea and Lucy would love that, too. She's going to call your daddy real soon to arrange it. Would you like that?"

She still doesn't answer.

"Is your daddy home, Emma?" Greg asks. "We'd really like to talk to him if he's here."

She shakes her head.

"Are you here alone, Emma?" he asks, keeping his voice calm.

Again she shakes her head.

"Who's with you?"

"Lucas," she finally answers, her voice a mere whisper.

"Your older brother?" Greg replies. "May we see him, please?"

The tiny girl with the light-coloured hair and pale skin looks at him, her brown eyes blinking quickly, as if they are on automatic pilot. She finally opens the door wider, but says nothing more.

Stepping inside the vast house, both officers remain in the entry lobby. Cliff can only imagine how many guests came and went in that period, when the historic house was a busy tourist destination. But it's long past its glory days, Cliff decides, glancing around the large foyer. He can't believe how quickly the place has become run down. It's only been four months since these people moved in and already he sees the place is suffering from neglect. He's disappointed to see the shape it's now in and he thinks his friend, Viola Toole, would be heartbroken if she knew the condition it was in. It's clear the current occupants have no respect for the building's legacy and clearly don't recognize the potential of the place, or possibly they just don't care.

Crouching again, Greg says to the girl, "Can you please go and ask your brother to come and see us? We'll stay right here until you come back."

Keeping her eyes glued to the two large men who tower over her like stately oak trees, she nods, but says nothing.

The officers watch as the girl sprints up the winding staircase, her short legs stretching to take the wide steps.

"Strange kid," Cliff whispers to his friend.

"Yes," Greg says. "Really strange, but this whole thing is strange."

"I get that," Cliff agrees, feeling vibes from this place he's never felt during any of his previous visits to this once proud structure. "Vi would be beyond upset if she saw this place now. After all the work she and Ronald put into this property, she would be devastated."

"That's the previous owner, right?"

"Yes," Cliff says, his eyes scanning the walls and floors and noticing that much of the rich oak and mahogany that was used in the trim and finishes throughout the foyer has either been damaged or is now covered with layers of dust. "You never met her, but she was a great lady and to say she would not be impressed, would be an understatement. The Tooles were meticulous when it came to this place. It was their pride and joy."

"Clearly," Greg says, glancing around. "These people don't care how they live."

*****

It's been several minutes since the little girl went up the stairs and both the officers are becoming restless, wondering what's taking so long for her brother to come down.

"This whole thing feels off to me," Greg finally whispers, scanning the room and looking for anything that might tell him more about the family. "This man lives here with three children, right?" he asks his friend.

"Yes." Cliff nods. "The brother is quite a bit older, but there are three children. Lucas and two young girls, Emma and Sophie."

"Do you find it odd that there are no toys or dolls lying around down here?" Greg asks.

"I don't know," Cliff shrugs. "Maybe."

"Trust me," Greg says. "Take it from someone who has a little girl in the house, it's normal to see dolls lying around. I'm tripping over them all the time. Don't you remember?"

"Yes. . . . Now that you mention it, I actually do remember that." Cliff nods again, recalling those days when his daughter, Carly, was small. "I do remember and you're right. They do tend to leave them wherever they're playing."

"Look around," Greg says, motioning with his hands. "There are no signs of little kids anywhere. Not one doll. Not one piece of kids' clothing. There's nothing."

"Good observation," Cliff replies, scanning the room again. "And do you know what else is weird?" he adds.

"What?"

"There's not one single picture of any of the children anywhere to be seen."

"You're right," Greg agrees. "It's like these children don't exist or as if someone is trying to hide them."

"Come to think of it," Cliff continues. "You hardly ever see them outside and when you do see them, they're always with their father."

"He sure does keep a tight rein on them," Greg says. "What do we know about this Murdock McCarthy?"

"Not a lot," Cliff answers. "Never really thought much about looking into him."

"Maybe it's time we did," Greg says, hearing the sudden pounding of feet on the massive wooden staircase. Glancing up he sees the little girl coming back down and behind her is a slender male with light-coloured hair who looks to be sixteen or seventeen.

"Officers," Lucas says as he reaches the bottom of the staircase and greets the two men standing by the front entrance. One is wearing an official RCMP uniform under a police navy overcoat and the other is dressed in jeans and black coat, which makes him look more like a thug than a police officer, but he's met this man before and he knows him to be Corporal Cliff Graham from the local detachment. "What can I do for you?"

"Hi, Lucas," Greg quickly answers, extending his right hand to the young man who grabs it firmly and shakes it. To Greg's surprise, he's stronger than he appears. "We were hoping to have a few words with your father."

"Sorry, officer," Lucas says. "But he's not home right now. Is there something I can do for you?"

"Not really." Greg shrugs, studying the young man's face. "We just had a few questions for him."

"About what?" Lucas asks, his eyes narrowing.

"It can wait," Greg answers. "We'd rather talk to him."

"Is there something wrong, Sir?" Lucas probes and Greg knows this boy is curious by their sudden appearance.

"Oh, no," Greg says. "Nothing like that." He pauses, thinking about what he can say to put the boy's mind at ease. "Okay," Greg finally says. "Truthfully. It's a minor thing. I was just following up on a routine stop I made the other day. Your father promised me he'd have snow tires installed on his van and I was just double-checking to make sure he had done that for safety reasons. Do you know if he's taken care of that piece of business?"

"Honestly," Lucas says and shrugs. "I'm not really sure. He doesn't tell me much about his business, but I can tell him you were checking and maybe he can call you."

"Yes," Greg says. "That would be fine, thanks."

"You drove all the way over here to ask my father about tires," Lucas asks. "Couldn't you have just called him?"

"Yes," Greg concedes and nods. "I guess I could have. But I was just in the neighbourhood and thought about it. Figured I may as well kill two birds with one stone, so to speak."

"I see," Lucas says and then pauses. "Well, Sir. As I said, I will tell him you stopped by to check and I'm sure he'll call you."

"Great," Greg says, glancing toward Cliff who has remained quiet during the exchange. "We should be going," he says to his friend.

Cliff nods but says nothing.

Before leaving, Greg crouches to speak with Emma again. "So listen, young lady," he says. "I promise you can come and play with Lucy real soon. We'll make it happen."

She says nothing but he studies her very closely, scanning her body from head to toe and lingering at her neck. Finally, he says, "That's a beautiful silver cross you've got there, Emma. Mind if I ask where you got that? I'm thinking that would make a wonderful Valentine's Day gift for Lucy. I was wondering what I could buy her and that would be perfect. Did you get it around here? I could stop and buy one on my way home this afternoon."

The girl doesn't answer, but her brother speaks up. "No," he says. "She didn't get it here."

"That's too bad," Greg replies standing straight again. "Where'd she get it?"

Lucas studies the man before answering. "She's had it for a few years. It was a gift from our mom."

"I see." Greg nods. "She's deceased, right?"

"Yes," Lucas whispers. "For four years."

"I'm sorry," Greg says, thrusting his hand toward the young man once again. "I didn't mean to pry. We'll be going now."

"It's okay," Lucas says, taking the man's hand again and squeezing with a force that, based on his slender appearance, Greg would not have guessed he possessed. "She's gone and we've accepted it."

"We all have to do that sooner or later. It's part of life," Greg whispers. "Please tell your father I'd like to talk with him. . . . thank you for your time."

"Yes, Sir," Lucas promises, moving toward the door. "I will make sure he receives your message."

Chapter 19

Pulling into the lot behind the RCMP detachment, where only members and support staff are permitted to park, Greg notices the other cruisers have returned from the trail where the remains of Hillary Lawrence were found this morning.

"Our guys must be finished at the scene," he says, glancing at Cliff who has remained quiet ever since leaving the McCarthy home several minutes ago. "I'll stop by later to see if the guys from the Major Crimes Unit need anything else from us, but I'm sure they've got it well under control. They're good at what they do and I can use the help back here."

Cliff doesn't respond.

"So," Greg says, turning off the ignition and leaning back in the seat, pushing his head against the rest. Rubbing his eyes as if he's trying to erase the stress, he asks, "What did you think?"

"Honestly?" Cliff finally answers, but not before letting out a long sigh. He continues to stare out the passenger's side window at the detachment's brick façade as he speaks. "I can't be one hundred percent sure, but I think it is. What about you?"

"I don't know," Greg shrugs. "I can kind of see it and then I can't. And that's the problem. We've got to be absolutely certain about this before we can do anything. If we're wrong, we're screwed."

"That's kind of where I am—almost sure but not really," Cliff admits, turning to look at his friend now. "So what are you going to do next?"

"Every goddamn thing I can think of to get to the bottom of this," he answers. "We've got to figure this out before we have the body of another missing kid on our hands."

"Is there anything else I can do to help," Cliff asks. "I know I'm not back on official duty yet, but it felt really good kind of being in action today. I didn't know how much I really missed working until I went with you."

"When police work is in your blood, it becomes part of who you are," Greg says. "That's what makes you such a good cop."

"So what can I do to help? I'm all yours."

"I'd love nothing more than to have you come back right now. It would certainly take the pressure off me," Greg says, throwing a smile in his friend's direction. "But you know it's not up to me. If you came back on this case without the proper approval and something happened, there would be hell to pay and both of our asses would be fried."

"True," Cliff nods. "But I'd like to help somehow."

"And you can," Greg says, cocking his eyebrows toward his friend and grinning slightly. "Just because you can't come back at official status right now, doesn't mean you can't keep your ears and eyes open. There's nothing that says you can't do that as long as you remember you're not back on duty."

"You mean you want me to spy on this guy for you?"

"You make it sound so sneaky and underhanded when you say it like that," Greg says. "But, yes. I guess that's what I'm saying." He pauses and glances around the parking lot, as if looking to see if someone is watching them. Then he adds, "Do you want to keep an eye on him from a distance and let me know what you see?"

"I could do that," Cliff says, grabbing the handle to the passenger's side door. "Actually, I'd love to do that." He smiles.

"On the QT of course," Greg adds.

"Of course," Cliff says. "Is there any other way?"

"With you?" Greg laughs. "I never know."

"I'll be good. I promise."

"And careful?" Greg adds, grabbing his friend's left arm. "Will you be careful?"

"Yes." Cliff grins. "And careful." He smiles at his friend. "I'll be careful and now, I should be heading home because I told Carly I wouldn't be long. Are you and Andrea still going out for dinner tonight or are you calling it off because of everything that's happened today?"

"If it was just for me, I'd say we're not going because I'm really not in the mood," Greg says. "But I know Andrea has been looking forward to an evening out for some time now and I don't want to disappoint her. But my heart certainly won't be in it. I don't feel much like celebrating a birthday right now."

"You can't stop living, Greg. You're not responsible for any of this so don't take it personally. As sad as this is, you still have a family and you have got to think of them. They have to come first," Cliff advises his friend. "Maybe getting your mind off this stuff for a little while will be a good thing for you. It might clear your head."

"Of course," he says. "I know you're right. But it's hard to think of anything else these days other than those poor little girls and what hell they've gone through. And I'm really afraid for Ruby Smith. God knows what he's doing to her right now."

"I get that, but do me a favour and try to put it out of your mind for just a little while," Cliff says, finally opening the door.

"I will pick up Carly around five," Greg says as he watches his friend slide out of the cruiser. "And you'll be home this evening, right? Just in case she needs you."

"I will," Cliff says, throwing his long legs out of the vehicle. "I'm only a few minutes away if she needs anything and I'll call regularly just to check on her."

"That's good," Greg says. "And Cliff. Thank you for your help today. I appreciated having another perspective. It was good working with you again."

"Any time, buddy," Cliff says, pulling himself out of the car and then leaning his head back into the vehicle. "You know you can always count on me any time you need something, even if it's just to talk."

"Thanks, man," Greg smiles. "Appreciate it. Now get home so I can see how things are going inside."

*****

It's quiet inside the detachment. As Greg enters he sees Constable Emily Murphy and three other officers sitting in the administration area. They're writing reports or reading information, but none of them are talking. The mood is heavy and Greg knows they're all stressed over what they've just witnessed. The energy in the room is so dark that he thinks he can practically see it.

Nodding to Constable Murphy he smiles. "What's up?" he asks. "Something else happen? You all look like you've just received more bad news."

"No, Sir," she says, the cracking in her voice betraying her emotions. "We stayed until the Medical Examiner cleared the body for removal and then we left the scene so the Major Crimes guys could take over. It was a hard thing to watch and I think we're all just feeling that."

"Of course you are and when you guys have finished your reports, I want you all to go home and unwind," Greg says, motioning toward his office. "Can you please come with me?"

Once inside, he motions for her to sit down in the chair across from his desk. She follows his orders while he removes his overcoat, hangs it up and then sits in the green swivel chair behind his desk.

"Is everything okay, Sir?" she asks, trying to make herself smile.

"Yes," he says and then pauses. "Well, actually, I'm really not sure."

"I'm afraid I don't understand," she says with a shrug.

"Of course you don't," he admits. "Why would you? I'm talking in circles and I don't understand it myself." Taking a deep breath, he begins again. "Okay, so here's the thing. As of right now, I want you to concentrate all your efforts on finding out everything you can about a Mr. Murdock McCarthy."

"Who is he, Sir?"

"He's a local resident. He owns the Haddon House."

"Okay." she nods while shooting him a puzzled look. "So why are we looking into him, Sir?"

"Just humour me, please."

"Of course, Sir. What do you want to know about him?"

"Everything there is to know," Greg explains. "All I can tell you right now is that he's in his mid-to late-fifties and moved here last November from Winnipeg. That's it. We don't know what he does for a living or anything else. I want to change that. I want every scrap of information you can dig up on him and his family and I want it ASAP."

"That won't be easy on a weekend, Sir," Constable Murphy explains. "Most of the offices are closed until Monday."

"Do the best you can," Greg says. "And for the time being, just keep this on the QT."

"Okay, Sir," she says and then pauses. "Is there a reason why we're investigating this guy? Did he do something I should know about? . . . Is he connected to this case in some way?"

"You know, constable, I'm not really sure," Greg admits. "Truthfully, right now I'm playing a hunch. It might turn out to be nothing, but for now this is a priority for you."

"And the missing girl case?"

"I'll keep working that file with the other members and the Major Crimes Unit, but I want you to concentrate on McCarthy."

"Very well, Sir," she says, rising from the chair in front of Greg's desk. "If that's what you want."

"It is," he says and smiles at her. "Trust me . . . this is important and that's why I want you to handle it."

*****

It's almost 4 p.m. and all the officers except for Greg and Constable Murphy have left the detachment. He's finishing the first draft of his report on the day's activities when he hears the phone out in the administration area ringing. He hears Constable Murphy pick up after the second ring.

"Liverpool RCMP," she says. "How can I help you? If this is an emergency then you should call 911 as our office is not open today."

He listens as the constable stops talking, then he hears her call his name.

"Sir," she says in a raised voice. "This call is for you. Would you like for me to tell him you are not here?"

"Did he give his name?" Greg calls back.

"It's Murdock McCarthy," she answers. "He wants to talk to you and he sounds upset."

"I'll take it," Greg says, picking up the phone in his office and pressing the flashing red light. "Sergeant Paris here. How can I help you?"

"I understand you stopped by my house this afternoon while I wasn't at home," the man begins and Greg can tell he's pissed.

"That is correct, Mr. McCarthy," Greg says.

"What did you want?"

"I just wanted to speak to you."

"About what?"

"Several things."

"Such as," Murdock asks, pressing for details. "And don't give me that shit about wanting to follow up on the snow tires like you told my son. I don't buy that crap."

"Since you brought it up, Mr. McCarthy," Greg says. "Have you taken care of that yet? You know it's not safe driving around without proper tires in these conditions."

"Not yet," Murdock snaps. "I've been busy, but you didn't come by my house to ask me about tires, did you?"

"No," Greg admits. "Not really."

"So what did you want?"

"I prefer not to do this over the phone, Mr. McCarthy."

"And I prefer that you not talk to my children when I'm not around and I'm asking you not to do it again," Murdock fires back. "Actually, I'm not asking. I'm telling you to keep away from my kids."

"Why?" Greg pauses and he can hear the man's breathing become laboured, his stress level rising. Pressing him for more details he continues, "Do you have something to hide, Mr. McCarthy?"

"What the hell does that mean?"

"It doesn't mean anything," Greg quickly replies. "I'm just wondering why you wouldn't want me to talk to your children. You seem pretty adamant about that."

"I am," Murdock fires back. "If you come near them again when I'm not around I will be going straight to your superiors and believe me, Sergeant, that is not an idle threat."

"That is your prerogative, Mr. McCarthy," Greg answers. "Would you like the phone number for H Division so you can reach the superintendent? That's where he's stationed."

"Are you trying to be a smartass?"

"Not at all," Greg says, keeping his voice calm. "I'm trying to be helpful, Mr. McCarthy. If you feel the need to contact my commanding officer, then by all means you have every right to do so. I'm just trying to save you the trouble of trying to find the number."

"Don't patronize me," Murdock says and Greg can tell he's pushing the right buttons. "What did you really want?"

"I need to speak with you, as I said, but not over the phone. Can I see you tomorrow?"

"I may not be home tomorrow."

"Can I call you in the morning?"

"You can try, but I'm not sure I'll be home."

"You're not sure you'll be home?" Greg pauses. "You don't know where you'll be tomorrow?"

"I said I wasn't sure," Murdock snaps. "You can call and if I'm home I will see you. If not, then oh well. Some other time."

"That's fine," Greg says. "Thank you for your time."

"Remember what I said, Sergeant," Murdock snaps, his voice revealing his anger. "Stay the hell away from my children."

"I understand your wishes, Mr. McCarthy."

"It's not just my wishes," he answers and Greg can tell he's really pissed. "It's an order."

"Well, Mr. McCarthy, I don't take kindly to orders."

"I'm serious, Sergeant," the man screams.

"Calm down, Mr. McCarthy," Greg says, refusing to raise his voice. "I understand what you're saying, okay. Is that good enough?"

"Not really," Murdock says.

"We can talk about this some more when we meet tomorrow," Greg says, keeping his composure. "Just try to remain calm."

"You haven't seen me when I'm not calm, Sergeant," Murdock fires back. "Remember what I said. Goodbye."

With that, Greg hears the phone slam in his ear and he knows that for whatever reason, he and Cliff hit a nerve with their visit to the McCarthy household this afternoon. Now, he thinks, as he stares at the phone, he just has to figure out why.

Chapter 20

A lot happened today, Greg thinks. He is standing in the bedroom, tucking his powder blue Brooks Brothers shirt into his navy dress pants. He fastens his pants around his thirty-eight inch waist and then buttons the shirt collar. *More than I can digest right now*, he admits, even though he does so begrudgingly.

Sighing heavily, he grabs the navy tie—the one with the tiny red flecks that looks like a mad artist threw drops of paint on it—from the hanger and wraps it around his muscular neck. Quickly tying the knot and smoothing the collar down in place, he steps back. Checking out the tie in the full-length mirror, he decides it looks good. Tying a tie is an art form and not one everyone can do, but he's been doing it for so long now, he thinks he can probably even do it with his eyes closed.

Grabbing his navy jacket from the back of the white wicker chair that's been in his wife's family for three generations, he slips it on and looks in the mirror again. Not that he's vain, it's just that he takes pride in how he looks and he thinks he looks pretty good for a fifty-five year old. More to the point, he chuckles to himself, he's actually checking for dandruff, as that can be hellish on a dark jacket.

Automatically brushing off his left shoulder and then reversing the routine with his right shoulder, he takes in a deep breath and stares blankly into the mirror. Try as he might to convince himself, he's not sure he should be going out for dinner tonight. Even if it is for a special occasion, it just doesn't feel right to him. Andrea has made reservations at the best place in town and has been planning this night for the past week, but he's simply not comfortable about leaving the house after everything that's happened the past few days. He's sure if he told Andrea everything that he's seen in recent days, she'd quickly change her mind as well. But he can't tell her, not that he thinks she'd blab about it to anyone. He can't talk to her about the case because it's an ongoing investigation and he's got to keep the details well guarded.

Besides what good will it do to make her worry? God knows, he sighs, he's doing enough of that for the both of them.

"Andrea," he says to the pretty brunette rummaging through her dressers as if looking for a long-lost treasure. It never ceases to amaze him even after two years with this woman that she can never decide what to wear until the very last minute, even though she's known for days they were going out to celebrate his birthday and Valentine's Day. In fact, the entire event was her idea so he's amazed she hasn't already thought about what she will wear. "It's almost five, honey, and I'm ready, so I'll go and pick up Carly. Will you and Lucy be okay while I'm gone?"

She stops what she's doing and looks at him.

"Of course we'll be okay, Greg," she replies. "Why wouldn't we be okay in our own home? You're only going around the corner, not to China."

"No reason," he quickly answers, realizing his question was a slip he now regrets. "Just meant is it okay for me to leave Lucy while you're getting ready?"

"That's not what it sounded like," she says, studying him. "Is everything okay, Greg?"

"Yes," he says, wondering if he should just tell her that he doesn't think it's a good idea for them to be going out this evening.

"I don't know," she says. "You've been acting really strange these past few days and now I'm getting the feeling you don't think we'll be safe in our own house without you here. We've lived here for two months and this is the first time you've given off those vibes. Are you sure everything is all right? Are you feeling well?" He can see the disappointment cross her face as she adds, "Do you want to stay home tonight? . . . We can go out some other time if you're not up to it."

"No, no," he lies. "I'm fine. Just tired. It's been a few rough days. . . . This case has taken a lot out of me and I'm distracted, that's all. . . . And tired. I'm thinking that a few hours out will do me some good. It might help to take my mind off things."

"Okay, but only if you're sure," she says, turning her attention back to rummaging through the dresser. "I promise that you can sleep in tomorrow morning for as long as you want . . . all day if you feel like it."

"Deal." Greg chuckles, knowing there's no way he'll sleep late. He hasn't slept past seven a.m. since he was thirty and most mornings he's up before five a.m. He's heard that the older some people get, the less sleep they need and that certainly seems to be the case for him.

"I'm going to grab a quick shower while you're gone," Andrea says, pulling a black bra out of her drawer and studying it as if she hasn't seen it in years. "Here you are," she says to the item of clothing. She adds, "Lucy's playing dolls in her room and will be fine until I'm done."

"Do you want me to wait until you're out of the shower? Because I can. Carly won't mind waiting a few more minutes."

"No, Greg," she says, slipping her pink housecoat over her white, creamy skin. "She'll be fine. I'll only be a few minutes." Staring at him again, she adds, "Are you sure everything is okay? You seem a little jumpy tonight."

"Just had a bad day," he says and smiles, admiring his wife's natural beauty. "I'll get Carly. She's probably wondering where I am."

"You're sure?" she asks, sliding up to him and pulling him close, her naked body under the housecoat presses against him.

"I am." He grins, dropping his large hands to her lower back and hugging her to him. "And if you're not careful, I won't be going anywhere except for that bed right over there."

"Later," she laughs, giving him a quick kiss on the cheek as she pulls away and heads to the bedroom door. "Now, go and get our babysitter while I get ready. You're distracting me."

"I'm distracting you?" He laughs, watching as her slender form disappears around the corner of the door.

"Yes," he hears her laugh before she goes into the bathroom just next door.

That's a matter of perspective, he thinks, but says nothing.

Grabbing his wallet from the dresser and sliding it into his right back pants pocket and then slipping his watch around his wrist, Greg leaves the bedroom and heads down the second level hallway. He stops at his daughter's bedroom and pokes his head inside the door where he finds her sitting on the bed playing with her dolls.

"Lucy, honey," he says, keeping his voice calm. "Daddy's going to get Carly and Mommy's having a quick shower. You stay in your bedroom until Mommy's done, okay?"

"Okay, Daddy," the tiny, blonde-haired girl smiles up at him— her innocent beauty melts his heart.

"Remember, if the phone rings don't answer it. Let it go to the answering machine," he tells her. "And if you hear anyone at the door, just ignore them until Mommy is out of the shower. Then you go and tell Mommy that you heard someone, okay? Do you remember those rules, honey?"

"Yes, Daddy," she smiles again and then turns her attention to the doll that's wrapped in a pink blanket and lying on the bed. "I remember," she says.

"Good girl." He smiles back. "Now, I'll be right back with Carly. You'll have fun with her. She really likes spending time with you."

Even though he's only going to be gone for about fifteen minutes, Greg detours to the kitchen where he checks to make sure the back door is locked. Flicking on the back light and pulling aside the door blind, he scans the snow-covered backyard, but sees nothing except snow-covered trees and rocks. It's a virtual winter wasteland back there, he thinks. Turning off the light and then trying the door several times, he's convinced everything is secure.

Heading through the living room and to the front door, he scans the house as he goes, eyeing every corner and stopping at the windows to close the blinds. Reaching the front door, he pauses briefly before turning the knob. Finally, taking a deep breath, he opens the door and steps out into the cool February evening, the wind tossing snow around as if it is as light as cotton. His breath forms tiny white clouds as he exhales. Stopping to lock the door behind him, he suddenly feels uneasy about leaving the house with his family alone on the inside. For a split second, he considers calling the whole thing off, but when he thinks about how disappointed Andrea will be, he decides he can't do that.

With goose bumps dancing up his spine, he quickly spins around and casts his gaze over the front yard, lingering at every tree and bush he sees, thinking someone could be hiding there and watching, waiting for him to leave. Minutes later, he tells himself he's being paranoid. There is no one out here. It's just his imagination.

Easy Greg, he thinks. *You can't let this case control your life.*

Taking a deep breath, he turns and tries the locks on the front door once more. Satisfied they are secure, he makes his way down the front walkway toward the driveway, peering through the shadows and glancing both ways as he goes. If someone is out here, he thinks, they're doing a good a job of keeping themselves hidden. *That's not a good thing*, he thinks because if he found someone lurking around his property, he isn't sure what he would do, but he knows they'd be sorry.

Reaching his Honda Civic, he presses the keyless remote. He hears the click and sees the interior lights flicker on. Opening the driver's side door, he looks around one more time before getting in behind the steering wheel.

"Greg," he says while scanning the yard and street that's void of any traffic, the streetlights casting an eerie orange glow on the lightly falling snow. "Get a grip, man. . . . You're losing it."

Sticking the key in the ignition, he listens as it starts. As the headlights snap on, the bright beam of white light illuminates the yard, creating large, almost obscene shadows on the unbroken snow. *Creepy*, he thinks, as his eyes roam the surroundings, but reveal nothing. Grabbing the stick shift, he pauses before putting it in reverse.

"Come on, Greg. You're better than this," he says, quickly blinking his eyes in rapid succession several times. "You're going to lose your fucking mind if you don't cut this shit out."

*****

He's been staring at the large juicy rib eye on the plate for several minutes. The perfectly cooked steak is smothered with sautéed mushrooms and caramelized onions and is nestled between a mound of garlic-infused mashed potatoes and a medley of mixed garden vegetables, but as tempting as it looks, and smells, he still hasn't taken a bite. His mind is elsewhere.

"Greg?" Andrea asks studying his face. "Honey?" she probes again. "Is everything okay?"

"Huh?" he replies, his eyes glancing at the woman sitting across the table from him, her finely chiselled features softened in the glow of the shimmering candle stationed in the heart-shaped lantern in the middle of every table in honour of Valentine's Day. *She's hot tonight*, he thinks, as he admires his wife in the black dress he likes so much. He wonders if he has told her yet how beautiful she is this evening. "Sorry," he mutters. "What did you say?"

"I said, is everything okay?" she says when he doesn't answer her. "Is there something wrong with your steak? At thirty-eight dollars a pop, it better be damn good."

"Oh," he whispers, forcing a smile. "Sorry. No. . . . It's great."

"How would you know?" Andrea says. "You haven't touched it."

"I was just about to dig in." Greg laughs, picking up his fork and steak knife. "It smells fantastic. I can't wait to sink my teeth into it." Glancing at her, he asks, "How's the haddock?"

"I imagine the haddock is delicious, but since I'm having the homemade fish cakes, I wouldn't know for sure," she answers, her eyes carefully studying her husband's face. "If you had been here in the restaurant with me instead of some other place, then you would know what I had ordered. So again, honey, I'm asking what's going with you? Your mind has been someplace else ever since you came home this afternoon and you're worrying me. I know this case is hard on you, but I really want you to let it go tonight and have a good time. It's Valentine's Day, it's your birthday and we're celebrating our good news about the baby. Can't you just concentrate on that for a few hours and block out all that bad stuff?"

"Yes. . . . Right. To the good news." Greg smiles, tipping his glass of Cabernet Sauvignon into the air in a half-hearted toast. "I'm sorry, honey. I don't mean to spoil your evening because I know you've been planning this all week, but you're right. It is this case. It really is starting to get to me."

"Would it help to talk about it?" She returns his smile, tipping her glass of water in his direction. "Sometimes, that helps."

"Trust me, sweetheart," he shakes his head and takes a sip of the wine. "It's not the kind of thing you want to talk about over a birthday dinner. It's not even something I want to think about, but I can't get it out of my mind and I can't stop wondering if I'm doing enough to stop whoever is responsible for all of this."

"Gregory Paris," she fires back. "If there's one thing I know in this whole wide world, it's that you are an excellent police officer and there is absolutely no doubt in my mind that you *are* doing everything in your power to catch this creep and more. I am one hundred percent certain of that."

"So, then why do I feel like I'm failing those poor little girls?"

"You can't put this on yourself. I know you are doing the best you can, but you are only human," she assures him, reaching across the table with her right hand and softly grabbing his. "Honey. You can't beat yourself up over this. You're not going to help anyone if you have a meltdown."

"I'm trying," he says, and he's sure if he weren't in a crowded restaurant where everyone is celebrating Valentine's Day, he'd promptly break down and cry, which is something he rarely ever does. "But I think this is the most hurtful case I've ever worked on."

She looks into his eyes. "Should I be worried, Greg?" She whispers, her eyes conveying her concern for her husband. "We moved to this small town because we thought we would be safe here and now we are stuck in the middle of a child murder spree that's about to drive my husband crazy." She pauses. "This isn't want I wanted."

"It's not what I wanted either," he whispers and swallows hard, the saliva feeling like shards of glass as it passes down his constricted throat. "Maybe it was all a big mistake. Maybe we should never have come here in the first place. It's been one thing after another ever since we got here last fall. The past six months have been like a freaking nightmare. Our daughter has had two serious accidents and almost dies not once, but twice. My best friend has a major heart attack and almost dies. I'm forced to take a job that I didn't ask for and now I'm chasing a crazed child abductor and killer that I can't figure out. It hasn't exactly been our dream location."

"Everything happens for a reason, I firmly believe that," she says, remaining calm. "Maybe you were meant to be here because you are the best person to solve these heinous crimes. Maybe you were supposed to be here to take over for Cliff when he had his heart attack because he really needed you. As for Lucy, yes, that was a horrific time for us, but she's fine now and doesn't seem to be suffering any ill effects from either accident, so you can stop beating yourself up over that. Besides, neither of those were your fault. They were accidents."

"Don't ask me how, but you always manage to put a positive spin on even the worst things." Greg smiles and winks at her. "I think that's one of the things I love so much about you. Somehow, you always find a way to keep me grounded and I'm sure I couldn't get through this without you."

"I *am* the best thing to ever happen to you, aren't I?" she giggles and he thinks she sounds like a schoolgirl. He loves how she sounds when she laughs.

"There's no question about that, my dear," he says, squeezing her hand tightly. "Absolutely no question. You and Lucy are my whole world."

"And in a few months, we'll have another little bundle of joy to brighten our lives," she points out, glancing toward her belly as her eyes light up. "What are you wishing for?"

"It doesn't matter to me," he says. "Just as long as he or she is healthy, I'll love him or her just as much as I love his or her mother."

"That's sweet," she says. She gives him a genuine smile and squeezes his hand in return.

"Let's eat before our food gets cold," he says, letting go of her hand. Cutting into the steak, he adds, "I had a great chat with Cliff today and he's doing much better. Looks to me like he'll soon be ready to head back to work."

"What does that mean for you, honey?"

"It means I'll be free to take another posting," he explains between chews. "Maybe I'll finally get the job in Halifax I was promised when I came here in the first place."

"Is that what you want?"

"Honestly," Greg says after swallowing. "I'm really not sure anymore. I'm hoping they'll give me a few weeks after Cliff returns to assess everything, so I can figure out what's best for me . . . and for us."

"I'm sure they will," she says. "They owe you that much."

"They certainly do—and then some," he agrees while glancing at his watch. "So listen, Andrea, it's been almost fifty minutes since we left the house, would you mind if I called Carly? I just want to make sure everything is okay."

"Will that put your mind at ease?"

"It will," he says.

"Okay, honey." She smiles and says, "You go right ahead. Truthfully," she admits with a reassuring smile, "It will make me feel better as well."

Chapter 21

His thermal socks and thick, lined boots are doing the trick. He's been standing in the frigid night air for close to an hour now, but that doesn't matter to him. He doesn't feel the wind slapping his face and breaking through the knitted material that covers his cleanly-shaven skin. His black ski mask is doing an adequate job keeping out most of the wind. Besides, he's endured far worse than these conditions and with practice, he's learned how to block the pain. He's forced himself to ignore the cold as he's stood and watched while life at the house across the street moves along, its inhabitants blissfully oblivious to the fact that someone could be outside studying their every move.

Earlier this evening, he watched Sergeant Greg Paris come out of his house and try the front door several times before getting into his car and driving away. But he waited in the shadows among the bushes and observed from across the road where he was sure no one could see him.

About twenty minutes later, he watched as the sergeant returned with a young girl in the passenger seat. And he watched as they both got out of the car and went inside the house. He thought she was cute, but not really what he was looking for this evening.

About fifteen minutes later, the tall man, with the thick, black hair, came out of the house along with a slender, brunette woman. He observed the man check the front door lock and then check it again for good measure. He watched as the pair got into the car and drove away, but not before the police officer slowed in front of the house and looked around, as if he was searching for something, but then he quickly sped away.

He waited for several more minutes to make sure the coast was clear before stepping out from his dark hiding place. He's been waiting a lot this evening. Waiting for just the right time to make his move and now that he's sure the sergeant isn't going to return for some time, he knows the right time has finally come.

Glancing up and down the empty street he's confident no one can see him. He grabs his black kit bag and emerges from the shadows of the tall pine trees that tower over the road and the yard where the Paris family is temporarily staying. Checking one more time to make sure there is no traffic, he quickly crosses the road and darts around the house to the backyard, pushing through the thigh-high snow as he goes.

Back here, he knows he'll be secluded. He knows this for a fact because, just like all his previous targets, he's surveyed this place several times over the past two weeks, but not since it snowed. He knew that if he came back after the snow fell, the RCMP officer would have seen his footprints and at that point, his plans would have been stopped dead in its tracks. He knows he can't take a chance with this officer. He's aware of the man's reputation.

Plowing through the deep snow, he doesn't care if it spills over the tops of his boots that he carefully covered with white kitchen-catcher plastic bags to disguise his footprints. The cold means nothing to him. He's in his own zone right now and when he's there, he's able to block out everything else, including the elements.

Ascending the snow-covered wooden steps, he glances around again just to make sure he isn't seen. This is his most risky mission to date and he knows he can't be too cautious. Slowing his breathing, he carefully leans against the back door and presses his ear against the wood. He listens. It's muffled, but he hears the phone ring.

*****

"Hello," Carly says after the third ring. "Paris residence."

"Hi, Carly," Greg says. "It's me."

"Hey, Uncle Greg," she replies. "How's dinner?"

"Delicious."

"Great," she says. "Try to have a good time and eat something really good for dessert. It's your birthday after all and it's Valentine's Day, so go ahead and indulge in something really fattening."

"We are," he assures her. "So how are things there, Carly?"

"Fine. We're playing the Memory Card Game and Lucy's a pro at that. She's already beaten me three times and is well on her way to her fourth victory."

"She is the Memory Card Game Champion of Liverpool," Greg laughs. "Don't play Crazy Eights with her or she'll take you for every nickel you have. She's a card shark that one."

"I believe it."

"Has anyone called, Carly?"

"No, Uncle Greg, only Dad. He's called many times," she answers. "Are you expecting someone to call?"

"Nope. Just checking."

"Well, other than you and Dad, that's it."

"So no one's been around the house, have they?"

"Nope," she answers. "Is everything okay, Uncle Greg? You're starting to freak me out a little with all of your questions."

"Yes, honey," he says. "Everything is fine. It's just that this is the first time Lucy has had a babysitter in the new house and I'm just double checking to make sure she's not giving you a hard time."

"Well, you can stop worrying," Carly says. "She's being a little angel. I couldn't ask for a better child to babysit."

"She is a good kid," Greg agrees. "I guess I should be going to finish my steak. We won't be late Carly."

"No problem, Uncle Greg. You guys have a good time. Once we finish this game, Lucy and I are going to watch a movie. She's picked out three she wants to watch," the young girl laughs. "I told her we'd only have time to watch one before she had to go bed so we'll see how that goes."

"We may actually be home before she finishes the movie," Greg says.

"You don't have to rush. We're fine, really," she assures him.

"Dad's been calling every half hour, sometimes even more often, so we're okay."

"All right, honey. You have my cell number and if you need me don't hesitate to call," Greg says. "Go and finish your game, but watch out for that little card shark."

"Okay." Carly laughs. "I'll see you when you get home."

"Bye, honey."

"Bye, Uncle Greg," she says, switching off the cordless phone and laying it on the table. Turning back to the little girl sitting across from her at the dining room table, she says, "Okay, you little devil. It's my turn and you better be careful. This game's mine."

"No way," she giggles.

"Yes way," Carly says and laughs, flipping over a card, finding a picture of a red apple. "Prepare to lose."

With his ear pressed against the back door, he's surprised that even though it's a bit muffled he can still clearly hear the two girls talking and laughing. They seem to be having a good time.

He remains still, frozen in this particular spot on the back doorstep and being careful not to make any noise. He must wait until they leave the kitchen-dining room area before he can make his next move.

Timing, he knows, will be very important. This is the first time he's done this while anyone is awake in the house, but he knows if he doesn't make his move tonight, he won't get another chance. He senses the police officer is locking down the family and his home and it will soon be an impenetrable fortress.

He knows it's now, or never.

"Okay, young lady," Carly says, picking up the cards and stacking them back in the box. "That's enough of that. You beat me four games to none. I've had enough." She laughs as she places the box on the table.

"Can we watch the movie now?" Lucy asks.

"We sure can," Carly says. "You go into the living room and decide which one you want to watch first. I'm just going to clean up in here and put the game away, then I'll be right in to watch it with you."

"Can I have a drink?"

"Sure. What would you like?"

"Apple juice, please."

"Apple juice it is," Carly says. "I'll bring it with me when I come in."

"Okay, thanks," the four year old says climbing down from the wooden dining room chair that matches the table and five other chairs. "Can I have a snack, too?"

"I suppose," Carly says. "What would you like?"

"Ritz Bitz, please."

"Do you know where they are?"

"Mommy keeps them in the treat room," Lucy says, pointing to a small pantry-like closet off the kitchen. "That's were all the treats are. She hides them there from me and Daddy, but Daddy can find anything."

"Okay. You go in the living room and decide which movie you want to watch first. I'll be right along to put on the DVD."

As the tiny girl heads down the hallway, Carly makes her way to the "treat" room as Lucy calls it.

*****

\This is it, he thinks. It's now or never. If he doesn't get inside now, he may not have another chance. He has to be precise. He never wants to rush when he does this because he knows that rushing increases the chances of him making mistakes, but he senses there isn't much time.

Pulling the thin wire from his black kit bag, he inserts it into the lock and turns. He hears the lock click open. *That was easy*, he thinks, recalling how he learned the skill many years ago when he first started breaking into homes to steal cigarettes, booze and money.

That little trick has certainly come in handy lately, he thinks.

Returning the lock pick to the bag, he then removes a pair of tin snips. Carefully turning the doorknob, he pushes it open just a crack until he sees the chain lock on the door. Easing the points of the snips through the crack, he applies pressure and the chain snaps. Pulling the snips back out he hopes the babysitter didn't hear the noise from the chain scraping against the wood, but he doesn't think so as he's pretty sure she's gone to the pantry.

Placing the tin snips back inside the bag, he closes the zipper and slides the bag over his right shoulder. He pushes the door open just wide enough for his head and looks around. He sees the kitchen is empty. He then eases the door open just a bit wider and slides his body through. He slowly closes the door behind him.

He stands by the door with his hand on the knob just in case he has to make a quick getaway.

*****

"Okay," Carly says as she scans the shelves in the tiny storage room that are filled with an assortment of boxes, bottles, packages and cans. Hoping Lucy can hear her in the living room, she adds, "I'll be right there."

It looks like a grocery store in here, she thinks. *If I was a box of Ritz Bitz, where would I be hiding?*

"Vegetable thins. Wheat thins. Granola bars," she says, reading all the boxes. "Triscuits with cracked pepper and olive oil. Fruit roll ups. Pudding cups and . . . Ritz Bitz," she says. "Here you . . ."

She's suddenly cut off as the door to the tiny room closes and she hears the lock click.

"Lucy?" she calls out. "Is that you? Lucy?" she yells, dropping the box of crackers and rushing to the door. Grabbing the knob, she tries to force it open, but it won't budge.

"Lucy?" she yells louder this time, realizing she's trapped inside the small room and the phone is out on the dining room table. She reaches for her cell in her jeans pocket but suddenly remembers it's also on the table.

"Did you lock the door?" There's no answer. She scans the room to see if there is another way out. To her horror, there isn't. "Come on Lucy. . . . This isn't funny, young lady."

She listens, but still hears nothing.

"Lucy?" She begins to pound on the door. "Open the door this minute, Lucy or you'll be in big trouble when your daddy comes home."

Pressing her ear against the wooden door, she listens for movement in the kitchen.

"Lucy?" She begins to cry as she realizes something is obviously not right. "Lucy," she calls again, leaning against the door and then slowly sliding to her knees. Tears now stream down her face. She is afraid for the small child in her care.

"Lucy," she calls again. "Please open the door. Please."

*****

Sure that the door to the storage room is secure he begins moving toward his real target. Making his way from the kitchen he peeks around the corner just to make sure the little girl isn't in the hallway.

She isn't. He knows she's in the living room where the television is located. He can hear her moving about even though the volume is really loud. . . . He hates loud noises.

Glancing one more time at the storage room door just to assure himself it's secure, he can hear the babysitter calling the little girl's name but it appears as though either the girl can't hear her over the television or she's ignoring the sitter's pleas for help.

Easing his body around the corner from the kitchen and into the hallway that leads to the living room, he moves slowly, taking very small steps to reduce any sound that his coat and boots might make. He knows that if he spooks his prey and she runs from him, then he will fail in his quest.

Slowing his breathing, he moves stealth-like down the hallway. With each step he takes, he hears her more clearly. Suddenly, she calls.

"Carly," she yells, her tiny angelic voice sounding like sweet music to him. "I'm waiting."

Pushing his body as far back against the wall as he can, he hugs the painted drywall and forces himself to remain still. But he is poised and ready to pounce. Should she come down the hallway, he'll be ready to grab her.

Seconds later, he decides the danger has passed. The little girl has probably decided to wait in the living room for the babysitter to start the movie.

Moving on, he reaches the edge of the hallway and from this position, he scans the entire living room. He can see the television, a coffee table, one large sofa, several large easy chairs and the little blonde-haired girl sitting on the sofa with her back to him. She's holding a movie case and looking at the bright pictures on the cover, turning it over in her hands like a book.

This is it, he thinks. The timing will never be better and he knows if he doesn't do it now, he will never have another chance.

He advances toward the sofa, with the precision of a large cat, quiet and ready to pounce. He's practically willed himself to stop breathing.

Within seconds, he's standing directly behind the sofa and towering over the child he covets. She's been the real subject of his obsession for months now, ever since he saw her one day with her father while they were Christmas shopping. All the others have partially filled his fantasy, but really, they were only a diversion, a distraction as he formulated his plans that led up to this moment.

This little girl is the one he really wants.

And now he has her.

Chapter 22

Andrea removes her leather glove and reaches out to her husband, softly placing her hand on his. His skin feels so warm—it feels like home to her. She sighs as she studies his ruggedly handsome face that seems to be perfectly back-lit by the glow of the passing streetlights and the occasional light from the neighbourhood homes.

"Are you really happy?" she asks, squeezing his hand tenderly, smiling at him even though she knows he can't see her with his eyes glued to the slush-covered street.

"You're kidding, right?" he whispers, pulling his hand free and then placing it on top of hers. "I'm the happiest I have ever been in my life. Actually, I'm the happiest man in the whole wide world right now. What would make you ask such a thing?"

"Just checking," she answers, her words soft and lingering in the darkened vehicle. "Sometimes when men find out they are going to be fathers, they run away. They don't think they can handle the responsibility. . . . You know. They can't take the pressure."

"I'm not like that," he reassures her while squeezing her hand. "I know you've been burned before, but that guy was a loser. You know you can count on me to be with you every step of the way. I'm very excited about the thought of being a new dad. Not that I don't love Lucy, because you know I love her with all my heart. She may not be my biological daughter but I love her as if she is, and I will have lots of love for the new baby, and his mother, too, of course." He pauses and softens his tone. "I will always have lots of love for his mother."

"Ahhh," she coos from the passenger seat. "So, you are wishing for a boy," she chuckles. "What is it with you men wanting to preserve your lineage? Do you think it makes you more of a man to father a boy?"

"Never really thought about it that much," he insists and chuckles. "Although, I will confess that the thought of having a son is very exciting. Besides, I already have a daughter. What's wrong with wanting one of each?"

"Nothing." She laughs and looks at his silhouette, wishing she could reach over and give him a big kiss. "That will make us the perfect nuclear family," she chuckles. "But seriously, we can try to find out what we're having if you want to."

"No," he snaps. "I like the suspense and the idea of being surprised in the delivery room is part of the fun."

"Okay, honey," she says. "It was just a suggestion."

"Sorry," he replies, squeezing her hand again and putting on his signal light to make a right turn down the narrow street that leads to their neighbourhood, a quaint location with only a few other modest homes. "Didn't mean to snap at you like that."

She laughs again. "Relax, honey," she whispers. "We've got at least seven more months to go, and at the rate you're going, you're not going to make it before you explode."

"I know," he says. "What the hell?" He straightens in his seat, as if trying to get a better view as their two-level house comes into sight.

"What is it Greg?" she asks, detecting the sudden urgency in his voice. "What's wrong?"

"Not sure," he mumbles easing the car over to the curb across the street in front of their house instead of pulling into the driveway. "But that's Cliff's truck parked right there," he adds, pointing to the black club cab near the walkway.

"I hadn't noticed," she answers following his finger. "What's he doing here?"

"I don't know," Greg says, putting the Honda Civic in park and turning off the ignition. "But I don't like it," he adds, releasing his seat belt, opening the car door and stepping out into the cold night air—all in one swift action. "Maybe you should stay here until I see what's going on."

"Not a chance," she tells him, releasing her seatbelt and opening the passenger door. "I'm coming with you." She practically jumps out of the vehicle.

"Fine," he says bolting around the front of the car and meeting her in the street. Taking her hand, he adds, "But you stay with me."

"Greg," she answers, her breath coming in gasps. "You're scaring me. Cliff probably just dropped over to check on the kids, that's all."

"I hope that's all." Checking for traffic, he then steps out into the street and, holding her hand tightly, takes long strides to the other side. "But it doesn't feel like that."

"Now you're really scaring me," she tells him. "Why do you think something's wrong, Greg?"

"It just feels wrong," he answers, leading her up the walkway to the front of the house. "Watch your step," he says, noticing the ice in their path.

"What do you mean?"

"It means that Cliff wouldn't be here unless something was wrong," Greg says, approaching the house just as he sees his best friend emerge from the shadows near the right-hand corner with a flashlight in his hand. "What's going on?" he quickly asks.

"I don't know," Cliff says. "I just got here and knocked on the front door but no one answered. I was starting to make my way around to the back door when I heard you guys pull up. I came back to see who it is."

"What are you doing here?" Andrea asks.

"I've been calling every half hour just to check in with Carly," Cliff says, eyeing the snow that surrounds the house. "When she didn't answer the last time, I tried again. After three tries, I hightailed it over here. The lights are all on, but I don't see anyone inside. I can't imagine Carly not answering the door when I yelled for her. And," he says glancing at Greg, "unless these are your footprints, it looks like someone was back here."

"I haven't been in the backyard since it snowed," Greg says. "I haven't had time."

"Well," Cliff continues, shining his flashlight on the ground and following the tracks around the corner. "Someone's been here and recently."

"They weren't here earlier. I know for certain because I checked and I would have seen them." He glances at his wife who is visibly distraught. "Wait for me, Cliff," Greg says while turning to Andrea. "Listen to me, honey. I want you to go back to the car. Get in and lock the doors. Then call 911 and tell them we need assistance at our house. Tell them you are my wife and we believe there is a prowler."

"Greg," she cries. "Let me go with you."

"Honey," he says, his voice becoming urgent. "Just *please* do as I say. There's no time to argue about this. Do not get out of the car until you see Cliff or me come out the front door. Do you understand, Andrea?"

"I can't," she sobs. "I want to see Lucy."

"Please, Andrea," he insists, becoming stern. "Just do as I say."

"Okay," she finally says, turning and making her way back down the front walkway as he watches. "Okay, but please, be careful," she says. "And try not to frighten Lucy."

"Remember to lock the car," he calls as he turns to join Cliff. "Okay." He sighs, trying to keep himself from panicking. "Let's go."

Without another word, the two large men step slowly through the banks of snow, some drifts so high the snow reaches their mid thighs, but neither complains. Sadly, neither has a weapon since they are not on duty, although both wish they had their Smith & Wessons with them.

Reaching the back corner, Cliff pauses and studies the footprints that were made sometime earlier this evening.

"There's something really weird about these footprints," he says to Greg. "There's no tread and there's not really any definition to them. It looks like every print is different."

"I noticed that, too," Greg says. "It's like whoever made these, had something wrapped over his boots." He pauses, catches his breath and then says, "This isn't good, Cliff. Something's definitely wrong here."

"Don't panic," Cliff cautions as he pushes on through the deep snowdrifts toward the back door. "We don't know what's going on. There could be a good explanation."

"Such as?"

Wishing that he could come up with one they would both accept, Cliff chooses not to answer but instead turns the corner and spies the back door, which he can see is open a crack. The snow is blowing in, forming a small pile on the tiles.

"Shit," he says, breaking into a sprint.

"What?" Greg asks as he picks up his pace and follows his friend.

"The back door is open." Cliff scrambles up the steps and eyes the latch. "It's broken. . . . Actually, I think it's been cut."

"Jesus Christ," Greg says, feeling his heart sink. "The kids?"

Being careful not to touch the doorknob, Cliff uses his elbow to push the door open wider and then steps inside as Greg follows close behind.

"See anything?" Greg whispers.

"Nothing," Cliff answers while stepping softly through the entrance.

Standing inside the kitchen, they scan the room. They see the cordless phone on the dining room table along with a cell phone and the box containing the Memory Card Game sitting beside it, but there are no children.

"Fuck," Cliff says. "This ain't good, friend. Someone's got them."

"Goddamn it. . . . Lucy?" Greg calls as he moves from the back door to the centre of the kitchen. "I knew it. I knew something was wrong. I knew we shouldn't have gone out tonight. I just felt it."

"You couldn't have known this was going to happen," Cliff answers as he frantically eyes the room, looking for any clue as to where his daughter and Lucy might be. "And this isn't the time to beat yourself up."

"Listen," Greg urges him. "Do you hear that?"

"What?" Cliff says, standing perfectly still.

"I hear something. It sounds like pounding." Moving toward the door of the small storage room, he listens. Nodding to his friend, Greg whispers, "It's coming from in here."

"It's pretty faint," Cliff says, moving into position beside the door. Grabbing the knob, he glances to his friend and asks, "Are you ready?"

"I am." Greg nods as he prepares to jump whoever might be on the other side of the door, praying he doesn't have a weapon. Watching as his friend unlocks the door, he can hear his heart pounding in his ears. He swallows and says, "Let's do this."

As the door swings open he's shocked but relieved to see Carly kneeling in the entry, her face blood red from crying and her cheeks wet from sobbing.

"Honey," Cliff cries, dropping to his knees and pulling his daughter into his arms. "You're okay now, honey. What happened?"

"I don't know," she sobs, staring at Greg as her father hugs her tight. "I went in here to get some Ritz Bitz for Lucy and then the door went shut. That's all I know. I didn't see or hear anything after that." She sobs again and struggles to catch her breath. "I tried to get out. I tried to call Lucy but I was stuck in here."

"Where's Lucy?" Greg can feel the urgency building in the pit of stomach. "Where is she, Carly?" His panic is growing more intense with each second that passes.

"I don't know," the teenager sobs, her body shaking violently as she cries. "I don't know. I'm sorry, Uncle Greg. I'm so sorry," she cries as Cliff holds her tight. "I'm sorry."

After that, everything becomes a blur to Greg. It seems that within minutes the place is crawling with RCMP officers and he's hugging his wife, telling her not to worry. He's trying to reassure her that everything will be okay when he knows it won't.

*****

She didn't hear him. She didn't see him. If she would have, she would have run away.

She didn't know anyone was behind her until it was too late.

All she knows is that someone grabbed her from behind and picked her up off the sofa where she was waiting for Carly to start her movie. Whoever grabbed her, quickly put something sticky over her mouth. He then wrapped her in plastic and tied her feet and hands.

She couldn't get away and she didn't get a good look at his face because he had something black over it. She thinks it was a mask because she's seen her daddy wear something just like that when he sometimes goes out running in the snow.

She tried calling Carly to help, but she couldn't open her mouth. He had taped it shut. She wishes she could have pulled it off and yelled for Carly, but her arms and hands were wrapped tightly against her body. She could see what was happening though. He didn't cover her eyes. So she watched helplessly as he carried her through the kitchen and out into the backyard where she could see all the snow. . . . It was cold.

All she could think about was her mommy and daddy, but he carried her out the driveway and then across the road through the bushes and then just dropped her in the back of a truck. She hurt her head when she fell onto the cold, hard metal.

After that, everything was dark and she has no idea where he took her.

Chapter 23

Guiding the vehicle down the empty streets, he can't help but gloat. In fact, he's pretty damn proud of himself. He's so proud of himself that he's practically climbing out of his own skin but he's trying hard to contain his excitement. The tiny hairs on the back of his neck rise with anticipation of what comes next. He wishes he could yell at the top of his lungs and let the world know how clever he is. But he can't, so instead he settles for feeling like a young child on Christmas morning, waiting to unwrap the biggest present under the tree. The giddiness almost overwhelms him.

He's longed for this minute for weeks. The girl has been the object of his obsession, something he's coveted since that day before Christmas when he ran into her at the hardware store while she was shopping with her father. Holding his large hand, her tiny hand getting lost in his, she was bubbling with childhood awe as she stared at the bright decorations and sparkling lights. She was so lost in her wonderment that she didn't notice him, but she caught his eye right away among the horde of shoppers pushing and shoving to fill their carts with presents for their loved ones, something he's never experienced. But he wasn't thinking about any of that. He was concentrating on her.

He had recognized her father from the papers so he knew her father was a cop. He knew her father would notice someone lurking about so he kept his distance and watched as they shopped. He was careful not to be seen, ducking behind tall counters and hiding amid groups of shoppers to avoid being detected. In a strange way, he felt like a cop himself, a cop on surveillance duty. From these angles, he observed her, following every move she made and becoming fixated on her light-coloured hair and tiny features.

He's been living his fantasies for many years, but he's been fighting the impulses to act, just waiting for the right time and to find the right one. He knew she was the one, the moment he saw her smile, the minute he heard her laugh—but he knew he couldn't just rush and take her. Instead, he needed a plan. He needed to cast suspicions elsewhere, so he hatched his grand scheme, knowing full well that while the authorities were concentrating their efforts elsewhere, he could exist within their midst and they would never suspect him. Why would they?

And all his efforts have paid off, he thinks, keeping his hands glued to the steering wheel and his eyes scanning the streets for any sign that someone might be following him. But the streets are empty and he sighs contently. She's finally his, and he will never—ever—give her back.

"She's mine," he says.

Quiet! Be calm, he tells himself as he maneuvers the van through the town streets, which have practically been reduced to narrow paths by the mountains of snow following the massive storm. He makes sure he keeps to the speed limit as breaking that law might inadvertently attract attention, putting an end to his plans. He'd be devastated if he failed at this point—after everything he's done and just when he's so close to having everything he could ever imagine.

Holding his breath as he drives through the centre of town, he glances in the windows of the other vehicles as he passes them.

Are they watching me? He wonders.

They are watching him, he's sure of that.

People always watch me, he thinks.

And they're probably talking about me as well. Making fun of me and laughing at me. They always do that, too, he thinks.

But he doesn't care now because he has the one he desires.

Everyone else in the world may as well be dead as far he is concerned.

The pounding in the back of the van infiltrates his thoughts and he knows she's kicking at the floor with her feet, which he's sure are bound tight.

"Quiet," he screams at his young prisoner who is sprawled on the back floor of the van like a fifty-pound bag of potatoes.

"No one can hear you," he yells. "And no one can help you."

The pounding continues.

"I said stop it," he screams again. "Don't make me stop the car and come back there. Trust me," he seethes. "You don't want me to do that."

The pounding stops just as he approaches the street that leads to his destination.

"Now be quiet," he yells again. "We're almost to your new home. You'll like it here with me. I even have a friend for you to play with.". . . *For now*, he thinks.

Slowing the van, he turns into the narrow driveway and stops near the house. Scanning the house he sees only three rooms on the second floor have lights on and the entire main level is in complete darkness. He smiles. He's sure no one even knew he was gone. By telling them that he's going to work, he's been able to sneak out a lot over the past few weeks, hiding under the cloak of darkness and creeping back in just before the morning's light. He's cut it close sometimes, but he's never been caught. He's proud of that. He credits his success to careful planning and meticulous attention to detail.

Easing the van down the long drive that leads around to the back of the house where he can't be seen from the main road, he pulls the vehicle to a complete stop, puts it in park and turns off the ignition.

"Made it," he says and lets out a long sigh, glancing this time at the back of the house.

He's relieved to see complete darkness. The coast is clear.

Opening the driver's side door, he slides out, his boots that are still covered in the plastic bags, land in the slush. He gently closes the door behind him, being careful not to slam it.

He stops and glances at the house again looking for any sign of life from inside. He sees nothing.

Pulling the plastic bags off his feet, he stuffs them in his coat pocket and rejoices in his success. *It was difficult*, he thinks, *but well worth the effort.*

Quickly moving to the back of the van, he throws open the cargo doors and admires the package that's squirming there on the floor. She's tiny, but not too small, he thinks.

"I've got you . . . you're mine now," he says, reaching into the van and pulling the plastic wrapped girl from the vehicle. "Just stop squirming so much," he commands.

But she continues to fight. And he resists the urge to yell at her again for fear of attracting attention. As it is, he's sure the people who live in this house don't even know he's here, so he wills himself to be careful and to not make any noise so as not to tip them off.

"Stop," he whispers harshly as he throws her over his right shoulder and she continues to flounce around. "If you make me drop you, it will be you who will be hurt, not me." Forcing himself to remain calm, he adds, "I don't want to hurt you, Lucy. I like you and we're going to be happy together. Just don't make me drop you."

To that, she squirms again and he gently closes the two doors. He squeezes her tightly as her cries are muffled under the duct tape.

Glancing around once again he's convinced no one has seen him arrive.

Firmly gripping the tiny girl in place over his shoulder, he moves past a series of dilapidated buildings located at the rear of the main house and under a clump of snow-laden trees. Following a narrow path that passes between two of the rotting and falling-down structures that were at one time used for storage when the original owners operated this place as a farm—even though it wasn't intended for that use when it was first built two centuries earlier—he follows a route that's been beaten down in the deep snow. Since then, the property has had many usages.

He pants as he goes because of the extra exertion from the added weight. He thinks this routine is becoming a major chore for him as he's seriously out of shape.

Heading toward another dilapidated building several thousand meters away from the big house and tucked obscurely within a dense growth of pine and fir trees, he stops midway and turns around to make sure no one is following him. He's sure they aren't as he's positive no one comes to this part of the property—except him. He's never seen any other footprints in the snow, so he's confident in that assumption.

Turning back to the path in front of him, the moonlight bouncing off the newly fallen snow and glistening like thousands of tiny diamonds, he pushes toward his destination. It's the building he discovered last fall while he was investigating the property and he knew right away that it was the slaughterhouse used by the original inhabitants when they kept cattle, pigs and chickens. As there were no grocery stores two hundred years earlier, the homeowners would bring the animals out here to kill them because their cries could not be heard from the big house.

He's sure it's been many years since any animals were killed here, but it's the perfect place to hide his prey. No one comes out here except him and no one can hear them if they scream. In fact, he's stood back in the yard and listened for their cries, but he could not hear them so he's confident he's chosen the best location to keep his trophy.

"You'll like it here," he says, shifting the weight on his shoulder to lessen the burden. "It's real nice."

He hears her muffled cries, but he can't understand anything she is saying.

"Don't worry, honey," he speaks softly. "We're gonna have lots of fun together. And wait until you meet Ruby. She's a real sweetheart. I'm sure you're gonna like each other a lot."

Reaching the door, he pauses before he pushes it open and glances around one more time. As the moonlight floods the path over which he just travelled, the dark shadows dance over the snowdrifts and he smiles.

Safe, he thinks. *Safe and sound . . . and alone.*

Chapter 24

February 15

His eyes snap open and he stares at the ceiling. Flakes of paint line most of the structure, which is in obvious need of repair. The once white paint is now yellow with neglect and gives off an ethereal, almost eerie glow in the light of the single bare bulb. He stares at the cracking paint, the tiny lines running off in all directions as if they were a roadmap leading to nowhere. Glancing out his bedroom window he sees the full moon starting to slide from its perch high in the early-morning sky.

He turns his head to the right to get a better look at the clock on his bedside night table.

Four minutes after three, the glowing red numbers scream out and he knows that if he's going to take care of his business and get back here before anyone else gets up, he's got to move now.

Throwing the cover back, he slides out of bed and pulls on his dirty jeans, one of only two pair he owns. Since he's slept in his socks and his plaid shirt, he doesn't have to stop to put them on, so that will save him time.

Moving to the bedroom door he places his right ear against the painted wood. Like the ceiling, it is dirty and starting to fade from months of neglect. He listens. Nothing. The house is completely quiet.

Good, he thinks, slowly turning the knob and listening as it clicks. *Perfect*.

Opening the door, he slides out of his room and into the hallway. From there, he quickly moves down the stairs and through the darkened house to the kitchen where he's left his boots by the door and his coat on a nearby hook. With his outer wear now on, he unlocks the back door, opens it just wide enough for him to slide through. The cold immediately takes his breath away. The frigid air grasps at his face and burns his nose as he tries to inhale. But he's ready to do this.

Passing between the dilapidated outbuildings, he follows the same path he walked earlier tonight, but he doesn't need a flashlight to see his way. He's familiar with this route and the full moon is providing just enough light that he can clearly see his way. Besides, if he uses a flashlight, someone might see him and his cover would surely be blown. He knows the darkness is his ally and he's learned to embrace it.

Reaching the abandoned building on the far end of the property, he pauses near the door and listens for any sound from inside. All is quiet.

He slowly pulls off his right glove and then fishes in the pocket of his jeans where he finds the key to the door. He bought the lock at the same hardware store where he first saw his angel just before last Christmas. He installed it himself, all the while dreaming about the day he would use the key as he is now. When it comes to "handy work," he doesn't consider himself very good, but this chore was simple and he's proud of his accomplishment—and the others he's achieved over the past few weeks. He installed the locks not so much to keep anyone out, as he's sure no one else comes back here, but to keep everyone on the inside. It would not do well to have one of his chosen ones get away. He decides who comes and goes and when they go. This morning, he's decided it's time for his number three to leave—for good.

Sliding the key into the lock, he turns it and hears the metal click of the frozen iron. Sliding the bolt to the right and pushing the heavy wooden door open, he slips into the windowless building and pulls the planked door closed behind him. Reaching onto a small, wooden shelf that's located to the right of the door, he finds the battery-powered lantern he put there several weeks ago along with spare batteries and other supplies including rope, rolls of duct tape and a lighter in case he needs to burn anything. He pulls the lantern down and presses the on button. A cold light immediately floods the room, the ground floor looking darker than normal in the shadows, the dirt saturated with the blood from an untold number of animals that would have been slaughtered here decades ago.

Standing by the door, he scans the dreary room looking for his latest prize. He didn't bother to tie her up once he brought her here last night because he didn't think she would try to escape and even if she did make an attempt to free herself, he was confident she would not have succeeded.

"There you are, my little angel," he says and smiles when he spots the tiny, light-haired girl cowering in a corner. His smile quickly fades, however, when he sees that the small child—his treasure—is trying to get as far away from him as she can. He can also see she has been crying.

"Don't be afraid, Lucy," he says, speaking softly as he crosses the room and approaches her. "I'm not going to hurt you. I promise." He smiles at her again. "You can trust me. I just want to be your friend, that's all."

She says nothing but instinctively turns her back to him and claws at the stone and cement walls, trying to dig her way free. Her fingertips are raw and bloody from an obvious earlier attempt to free herself.

"Lucy," he whispers. "Don't do that. You can't get out and you might hurt your little hands."

Bending to her level, he adds, "I wouldn't do anything to hurt you, I promise."

He reaches out to her and takes her small head in his hands, turning her to face him. "Did you like playing with Ruby? Isn't she nice? I thought you two would like each other."

Lucy says nothing but stares blankly at the man who has taken her away from her parents and the safety of her home—or at least what everyone thought was safe.

"Well," he says, standing up and towering over her. Glancing toward the girl tied, naked to the bed, the lone piece of furniture in the room, he adds, "If you didn't, it's too late now because it's time for Ruby to go."

*****

He felt nothing when Ruby Smith closed her eyes for the last time in her young life. He would have to be able to empathize with her in order to do that. But he has no emotions. He isn't capable of thinking about other people or feeling remorse for anyone—or anything. That part of him died many years ago.

She didn't put up much of a fight when he put her in the back of the van. And she was clearly too weak to struggle when he placed his glove-covered hand over her tiny nose and mouth so she couldn't breathe. She went quickly, unlike the previous two girls who squirmed and wiggled under his weight, trying to break free. *She knew her fate*, he thinks.

His eyes burn and water as he scrubs down her body with the brush and strong ammonia. He ignores the painful fumes, as he is more concerned about how he will get the dead child out of here and dispose of her remains before the sun comes up.

When he is confident he has removed any evidence of himself from her tiny body, he tosses her in the back of the van with as much concern as he would have for a pile of dirty laundry. He stands back briefly and looks at her fragile body, now crumpled in a heap. Her skin is red from the harsh chemicals, which means he has done his job. He's confident he's removed any trace evidence from her body that might lead police to him. Her skin will soon turn a pale white when the blood settles and pools. And once he dumps her like the other girls, the harsh winter air and the brisk coastal winds will take care of everything else.

One more thing, he thinks, pulling the piece of jewellery from his coat pocket.

"There." He slides the thin silver chain around the girl's neck and positions the silver cross on her chest. "Now you are perfect," he says and sighs.

Although he doesn't consider himself to be religious and in fact, has never stepped foot inside a church, the cross is a symbol of his connection to his past and to someone who was very close to him. He sees the cross as a token of his appreciation to the girls who have been a part of his much larger plan. It matters little to him that he's snuffed out the lives of three young children. In his mind, the girls are essential components in a plan that was devised to ultimately lead him to his real target. Their deaths are inconsequential. They are merely collateral damage.

Spreading out the plastic in the back of the van, he then rolls the girl's body onto it, ties it tightly with a piece of yellow nylon rope and softly closes the cargo doors.

He opens the driver's side door that squeals and echoes in the bitter cold. He freezes for a moment and looks around, then slides in behind the steering wheel. He waits a few more seconds and then starts the van. *One more stop tonight before his work is done*, he thinks.

The man puts the van in drive and glances at the house to make sure no one has heard him, but the building is in complete darkness. He is safe to complete his task.

*****

He chose this park as it is shrouded by stately pine trees so he feels safe in this place. It also borders on the outskirts of town so while it's secluded it's still easy to access. He can deposit the body here and be back home within the hour. He'll have sufficient time to clean up the van and still be in bed well before anyone else in the house wakes up.

No one will even know I've been up for most of the night, he thinks, again basking in his own brilliance.

He pulls into a parking spot near several picnic tables that are almost buried under the low hanging pine branches, their boughs bending under the weight of the snow. He puts the van in park and turns off the ignition. He pauses and takes a deliberate deep breath in an effort to gather his strength and calm his nerves.

Adrenaline courses through his body. He relishes the sensation and wonders if this is what it's like to be high or maybe to have an orgasm. He wouldn't know, as he's never experienced either.

Once he's steadied his nerves, he glances around the parking area before opening the door. He knows it's probably just paranoia, but he's being cautious as he always is. It wouldn't be smart to get caught at this stage.

Satisfied that no one is watching, he pulls his hood up over his head and ties it snuggly under his chin. Then he checks to make sure his gloves are good and snug. They are.

Good to go, he thinks.

He opens the door and slides out into the cold. He looks down at his boots, which he's covered again in the white plastic bags, as he immediately sinks in the deep snow. He could have chosen an area that was plowed but he likes the seclusion this spot provides under the cover of the drooping pine branches.

He trudges through the thick snow as quickly as he can and makes his way to the back of the van where he pauses and looks around once more. He sees no one, but he hears a dog barking. The commotion seems to be off in the distance somewhere but he can't tell exactly from which direction. That concerns him because he can't tell if it's close to his location as sound often carries in the cold air. The last thing he needs is to be ambushed by an angry dog. . . . He hates dogs. They're noisy and messy, but more to the point, he's afraid of them.

Maybe this wasn't such a good location after all, he thinks, but it's too late to change his mind now. When he started this adventure, he knew the risks but he promised himself he would never second-guess his decisions and he never has and, damn it he's not about to start today. He trusts his first instincts.

He yanks on the cargo doors that are sticking in the winter air. They break loose but not before clanging, the sound echoing through the pine trees. He stops again and waits a few more seconds to assure the coast is clear. It is. He then grabs the plastic-wrapped body, throws it over his right shoulder as if he's transporting a sack of potatoes, and closes the doors. Quietly. He spins around as he hears the dog barking again.

Goddamn it, he thinks, his eyes scanning the parking lot and wooded areas in case someone is hiding there, his breath catching in his throat. *Where the hell is that fucking dog?* he wonders, but decides to push on with his plan.

He grips his package tightly as he trudges through the snow, passing through the park's inner gate and then following an isolated trail, the full moon providing sufficient light for him to see where he's going. Since there are houses in the vicinity, he chooses not to use a flashlight as the locals might think it odd to see a light in the park at this time of day. Providing anyone is up at this hour.

No matter, he thinks, slowly placing one foot ahead of the other so as not to slip and fall. *Don't need one.*

He's been to this park before and he knows the perfect spot to leave his package. He wants it to be found by people who he knows enjoy the park, but not for several more hours. That's part of his game.

He finally reaches his destination but he is concerned. In the moonlight and under a thick blanket of snow, he thinks the place looks different. He panics for a brief second but is able to identify an outcropping of rocks, so he knows he's reached the chosen spot.

He tries to gently place the body on the ground but she slips from his arms as the plastic slides off his gloves. *Damn it!* He looks around again, but nothing seems out of the ordinary. He quickly unwraps the tiny body and then places it on top of the snow-covered flat rock. It seems fitting as it reminds him of a bed. He then makes sure her cross is resting squarely on her chest. He takes her hands, and folds them on her chest so they rest just below the cross. He then makes sure all her blonde hair is pulled down to her shoulders so that it frames her face.

"There." He sighs as he steps back and admires his handiwork, her raw white skin almost glowing in the bright moonlight.

Not so bad, he thinks. *She looks nice.*

"Well," he finally says grabbing the sheet of plastic, which he balls up and puts under his right arm, "time to get going."

Retracing his footsteps in the snow, he listens for any noise but all is quiet this early morning under the tall, snow-laden pine trees. When he reaches the parking area, he pauses and listens.

"Shit," he says, hearing the dog bark again. "Where the fuck are you?"

He decides it's time to leave—now. He jumps in the van, turns on the ignition, puts the vehicle in reverse, and leaves. He is not concerned about leaving tire tracks in the snow since he's using Goodyear all-weathers, a fairly common brand in these parts, which would make them impossible to trace.

I've thought of everything, he thinks.

Turning the van right onto the highway, he heads home feeling pretty confident that everything went according to plan.

All but the goddamn dog, he thinks, pointing the van toward his neighbourhood.

Chapter 25

Greg Paris makes his way out onto the small back doorstep. His mind is reeling with terrifying thoughts. He can feel his stomach twisting with each horrific image that flashes across his mind—images of what the monster who snatched his little girl right out from under him is doing with her at this very minute. He tries to block them out, so he can think—strategize—about how he will get her back when he suddenly stops and stares at the odd-shaped footprints that fill the deep snow. They stand out on the dimly lit layer of white as the two porch lights reflect back on the blanket of snow.

He curses, squinting so he can get a better look at the tracks the son of a bitch left when he ripped his baby girl out of her home—a place that should have been safe. He shivers as the image of Carly, trapped with the serial killer, probably trying to call out for help—for her father—who wasn't there to save her, to keep her safe. Tears begin to streak his face as an odd mixture of anger and guilt finally explode from deep within his gut.

"You Fucker!" he screams, looking up into the dark, star-filled sky. He doesn't know who he is angrier at right now—the killer . . . himself . . . or God . . . for letting this evil man take his innocent child.

"I swear, if I ever get my hands on you, you fucking bastard, I am going to rip you limb from limb and feed you to the wolves," he shouts, hoping his threat will be carried on the brisk, easterly wind to the perpetrator's ears. "You're dead!" The words spill from his mouth. "Do you hear me? You're dead, you motherfucker. When I catch you, and I will, you're going to wish you never heard the name Greg Paris."

His thoughts turn back to his daughter, the image of her innocent, sweet face, tearing at his heart. He suddenly collapses to his knees.

"Hang on, honey," he whispers. Warm tears continue to drench his cheeks, now cold and red from the brisk, night air. "I will find you. I promise. Daddy will find you."

A sudden sharp caw startles him, allowing him a brief reprieve from the horrible images that fill his heart-broken mind. He jumps to his feet as a second guttural caw cuts through the frigid, night air.

"Jesus," he says, spinning around on his heels to see five, large black crows perched in the branches of a nearby birch tree, its leaves long gone and buried deep beneath a foot of snow.

"What do you want?" he screams at the birds.

The largest bird—the one that is clearly the leader of the flock— cackles. It's a bone-chilling, guttural sound that sends goose bumps racing across his body. Greg steps toward the tree just off the back doorstep.

"You knew, didn't you?"

He pauses and studies the birds again—not sure whether he should be angry or grateful they are here.

"Point me in the right direction," he pleads. "That's all I need. If silver is the clue, just show me where he is and I'll do the rest. I *promise* I'll take care of business, if that's what you want. But you have to help me." His voice cracks as he tries to stay strong for his little girl. "Just show me the way."

The birds move their heads in unison, like tiny robots or a child's toy. Their ten pellet-like black eyes blink as one, reminding Greg of something straight out of a horror show.

"You're still talking to the birds?"

"Shit," Greg gasps, turning around to find Cliff Graham standing directly behind him. "I didn't hear you come out of the house."

"Sorry, buddy" Cliff says, speaking softly. "I didn't mean to scare you. Looks like the forensic guys are pretty much ready to wrap up in there. Just finishing up in the storage room where Carly was trapped."

"They aren't going to find anything, Cliff," Greg says as he lowers his head. The frustration oozes from his words. "We've seen how good this guy is. He's always one step ahead of us. I don't know who he is, but I can't wait to look him in the eyes . . . before I rip them from his head." He clenches his fists. "He obviously knows something about forensic evidence because he's learned how to cover his God-damn tracks pretty well. . . . He's thorough, I'll give him that much."

"I know." Cliff speaks softly. He can feel his friend's pain. "Truthfully," he pauses and studies Greg's face for a few minutes and then continues, "I wasn't going to say anything but I've been wondering . . ." He pauses again as if looking for the right words.

"Come on, Cliff," Greg finally says, clearly losing his patience. "Just spit it out. What's on your damn mind?"

"Okay," Cliff says and lets out a long sigh, closely watching his buddy's reaction. "Maybe this guy is a cop. I'd hate for that to be true, but to me, he thinks like a cop."

Greg clenches his fists again. "I have to be honest, I'd be lying if I said I hadn't thought of that as well, but then I realized you don't have to be a cop to know these things. You can learn all about foren-sics on the Internet. The Web is full of sites about forensics—about anything for that matter." He spits out this last sentence. "I've checked out a few myself just to see what we're up against and I can tell you it's not hard for anyone to become an expert on anything these days."

"That's true." Cliff nods, his eyebrows knitting together. "So then," he says, "we both agree . . . we've got nothing."

"That's pretty much it." Greg shrugs, turning to look at the crows again only to find they've gone. He's not surprised. They seem to come and go a lot these days. "How's Carly?" he asks.

"She's shaken up pretty bad," Cliff says. "It took me a while to finally get her to calm down. She kept crying that he was coming back . . . and she's afraid she's let you guys down."

"She hasn't. I know it's not her fault and Andrea doesn't blame her. . . . This guys a monster."

"I think she finally dozed off around three," Cliff says. "She's been sleeping ever since and I don't want to wake her up. The poor kid's been through a lot. I'll let her sleep as long as she needs."

"That *bastard*." Greg tries hard to contain his hate. "Why is he doing this?" His voice reveals his desperation.

"Your guess is as good as mine," Cliff shrugs. "But if I get my hands on the prick, I'll be break his goddamn neck, and that's a promise."

"Listen," Greg says. "I want to head into the detachment to work the investigation from there. Can you stay here with Andrea? I can't leave her alone right now. Her parents are catching the first flight out of Toronto this morning, but they won't get here until later this afternoon and since Carly's sleeping, I'm thinking this might be a good time for me to go. Dr. Webster's been with Andrea for a while now, trying to keep her calm, but he can't give her anything because of the baby. He came right over when I called, but I'm not sure she's going to calm down until I bring Lucy home. And," he stares at his friend, his eyes turning to narrow slits, "I'm going to bring her home, but I can't do it from here."

"I know you are," Cliff assures him, reaching out and squeezing his friend's shoulder. "And sure, I'll stick around. I don't mind and it's not like that pervert's going to show his face around here again, but if he does, I'll be more than happy to knock his fucking head off his shoulders. You can bet I won't ask questions."

"Cliff," he begins and then stops.

"Come on, Greg. What's on your mind?"

"Why did he take Lucy?" Greg asks. "I mean, she's not even the same age as the other missing girls and the whole scenario is different from the previous cases. Why has he deviated from his routine this time?"

"Who knows how these sick bastards think?" Cliff shrugs.

"I do." Greg lets out a loud sigh. "But I admit, I can't figure this guy out. This whole thing has thrown me for a fucking loop. It's like he's been thrown off his game by something. He's had us going in one direction for the past couple of days and now, he's done an about-face. These bastards don't usually do that. Most times they stick to their game plans unless he's devolving and feeling trapped, maybe desperate, which means he could snap at any time. And if he does, then Lucy's in deep trouble."

"We'll get him," Cliff assures his friend. "I promise you . . . we'll get him."

"I just hope that when we do, it's not too late for Lucy."

*****

Floyd Winchester has had enough of the barking and whining.

"Okay. Okay," he says, gulping down the last mouthful of his first coffee on this cold Sunday morning. The sun has just barely come up over the river that flows past his backyard, but it's clear, if he's going to get his dog to settle down, he's going to have to take the animal out for a run.

"Settle down, Rocky," he urges the dog, as it runs around his legs and rubs up against him. "I don't know what's gotten into you this morning, but let's get your leash and head over to the park so you can blow off some steam."

Rocky, his nine-year-old German Sheppard/Golden Retriever mix has been going crazy since around three o'clock this morning. The large animal has been barking and running around the small house for several hours and no matter what Floyd tries to calm him, the dog just won't relax. He's never seen Rocky so wound up.

Something must have spooked him, Floyd thinks as he glances out the kitchen window toward the park. The towering pine trees are draped in thick layers of snow. He immediately decides it looks cold—really cold. He would rather stay inside for a while longer. He typically walks Rocky later in the morning, but since the dog is literally bouncing off the walls, he figures it's best if he takes him to the park now so he can run off his pent-up energy before the poor thing explodes.

He reluctantly pulls on his insulated steel-toed workboots—a must have when working with the local logging company. He laces them up to the top so the snow doesn't get in.

"Just a minute, Rocky," Floyd says to the dog as he slips his arms through his thick, down-filled coat and pulls the zipper up to his chin. As the dog jumps and runs around the modest kitchen where Floyd and his wife, Gail, have lived for the past seventeen years, he adds, "I've got to get dressed, buddy. It's damn cold in case you haven't noticed. Just give it a rest for a few minutes."

Sliding the toque over his head as the dog jumps on him, Floyd is finding it hard not to lose his temper with his loyal and usually obedient companion.

"What has gotten into you this morning?" he says to the dog. "Just calm down and wait a minute. You can't be that anxious to get out into the snow. You've seen snow before, for God's sake."

The dog barks.

"Quiet," Floyd commands. "Are you trying to wake up Gail? . . . She'll be pissed at the both of us if you wake her up this early on a Sunday morning."

The dog whines as it drops to its haunches and watches his master pull on his thick gloves.

"Okay, Rocky," he says as he snaps the leash to the dog's collar. "We'll go to the park and you can have a quick run. Then we'll come back and have some breakfast. By then, Gail should be up and hopefully, whatever's going on with you will have worked its way out of your system."

Opening the back porch door, Floyd holds the dog's leash firmly and steps out into the early morning light.

"Jesus." He sighs as the cold air quickly bites the exposed skin on his face. "Couldn't you have waited a while longer—at least until it warmed up a little?"

The dog immediately bolts from the doorstep and attempts to sprint toward the park, the chain leash pulling tight in Floyd's hand.

"Hold it, Rocky," the man insists as he's literally pulled behind the dog. "Not so fast. If all of this is over some freaking squirrel or raccoon, I'm not going to be very happy with you."

The dog ignores his master but instead continues to pull the man toward the park's main entrance. Once inside the gate, Floyd notes only a portion of the parking lot has been plowed. It puzzles him since this park gets a lot of use by walkers, snowshoers and cross-country skiers.

If you go through all the trouble of bringing in a plow, why not clean the entire lot, he wonders, as Rocky continues to pull him through the plowed area and then through the deep snow where clearly a vehicle has recently travelled.

Odd, Floyd thinks. He wonders why any driver would choose to park in the snow when there are clearly plenty of other spaces cleared out.

What the hell, he shrugs, thinking it's really not his concern where someone decides to park.

As Rocky continues to lead him to the spot where the vehicle was obviously parked, Floyd looks around as the dog suddenly becomes more anxious and agitated, sniffing the area with an increased frenzy.

"What has gotten you so fired up?" he says to the dog while wrapping the leash tightly around his right hand several times to make sure the animal doesn't break clear. The last thing he needs this morning is to have to chase the dog through the park.

Not a good thing, he thinks as the dog zeros in on a set of footprints that lead from the spot where the vehicle was parked and then through the park's inner gate, which is made out of old logs.

"Whatcha got, Rocky?" he asks, as he runs, almost stumbling, along the trail of footprints in the deep snow.

The dog barks and spins around several times.

"Easy, boy," Floyd whispers as a sudden rush of apprehension grips his body. While the dog begins to pull him along the trail of footprints, Floyd tries to pull back.

"I'm not sure about this, Rocky," he cautions, fighting with all his strength to hold the dog in this spot, which eventually ends up being a losing battle.

Pushing through the mounds of deep snow, Floyd struggles to keep up with the dog, which has become relentless in its determination to follow the footprints.

"Okay, Rocky," he finally says, breaking the drifts, which are up to his thighs in some places. "This better be good, whatever it is."

The dog barks and Floyd chuckles. "So much for seeing who's the real master here."

Moving deeper into the park under the snow-laden trees that are casting eerie shadows on the fresh, white snow, Floyd becomes more unsettled as the dog continues to strain under the leash.

"I don't like this, Rocky," Floyd says as the pair moves under the drooping branches and follow the trail of footprints. "Something doesn't feel right here. I think we should go back."

With his nose buried in the snow, the dog pulls his master deeper into the park until he finally reaches an outcrop of rocks where it stops and barks. Glancing back at his master, he barks again and then whines, something the dog rarely does.

"What is it, Rocky?" Floyd asks. "What's there?"

Seeing his dog is totally agitated, he ties the leash around a nearby tree and glances around. Noting Rocky's unusual behaviour, he says, "All right, all right, let me have a look around."

Stepping carefully through the deep snow, Floyd eyes the rock formation. From this angle, he sees what he thinks appears to be a tiny human foot sticking out around the edge of one rock.

Swallowing hard, he turns back around to face the dog, "Just sit still, Rocky. If that's what I think it is, I know what's going on with you."

As the man steps toward the rocks, the dog drops to his belly in the deep snow and watches his master. He whines occasionally, a mournful sound that Floyd doesn't like.

Moving carefully and avoiding the footsteps previously made in the area, Floyd makes his way through the underbrush that surrounds the rocks until he's in a better position to see whatever's been left on the rocks.

"Oh dear God," he cries, dropping to his knees. A tiny body rests on the table-like rock formation. "No, no." He immediately wishes he could remove the horrific image from his mind.

Chapter 26

Holly Conrad's autopsy report is already sitting on Greg's desk when he arrives at the detachment. He picks it up and pauses, letting out a long, exaggerated breath before he begins to review it. After several minutes he looks up from the papers and stares at the young constable seated across from him. Emily Murphy had slipped in while Greg was nose-deep in the report. At first, he was surprised to find her there at this hour, but then he realized this case has gotten to her as well. He sees a lot of himself in the young officer. He was just like her when he was starting his career—he understands her dedication.

"Death by asphyxiation," he reads aloud.

"Yes." She nods. "And the Medical Examiner didn't find any fibres or debris in the airway so he's determined the killer used his bare hands to smoother her. Then he scrubbed the body down and removed any trace of himself on her skin." She sighs, looks away, and adds, "That's pretty gruesome, if you ask me."

"It's a very personal way to kill someone," Greg says. "It means whoever did this was looking into that little girl's eyes when she died. We know for certain this guy is a sociopath, but to be able to disassociate in such a heinous manner is truly evil. . . . This guy has no soul."

"I can't imagine what kind of monster could do that, Sir," the constable replies, turning back to face her commanding officer. "It takes a special kind of creepy to be that callous. It's so . . . so cold-blooded."

"Indeed." Greg nods, scanning the report again. "The Medical Examiner says there were no signs of sexual assault," he whispers. "That's one saving grace. At least the poor child didn't suffer that indignity before she met her untimely end."

"Yes, Sir. I suppose." She looks to the floor in an effort to conceal the tears that are threating to burst forth. "It's a small consolation though."

"That fact tells us a lot about this guy. We know he's not doing this for sexual pleasure, at least not in the normal sense." He watches the officer's facial expressions for several seconds then finally says, "What's on your mind, Murphy?"

"Sir?" She responds.

"Tell me what you're thinking," Greg answers, staring at her.

"Well, Sir," she says. "If I may speak candidly?"

"You may," he nods. "I would expect nothing less from one of my officers."

"Very well. . . . I'm just wondering, Sir, if you feel okay to be here? I mean," she pauses and swallows, "what with everything that's just happened to your family."

Greg pauses before answering and then says, in a purposefully calm and relaxed voice, "I know you may think that I should not be working, considering the situation constable, but believe me, this is the best thing for me right now. I have to do this. I have to catch this son of a bitch."

"Yes, Sir." She nods. "And we will, but . . .?"

"But what?" he interrupts her. "Am I capable of keeping a clear head? Can I think straight or will I become a hindrance to this investigation?"

"Sir," she says, swallowing hard. "I didn't mean to . . ."

"Yes you did," Greg interrupts again, raising his right hand to tell her to stop talking. "You did, and that's fine. That's what makes you a good cop. You're worried about the case and that's as it should be, because nothing should get in the way of the case, but you can believe me when I say I will be more focused now than ever. When that son of a bitch invaded my home and took my daughter, he chose the wrong man to piss off. And if he hurts one tiny hair on her beautiful head, I will personally cut his balls off and shove them down his throat. I will feed them to him one at a time. That's a fact, Constable, so you can believe me when I say I won't do anything to impede this investigation."

"I'm sorry, Sir, if I implied . . ."

"Don't be sorry, Constable," Greg says offering her a reassuring smile. "You have every right to question my mental capacity. I'd do the same thing if the roles were reversed, but I'm telling you, I'm good to go. Whenever you think I've lost perspective, you have my permission to step up to my face and tell me to sit the fuck down. Okay? Whenever you think I'm getting in the way of this investigation, tell me to go home. Understand?"

"I would never do that, Sir."

"Yes you would," Greg insists. "Because that's an order. Whenever you think I'm out of control, you kick me in the ass and don't worry about rank. You got that?"

"Yes, Sir," Constable Murphy says and smiles reluctantly. "I got that."

"Good." Greg smiles at her again. "Now that we've got that out of the way, let's get down to business. I want to know what you were able to find out about Murdock McCarthy."

"Honestly, Sir," she begins, scanning the notes she's written on a pad attached to a black clipboard. "There's not much to tell. It's the weekend and some of the records I'd like to see are hard to access without people in the offices to find them, but I've found enough discrepancies to raise alarm and to confirm your suspicions that something's off with this guy."

"Please explain," Greg says, pulling himself up straight in the green swivel chair and placing his elbows on the desk. He then puts his chin in his hands and listens as she reviews her findings.

"Okay," Emily Murphy begins. "Here's the thing. I've not been able to track down any official birth certificate for Murdock McCarthy."

"Nothing?"

"No, Sir," she shakes her head. "I started my search in Manitoba where he says he came from and when that turned out to be useless, I broadened my search. I went west and then east and there's no record of his birth registered in any Canadian province. I've turned up a few others by that name, but they are either younger or older. Clearly, he's not twenty-three, seventy-one or eighty-six, is he?"

"No." Greg shakes his head. "That is certainly weird," he says. "But he has a vehicle and that must be registered because it's still got Manitoba plates."

"I thought as much, too, but there's no vehicle registered in Manitoba under that name."

Greg studies her face and then says, "I made a huge mistake the other day."

"Sir? . . . How?"

"I stopped him because he skidded through the red light and almost hit my car, but when I pulled him over, I didn't run the plates because technically he hadn't broken any laws . . . and because I knew the guy, I didn't want to upset him. I just wanted to give him a warning about his tires. I should have known better. One of the first and most important rules of police work is to never take anything for granted, even with people you think you know."

"What was he driving?"

"A white Chevy van and judging by the shape it was in, I'd say it was around a 2000 or 2001."

"I'll go back later and run a check on all van registered in Manitoba from those years. It might give us something."

"Good idea," Greg says. "Find anything else that might be helpful?"

"Not really. As I said, there are no records for this guy. No record of employment or health coverage or anything." She pauses. "It's like he doesn't exist."

"That's bizarre," Greg agrees. He studies the young officer again and then says. "Let's try something else. Murdock says his wife died in a traffic accident about four years ago. Let's go back over the past five years and see if the system can find any deaths registered to any female with the last name McCarthy. Legally, she may have kept her own last name, but her husband's name should show up on the record as next of kin. That should be in the RCMP database somewhere, but something's telling me you won't find it."

"I'm having that same thought," Emily nods as she makes notes on the pad she's holding on her lap. She adds, "Anything else, Sir?"

"Yes," he says. "Let's run the children. The oldest boy's name is Lucas. There are two younger girls, Sophie and Emma. There must be birth records or school records for them. They have to be somewhere in the system."

"You would think so," the constable agrees.

"What about property records?" Greg asks, as if he's just had a bright idea.

"Already running that search," she answers. "That one's a bit more complicated and will take considerably more time since all property transactions are registered by the Municipality or City and it's possible he owned property under a different name, maybe even a numbered account. You can do that legally in most provinces, so it's going to take several days to go through the entire data base, but the computer is searching and I've asked members in Manitoba to give us a hand with it."

"Very good," Greg says, leaning back in his chair and looking at the ceiling as if contemplating his next words. Then he says, "You know, Constable, something didn't feel right about this guy from the first time I met him several months ago. I could never put my finger on it, but there was just something about him that didn't sit right with me. There was something about the way he carried himself and about how his children act around him. Ever get that feeling with someone you met, Constable?"

"I have, Sir," she nods. "Many times, and I've learned over the years that no matter what my mind says, I should always go by what my gut is telling me."

"Yes," Greg says and then sighs. "I learned that lesson a long time ago as well, and now, because I didn't act on my instincts, this guy who is clearly hiding something has been living in our community. The question is, what's he been doing? Is he hiding from someone? Has he broken any laws?"

"Is he the guy who's doing all of this?" Constable Murphy jumps in.

"Nothing like cutting right to the chase, Constable," Greg agrees, nodding. "But yes, that's what I'm wondering, too. The question is how to either confirm that or rule him out as a suspect? We can't just barge into his house and accuse him of something like that without solid proof to back it up."

"Hopefully, our searches will give us something," she answers.

"They better, and really soon," Greg says. "Because right now, we don't have a hell of a lot to go on."

She's about to respond again when the communication centre in the administration area springs to life. Both Greg and Constable Murphy remain quiet and listen as the dispatcher's voice breaks into their conversation, sending a page on a secure channel to all officers in the Liverpool detachment.

"10-32. Liverpool. All available units needed at the picnic park on the northern edge of town off Highway 8. Nine-one-one has just received a call about the discovery of a body in the woods. No further details available at this time but EHS is already rolling," the female dispatcher says, her words echoing through the vacant detachment and hitting Greg like an iron fist to the face. "I repeat. All available units please respond."

Jumping from his chair, Greg says to the constable, "You drive."

*****

Neither has spoken during the six-minute trip from the detachment to the park, but they know what they expect to find once they get there. Both fear the body of young Ruby Smith has just turned up.

Entering the park's main entrance, they are the first to arrive on the scene. Noticing a lone male and a dog pacing near the park's inner wooden gate, Greg opens the car door and jumps from the cruiser, even before it comes to a complete stop.

"You secure the entrance, Constable. I will talk with the gentleman," he says to Emily.

"Yes, Sir," Constable Murphy nods, waiting until her commanding officer is clear of the vehicle. She then does a circle in the parking lot and parks near the main entrance. Turning off the engine and grabbing her brown fur hat from the dash, she leaves the vehicle with its red and blue lights flashing and stations herself at the gate. Only emergency personnel will get past her this morning.

Approaching the man who's holding a dog on a leash, Greg asks, "Are you the caller?"

"Yes, Sir," the man nods, his voice barely a whisper in the cool breeze.

"I know this is hard, but can you please speak up," Greg instructs him. There is no time for pleasantries.

"Yes, Sir," the man says again, only this time several octaves louder. "I called 911."

"Where is the subject?" Greg asks.

"Back that way," the man answers, pointing toward the path that leads through the inner gate. "On a rock under a stand of pine trees."

"Can you please show me?"

"I can," he nods, wrapping the dog's leash around a tree and tying it in several knots. The dog remains calm and hangs its head. "But I don't have to look at it again, do I?"

"No," Greg assures him. "Just show me the location, please."

"This way," the man says, turning and making his way through the gate as the officer follows him. Turning to the dog, he adds, "Rocky. You behave and I'll be right back."

"What is your name?" Greg asks as they begin their trek through the deep snow.

"Floyd Winchester."

"I am Sergeant Greg Paris," he says. "Do you live nearby?"

"Yes, Sir," Floyd says, nodding toward a small house on the riverbank that is barely visible through the snow-covered trees. An outside light flickers from the house in the grey morning sky.

"What are you doing out here so early, Mr. Winchester?"

"Old Rocky back there was going crazy all morning so I brought him over here for a run."

"You do that often?"

"Every day."

Noticing a familiar set of footprints along the trail, Greg asks, "Did you make these?"

"No, Sir. Rocky and me may have gotten into some of them tracks, but we broke our own trail when we came in and when we came back out. Rocky likes going through the snow and I had no choice but to follow him."

"Okay," Greg says. "Please try not to disturb those prints if you can help it."

"This way, Sergeant," Floyd says as he leads Greg around a sharp bend in the trail and up a slight rise.

"You said your dog was acting crazy this morning," Greg

continues as they trudge through the snow. "What did you mean by that?"

"He just wouldn't settle down," Floyd answers. "He started whining and jumping around at about three o'clock this morning and I just couldn't get him to calm down. Something had obviously spooked him."

"That's not normal for him?"

"No, Sir," the man replies. "Usually he sleeps through the night until about eight in the morning but even then, he's still pretty sluggish."

"So what do you think got him riled up this morning?"

"I'm not sure," Floyd explains. "But I'm thinking now that maybe he must have heard something that spooked him."

"Can you hear people in the park when you're at your house?"

"Sometimes."

"So then it would be possible for the dog to hear someone over here?"

"Oh yes." The man pauses and then sighs heavily while nodding. "Yes, Sir. I guess it would."

"Does he normally behave oddly when he hears people in the park? I mean this park gets a lot of use, doesn't it?"

"It does," Floyd agrees, taking a final turn on the trail. "And, no. Normally Rocky don't seem to mind it so much."

"What about you, Mr. Winchester?" Greg asks. "Did you hear anything?"

"No, Sir. I was asleep until Rocky woke me up."

"I see," Greg says as the man comes to a stop.

"It's over there," Floyd says, pointing to a crop of rocks. "On the other side, but I don't want to go any further."

"You don't have to, Mr. Winchester," Greg tells him. "I can go on from here on my own. But I would like for you to stay right here until I come back, okay?"

"Okay?" Floyd nods.

"Are you all right, Mr. Winchester?"

"Not really," the man admits as the tears he's been fighting back, finally break the dam. "I've never seen anything like that before and I'll never get that image out of my head. . . . She was so young . . ."

"I know it's hard, Mr. Winchester," Greg says. "But unfortunately, you've already seen it, so all we can do now is try to figure out what's going on around here so we can stop it."

"Is it him? Is it the same guy who's been killing all those little girls?"

"We can't say for sure," Greg admits, beginning to make his way toward the rocks. "Can I ask you if you got out of bed when your dog started barking? I mean, that's the normal thing to do, isn't it, if a dog starts going berserk like you say he was?"

"I did."

"You did? What did you do when you got up?"

"I checked around the house and looked out a few of the windows because I thought that maybe Rocky had heard something outside. We have a lot of raccoons around here and they like to get into our composters."

"And did you see anything?"

"No, Sir."

"Did you happen to look over here at the park?"

"I did."

"See anything over here? Headlights from a vehicle maybe?"

"No, Sir, not in the park."

"Not in the park? What do you mean?"

"Well, the park was totally dark when I looked over here as it usually is that time of night, but I did happen to catch a glimpse of a vehicle when it went by the house and headed back into town."

"I imagine you see a lot of traffic on this road every day."

"Yes, Sir. A lot."

"Is it unusual to see traffic on the road at three in the morning?"

"We don't see a lot at that time of day, but there's some."

"Can you tell me what kind of vehicle you saw this morning, Mr. Winchester?"

"It went by the house really fast and even though the moon was bright, it was still pretty dark, so I couldn't tell the make or model, if that's what you mean."

"What can you tell me?"

"I can tell you it was a white van."

Chapter 27

"Do we have enough information to confront him," Constable Emily Murphy asks. She carefully steers the police cruiser along the narrow, snow-filled streets that pass through the picturesque seaport and lead up to the large, historic home that sits on a hill fronting a massive, sprawling property. The home was built over two hundred years ago by a rich sea trader as a wedding day gift for his only daughter. Since then, the property changed hands many times over the years. At some point, it even became the site of a busy farming operation. In more recent times, it was the site of a very successful bed and breakfast. Today, sadly, it's but a ghost of its former glory.

"We do," Greg says, scanning the property as the constable eases the vehicle up to the street curb, which is essentially almost two feet of snowbanks. She puts the cruiser into park and turns off the ignition. "But right now, we're just going to talk with Mr. McCarthy and ask him a few questions . . . that's all. We're not going to come right out and accuse him of anything. We certainly don't have enough for that."

"Are you afraid we'll spook him?" she asks, as Greg opens the passenger side door and prepares to step out into the slush that covers the street. "I mean, if it's really him, won't we tip him off that we may be onto him?"

"Oh, yes," Greg answers. "There's no question he'll panic, especially if he really is guilty. From this point on, we're going to have to keep a close watch on him." Pulling his tall, slender body out of the vehicle, he adds, "Let's go Constable Murphy. I'll ask the questions and you keep an eye on the surroundings. If the kids are there, I want you to watch their reactions. You're looking for certain things. Do they make eye contact with us or with their father? Do they appear overly nervous? Do they take their cue from their father? Are there any visible marks on their bodies that might tell us something about what's going on in that house? Is there anything in the house that looks like it doesn't belong there? You know the drill."

"Yes, Sir," she says but Greg senses her apprehension. She walks around the cruiser to join her commander on the sidewalk, which by now has been cleared to the concrete by the town workers.

"Are you nervous, Constable?" he asks.

"A little," she admits.

"That's good," he tells her. "Being a little nervous will give you an edge. It's never good to feel overly confident during an investigation like this." Leading the way as they go up the front walk, he adds, "Just don't let your nervousness guide your reactions. Stay on your toes. Stay sharp. Sometimes even the most subtle gesture can be a clue."

"Yes, Sir," she says, scanning the property that's covered in a thick blanket of snow. "Sir," she says, noticing the vehicle parked in the driveway, which runs alongside the massive and once glamourous house. "I see a white van."

"I see it, too, Constable," Greg says, taking the steps one at a time that lead up to the sweeping veranda and the front door as she follows closely behind. "Since we don't have a warrant, we'll need his permission to look at it."

"Right," she replies, standing behind him as he knocks on the door.

They wait for several minutes and Greg's about to knock again when the door opens and a tall, balding middle-aged man stands in front of them.

"Sergeant Paris," the man says, his eyes jetting back and forth between the two officers. Clearly he's surprised by the unannounced appearance of two RCMP officers on his front doorstep.

"Good morning, Mr. McCarthy," Greg says trying to sound pleasant. "May we have a few minutes of your time, please?"

"On a Sunday morning?" the man replies. "Can't it wait? My children and I have just gotten up and we haven't even had breakfast yet."

"Sorry, Sir." Greg shakes his head. "But, no, it can't wait. We really would like to speak with you now. May we come in, please?"

"What's this about?" Murdock asks while holding the door open just enough that the officers can see him, but not into the house.

"We would just like to speak with you for a few minutes, that's all," Greg says. Motioning to the officer behind him, he adds, "This is Constable Emily Murphy. We have a few questions we're hoping you can help us with."

The man studies the two officers but Greg can't get a good read on what the tall, lanky man is thinking. After several seconds of silence, the homeowner sighs and then says, "Okay, Sergeant. Please come in." He opens the door wider so the officers can easily pass through. Leading the pair into the large foyer, he asks, "Would you like to come in and sit down?"

"This is fine, Mr. McCarthy. Thank you," Greg answers. "Our boots are wet and we don't want to track water through your house."

"So, Sergeant," Murdock quickly asks. "What do you want?"

"For starters," Greg begins, as Constable Murphy looks around the expansive room, visually roaming up the massive, oak staircase. On the top step she notices a small-featured girl with light-coloured hair sitting and watching the visitors. The officer smiles, but the child remains stoic. Emily continues to observe the girl as her commander begins the questioning. The child seems to be hanging onto his every word. "We'd like to know a little bit more about you and your family," Greg says.

"What?" The man immediately reacts and the tension in his voice quickly becomes obvious. "Why?"

"Honestly, Mr. McCarthy," Greg explains, meeting the man's eyes. The seasoned police officer is immediately taken by the depth of coldness and distance found there—his glare sends a shiver of apprehension up his back. He immediately shakes if off and continues. "We were doing a routine traffic follow-up from that incident the other day and we discovered some interesting things we'd like to address with you."

"You discovered something interesting?" Murdock repeats, his skinny face turning red. "Like what?"

"Like, for instance, despite your plates, your vehicle is not registered in the province of Manitoba where you say you came from. Why is that?"

Murdock pauses for several seconds and studies the officer's face. Finally he shrugs, "I have no idea why that would be. I suppose it must be some kind of computer glitch."

"I see." Greg nods. "A computer glitch?"

"I suppose so," Murdock confirms. Shrugging, he asks, "Anything else?"

"Do you have a birth certificate, Mr. McCarthy?"

"A birth certificate? That's an odd question. Why do you ask?"

"Just curious," Greg says. "Do you have one?"

"I do," the man sighs. "But I don't understand."

"May I see it, please," Greg asks.

"Yes, I suppose you could if I knew where it was," Murdock tells the officer.

"You don't know where your birth certificate is?"

"No, Sir." Murdock shakes his head and averts his eyes. "When we packed up our things in the other house to move here, we misplaced all our important papers and haven't come across them yet. Of course, we still have more boxes to unpack, so I'm hoping they're in one of those and that we didn't accidentally throw them out or leave them behind."

"I see," Greg says, trying to remain professional despite the pitiful excuses the man is obviously providing. "So then you don't have any papers for the children either? No birth certificates, school records or possibly even medical records?"

"No, I'm afraid not. I believe they must all be together, wherever they are," he answers and Greg can see he is quickly becoming agitated by the questions. "So what's this really all about, Sergeant?"

"It's routine."

"Doesn't sound routine to me," he fires back and Greg notes the man's eyes draw to narrow slits, as if squinting. "Am I under suspicion of something?"

"No," Greg answers. "However, I am curious about something,

Mr. McCarthy. I note you have not yet enrolled your children in school even though you've been here for several months now. Is there a reason for that?"

The man remains silent, his eyes darting between the two officers. Finally he says, "I homeschool them."

"You teach them here?"

"Yes," he nods. "My wife and I did that in Manitoba and I decided to keep doing it after we moved here. As far as I know that's not against the law in Nova Scotia, is it?"

"No, it's not, but you are required by law to notify the school board." He locks eyes with the man. "Have you done that, Sir?" The man begins to squirm, shuffling his feet as he looks to the floor that is now wet with the melted snow from the officer's boots. Before Murdock can answer, Greg says, "May I ask why you have chosen to homeschool your kids?"

"I don't trust the public system to give them a good education."

"I see," Greg replies.

"This all seems rather unusual to me, Sergeant and way too personal to be routine," Murdock finally says. "Now, unless you can tell me what you're looking for, then I believe I will ask you to leave—and the next time you want to see me, please phone before you just show up. It's very inconsiderate of you and it frightens the children when you show up without warning."

"Very well, Mr. McCarthy," Greg says, glancing toward Constable Murphy. "But before we leave, can I ask you about your van?"

"Is this about those snow tires again?" Murdock fires back, his temper beginning to flare. "I told you I would get new ones put on and I will. I just have to make the time to do it."

"Actually, no, Mr. McCarthy," Greg says shaking his head. "It isn't about the tires."

"What's it about then?"

"What do you use the van for?"

"To transport things."

"Things? . . . Like what?"

"Oh, I don't know. Everything," he snaps, studying the two officers standing in his foyer. "What's this about?"

"Nothing specifically," Greg says. "May we look in your van, Mr. McCarthy?"

"I'm not sure that's a good idea."

"Do you have something to hide?" Greg asks as he maintains eye contact with the man.

"Do I have something to hide?" Murdock repeats and then pauses before he says, "No. I don't have anything to hide. Let me get my coat. The keys are in my pocket."

Watching Murdock closely as he moves to a coat rack near the front door, Greg nods to Constable Emily, a silent gesture telling her they're going back outside.

"Follow me," Murdock says, slipping on his coat and opening the front door. "I don't know what this is all about, Sergeant, but I have to tell you I don't like it."

"Duly noted, Mr. McCarthy," Greg says. "We'll only be a minute."

"Let's just get this over with," Murdock says, sprinting out the front door and making his way to the van parked in the driveway. Unlocking the back cargo doors, he opens them wide and steps back. "There," he says. "Go ahead and look. Just be quick about it."

"Thank you," Greg says, stepping up to the vehicle while Constable Murphy remains back and keeps her distance. She watches Murdock McCarthy closely as her commanding officer inspects the van.

"Find anything?" Murdock asks after several minutes.

"All clear," Greg says and steps back from the vehicle to address its owner. "It's fine. Sorry to inconvenience you on a Sunday morning, Mr. McCarthy." To his colleague, he adds, "Okay, Constable. We can go now."

"So, that's it?" Murdock steps up to the officer coming danger-ously close to his face. As a police officer with years of experience, Greg can tell when a situation is about to explode. He can see the anger rush to the surface as the man's face turns a blotchy red, his eyes narrowing again to tiny slits. "Just like that?" Murdock fumes, froth gathering at the corners of his mouth. "You come to my home on a Sunday morning asking all kinds of questions without any ex-planation. You scare my kids half to death and now you're just going to leave without telling me anything? This isn't over, Sergeant. Police harassment isn't tolerated in this country and I will be taking this to your superiors. You can count on that."

"Yes, Mr. McCarthy. As I've told you before, that is your right," he says. "And your prerogative."

"Whatever," Murdock snaps as the officers begin to make their way down the driveway. "Just don't come back here anymore unless you are prepared to tell me what the hell's going on. And the next time, you better have a search warrant."

"Yes, Mr. McCarthy. We understand," Greg says. To his constable he whispers, "Just keep moving and get in the car. Don't look back. I can see him if he makes any sudden moves."

*****

Constable Murphy waits until they pull away from the curb before she asks any questions, "So, how did that go?"

"Not entirely well," Greg replies, watching the man in the side-view mirror as they drive away. He notes that Murdock McCarthy is standing in the driveway looking puzzled—obviously unaware of why they were really there. Greg can also tell the man is fuming. He believes Murdock has a very short fuse. It's clear he was struggling to contain his temper and if they hadn't left when they did, the situation would likely have escalated.

"How so?" Constable Murphy asks.

"He didn't give us much," Greg sighs, keeping an eye on the man in the mirror. "Not that I expected he would."

"The van?"

"Nothing that I could see," Greg answers. "Nothing with the naked eye at least but it looked pretty normal to me. I'd like to have a forensic investigator go over the vehicle, but we'll need a warrant to do that. We should have it checked out just to be sure, but something tells me that it's not the one we're looking for."

"Damn," Constable Murphy sighs.

"But it's not a lost cause," Greg adds.

"How so?"

"We've got his license plate. When you get back to the detachment, you can run the numbers through the Manitoba registry and see what turns up."

"I'll do it right away," she nods. "And the questions? How did that go?"

"Better," Greg says.

"How so?"

"There really is absolutely no question this guy is hiding something major."

"How can you be so sure, Sir?"

"There were several clues in the way he answered. For example, he often paused longer than normal before answering some questions. That's a sure sign he was trying to come up with believable answers, and that's not necessarily the truth," Greg explains. "And the way he repeated some of the questions back to me before he gave an answer is another clue he was stalling and not telling the truth. His eyes were also shifting quickly, another clue he was thinking on his feet. When you don't have anything to hide, you answer quickly because the truth comes naturally. It's simple body language. How people react to a question can tell you a lot about them. I think the man's probably a good liar but we caught him off guard this morning. He certainly wasn't expecting us to show up out of the blue and that left him vulnerable, which is exactly what we wanted."

"So do you think we know enough to determine if he's our guy?"

"Not yet," Greg says, as they round a corner and the house disappears out of sight. "But now that we've been there, he's going to be spooked. If he is our guy, then he's likely going to be on the move. From now on, we've got to keep close tabs on him. He could be a flight risk if he thinks we're closing in on him. And if he isn't our suspect, then there's still something going on with him. He's definitely hiding something and we need to find out what it is."

"You certainly seemed to strike a nerve with some of your questions."

"Yes, I did, didn't I?" Greg nods. "What about you? Did you notice anything that might be useful?"

"There's not much in that house to see but that's odd in itself," she says continuing to guide the vehicle down the town's narrow streets. "Certainly not many signs that someone lives there and there's nothing that would tell you there are any kids in the house. I did see a little girl at the top of the stairway. I tried smiling at her but she didn't even bat an eyelash. It was like she was staring right through me."

"Was she really tiny with light hair?"

"Yes."

"That would be Emma," Greg says. "I'm not really sure what's up with her."

"You know her, Sir?"

"Yes. I've met her several times since the family moved here, but she's a strange little girl," Greg says. "Really cute, but she doesn't talk much and forget about getting a smile out of that one. It just doesn't happen. Every time I see her, I'm left with this overwhelming feeling of sadness—it's like she emanates sadness. . . . I know something isn't right with her."

"What about the other kids?" Constable Murphy asks.

"I've encountered the son, Lucas, several times as well. He's an odd duck," Greg replies. "But I've only laid eyes on the other daughter, Sophie, once or twice and she's even stranger than the other girl. It's like she's trying to jump out of her own skin. Truthfully, the whole family kind of creeps me out," Greg admits.

"I can't shake the feeling there's something really weird going on with them," she says as she snaps on the signal light to make a turn that will take them back to the detachment.

"I'm with you there," Greg says, adding, "Instead of heading to the detachment, let's go back to the park to see how things are going. The Major Crime Unit should be well into their investigation by now and I'd like to check on things."

"Yes, Sir," Constable Murphy answers as she turns off the signal light then guides the cruiser down Main Street toward the north end of town.

"This whole case just keeps getting stranger and stranger by the minute," Greg says as he glances out the window and watches the passing buildings and trees. He's just about to share another thought with the constable when he quickly notices five black crows perched on a telephone wire. He gets the feeling they're watching the police cruiser. "Are we on the right track?" he whispers as they pass by the birds.

"Sorry, Sir?" Constable Murphy asks. "I didn't hear you clearly."

"Huh? Oh, sorry, Constable. It was nothing," Greg quickly answers, turning his attention back to his colleague. Recalling what Clara Underwood had told him about looking beyond the obvious, he adds, "I was just thinking out loud. It was nothing serious."

Chapter 28

The two officers arrive back at the park where the remains of Ruby Smith were found earlier this morning. Greg sits in the cruiser and watches as the young female constable talks with several officers from the detachment who have been charged with maintaining a secure perimeter around the entrance. He pulls his cell phone from his jacket pocket and dials his friend.

"Come on, Cliff." He sighs as he watches the officers through the cruiser's windshield, now foggy with condensation. He knows this case is hard on everyone and he would give anything to catch the sick bastard who not only stole his little girl but also kidnapped three helpless girls right out of their homes, only to kill them. For the first time in his distinguished career, Greg also feels helpless, like he's on the outside looking in as a gruesome horror movie unfolds before him. "Come on," he says again, wishing his friend would move faster. "Come on. Pick up, Cliff. . . . Where the hell are you?"

He watches the officers swarm around the park, looking for anything that can provide them with even the smallest clue as to who dumped the tiny body of Ruby Smith and then simply left her lifeless remains under the tall pine trees, like nothing more than a bag of garbage. His anger grows as he thinks about the almost sterile-like home they just left. Greg knows with every cell in his body that it's not a good environment, especially for those young children, but his hands are tied by procedure right now.

He makes a mental note that on Monday, however, he'll contact the local offices of Community Services and express his concerns to the proper people. He knows his interference will likely piss off Murdock even more, but he couldn't care less about that. That's the least of his worries right now. He believes someone should really check out the situation in that house. And if he doesn't have enough evidence to proceed with an investigation, then he's sure there's enough reason to at least send in the social workers to check out the children. If there is any question about the safety and wellbeing of children, he has the authority and an obligation to report it. While he can't put his finger on it just yet, he's sure the situation in that home isn't normal and he'd never forgive himself if he didn't have those children checked out and then something happened to them.

He watches as a team of three officers makes a mold of the tire tracks they discovered in the snow. He's pretty sure it's a dead end—the child-killer is too smart to leave such an obvious clue behind. Clearly, Greg thinks, the guy doesn't believe the tire tracks will lead the police to him or he would not have parked there. Furthermore, he knows there's nothing to confirm the tire marks were even left by the creep, but on the off chance they were, the evidence still needs to be collected—sometimes a clue can present itself in the most obscure place—even as a tire track.

Anything that might help must be considered since the investigation seems to be stalled. He's about to hit the panic button when Cliff finally answers on the third ring.

"Hello," Cliff says, sounding out of breath.

"Cliff? Are you okay?"

"Yup. I was just outside on the back steps and didn't have the phone with me," Cliff explains. "Thought I'd take another look around."

"Everything in order?"

"Yup. No sign of anything out of the ordinary. I don't think that son of a bitch would dare show his face around here again." Cliff clears his throat. "If he does, I'm ready for the bastard. If he comes back I guarantee he won't see tomorrow."

"So," Greg hesitates and then says, "How are things at home?"

"Not so great, I'm afraid."

"Andrea?"

"She's not in a good way, friend."

"I'd expect that." Greg pauses. "Are you okay to stay there for a while longer? I'm kind of up to my ass in it right now."

"Yes, I'm fine," Cliff confirms and Greg feels relived his friend is there with Andrea. He'd trust his own life with Cliff and he knows the off-duty police officer will protect his wife at all costs. He's sure his home is well protected in the off chance the perpetrator decides to return to the scene, for whatever reason, although he doesn't feel it's likely. It doesn't fit the killer's profile.

"Thanks, Cliff," Greg answers, continuing to watch his officers as they go about their duties at this once pristine park—now nothing more than a police crime scene. Lines of yellow and black tape are strung around the perimeter standing out like a ghostly reminder of the death and carnage that littered the virgin snow only hours earlier. "It makes me feel better knowing you're there with Andrea."

"Anything for you guys. You know that. . . . You don't even have to ask," Cliff replies, wishing there was more he could do to help the investigation but he knows if there is one person in this country who can catch this creep, it's Greg Paris. "How's it going over there?"

"Not so well," Greg says as he releases a long, hard sigh, the weight of another young victim becoming an immense burden on his heart. "I certainly didn't need to have another body turn up this morning on top of everything else that's going on."

"I know," Cliff says. "That's a real kick in the ass, but stay focused. . . . Got any leads?"

"Nothing substantial."

"You'll get him, Greg," Cliff tells his friend. "I'm sure of it."

"Thanks, but I wish I was as confident as you seem."

"Don't give up," Cliff says, wishing he was there with his friend to help out but he knows he can't go anywhere near the crime scene until he's back on active duty. "By the way, Andrea's mother called about an hour ago from Toronto. They're on their way. They were at the airport just waiting for their flight so they'll be here sometime this afternoon, providing everything goes all right with the flight and their car is ready when they get to Halifax."

"I wish I could be there to meet them when they arrive."

"Your time is better served doing what you're doing," Cliff assures him. "You need to concentrate on finding Lucy so you can bring her home to her mom."

"What if I don't find her in time?" Greg says, the words barely able to leave his mouth. "What if it's already too late?"

"It's not," Cliff quickly answers. "Stop thinking like that. It's not too late." His voice is hard and stern.

"How can you be so sure?"

"I just know it because I know you," Cliff fires back. "Now stop sitting on your goddamn ass and go out there and find that son of a bitch and when you do, put a bullet right between his fucking eyes."

"You're right." Greg nods, even though he knows his friend can't see him. "But you will call me if anything happens there, won't you?"

"Right away."

"You take care of Andrea and Carly," Greg whispers, rubbing his eyes and then quickly glancing around to see if anyone is looking.

"I've got them," Cliff assures his friend. "Don't worry about them. You concentrate on finding that bastard."

"Thanks," Greg says. "Gotta run now. Bye."

"Keep me posted," Cliff says as Greg turns off the phone and sighs again. He knows he has all the skills, knowledge and experience to catch whoever is doing this, but he feels stumped—there are no solid clues.

He slips his phone back inside his coat's inner breast pocket and opens the car door, stepping out into the slush. The cold morning air immediately reminds him of the nightmare in which this town is currently immersed. He knows he's not going to solve this case by sitting here stewing over it.

*****

"Lucas?" Murdock McCarthy yells as he storms through the large house, banging the room doors and searching for his son. "Lucas, you skinny son of a bitch. Where in the hell are you?"

Stomping up the spiralling oak stairway that leads from the foyer to the second level where the bedrooms are located, the lanky middle-aged man pounds on his son's bedroom door, the force so powerful that it rattles on its hinges.

"Lucas. You useless piece of shit," he screams. "Are you in there? What the fuck are you doing? If you're in there, you better get your goddamn lazy ass out of bed right now. Do you hear me? . . . We have a problem and I need your help."

When the younger man doesn't answer, Murdock tries the door latch. "Locked. You bastard," he says, spit frothing at the corners of his mouth, his face red. "What have I told you about locking your goddamn door?"

"Daddy?" the tiny voice from behind him interrupts his rant.

"What?" he says through gritted teeth, spinning around and finding his youngest child, Emma, standing in her bedroom doorway.

"Is Lucas okay?" she asks, her trembling voice nothing more than a wisp of air.

"That son of a bitch is fine, but he won't be when I get my hands on him," he answers her hatefully, his eyes bulging as if they could pop from their sockets at any minute. "Now go back into your room and close your door," he orders. "Don't come back out until I tell you to," he screams.

The tiny girl stays put.

"Do it!" her father commands. "Do it, now!"

Without another word, she complies with her father's command, like an obedient dog that has been beaten into submission.

She retreats into her sparsely furnished room and softly closes the door, not making a sound, as Murdock begins screaming at his son again.

"Open this fucking door kid or else." Spit flies from his mouth and lands on the chipped paint of the old wooden door. The enraged man continues to vent his anger, as the door remains closed.

"You little prick," he seethes, kicking the door as his anger nears explosion. "Wait until I get my fucking hands on you. You'll be so damn sorry you pissed me off this time."

Standing back from the door, the older man fumes. "You won't open the door . . . then I'll fix that," he says, throwing his shoulder into the hardwood door several times, each time the door frame buckling, showing signs of weakening until on the fourth time, it finally cracks and the door flies open, snapping back on its hinges and the inner casing exploding into splinters.

"There," Murdock snarls. "You won't lock it anymore, you skinny little bastard. No more goddamn locks on this door."

Stepping into his son's bedroom, he's surprised to find it empty. The younger McCarthy male is not there.

"Where the hell are you?" Murdock screams. He's seething, even more pissed off now that he's discovered the room is empty—his temper passing the boiling point. "Where the hell are you, you little prick?" he says, as he stands in the centre of the sparsely furnished room and looks around. There's not much in the room apart from a bed with only one blanket and a thin pillow covered by a dirty, white pillowcase that betrays his son's lack of personal hygiene. A single dresser that holds the young man's socks, underwear and T-shirts stands alone against the far wall. The closet is empty except for one red, plaid shirt hanging on a metal hanger along with several other empty hangers.

Just the bare essentials, Murdock thinks. He doesn't believe in giving his children material things because they don't deserve them. He believes that material things make children greedy and impertinent. He will have none of that in his children.

"What the hell are you up to, boy?" Murdock says as he casts his eyes around the room looking for any clue as to where his son might have gone. Then he remembers the wooden box his son keeps stashed under the bed. It contains all his trinkets—his treasures—as he calls them.

Dropping to his hands and knees, Murdock reaches under the bed and gropes around in the dark until his right hand lands on a wooden object that he knows to be the box Lucas covets. He knows that whatever secrets his son is keeping, they are locked within this small pine chest. Quickly sliding it out from the darkness, he lifts it onto the bed and, places it on the thin mattress, visually examining the small chest. It's locked.

"Shit." He runs his long, skinny fingers over the latch as he examines the lock and hinges.

"I can fix that," he finally says, reaching into his back pants pocket and fishing out a pocketknife he carries with him. He's had the knife with the brown handle and four-inch blade for as long as he can remember. He took it from a punk many years ago in a drunken street brawl. When the asshole thought he could take Murdock in a fight, the older man showed him who the boss was. Now, he smiles at the memory of seeing the other younger man lying in the street covered in his own blood and he keeps the knife on him at all times as a reminder of his prowess.

"Let's see what you've got in here that's so goddamn important to you," Murdock says as he sticks the blade into the lock and attempts to pry open the box. "There." A huge grin of satisfaction spreads across his face as the lock pops open and he lifts the lid to expose its contents.

"What the fuck are you doing!"

That's the last thing Murdock hears as he feels the sharp edge of the hardened steel axe head enter his skull. As the box and knife drop from his hands and bounce on the mattress, the middle-aged man slumps backward on the bare wooden floor, his body crumpling into a heap beside the bed. As his body quivers and twitches, a thick river of blood quickly gushes from the massive wound in the man's head. His lifeless eyes stare blankly up at his son.

Lucas stands over the man he called his father, still clenching the blood-soaked axe in both hands. Thick red droplets of blood drip from the blade and land on the floor to form a pool at his feet.

"Fucker," he screams, spitting the word from his drawn, taunt lips like venom.

Murdock McCarthy was careless. He underestimated his son's anger. In his rage, Murdock didn't hear his son sneak up behind him, a fatal error since he didn't know Lucas was wielding a weapon that he was finally prepared to use. He had no idea that when he crashed through his son's bedroom door this morning, he would soon be drawing his last breath.

"I told you that is mine," Lucas yells at the bloodied, quivering mess at his feet, his eyes bulging with anger as he curses. "I told you to never come in here or touch my things, but you wouldn't listen." He rants, never pausing to take a breath. "You never listen to me. You never care about me."

Moving to sit on the edge of the bed, he looks at his father's face, the man's eyes are still open in a death stare, the shocked expression still registered there. Lucas feels no remorse for what he has just done. Instead, he suddenly feels a heavy weight has been lifted—he finally feels free. He warned his father never to come into his space, but the older man would not listen.

"Now," Lucas says, smiling, his eyes narrowing, "you can't hurt me anymore. You can't hurt the girls anymore."

He sighs, the tips of his fingers turning red as he wipes his father's blood from the edge of the axe blade and then runs his hands through his greasy hair, leaving behind streaks of red in the messy strands.

"We're free," he whispers, a smile forming at the corners of his narrow mouth. "We're free."

Watching as the red liquid oozes from the hole at the back of his father's head and the grey matter that was once Murdock McCarthy's brains, spills from the massive gash, he smiles. He's finally content. He finally feels safe for the first time in his life.

*****

Lucy Paris isn't even five years old yet and she has no idea what's happening to her. She's cold, hungry and she feels dirty. She wants her mommy and daddy. She's not used to being alone like this and she wishes Mr. Ted was here with her. At least her teddy bear would keep her company and help to keep her safe. He'd know what to do, she thinks.

If Mr. Ted had been with her last night when she was getting ready to watch the movie, she's sure whoever took her would never have gotten away with it. Mr. Ted's her hero, just like her daddy. Whenever her daddy isn't around, Mr. Ted is there to protect her, but last night, he was upstairs in her bed, just waiting for her to come up. He always keeps her safe when she goes to bed. He keeps the monsters away. If he were here now, she thinks, he'd keep this monster away.

She's tried walking around the room, but it's too dark and she can't see so she sits on the edge of the bed, the same bed where that other little girl was held prisoner. She can't remember the girl's name but she knows she was sad and very scared. She also knows the little girl missed her mommy and daddy, too. Lucy wanted to help her, but she didn't know what to do.

Sitting on the bed in the darkened room, she listens and waits for the man to come back. The same man who took her from her home last night. She doesn't want him to come back. She hopes he never comes back.

Lucy suddenly hears the outside lock click open. She hopes her daddy's come to get her and take her home, but as the door creaks open and the light from the outside spills in and breaks the darkness, she sees it's not him. Her heart stops and she takes a deep breath, instinctively pulling her knees to her chest.

"No," she cries as the hateful man strides into the room.

"No crying," he commands as he pulls the door closed behind him. "I don't like it when kids cry."

Chapter 29

Even though it's Sunday evening, the Liverpool detachment is a hub of hurried activity. RCMP officers from across the province are gathered to discuss the case of the abducted and murdered girls. The case has rocked many communities over the past week and everyone is eager to catch the bastard that has stolen four beautiful souls, leaving their families devastated and communities feeling vulnerable.

Sergeant Greg Paris has called an emergency meeting of all officers working the case and those with first-hand knowledge of the investigation. Commanding officers from the Windsor, Yarmouth and Bridgewater detachments, where the murdered victims were taken, as well as Corporal Cliff Graham, the official, but unofficial at this point, commander of the Liverpool detachment, where the latest abduction has occurred, are all gathered to share what they know about the sick child killer. Although he is still on sick leave, Cliff hopes to return to work shortly so Greg has kept his friend in the loop in the event the case is still active when he resumes his command. He knows continuity is vital in such an investigation.

As Greg watches the dozen police officers take their seats in the Liverpool detachment's crowded officers' lounge, he prays the case is solved soon or it will likely mean he'll never see his little girl again—not alive at least. He hopes that by sharing information, the officers might be able to connect the dots that could ultimately lead them to whoever is responsible for these heinous crimes.

"Gentlemen," he says, raising his voice to get the attention of his colleagues who are engaging in small talk and discussing various aspects of the case. "Guys," he says, almost shouting this time. "Can we get started, please?" he urges those assembled. "We've got a lot to talk about."

He gives his colleagues a few seconds to get comfortable and to turn their focus back to him before he speaks.

"Thanks for coming," he finally begins, his eyes scanning the room full of RCMP officers with various levels of experience and years of service to their credit. He knows most of the people in the room, but some are strangers. However, no matter their level of service, they've all heard the stories of Sergeant Greg Paris, the renowned and well-respected forensics psychologist who has worked many high profile cases across the country and beyond. They listen with the utmost respect because they know they are fortunate to have an expert of his calibre in charge of the investigation, even if it is the result of a mix of circumstances that seemed to have conspired to bring him here.

"As you know," Greg continues. "We have an individual roaming the south-western end of the province, preying on little girls. We know he abducts them under the most challenging circumstances and I believe the thrill of the abduction is part of what excites him the most. We also know, that based on the autopsies, the killer has not sexually assaulted the victims, which rules out sex as the motive for the crimes. For him, it's all about the game—the hunt, the stalking, the dominance and the sense of being in charge. That's why he chooses little girls. He knows they are the least likely to put up any substantial resistance. Perhaps the dominance is a form of sexual release, but it's more likely this guy is sexually inept, physically speaking. I believe the killer, no matter how old, has never had a real sexual experience. In fact, any experiences he's had have likely not been satisfying. His world is a fantasy. He's awkward and feels inferior around both males and females his own age, which further explains why he preys on children."

"Okay, so it's about dominating his victim, but that's a leap from abduction to murder. What would make someone do something so callous and cruel as killing little girls and then disposing of their bodies in such a public and humiliating way?" asks Sergeant Blake Brown, the commander of the Bridgewater detachment where the third victim, Ruby Smith, was taken. "To me, that's the last, ultimate act of degradation he can perpetrate against these helpless victims."

"This man is damaged goods," Greg answers without hesitation. "And let's be clear about this. I am positive our perpetrator is a man."

"How can you be so sure?" Sergeant Brown asks again.

"Good question," Greg admits. "Make no mistake about it, we know that women can be killers and they've been known to abduct children, but because the victims in this case are young girls and their nude bodies are disposed of in such a public way, I don't believe a woman would do this. Even in a warped sense of reality, a woman's maternal instincts would override her anger and she would not put these little girls on public display like this killer has. If a woman were the abductor and if she killed her victims, we would likely never find the bodies in such a public fashion and if we did, they'd be covered up or concealed. This represents total disregard for the girls' dignity and for that reason, I'm sure that ninety-nine percent of women who kill would not take that leap."

"Is it possible that you're giving the perp too much credit and that it's possible there is a female out there who doesn't fit the profile?" the Bridgewater commander asks again.

"Of course that's possible. Everything is possible when you're dealing with a deranged individual such as this," Greg answers. "But I don't believe that to be the case here. The human mind works in mysterious ways, but even when you're damaged, your basic instincts usually remain intact. I am confident no woman would do these indignities to these little girls."

"Okay," Sergeant Brown says. "You're the expert on these assholes, so I trust what you're saying. . . . The big question remains, though, how do we get this son of a bitch before he does it again?" Pausing, he glances at Greg and adds, "We all know he has your daughter, Greg, and we'll do anything we can to help you get her back before . . . " he pauses, as though choosing his words carefully, ". . . something terrible happens to her."

"Thanks, Blake." Greg nods and smiles at the sentiment. "I appreciate the thought, but if we're going to be effective here, I urge you to forget the fact that my four-year-old daughter was his latest victim. Our only hope of bringing Lucy home is to get this guy, so don't let your emotions cloud your thinking. Be objective. Treat my family's case just as you would anyone else."

"And I appreciate your approach," Blake says. "But don't be the hero, Greg. Don't be afraid to lean on us if you need our help. We're here for you. You just tell us if you need anything—anything at all."

"I understand." Greg nods and scans the room. "But the best thing you can do for me is to help me get this bastard."

"So, then, let's do it," Blake replies. "What do we do?"

"I think the best thing we can do, is to start at the beginning," Greg says. "And for that," he adds, glancing at Emily Murphy, "I'm going to turn the proceedings over to Constable Murphy. She's been in on this investigation since the discovery of the first body, five-year-old Holly Conrad."

"Me, Sir?" Constable Murphy replies, glancing at her commanding officer.

"Yes," Greg says, sitting down as all eyes in the room turn to the young female officer. "The floor is yours, Constable. Please take it from here. Remind our colleagues what we have."

"Thank you, Sir," she answers, slowly rising from her chair. Glancing at her notepad and flipping back several pages, she begins. "As Sergeant Paris said, the first victim was abducted in Windsor about a month ago and was found four days ago in the dunes at Beach Meadows beach, approximately twenty minutes outside Liverpool. The second girl, seven-year-old, Hillary Lawrence, was abducted from Yarmouth three days ago and her body showed up less than forty-eight hours later on a popular hiking trail right here in the centre of town. That was the first sign he was escalating. The third victim, eight-year-old Ruby Smith, abducted from Bridgewater two days ago, turned up this morning at another popular location, just on the outskirts of town, another escalation."

The constable pauses and glances at Greg Paris.

"And," he says, returning her stare.

"And," she continues. "A fourth victim was taken last night from a Liverpool home. She was four-year-old Lucy Paris. She has not been seen or heard from since."

The room remains quiet until Cliff Graham speaks up.

"So, those are the cold, hard facts," he says to the constable. "What else do we know? I mean, what do we know about the victims?"

"Well, Sir," Constable Murphy replies, scanning her notes and then addressing his question. "We know that physically speaking, they are similar in appearance. All have light-coloured hair and they are all very young, all less than ten years of age."

"What else?" Cliff asks.

"All the victims were . . . uh, are . . . single children," she answers, looking directly at Greg Paris.

"Is that a clue?" Cliff asks.

"It is," Greg interjects, throwing a quick glance at Constable Murphy to tell her he'll handle this question. "This perp chooses children who are the most vulnerable. Fewer children in the home, means fewer chances of getting caught."

"Makes sense," Cliff says.

"In the case of the Smith girl," Blake adds, "she was taken from a bedroom while the parents were sleeping right next door. They didn't hear a thing. Slept right through it, and you better believe that's playing hell on them."

"That's pretty brazen," Cliff observes. "The guy's got balls, that's for sure."

"He's also a coward," Greg suggests as the others in the room look at him. "Think about it. He chooses little girls when they're the most vulnerable—either sleeping in their beds or when they're alone on a school ground. He's a coward."

"He was pretty brave to take your daughter," Blake says. "I mean, you can't get much more brazen than going into the home of a high-profile and well-respected RCMP officer and stealing his daughter. That's either pretty bold-faced or pretty stupid."

"Or both," Cliff suggests.

"It's an act of desperation," Greg says. "This guy has escalated to his breaking point. When he took Lucy, I believe he was acting out his final fantasy."

"That doesn't sound good," Blake says, immediately regretting his words.

"It's not," Greg admits. "When these perps reach this point, they're on the verge of self-destruction. I am totally convinced that Lucy was his real target from the beginning. I say this because he was willing to risk getting caught when he took her right out from under the nose of her babysitter. He took the other girls to fill some type of void in his life, but it was Lucy he really wanted. Now that he has her, the end game is near for him."

"What does that mean, exactly?" Blake asks. "What's his end game?"

"It could mean many different things," Greg speaks candidly, trying desperately to forget he's talking about his own child. "It could mean he may run, he may go into hiding and take his victim with him or," he pauses and swallows hard before continuing. "Now that he has the one he truly wants, it could mean he's ready to end it."

"Is he likely to be suicidal?" Blake asks, albeit timidly, as if he knows that any suggestion of that nature might also suggest he will take the young victim with him.

"Possibly," Greg says, trying to find any remaining spit in his dry mouth. Although he covers it with a practiced bravado, the stress of the situation is playing hell with his emotions. "Especially if he thinks we're close to catching him."

"Are we close?" Blake asks. "*Are* we closing in on him? I ask, because it doesn't feel that way to me."

Greg pauses and contemplates the question. Finally, shrugging, he sighs, "Not as close as I'd like." Glancing around the table, he adds, "We have a couple of clues but so far they've turned up nothing concrete." He turns to Constable Murphy and says, "Let's talk about the clues."

"Yes, Sir," she says, scanning her notes again. "First of all, we found a thin, silver chain and small silver cross on each victim. In each case, the parents of the victims confirmed their daughters did not have any such jewellery."

"So what does that tell us?" Blake asks, directing his question to Greg, the noted expert on such things.

"This," Greg answers, "is clearly the perp's signature. He's using these crosses to tell us something."

"Like what?" Blake probes.

"I believe the cross is a link to his past and to someone important to him," Greg replies. "I also believe that person was or still is a religious fanatic and most likely ruled the household with an iron fist. You know, like the *Bible* says, spare the rod, spoil the child. In this case, that person did not spare the rod but they left a lasting impression on the child who eventually became our perp, and now he's emulating the behaviour. It's an important clue."

"How so?" Blake asks.

"The *Bible* says," Greg begins, "He who spareth the rod hateth his son: but he that loveth him correcteth him betimes. (Proverbs 13:24) and Withhold not correction from a child: for if thou strike him with the rod, he shall not die. Thou shalt beat him with the rod, and deliver his soul from hell. (Proverbs 23:13-14). . . . There's the connection to the cross. I'm certain that when we do find this guy, we will also find that he is the product of what I and many others in the field call the 'Tough-Love Syndrome.'"

"Sometimes, parents can be cruel taskmasters," Cliff says. "We've all seen it in our careers. We've all had tough cases of child abuse where parents will argue they were just trying to make their children do as they were told by using physical punishment. I know I have," Cliff says, "and it still makes me sick to think of some of the situations I've encountered."

"And the parent—or guardian—in this perp's life, likely took it to the extreme," Greg explains. "As a result, they damaged this guy's psyche and now he's likely experiencing a major psychotic break. This is likely what led to his current fantasies."

"That may help us understand what motivates him," Blake says, "but how does that help us catch him? It doesn't really give us a clue to follow. Those cheap silver crosses can be bought at any dollar store in the country and there's got to be thousands of them around. We'll never be able to trace them."

"True," Constable Murphy speaks up. "But we do have another, more tangible clue. We have a witness who spotted a white van in the vicinity of the park where the remains of the Smith girl were found this morning. At least that's a starting point."

"Yes, it is," Blake says, "but let's not get overly excited. "There are dozens of white vans on the roads, but at least it gives us something to look for. We need to spread the word. We need to check every white van out there."

"We're doing that, Sir," Constable Murphy replies. "We've issued a bulletin on the wire to every detachment in mainland Nova Scotia.

We believe there's a very good chance this guy lives and works in this end of the province, but he could be on the move if he believes we're closing in on him."

"Very good," Blake says. Glancing at Greg he asks, "So, honestly, Greg. How much time do you think we have before this guy snaps?"

Carefully considering the question, Greg finally, answers, "Not long. Based upon his accelerated rate of abductions and killings, I fear he's about reached his breaking point."

"Well then," Cliff clears his throat. "Why the hell are we sitting here? Let's get off our freaking butts and get this asshole before he hurts that sweet little child."

"Amen to that," Blake says, rising from his chair and grabbing his uniform hat from the table. Addressing Greg, he adds, "Let's put an end to this for your daughter's sake."

*****

"I'm going to head home for a few hours," Greg informs Constable Murphy who is sitting in front of the bank of computers that line one wall of the detachment's communications centre. "Andrea's parents have been there for a few hours now and I haven't seen them since they arrived. I feel I should at least bring them up to date on what's happening, and I also need to see how Andrea's doing. . . . She's having a rough time. Do you need me for anything before I go?"

"No, Sir." The constable shakes her head while keeping her eyes glued to the screens that are flashing a series of photographs and addresses. "I'm going to stay here for a while longer. I've got some searches running and I want to see what turns up."

"Very well," Greg says, watching as the images flash across the computer screens. "One of those searches wouldn't happen to be for the license plate number from the McCarthy van, would it?"

"It is, Sir," she answers without diverting her eyes. "I've just started it because I didn't have much time to do it before our meeting."

"That's fine," he says, pulling on his overcoat. "Will you please call me at home as soon as you get a name?"

"I will," she confirms. "Could be a while though since it's Sunday and I haven't spoken to anyone in Manitoba. I've got a call through to the detachment in Winnipeg. I hope to speak to someone who can help me with some of this on their end. I will give you a call as soon I've got anything to report."

"Thank you, Constable," Greg says, "and thanks for your effort on this case. It's been noticed."

"I just hope we get the guy before it's not too late," she says. "I mean . . ."

"I know what you mean, Constable," Greg says, heading toward the door. "And it's all right. We can't skirt around the truth, no matter how much it hurts us. Please give me a call the minute you find get anything."

"Yes, Sir," she says. "The minute anything happens you will know about it."

Chapter 30

The lights begin to flicker on, like tiny fireflies skirting from place to place as nightfall sets on the snow-covered town. Greg Paris hardly notices as he mindlessly navigates the police cruiser through the narrow streets, expertly avoiding the plows that are still working around the clock to remove the remains of the blizzard's massive snow dump. Like the frigid temperatures, the events of the past few days have left him feeling numb. The roar of the busy plows, as they push through the heavy, wet snow hardly register with him as he white knuckles the steering wheel.

He fights the urge to scream, to punch something—anything. He wishes he could simply crawl out of his skin, become the man he was before the demented killer invaded his life. But like any good cop, he knows he can't let his emotions get the better of him—he needs to be objective, especially now, if Lucy is to have any chance at all. He hates how out of control he feels, how his stomach churns and races every second his four-year-old daughter is with that madman. He hates that he now questions his abilities, his years of hard-earned skills . . . and even more, he hates that he has failed his daughter.

He was supposed to protect Lucy from the monsters.

He promised her he would always protect her. He instinctively scans the snow-covered streets and sidewalks, many of which are still blocked by deep drifts.

Is it him? Greg wonders, as he drives past one man at the end of his driveway shovelling snow.

Or maybe, it's him, he thinks, as he notices a single man dressed in a dark-coloured parka with its hood pulled up to protect his face from the biting cold as he pushes through the deep snow, going who knows where.

"Or him?" he says under his breath, spying another man standing on the balcony of his home, smoking a cigarette.

It could be anyone. Greg lets out a defeated sigh.

He knows how these predators operate, often hiding in plain sight, living seemingly normal lives until they're caught. He's that guy—the one that no one can believe would do anything so horrific. But he did, and he will continue to do so until someone stops him. Greg has encountered far too many of 'these guys' throughout his career and he knows all too well they exist, even in places that may seem immune to evil.

No place is safe.

These guys can be the next-door neighbour. The man at the grocery store. A teacher. The oil deliveryman. The clerk at the local takeout. A mechanic. A labourer or a professional. A trusted friend or family member. They are chameleons. They fit no slot and often defy logic. *They seem normal—whatever normal is*, Greg thinks, flashing back over his extensive career that has brought him face-to-face with some of the most horrifying people on the planet. The monsters that prey on the innocent and weak. He's encountered them all. He's witnessed things he wishes he could simply wipe from his memory, but the images are forever ingrained in his brain. They have defiled his mind and there is no coming back from it.

He lets out a callous, mocking laugh, as he thinks how naïve he was, thinking that if he dragged his family to a small town in rural Canada, he could raise his daughter in a safe and secure environment, far removed from the horrors of the big city. But now he knows that no matter where he goes, these bastards and their evil can reach his family. He berates himself, hoping to somehow relieve his guilt. *I should know better than anyone that small towns are not immune to tragedy. But how could I expect it to follow me here to the South Shore of Nova Scotia of all places. In my wildest dreams, I certainly didn't expect I'd be working a case in which my own daughter's life hangs by a thread.*

"Damn it!" He releases his claw-like grip on the steering wheel just long enough to pound his right fist on the dashboard.

Greg releases a loud sigh and turns his attention back to the road. He turns right onto the road that leads home. He can't shake the feeling that all the senseless killings relate back to him, that the predator was really out to hurt him. And if it turns out to be true, and anything happens to Lucy, he will never forgive himself. How can he carry on if it is his fault?

Pulling his cruiser into the driveway, he stops the car directly behind the rental sedan that his in-laws picked up at the Halifax airport earlier today. He puts the car in park and turns off the ignition and just sits for several minutes.

"Shit!" He stares at the dark blue car as he braces himself to face Andrea's parents. Normally, he likes spending time with Bill and Mona Leduc. Unlike many in-law relationships, he actually enjoys their company. They're also wonderful grandparents to Lucy, but today, he's dreading their questions that will undoubtedly come with inquisitive glances and even accusatory innuendos. He understands their need to blame him, and why not? He's been doing it from the moment he found out his baby girl was taken by the sadistic child killer.

"Well," he says, pulling the keys from the ignition, shoving them in his pocket and opening the driver's side door. Stepping out into the cold evening air, he sighs, "Time to face the music."

*****

"Hold still," he yells, yanking her skinny arms behind her back and wrapping the rope tightly around her tiny wrists, the thick rope seeming almost grotesque against her angel-like skin.

"It hurts," she cries. "I want mommy. I want to go home."

"If you'd stop squirming, it won't hurt so much." He sneers, tugging the rope tighter. He feels a rush of pleasure as he sees her pale skin redden as the rope cruelly chafes her small wrists.

"But it cuts my hands." She continues to cry, her sobs coming in quick bursts.

"I don't want to hurt you, Lucy, I really don't," he says, snarling as he pulls the rope even tighter. "But if you don't stop crying, so help me God, I will, and it will be all *your* fault. I don't like it when kids cry. I've told you that before, so just stop before you make me hurt you." He can feel a familiar rage begin to rise inside him.

"Okay," she whimpers, biting her bottom lip in an effort to stifle her cries. "I'll try."

"You better do more than try young lady," he tells her, pulling her small body up on the bare mattress.

"I'm hungry."

Stepping back, as if admiring the scared little girl like she is the prized calf at a beef auction, he studies his helpless prisoner.

"I brought you a sandwich," he finally snaps. "But you didn't eat it."

"I don't like peanut butter and jam," she whimpers again. "I just like peanut butter."

"Well, that's all you're getting and if you don't eat it, that's not my problem," he says, spittle spraying from his curled lips. "Now stop whining. I don't like that either. It's almost as bad as the crying." His dark eyes burn with anger.

"When can I see Daddy?" she whispers, trying to comply with the man's commands.

"*Never*. I already told you that," he snaps, watching as she tries to stifle her tears. "I told you! You are *never, ever* going to see him again. Now," he says, glaring at her through squinted eyes, as if contemplating his next move, "am I going to have to tie your feet?"

"No," she whispers, trying hard to control her sobs. "I won't move. I promise." Her tiny chest deflates as she speaks.

"Like I said," the man tells her as he roams the darkened room. "I don't *want* to hurt you and I'm trusting you to stay where I put you."

She watches his every move, forcing her eyes to adjust to the darkness, but she says nothing.

"I need you to behave yourself," he tells her, his tone becoming considerably softer. "It will soon be time for us to leave," he says. "I have a few more things to take care of and then I'll come and get you. Then we can leave this town and never come back. You're mine now."

"I want to see Mommy," she whispers, her voice barely a wisp. But he still hears her.

"Stop it," he suddenly screams. He rages back toward her like a panther about to pounce, spit flies from his lips spraying a wet path before him. "Do you hear me? Shut up! Shut up! Shut up! I don't want to hear that ever again." He rips the roll of duct tape from a nearby table. "Do you want me to cover your mouth?" he says, shoving the hard roll of tape into her face, banging her skull against the metal headboard.

She slowly shakes her head as a waterfall of new tears burn her fair skin as they stream down her frightened face.

"Then stop talking about her! . . . Forget her!" he fires back, his hateful words filled with such venom that they hurt her ears. "She's already forgotten about you," he tells her, trying to ignore her tears that are obviously meant for her *sacred* mother, not him. "She doesn't want you anymore. She *wanted* me to take you."

"I don't want to stay here," she says. "I don't like it here. I'm cold."

"I don't care what you want," he says. "This is what *I* want, so just forget about everything else you knew. It's all gone now. You're mine forever and you'll do what I say."

She knows she shouldn't cry because it will only make him madder, but the tears continue to flow.

"And no more crying!" he snaps heading back toward the heavy wooden door. "I'm going now, but I'll be back soon. You stay right there on that bed or you'll be in big trouble."

"Okay," she whispers, nodding her aching head feebly.

She watches as he opens the door just a crack so he can slide through. He slams it tight behind him causing the room to echo with a heavy thud. She cringes as she hears the lock click. She knows there is no way out until he comes back for her. She scans every inch of the dark room, her tiny eyes darting back and forth like a frightened caged animal looking for another way out—but she can barely see a few inches in front of her. With her hands tied behind her back, she knows she is trapped.

She wants to cry out, but thinking about what Mr. Ted would do, she fights the urge.

"Daddy," she whispers, closing her eyes and wishing she could fall asleep so she could leave this place, even if only in her dreams. "Help me, Daddy."

*****

Coffee will do the trick, Emily thinks, as she rolls her office chair away from the computer terminal and glances at the large clock on the wall, its bold, black numbers confirming that she's been staring at the screens for several hours now.

"Jesus." She sighs, rubbing her burning eyes with the palms of both hands and then stretches her arms high over her head. *Maybe I should call it a day and come back tomorrow with a fresh perspective*, she tells herself as she looks around the empty room.

"Na," she says, pushing her tired body out of the chair and making her way down the dimly lit hallway to the officers' lounge to get a refill.

Just a little longer, she thinks. She grabs the coffee pot and pours the last of the hot, black liquid into her ceramic cup. The coffee has obviously been sitting there for some time because it is now the colour of molasses, but she doesn't care. She can't shake the feeling that she's close to finding something that might be important, and that keeps her motivated. Every time she thinks of Lucy being held God knows where by the monster, that could be doing God knows what to her, she wants to vomit. She can't go home until she believes in her heart that she has done everything she can to find the little girl, and if that means working until morning to find answers, then that's what she's prepared to do.

Bringing her cup with her to the row of computers in the communications centre, she turns her attention back to the search. She's worked the computers on previous cases, so she knows how to *manoeuver* around cyber space, but this time she doesn't feel she's making progress. And it frustrates her that with all the programs and technology they have at their fingertips, she can't find the right programs to locate McCarthy's license plate number. *It's got to be registered somewhere*, she thinks, as she watches data flash across the screen while she sips her coffee.

"To hell with it." She picks up the phone and punches in the numbers that will connect her with the Winnipeg RCMP detachment. She's tried several other times throughout the evening, but maybe this time she'll finally have some luck and actually connect with someone there.

"Three. Four," she counts aloud as she listens to every ring.

"Five. Six. . . . Come on. Come on," she says, as though her words will make someone answer. "Pick up. Come on, somebody please be there."

"Winnipeg RCMP," a voice suddenly answers. "Constable Malcolm speaking. How can I help you?"

"Malcolm?" Emily replies. "As in Malcolm the last name or Malcolm the first name?"

"As in Ross Malcolm," the officer answers flatly. "How can I help you, miss?"

"Hi, Ross," she says, quickly overlooking the fact he just called her miss. "This is Constable Emily Murphy from Liverpool, Nova Scotia. I've been calling your office for hours and was just about ready to give up."

"I just got in," the Winnipeg Mountie tells her. "It is Sunday you know and our detachment is technically closed so you're really lucky to find anyone in here today."

"We're technically closed, too, but I'm here working and I was hoping I might be lucky enough to catch someone there."

"So now you've caught me," he replies, "what can I do for you?"

"I assume you've heard about the child abductions and murder case we've been working for the past few days?"

"I have," he confirms with a heavy sigh. "Who hasn't? It's made the national news and I understand why. It's terrible that someone would hurt children like that."

"It sure is and now I'm chasing a lead that's brought us to your city."

"To Winnipeg?" His surprise is evident. "What could possibly link us to your case?"

"A license plate number," Emily tells him. "I've been running the number through your province's data base for a while now, but I'm coming up empty."

"That's weird," Malcolm suggests. "Something should turn up. Want me to run it on my end?"

"That would be great."

"I've got a pen right here," he says. "What is it?"

She tells him.

"Who does the number belong to?" Ross asks.

"A Mr. Murdock McCarthy," she replies. "Are you really busy or can you run it for me now?" she asks, hoping he's got a few minutes to do it right now. "It's really important that I get this information as quickly as possible."

"I can do it now," he tells her. "Will you be there long?"

"I will wait until I hear from you," she says. "And thanks for doing this, Ross. It might not be anything but then again, you never know."

"Anything to help you guys get that son of a bitch," he says. "Sit tight, Constable Murphy. I'll get back to you as quickly as I can."

*****

It's been a long day, but Greg knows it's not going to get any easier. He wishes he had something to tell his wife that would give her at least some level of hope. He knows she's emotionally distressed, worrying herself sick about their daughter and he would do anything to take that worry away for her, but unfortunately, he's got nothing new to relieve her anguish.

This guy is good, he thinks, as he studies his wife's body language. He's been sitting on the edge of the bed for at least the past half hour watching Andrea sleep. Even though her eyes are closed, he knows she only managed to fall asleep because exhaustion finally overtook her. He also knows she isn't resting well. He can see in the way her face twitches and her eyebrows knot that her subconscious is working overtime. She's terrified for Lucy, as he is, and he wishes he had something encouraging to tell her when she wakes up.

He wipes his eyes, pushing back the few tears he's allowed himself to shed—he's convinced himself that emotions will only get his little girl killed. He is also afraid that unless they get a break soon, he may never hold her in his arms again. He's worked too many of these cases to know how they end.

"Greg?" she says, opening her eyes and staring up at him. "How long have you been here?"

"A little while," he whispers, brushing the brown hair from her face, her eyes puffy from the tears she's been crying since Lucy was abducted over a day ago now. "How are you?"

"You know how I am," she replies. "I need Lucy to come home."

"We all need Lucy to come home," he says, stretching out on the bed beside her and placing his right arm around her slender body.

Gently pulling her toward him, he says, "I miss her so much it hurts."

"I know," she replies, grasping his hand and hugging it close to her chest. "I really didn't mean to fall asleep."

"Don't feel bad about sleeping, Andrea." He speaks softly. "You need your rest."

"I just can't stop thinking that I need to be awake in case Lucy comes home. I wouldn't want to be sleeping and miss her when she walks through the front door. Somehow that would feel like I was letting her down."

"You would never let her down," Greg whispers, snuggling up to her. "You're the best mom in the world and Lucy knows that."

"If I'm such a good mother, how could I let this happen to my baby?" she answers and Greg sees the tears starts to flow.

"Don't," he says, pulling her face to his and looking into her brown eyes. "Don't put this on yourself. None of this is your fault. It's not my fault. The only person responsible is the son of bitch who took our little girl. He's the only one who can take the blame."

"But she was counting on me to protect her, to keep her safe," Andrea rebuts. "That's what mothers are supposed to do."

"That's what all parents are supposed to do and in a perfect world, that's how it would work," Greg says, gently wiping the warm tears from her eyes with his long, bony fingers. "But you and I both know this is not a perfect world and there is no way we can anticipate the sickness that some people possess. Some people are pure evil and the guy that took Lucy is sick, plain and simple."

"Will he hurt her, Greg?" she asks, swallowing hard.

"Honestly, honey," he pauses. "I wish I could say no, but I just don't know. I've studied these people all my life and if there's one thing I've learned about them, it's that they're all unpredictable. There really is no way to anticipate what he'll do next."

"If he hurts her like he hurt those other poor little girls, I don't know what I'll do," she cries. "I hope and pray he hasn't hurt her all ready and that you'll find her soon."

"I am doing everything I can to bring her home. I promise you that," Greg assures his wife. "That's why I haven't been here. I know you need me but I can't be here and out there looking for our daughter at the same time."

"Lucy needs you more than I do right now," Andrea tells him.

"Please find her soon."

"I'm doing my best," he says just as his cell phone rings. Sliding the thin phone from his pants pocket with his left hand, he presses the talk button and places the phone next to his ear. "Hello."

"Sergeant Paris," Emily Murphy answers. "I'm glad I caught you."

"What's up?" he says, sitting up on the bed and swinging his feet over the edge to turn his back to his wife. If the officer is calling with bad news, he doesn't want his wife to see his reaction.

"I know you just got home, Sir," Constable Murphy says. "But can you possibly come back right away? I've got something that you will want to see and it can't wait."

"Yes," he tells her, reaching back with his right hand and taking his wife's hand and squeezing it. "Is it a viable lead?"

"I'm not sure, Sir," the constable answers. "But it's certainly something that requires your attention."

"Very well," he says, releasing his wife's hand and rising to his feet. "I'm on my way. I'll be there in ten, fifteen minutes at the most."

"Okay, Sir," she says. "Bye."

"Thank you, Constable," he says before he ends the call.

"What is it, Greg?" Andrea asks, pulling herself up and leaning back against the pillows for support. She brings her knees up and hugs them to her chest. "Have they found Lucy? Is she okay?"

"I'm not sure," he says, turning to face her. "But I have to go. Will you be okay?"

"Mom and Dad are downstairs so I'll be fine, but I'll be better when you bring her home," Andrea whispers while wiping her eyes. "Go find out what this is all about."

"I'll try to keep you in the loop," he replies, bending and kissing her gently on the forehead. Wiping the tears from her eyes with his thumbs, he adds, "But depending on what's up, I may not have time to call you, which means you'll just have to sit tight."

"Just bring her home, Greg," she says as he walks around the bed and heads to the door. "Just bring my baby back to me."

"That's my plan," he answers, pausing at the door. "I love you," he adds.

"Me, too," she replies, as he slips down the hallway and out of sight.

Chapter 31

"Hey, Greg. What's up?" Cliff asks. The off-duty officer is convinced call display is definitely one of the best inventions ever. "I hope
you're calling to tell me you've got some good news on the investigation because honestly, I'm going nuts over here. I feel so useless just
sitting here waiting for the phone to ring. I feel like I should be out
there looking for that bastard and doing something constructive to help
you bring Lucy home."

"Truthfully, I'm not sure what's up," Greg says, sitting behind
the wheel of his cruiser still parked in his driveway. He lets out a deep
sigh and stares at the soft light glowing from behind the bedroom
curtains where he just left his wife. Pangs of guilt grip his body,
twisting his stomach into a tight, hard knot. In an odd way, he enjoys
the pain—as though it provides him some form of redemption—his
penance for not being able to protect his family. "I barely got home
before Constable Murphy called, telling me she's found something
she thinks I should see."

"What is it?"

"I don't know," Greg answers. "But she seems anxious. She
wants me to come back to the detachment immediately so I'm heading

back there right now."

"Hmmm," Cliff pauses then adds. "Maybe it's a break."

"I hope so . . . I could use one," Greg says. "What are you doing?"

"Just watching a little TV—trying to get that son of a bitch out of my head, but it's not working," Cliff answers, thoughtlessly switching from channel to channel without really paying attention to anything flashing across the screen. "Nothing serious." Pressing the power button on the remote, Cliff watches as the screen fades to black. "Why?"

"Can you come to the detachment?"

"I could," Cliff says, clearing his throat. "But you do remember I'm not on official duty, don't you?"

Greg pauses. "Of course I do," he finally says. Swallowing hard, he continues, "But something major must have come up if Emily is asking me to come back . . . and if it's bad news about Lucy, I'd really like you to be there with me. I might need the support of a friend. Besides, you could be taking over the detachment any day now so you need to be up to date on this case."

"I'll be there," Cliff quickly answers. "But first, let me call someone to stay with Carly. I can't just leave her home alone, not yet anyway. I won't be long. I've got a backup plan for these situations."

"I understand," Greg says, sliding the key into the ignition. "How is she doing, anyway? I feel so bad this has happened to her. I wish there was something I could do for her."

"She's keeping close to her room," Cliff says. "She's shaken, but I think she'll be fine once Lucy comes home."

"Won't we all." Greg lets out a defeated sigh. "So I'll see you at the office."

"You bet, buddy."

"And, Cliff," Greg adds. "Thanks for being here for me. I don't know what I'll do if it's something bad."

"You know you can count on me, friend," Cliff says. "I'm there for you no matter what it is, but I'm sure she's going to be okay."

"How can you know that?" Greg replies, turning the key and listening as the engine resists slightly with the cold and then fires up.

"I just feel she's okay."

"You feel it?" Greg answers. "That's a switch. Usually I'm the one that has these feelings."

"This one's a little too close for you, pal," Cliff says. "Now you head over to the station and let me make a call. I'll see you in a few minutes."

*****

The ten minutes it takes Greg to travel across town are nothing but a blur, but by the time he arrives, Cliff is already in the back parking lot waiting for him. When he sees the cruiser pull in, the middle-aged officer gets out of his club cab truck and waits near the detachment's rear entrance while his friend parks and locks up the cruiser.

"How the hell did you get here so fast?" Greg asks as he approaches Cliff.

"You know me," Cliff says as he shrugs and smiles sheepishly. "Broke a few speed limits, ran a few stop signs, ran over a few curbs," he replies, trying to keep the conversation light. "Nothing serious."

"Guess it's a good thing you know a few cops, buddy." Greg smiles. "Or else you might find your sorry ass behind bars for the night. But seriously, did you find someone to be with Carly?"

"Yup," Cliff answers while Greg uses a coded key card to unlock the security back door that's only accessible to members. He hopes it won't be long before he has that key back in his possession. "Called one of the off-duty female members who lives close by and she came right over, so you've got me as long as you need me."

"Which one?"

"Bridget."

"She didn't mind?"

"Nah," Cliff says, following his best friend into the rear of the detachment, through the service bay then the evidence storage area and finally past the two eight-by-eight holding cells where they usually put drunk drivers and individuals awaiting transfer to the larger provincial correctional centres in the metro area. "I had it all arranged with her just in case I had to go someplace quickly."

"Good thinking," Greg says, slipping off his heavy overcoat and throwing it onto the back of a chair near one of the desks, stealthily moving through the administration area on his way to where he hopes he'll get some answers that might help him find his daughter. "Obviously, you can't be too careful these days."

"We're going to find her, Greg," Cliff says as the officers then proceed to the communications centre located in the centre of the detachment where they find Constable Emily Murphy. She's still sitting in front of the computers where Greg had left her earlier this evening.

"We're here, Constable," Greg announces as they approach her from behind.

"Sir," she says, spinning around on the padded swivel chair. Her surprise at also seeing Cliff standing beside her current commander is clearly evident in her expression.

"Hey," Cliff smiles, his eyebrows quickly rising and falling as they have a habit of doing when he speaks in short sentences.

"Corporal," she replies, smiling slightly.

Greg speaks up when he notes the constable's reaction. "I called Corporal Graham and asked him to be here. If your news has anything to do with this case, then I want him in on it since this might soon be his investigation."

"Sure, Sergeant," the constable says and nods. "I understand." To Cliff, she adds. "Nice to see you, Sir."

"You can rest easy, Constable Murphy," Cliff says. "I'm basically here for moral support, but the Sergeant has told me how impressed he's been with your efforts on this case. It has been duly noted and won't be forgotten, I can assure you of that."

"Thank you, Corporal," she says and smiles slightly again, as if embarrassed about receiving praise from a superior officer.

"I believe good work deserves recognition, Constable," Cliff adds, glancing at Greg. "Right?"

"Without a doubt." He nods and turns to the officer and adds, "So, Constable Murphy, what have you found?"

"Well, Sir," she begins while glancing at her ruled notepad where she's scribbled several lines of information. "This whole situation about not being able to locate the license plate from the McCarthy van has been really nagging at me because if it's an active plate, as it appears to be since it's on the vehicle, then it should be registered and that registration should show up somewhere in a search, but I couldn't find it anywhere in the data base," glancing at her superiors, she pauses, takes a deep breath, then adds, "that was not until I managed to connect with Ross Malcolm, a member at the Winnipeg detachment. He helped me locate it."

"So what did you find?" Greg asks, watching the constable's expression for any clues that might give away her news, but she's good at keeping her enthusiasm in check. "Is it registered to Murdock McCarthy?"

"No, Sir," she quickly replies.

"Who then?" Greg probes, his curiosity now peaked.

"A dead woman," Constable Murphy quickly tells him, her voice betraying her obvious excitement.

"Excuse me," Greg answers.

"That's right, Sir," she replies as she struggles to contain her pride. She desperately wants to impress these men with her investigative skills, but she also knows she can't seem too obvious because this information isn't about personal glory or career advancement. It's about finding a missing little girl—the daughter of her commanding officer. "A dead woman," she tells them. "That's why I couldn't find it at first because I was looking in the active files. Somehow the plate number is registered to a woman who's supposedly been dead for four years, so the plate is no longer in service."

"How can that be?" Greg looks at her and she can see he's puzzled. "We've seen the stickers on the plates that clearly show they were renewed for this year," he says. "You and I clearly saw them earlier today when we went to the house."

"We did," she says and nods. "We're not sure how he did it," the constable says, "but Constable Malcolm believes that somehow McCarthy managed to get his hands on a new sticker from another vehicle and just applied it to the van plate. That way, it looks current, especially if an officer is following from behind and as long he doesn't get pulled over, he can drive around for God knows how long on expired plates. No one is going to think the sticker doesn't belong to that plate without provocation."

"Smart," Cliff says. "But illegal. And he's never been caught in four years?"

"Apparently not, Sir," she nods. "He's been extremely lucky. If his plates had ever been run, the discrepancy would have shown up right away."

"It's uncanny," Greg observers. "But luck always seems to be on the side of the bad guys, for a while at least. Eventually, though, they make mistakes like sliding through a red light and almost ramming a police cruiser." He pauses, studies the young constable. He can clearly see she's proud of her efforts, as she should be, he thinks. He then asks, "So, if the plate isn't registered to McCarthy, then who?"

"Well, here's the thing," she replies and he can tell she still has lots of news to share. She's practically bursting at the seams. She takes another deep breath and continues. "It took him a while and some digging, but kudos to Constable Malcolm. . . . He found the plate number actually belongs to a dead woman named Wanda Demings."

"Who the hell is Wanda Demings?" Cliff asks.

"That was my question, too," she says, smiling at Cliff. "And what's her connection to Murdock McCarthy? Digging a little further, Constable Malcolm discovered that Wanda Demings was killed in a car crash four years ago and at the time of her death, she was living in Winnipeg, supposedly with her husband and three children, or," nodding toward a document she's printed off, now resting near the computer, "at least that's what it says in the official accident record. Constable Malcolm sent me a copy."

"So that would be a Mr. Demings," Cliff suggests.

"That's what you'd think," she continues with a nod and then quickly shakes her head. "But maybe not."

"How so?" Greg asks as he tries to digest the information. "Demings must be her maiden name then."

"Here's the thing," Constable Murphy explains. "A further search of the records reveals that at the time of her death, her official residential address was listed at 65 Westmount Avenue in Winnipeg. However, on a deeper search, Constable Murphy found that 65 Westmount Avenue is now a vacant lot and it's been that way for several years following a devastating fire that decimated the house."

"Where the hell is all this going?" Cliff asks.

"Good question," Greg says. "Please continue," he instructs Constable Murphy.

"When Constable Malcolm ran that civic address he found the property is registered to a Mr. Ronald Silver."

"No way," Cliff says.

"And there's more," she says. "This Mr. Silver was married and his registered spouse, according to provincial records, was . . . guess who?"

"Wanda Demings," Greg answers.

"Yes, Sir. Wanda Demings," she replies, beaming again. "And this couple did not have any children or at least any children that were officially registered anywhere in the province. There are no birth certificates, health records or school records for any children from Silver or Demings. According to the province of Manitoba, those children don't exist, yet this death certificate for Wanda Demings shows that she is survived by three children."

"And," Greg adds, "Murdock McCarthy has three children."

"Exactly," Constable Murphy answers, glancing at both senior officers. "That's a major coincidence isn't it, Sirs?"

"A bit," Cliff nods.

"The question then," Greg adds, "is Murdock McCarthy actually Ronald Silver?"

"Jesus," Cliff suddenly adds, his complexion turning a pale grey as he stares at his friend.

It looks like he has just seen a ghost, Greg thinks. "What's wrong Cliff? Are you okay? You don't have chest pains, do you?"

"God no," Cliff quickly says as he shrugs. "But do you realize what you just said?" Cliff asks.

"You mean that McCarthy could be Silver?" Greg replies.

"Say that second name again," Cliff tells Greg.

"Silver," Greg says, as he suddenly understands what his friend is now implying. "Jesus," he sighs heavily. "Silver."

"Jesus is right," Cliff says, the colour returning to his face.

"Sorry, Sirs," Constable Murphy jumps in while glancing at the senior officers. "But you've lost me."

"I'm not surprised," Greg says and then glances at Cliff again. "I'm not surprised one goddamn bit."

*****

"Should we wait for backup?" Constable Murphy asks as Greg parks the RCMP cruiser around the corner from Haddon House, now the residence of Murdock McCarthy and his three children. He knows it will be out of sight in this location.

"Probably," Greg agrees, glancing in the rear-view mirror at Cliff whose tall frame is squeezed into the cruiser's back seat separated from the front by a Plexiglas partition. "But the last thing I want to do is spook this guy by having a couple dozen officers swarm this place. We don't know anything about him and if he panics, God knows what he'll do."

"I understand, Sir," she nods, peering out through the windshield that's smeared with mud and salt spray from the roads. She notes that a light snow has started falling, the fluffy flakes landing on the grimy window and turning it white, before melting and running down the glass.

"If you don't feel comfortable going in there like this," Greg says to her, "I understand. It won't be a reflection on your service in any way. I completely understand. You've done exemplary work on this case and no one will fault you for not wanting to risk your well-being. Certainly, neither I nor Corporal Graham will hold it against you."

"No, Sir," Constable Murphy says shaking her head, her short blonde hair bouncing neatly back into place with each determined movement. "I'm in. You can count on me. I'll do whatever it is you need me to do."

"What about you, Cliff?" Greg asks, glancing again at his friend in the rear-view mirror.

"I'm good to go," Cliff says, "but you know that if something goes down here we're both going to be in a shitload of trouble since I'm not on official duty. There could be hell to pay."

"I trust you for backup, Cliff, and we need you," Greg says. "But just remember to let either me or Constable Murphy make any official arrests, if there are any to be made."

"Okay then," Cliff says, nodding to his colleagues in the cruiser. "Let's go have a chat with Mr. Murdock McCarthy or Ronald Silver or whoever the hell he is."

Pushing open the heavy, reinforced door of the cruiser and stepping out into the cold evening air, the salty Atlantic wind nipping at his face, Greg suddenly stops and stares at a nearby streetlight, its beam picking up the gently falling snowflakes.

"Something wrong?" Cliff asks, standing beside his friend. "Is everything okay?"

"I'm not sure," Greg answers as he observes five large black crows swooping through the gently falling snow and gliding on the cold currents. As they land and perch on a nearby snowbank near the lamppost, the muted light caressing their shimmering feathers, he says to Cliff, "Do you see them this time?"

"I do, buddy," Cliff answers. "I certainly do."

Chapter 32

"Emma," the slender man-boy calls out as he climbs the winding oak staircase to the second floor bedrooms. "Come here," he demands. "Right now."

Without saying a word, a petite-framed girl with light-coloured hair suddenly appears at the top of the stairs and stares down at him. He knows she's been crying as he can see the stains on her pallid face.

"What are you doing?" he yells.

"Nothing," she answers, her words barely escaping her small mouth.

"What did I tell you about that?" He snarls, taking the steps two at a time, his face twisted with rage.

"Sorry," she whispers.

"Stop it!" he commands. "Do you hear me? Stop it right now." He glares at her. "Go to your room and put some things in a bag, but only one bag."

"Why?"

"Because I told you to," he fires back. "Now go. Do as I say. We don't have much time."

"What about Daddy and Sophie?"

"Don't worry about them," he tells her, reaching the halfway point of the staircase. "I will take care of them. Now go and do as I say, right now. . . . Like I said, we don't have much time."

Stepping back from the stairway, she's about to ask him another question when a loud knock on the front door interrupts her.

"Shit." Lucas stops in his tracks. "Who the hell is that?" he says, standing still and hoping that whoever is at the door will leave if he doesn't answer.

He's just about to take another step, when he hears another, louder knock.

"Fuck." Turning to the tiny girl he says, "I'll get rid of whoever's at the door. You go to your room and do as I said . . . and be quick about it. . . . Remember, only one bag."

Saying nothing, Emma obediently scampers away from the top landing. The scrawny young man whose physical appearance masks his real strength, takes a deep breath, turns and makes his way back down the stairs and through the large foyer that at one time seemed vibrant and full of life, but today is dreary and dusty, the oak woodwork and the floors requiring a good scrubbing. Reaching the front door, he opens it just a crack and peers through.

"Yes," he says, greeting RCMP Sergeant, Greg Paris.

"Hi, Lucas," Greg says calmly. "Is your dad at home this evening? I would really like to speak with him, please."

"No, Sir," Lucas answers, keeping the door open enough that Greg can barely see his face.

"Do you know where he's gone?" Greg probes.

"No, Sir," the young man replies. "No, I don't."

"Do you know when he'll return?"

"No, Sir. He didn't tell me."

"I see," Greg says and nods, inching closer to the door. "Who's at home, Lucas?"

"Just me and my sisters, Sir."

"May I come in and talk to you?" Greg asks.

"No, Sir," Lucas quickly answers. "I am not supposed to let anyone in the house when Dad isn't home. He doesn't like that."

"Even if it's the police?"

"It doesn't matter," Lucas says. "I can't let you in."

"Do you get in trouble if you let people come inside when he's not home?"

"I don't know," the young man answers, his voice unrevealing — remaining low and monotone. "I guess so."

"What does he do when he gets mad at you?"

"I can't say, Sir."

"You can't say or you won't say because you think your father will be angry at you?"

"I can't say, Sir."

"What does he do, Lucas, when he gets mad?" Greg continues to question the young man.

"I'm sorry, Sir," Lucas replies. "But I really can't be talking to you. I think you should leave. . . . Please."

"Well, you see, Lucas," Greg says, reaching out to grab the door. "I'm really not ready to leave just yet."

Anticipating the officer's move, Lucas quickly pushes the door closed before Greg can reach it

"Shit," Greg says as he hears the locks click into place. Glancing toward Constable Murphy and his friend, Cliff, who remain off to the side and out of view from the door, he adds, "We've got a problem here. This situation doesn't feel right. Something is seriously wrong inside this house."

"What are we going to do?" Constable Murphy asks, and Greg sees the adrenaline kick in.

"Easy, Constable," Cliff cautions. "Let's knock the goddamn door down," he then suggests as he quickly moves into position beside his friend. He's ready to turn his body into a battering ram if that's what he has to do. "Clearly, these people have something to hide and to me that screams probable cause"

"Lucas," Greg calls out as he pounds on the door. "Open the door, Lucas, or we'll come in. This is your only warning."

"Come on, Greg," Cliff tells him. "We're wasting time. If you think something's going on in there, then we should go in right now."

"I know," Greg replies. "But we can't break this door down. It's too heavy. . . . Give me your baton," he says to Constable Murphy, the only one of the trio who is in uniform.

"What are you going to do, Sir?" she asks, sliding the retractable, black stick from the hook on her belt and handing it to her commanding officer.

"I'm going to break in," Greg says, taking the baton, bolting off the veranda and, plowing through the thigh-high snow drifts, he makes his way to a window that he believes is in the living room. Swinging the baton and shattering the glass, he says to his colleagues on the front veranda, "Stay right there. I'll let you in."

Using the baton to clear the broken glass from the sill, Greg then pulls himself up and through the opening. First pushing his legs through the shattered window, he enters the quiet house. Landing on his feet in the sparsely furnished room, he quickly takes a defensive position and glances around in the darkness, the oppressive silence embracing him.

"Lucas?" he yells, pulling his gun out of its holster. He plants his feet slightly apart and stands firm.

"Lucas," he calls again. "Murdock McCarthy? Are you in here? It's Sergeant Greg Paris with the Liverpool RCMP. Please present yourself. I am armed. You need to know that."

Silence fills the massive house as Greg slips a flashlight from his coat pocket and slowly makes his way through the darkened living room, into the entry foyer and then to the front door.

"Lucas," he yells again as he turns the lock to the front door and swings it open to allow Cliff and Constable Murphy, their weapons drawn, to enter the house. He chooses not to ask Cliff where he got the gun since his friend is not officially on duty and should not be carrying a weapon. "Please identify your location," he calls out. "And again, I'm warning you that we are armed. Murdock, we need to talk. . . . I have no idea what's going on in here, but please come to us before something tragic happens."

The officers stand firm in their positions at the front door and listen for any sign as to where the young man could have gone.

The trio is greeted only by silence.

"Okay," Greg says to his colleagues. "Constable, you and Corporal Graham take the upstairs level. I will take the ground floor." Slowly inching through the foyer as Emily and Cliff move toward the stairway, he adds, "Be careful. We have no idea what we're dealing with here."

"You don't have to tell us twice," Cliff replies, his gun in hand as he follows Emily up the winding oak staircase, their flashlights showing them the way.

*****

"You take the rooms to the right, Constable," Cliff says as he and Emily reach the top of the staircase. "I'll take the left side, but watch yourself. . . . I don't feel good about this."

"Yes, Sir," she replies, her breath, which seems drier now than it's ever been, catches in her throat.

"Deep breaths, Constable," Cliff says as they each enter the first room on their side of the long, dreary hallway. "Deep and slow."

"Yes, Sir," she answers, approaching the entrance to the first room on her right where a door clearly was hung. Examining the splinters, she can tell someone was bound and determined to gain access to this room. Shining her light along the shattered remains of the door casing, she decides that busting through a heavy door like this would take someone with a great deal of power and considerable strength. Hearing her own heart beating, she wills herself to step into the room.

"Lucas McCarthy," she says with as much force as she can muster. "If you are in this room, please show yourself. I am armed so no sudden movements, please. Step forward so I can see you."

Standing in the doorway entrance she shines the light around the room, the beam breaking the darkness and illuminating the empty space. She sees a single dresser and a bed with only one blanket and no sheet on the mattress.

"Lucas," she says again, stepping further inside, the beam from her flashlight bouncing around the room until she spots what she is sure is an unmistakable blood stain on the floor near the bed. Scanning the floor, the light illuminates a trail of blood stretching across the room.

Without another word, she approaches the stain, squats and shines the light directly on the puddle.

"Blood. . . . Fresh," she whispers, quickly pulling herself up and turning to face the bedroom door. It has suddenly become eerily quiet. Quieter than it had been, *if that's possible*. She feels like she's suffocating, as if all the air has suddenly been sucked out of the small room and the darkness is closing in on her.

In this position, she can see back out into the hallway and as she moves the beam from the flashlight into every corner, she pauses when she comes to what is clearly the closet.

Swallowing hard, she approaches the closed door, points her firearm at the door and says, "Lucas McCarthy, if you are in the closet, please come out with your hands raised. Do not make any sudden moves or *I will* fire."

Seconds later, after waiting to see if the young man will show himself, she approaches the closet door, grabs the knob and pulls it open. The beam from her flashlight immediately lands on the blood-soaked body of Murdock McCarthy that has been propped up on the closet floor, his head split wide open, leaning forward allowing the man's brain to spill out. Resting on his lap is a bloodstained axe, which the constable immediately concludes is the murder weapon.

"Corporal," she calls out while backing away from the closet and fighting the urge to vomit. Swallowing hard and gasping for air, she says, "I've found Murdock McCarthy …"

*****

Stepping lightly and keeping his breathing under control, Greg makes his way along the darkened corridor that leads from the entrance foyer to the massive kitchen where he's heard the previous owner pre-pared wonderful meals that attracted widespread acclaim. Greg shines his flashlight as he goes, scanning the walls and floors as he looks into every corner and space for anything that might help him unlock the mysteries that surround this family.

He calls out as he approaches the kitchen doorway, "Lucas McCarthy. This is the RCMP. This is a warning. I am armed. Please step forward with your hands raised."

It would be too simple, he thinks as he steps into the kitchen, for the young man to give himself up.

Slowly moving past the table, full of clutter, dirty dishes and a cereal box, he pauses and looks at several recent issues of the *The Daily Post* that are piled there, all their pages turned to stories about the missing girls. He shudders at the thought. He knows the fact that these newspapers are here, doesn't necessarily mean anything because they are likely in thousands of homes—it's the big news right now—but he still can't shake the uneasiness that has suddenly washed over him.

"Lucas," he calls out again. "It's Greg Paris here. I want to talk to you. Please show yourself right now."

Moving away from the table, he notices the door leading from the kitchen to the backyard is swinging open and the snow is blowing in. He approaches the entrance and pauses at the threshold where he calls the young man's name again.

"Lucas McCarthy," he says, kneeling and examining the footprints that are visible in the freshly falling snow.

"Damn," he whispers. It's obvious that someone has just gone this way and he's sure it was probably the young man.

*****

"Constable?" Cliff calls out while exiting the first room he had entered. "It's clear and empty in here. Not even a bed. Please acknowledge."

"Sir," Emily replies, exiting the room where she's just found the remains of Murdock McCarthy.

"Are you okay?" he asks as the two meet in the corridor and he quickly glances in both directions to make sure they are still alone.

"Yes, Sir." She swallows hard, her mouth and throat feeling like they're stuffed with cotton balls. "I'm fine."

"The old man's dead, isn't he?"

"Yes Sir," she answers, pausing in the centre of the darkened hallway. "There's no doubt about that. Looks like he was bludgeoned to death with an axe. . . . It's a real mess in there."

"Well that's certainly up close and personal," Cliff says. "Clearly, there was a lot of hate in this house."

"Brutal," she agrees. "There's lots of blood and . . . other things that no one should ever have to see."

"Are you sure you're okay?" Cliff asks again. He knows this is the constable's first exposure to such violence and he's worried about how she will react in these circumstances, but he has also been impressed with what he's seen of her the past few days and believes he can trust her for back up.

"Yes," she says, gripping tightly to her weapon with both hands. "I'm positive. I can handle it."

"All right then," Cliff says. "Let's move on, but be careful. We don't even know if anyone's up here."

"Yes, Sir," she says before slipping out of sight into the next room down the hall.

Approaching the door to the next room on his side of the hall, Cliff sees it's closed. He slowly turns the knob with his right hand. It's unlocked. *Good*, he thinks as he carefully pushes the door open, squinting to look inside.

"Lucas McCarthy," he calls out, shining his light into the darkened room and scanning the small area. He immediately sees a bed directly in front of the lone curtain-less window. Beside the bed he sees a dresser and not much else.

He steps into the room and then quickly spins around, shining the light into every corner. He's suddenly taken by surprise when he discovers a small child cowering near the closet like an abused dog terrorized by its master. She's shaking so violently that he can actually see her moving in the beam of his light.

"Emma," he whispers, rushing to the little girl. Kneeling in front of her and lowering his weapon, he asks, "Are you okay, honey?"

She says nothing but cries and tries to pull herself into a tiny ball.

"It's okay, Emma. I am not going to hurt you," he says maintaining a soft, gentle tone. "I'm going to help you." Quickly scanning her quivering body, he asks, "Are you hurt?"

The tiny girl sobs loudly.

"Constable," Cliff calls out. "Are you clear in that room over there?"

"Yes, Sir," she calls back. "Are you okay?"

"I am, but can you please come here?"

"Sir," she says, joining him seconds later. "Is everything okay?"

"Not exactly," Cliff says. "We've got a small child here who seems to be in shock and needs immediate medical attention. Get that blanket off the bed, please."

"What now, Sir?" she asks, handing him the blanket.

"Easy, Emma," Cliff whispers as he pulls the tiny child toward him and wraps the blanket around her trembling body. "Can you come with us, please?"

The child says nothing but does not resist as he picks her up and tenderly folds her into his strong arms, as if he was hugging his own daughter.

"Good job, Emma," Cliff whispers again as he feels her shaking.

To Constable Murphy he says, "Here's what you're going to do. I want you to take this child out of this house. Take her to the cruiser and keep her there. You stay with her and call for an ambulance and backup. I'm not sure where Greg has gone, but we need some help in here."

"What about you, Sir?" she asks, taking the child from Cliff. She balances her in her left arm while still keeping her gun in her right. The child immediately buries her head into Emily's shoulder and the constable pulls the blanket up over the girl's shoulders and neck.

"I am going to stay up here and keep looking," he says. "We still don't know where Lucas has gone."

"Will you be okay, Sir?" she asks, holding the child tightly as she makes her way to the door.

"Yes," he replies, standing and watching them pass through the doorway when the child suddenly speaks.

"Sophie," Emma whispers.

"What about Sophie?" Emily asks, glancing back at Cliff.

"Is Sophie up here somewhere?" Cliff asks.

"Yes," the child says, nodding slowly and pointing to a room two doors down. "Her bedroom."

"Okay, Emma," Cliff says nodding to Emily. "I'll get Sophie and you go with Constable Murphy. You'll be safe now."

Chapter 33

Come on, Greg, the tall, well-built police officer thinks as he ponders his next move. To look at him, it would be difficult to tell that he just celebrated his fifty-fifth birthday yesterday. Most people agree he looks more like he's in his mid-forties, but he couldn't care less about that right now. Presently, he's more interested in finding out what the hell is going on in this house.

"Get a grip," he says softly, willing himself to take slow, steady breaths as he steps through the back door from the dirty, cluttered kitchen and into the sprawling back acreage. At one time, the land was rich and fertile, giving way to acres of fresh vegetables. Cows grazed in the backfield and the barn was home to a variety of animals. It was a full-working farm, long before the house became a world-class bed and breakfast that welcomed guests from all over the world.

Today, it looks nothing like it did during its halcyon days of tall ships and sailors or more recently, as a tourist destination where visitors flocked to sample the hospitality at the welcoming B & B. The stately property has undergone many incarnations since it was first built over two-centuries ago as a wedding gift for a rich merchant's daughter. But based on what he's heard from Cliff Graham and others who have seen the property in its glory days, the place is now a mess and after what he's just seen in the kitchen, he would agree, but right now he can't shake the feeling that they've walked into something dangerous, maybe even evil. The stench of fear and loathing is palpable, hanging in the air like dense smoke from a raging fire.

He knows this feeling all too well. This is not the first time that Greg Paris has walked into a potentially life-threatening situation. In fact, he's done it more times over his extensive career than he cares to remember. But the circumstances tonight feel different. Despite being an internationally renowned forensic psychologist who has worked some of the highest profile cases on this continent and overseas, he can't seem to get an accurate read on these people. And that scares him because he has no idea what he may have just gotten himself and his two colleagues into.

Steady he thinks, scanning his surroundings and thrusting his hands in front of him. Armed with his Smith & Wesson and a flashlight, he steps into the fresh layer of snow that's fallen since the trio of police officers entered the front of the house nearly ten minutes ago now. Spinning around to make sure no one is sneaking up behind him, he scopes out the area.

"Exhale, Greg," he whispers.

Standing firm in the backyard, ready to fire if he feels threatened, the gently falling snow quickly turns Greg's head and shoulders white as he glances around, trying to figure out where the young man may have gone. It's dark here, far removed from any streetlights and the moon is fully blocked by the clouds that are now dumping more snow on the region.

"Where are you?" he whispers, shining his light from one group of snow-covered bushes to another and through trees that line the yard's perimeter, many of their branches bending to the breaking point from the extra weight following the recent snow storms.

"I know you're back here somewhere," he says, studying every shadow and scoping out every corner of the property.

He shudders as an eerie stillness descends on the yard, embracing him in its icy grip. The mood is dense and heavy. He can feel it. The stench of evil hangs in the air. He can smell it. There is danger here. He can sense it.

Stepping slowly, his boots plowing through the quickly accumulating snow, he moves to the outer perimeter of the yard where he sees a group of rotting outbuildings that have clearly, long ago outlived their usefulness. Shining his light over the dilapidated structures, many of them without windows and doors, some with their roofs caving in from decades of neglect, he looks for any sign of movement from within the obsolete structures.

"Lucas McCarthy?" he says, raising his voice to ensure he's heard clearly. "Are you in there? If you are, please come out with your hands raised and don't make any sudden moves. I am armed and prepared to fire."

Nothing.

"Shit!" A loud and piercing cackle suddenly startles him. He stops and turns toward the noise. He knows what it is. He's heard it countless times in recent days.

"Okay," he says, spraying the beam of light over the yard and buildings. "I hear you but I don't see you."

Listening carefully, he then hears the familiar cackling again, but this time he follows the ruckus. Shining his light between two of the dilapidated buildings, he spies the five crows prancing on top of the snow, moving about on the ground as if they're desperately trying to get his attention.

"There you are," he says gently, while slowly approaching the gathering of boisterous black birds, the snow landing on their sleek, ember feathers, quickly turning them white. "What do you want?"

The larger bird—the one Greg assumes is the leader—caws and quickly beats its wings, flapping them furiously. Watching the routine, the police officer gets the unmistakable feeling these birds are here to help him.

"What?" Greg says, standing before them. "What are you saying?" Glancing toward the space between the buildings, he asks, "This way? . . . Do you want me to go this way?"

The bird cackles and its eyes blink quickly as its companions form a line behind it, their obvious leader, as if they are soldiers preparing for inspection, or maybe going into battle. Greg watches the manoeuver with a mix of awe and apprehension.

"Is that what you're trying to tell me? You want me to go this way?" he says, slowly drawing close to the birds. They suddenly become very still. Standing their ground, the five avian guardians watch as the human passes by them.

"Easy does it, guys," Greg whispers, stepping lightly on the newly fallen snow as he goes. He's afraid that any sudden movement might startle the birds. "Did Lucas go this way? Did you see him? Is that what you're trying to tell me?"

The lead bird caws softly while tilting its head first to the right and then to the left, its beak slowly opening and closing as if it's attempting to answer the man's question. It blinks steadily.

Shining the light along a nearly invisible path leading into a dense growth of trees that Greg sees off in the distance, he breaths deeply. He is certain the crows have just shown him the way.

"This is it, isn't it?" he says softly turning to face the birds. "This is the way, isn't it?"

The larger bird caws again, only this time louder.

"Thanks, guys," he whispers, the words floating off with the falling snow.

Okay, he thinks as he turns to follow the barely visible path now blanketed with snow, *that's just downright creepy.*

"Let's see where this goes," he whispers as he begins his trek through the deep snow.

*****

Grasping the doorknob with his right hand, Cliff holds his pistol and flashlight in his left and takes a deep breath. He has no idea what he expects to find on the other side of the closed door, but he knows there's at least one more child here, somewhere, and he has to find her. Based on what he's already seen in this house and going with the feeling in his gut, he knows that anyone in here could be in grave danger, especially a small child unable to defend herself.

"Sophie?" he whispers while slowly pushing the wooden door inward a crack. He peers through cautiously. It's as black as ink inside the room.

"Sophie?" he calls the girl's name again, this time opening the door a bit wider. "Are you in here, Sophie?"

He never understood what people meant when they said "the silence was deafening." But right now, in this moment, he knows exactly what that means. The "silence" actually makes him shiver.

"Don't be scared, Sophie," he says, cautiously inching into the room. "It's Cliff Graham? Remember me? We've met before. I'm with the police. I'm here to help you."

He pauses to listen and then says, "Just call out to me, if you can. Or make any noise at all. Let me know where you are so I can find you."

He listens for any movement—anything that might tell him that someone is in the room, but he hears nothing.

"Sophie," he says again while easing through the doorway. "I promised Emma I would come and get you and bring you to her. She's okay but she really wants to be with you. If you're in here, please say something. You're safe now. I'm the police and I've come to take you out of here. No one can hurt you anymore, I promise you."

Nothing but silence.

Stopping just inside the doorway, Cliff slowly pans the flashlight around the room until the beam finds its way to the bed where it lands on a figure resting there, the still and lifeless form instantly confirming his worst fears.

"God," Cliff cries as he feels his heart drop to his stomach. His breath catches in his throat and he fights the urge to vomit.

"God," he says again, this time it is more like a question. His mind searches for an explanation as to how anyone, including God, could allow such an atrocity to happen. He rushes to the bed, but he knows he's too late to help this child.

Standing over the bed, he roams the light over the tiny body that lays naked, on the bare mattress. He recognizes Sophie McCarthy right away and he knows she's been dead for a while. Her pale skin has turned an unnatural putrid grey.

"You poor child," he begins to sob as he steps closer to the bed. He suddenly falls to his knees, the flashlight's beam following to the girl's chest. Cliff doesn't have the will to move, so the light lingers on the centre of the girl's chest for several minutes while he tries to gather his composure. As he is about to rise, Cliff notices a tiny silver cross that has been purposely positioned on the girl's tiny chest. He can see a thin silver chain sparkle as it catches in the light beam.

"Jesus," Cliff says, the word catching in his throat. Spinning on his heels and bolting toward the bedroom door he hopes he's not too late.

"Greg," he calls out, darting into the dark corridor. "Where did you go? . . . Greg? Answer me. Where are you?"

*****

Stepping carefully to maintain his footing, Greg follows what he believes to be a path. It's clear that someone else has recently come this way, but with all the fresh snow still steadily falling, the trail is nearly obliterated. It's simply too difficult to distinguish any new footprints. Regardless, he's confident he's going in the right direction because this is where the crows have told him to go and for some reason that he really can't explain, he trusts the birds.

Thinking about the events of the past few days, he's now convinced the five crows have been guiding him all along through the maze that has been this investigation. He now believes they have been trying to lead him to this house and to this family from the very first time he saw them. He doesn't yet fully understand what it all means, but he's sure he will have a better picture once he's had time to study all the facts and gather all the information.

He can't explain the crows' unusual and bizarre behaviour. He's heard the stories about how the crows in this region seem to be involved in situations that defy logic and at first, he dismissed the talk as absolute nonsense. He's listened as his best friend, Cliff, has gone on and on over the years about how the crows have been in the middle of some of the most extreme cases he's ever dealt with.

And then, Greg thinks as he trudges on toward the patch of trees, there's Clara Underwood. He has no idea how to explain her or her uncanny abilities, but recalling the conversation he and Cliff had a few days ago in her home, he now knows the old woman's predictions were one hundred per cent accurate.

He swallows hard as the adrenaline kicks in. Pausing to wipe snow from his face, he focuses on the trees in front of him.

"*How can that be?*" he wonders.

He shrugs, moving forward again and accepting that he cannot explain the strange woman, but he's now convinced that somehow Clara has a connection to these crows that is beyond the bounds of nature, as he knows it.

"They know everything that happens around here," he remembers

Clara telling him and Cliff when they called on her as their investigation was just getting underway. She insisted the crows are intelligent and from where they roost, they can see everything that happens around his town.

He was skeptical at first, he admits that, but she told him the crows were like guardians charged to take care of their flock and if he was seeing them, then they were trying to reach out to him. Thinking about recent events he now knows that to be true, he just doesn't know why they would have chosen him.

The thing that amazes him is how Clara knew the significance of the number of crows and how they seem to fit into the case. He reaches the outer peripheral of the trees. As he steps through the snow, he recalls Cliff reciting the rhyme—"One crow sorrow, two crows joy, three crows a letter, four crows a boy, five crows silver . . . "

"The number five," he remembers the old woman saying, was a definite clue.

Pausing before he enters the line of trees, he recalls her words.

"Each number in the flock is a specific message," she had said. "If they are coming in a group of five, then that means something silver plays an important role in their message."

"Silver," Greg says aloud as he steps further into the woods, following the path that's leading him God knows where and into God knows what.

She was right when she told him that silver might be a reference to something made of silver, like maybe jewellery, but she also said it could mean something else and he now knows she was right about that as well.

"It's not always about the obvious," she cautioned. "Don't look for the easy meaning, it's not always that simple. And sometimes, there can be double meaning in their messages."

Greg swallows as he now believes that while the obvious connection to the five crows may have been the silver crosses found on the bodies of the young girls, it could have also been that the crows were trying to bring him to Ronald Silver or, as Greg now knows him, Murdock McCarthy.

He's still not sure about the man's connection to the missing girls and their murders and he still doesn't know if Murdock is somehow responsible for taking his daughter. He turns a bend in the trail and stumbles upon a ramshackle structure with no windows. It is hidden back under a stand of fir trees. It suddenly becomes clear to him that all of these circumstances have been designed to bring him here, to this place.

Chapter 34

"Get up," commands the man-boy with the gaunt, pasty complexion. His eyes are haggard and sunken into his rather large skull and encircled by large black rings as if he hasn't slept in many days.

The little girl winces as he yells at her. She tries hard to hold back her tears.

"I said, to get the fuck up," he now screams, rushing up to the bed and leering at the petite girl who is cowering on the dirty mattress like an old and beaten mongrel who has been caught stealing a scrap of food on the floor. "Get up. . . . I said that I want you to get up right now."

She tries to tell him that with her arms drawn behind her back and bound at the wrists, she isn't able to move quickly, but he doesn't give her enough time to respond. Instead, she just whimpers and tries to wriggle from his grasp.

"Ow," she cries as he grabs her by the shoulders and forces her to sit up straight. "It hurts." She sobs loudly at first. "I want to go home. . . . Let me go home," she sobs as she begins to plead.

Grabbing the end of the duct tape roll that he stashed under the bed after the last time he used it in here, he rips off several inches and pushes the grey strip of adhesive over her tiny mouth.

"Shut up. Shut up. Just shut up," he yells, pulling a length of yellow nylon rope from his jeans pocket and wrapping it around her ankles, rendering her completely helpless. "Just shut the fuck up. I can't stand it when you cry." He pulls the rope tight. "Kids should never cry. Kids are supposed to be seen and not heard."

She is now unable to move her body at all. He's made sure she can't cry out. She is totally vulnerable and entirely at his mercy.

Taking her by the feet he roughly swings them around while at the same time pushing her head back down to the mattress. She's now stretched out straight as he hovers over her.

"There's been a change in plans," he sneers, enjoying the fear he sees in his young victim's eyes.

"I was going to take you away from all of this and we were going to be happy together for a long time," he says, turning to a small wooden chest he had brought out here earlier today after his father tried to take his things. He had to keep the box safe from anyone else. "Just you and me," he adds. "It was just going to be the two of us. But now things have changed."

Retrieving the chest, he thinks about his father and remembers how much he enjoyed driving the axe into the old man's skull. He relives the rush he felt when the blade crunched through the bone, spewing blood in all directions. He remembers how he felt when his father's warm blood splashed on his face. He liked it . . . no, he thinks, *I loved it. The old bastard had it coming.*

He breathes deeply, sucking the air in through his thin, pert lips. As the image of his father slumping to the floor flashes before him, he relishes the memory and he smiles.

I showed him, he thinks, wiping at the froth that's bubbling from the corners of his drawn lips. *The old man will never touch me or my things ever again.*

"I warned him," he says to his tiny prisoner who's flouncing around on the dirty cot. He basks in the glow of her vulnerability. *I am the master.* "I warned him to stay away from me, but the old bastard wouldn't listen. But I showed him." Snuffing his nose, and glaring at the tiny girl, he repeats, "I showed him real good this time."

As the tears finally break through the dam he's been building for as long as he can remember, he cries, "I've made sure the old man will never touch my things ever again."

Clearing his throat, he watches the little girl squirm on the mattress. "Stop it," he says, bringing his hands to his eyes. "Stop it. I hate it when you cry. . . . Kids aren't supposed to cry."

Pulling back his own tears, he towers over the bed as he considers his next move.

"You were going to be mine," he tells the young girl as the spit froths at the corners of his mouth like a rabid dog. "You were going to be with me forever, just like the others were. Sophie. Emma. And all the others before them. . . . They were mine. I found them and took them away from those other places. Father was mad at me at first when he saw what I had done, but then he let me keep Sophie and Emma after I promised him I wouldn't take anymore. I kept them with me all this time. They were happy. They liked being with me and they forgot all about those other mean people they used to live with. I saved them from those people . . . from their *mommies* and *daddies*, just like I was going to save you."

She whimpers as the duct tape makes it difficult for her to breathe.

He rants, "After I saw you at Christmastime, I knew I couldn't keep my promise to father but I was never going to tell him about you . . . father would not understand. . . . I had to rescue you. It was my duty, my mission. You were going to be my secret, but father had to get in the way. He had to get into my things and ruin my plans. He paid for that. He will never get in my way ever again—ever."

Glaring at Lucy, the tears streaming down her face, he snarls, "You would have liked it with me and you would have forgotten about those other people, just like the others did. I would have made you forget, too, but now, those people have come and ruined my plans. . . . They've ruined everything I worked for. They ruined all my plans. Why do people do that? Why can't they just leave me alone? Father would never leave me alone. Do this. Do that. *Do what I tell you. Keep your mouth shut.* It was always about him, but now he's out of the picture for good. I've taken care of that."

Flipping open the lid on the pine box and removing a thin silver chain with a tiny silver cross, the man-boy with the pale skin looks longingly at it.

"Mother loved these crosses," he whispers, his eyes bulging.

"Father and mother took me, too, when I was your age and they helped me forget. They rescued me."

He pauses and swallows, again wiping his eyes.

"I don't remember much about my other life, because they told me I was supposed to be with them. They said that's how it was meant to be, that they were told I belonged to them. They gave me therapy through Jesus and showed me the truth. Mother said that no matter what happened, I would always find my power from the cross. She gave all her children one of these beautiful crosses and now I give them to my children. . . . Mother would have liked you, Lucy. Unlike father, she would have praised me for finding and rescuing you. She would have helped me to keep you and take care of you."

He looks down at Lucy, his eyes showing an inkling of compassion for a mere second. Then just as quickly, it is gone and the dead blackness returns as he stares back into the empty room. "She would have given you shelter and you would have become one of hers. She was so special." He lowers his head and begins to cry again. "I miss her so much. I don't know why she had to die. I wish it had been Father. I wish he had been the one to die and not her, but we don't have to worry about him anymore, do we? I saw to that. He won't be able to bother me now."

Touching the tiny cross with the index finger on his emaciated, bony right hand, its dirt-encrusted fingernails indicating he hasn't washed for some time, he pauses and closes his eyes as his tears stream down his cheeks.

"Mother . . ." He lets out a long sob. "I miss you so much."

He shakes violently for several seconds, sobbing with such ferocity that it moves the bed and the little girl trapped there.

Then, without warning, he stops and remains still. Silence descends on the dark room as his mood suddenly changes.

"I have one of these for you," he eventually says, his voice now surprisingly soft. "I don't have time to cleanse you like I did all the others, but I can still give you this wonderful gift."

Dangling the cross in front of her eyes, he tells the child, "It will link us for all eternity. You will be with me forever. . . . you'll be mine."

Holding the chain in his right hand, he stands over her as if he's about to preach to her.

"This cross will protect you no matter what happens," he says, leaning in to get close to the tiny girl who is trying desperately to squirm away from him.

*****

Approaching the heavy wooden door, built with large planks like he remembers seeing on historical buildings and museums, Greg pauses. *This place has been here for a while*, he thinks, his eyes quickly scanning the structure that looks surprisingly sturdy for its age. He knows it's essential to assess the situation before rushing into a building, let alone one where a suspect may be lurking, and this place looks pretty secure to him.

Pushing as close to the door as he can without touching it, he stills his breathing, calms his nerves and listens for any noise from within. It's quiet in here under the dense growth of trees—*too quiet* he thinks—so he should be able to hear any noise inside the building.

Although he is not a history expert, he would guess, considering the location of this structure on a secluded area of the property, that at one time, when this place was a fully functioning farm, this building was most likely a slaughterhouse. Far removed from the main property he knows livestock could be butchered here without disturbing the main residence. He shudders at the prospect and tries to forget about all the blood that must have been spilled here over the years. He also thinks the old building would be an ideal place to hide prisoners.

Blocking out his surroundings and other distractions, he strains his ears and while he cannot distinguish the words, he is certain he can hear someone talking inside. The words are muffled, but based on their tone, he's confidant he has just located Lucas McCarthy.

Thinking again of the five crows and how the black birds showed him the way, he feels a cold shiver rush up his spine. He knows he'll never be able to understand how or why the mysterious birds reached out to him, but he is thankful they did. *And thank you Clara Underwood*, he thinks, remembering her advice about allowing the crows into his heart and mind. He's certain that without the old woman's help, he would not have found his way here.

Firmly gripping his Smith & Wesson, he swallows hard and gently pushes on the heavy door, hoping he can open it, slip inside and take a defensive position well before the young man sees or hears him and has time to react because at this point, he has no idea what Lucas McCarthy might do if he feels threatened.

*****

Reaching around the girl's neck, Lucas brings both ends of the thin silver chain together and fastens the tiny clasp.

"There," he whispers, standing straight again. "It looks lovely on you. You are now complete. You look like an angel . . . my angel."

He stands quietly, hovering over the bed, as if admiring the small and fragile young girl who is squirming on the mattress and trying to free herself, her eyes bulging with fear.

He speaks again.

"Stop struggling," he tells her, his voice still calm. "It will all be over very soon. This is not how I wanted it to be for us, but when those people came to the door, everything changed. Now . . ." he pauses. Then moving in close to her, he adds, "Now I have to change my plans and that means I have to go away. I want to take you with me but there is no time to get you ready, so I am going to take care of you. . . . But don't be afraid, Lucy. With my cross around your neck, you will be safe. ... Mother will always be there to look over you."

Placing his bony right hand over her tiny face, he whispers again, "You will be safe with her."

As the girl tries to kick at him with her feet that are bound tightly together, he slowly applies pressure over her nose and mouth, still covered with duct tape.

"Lucas," a deep, harsh voice suddenly explodes in the darkness of the slaughterhouse.

Except for the glow of a lone battery operated lantern that sits beside the bed, there is no light in the building, but it's enough for the seasoned police officer to see the child on the bed and the young man physically assaulting her.

"Lucas McCarthy," Greg says, his voice stern and harsh. "Step away from the bed," he commands. "*Right now.*"

The young man-boy refuses to comply with the order but instead continues to apply pressure to the girl's face.

"Lucas McCarthy," Greg says again, louder this time. "This is your *last* chance. Move away from the girl or I will shoot. Again, I am telling you, this is your last warning. . . . Take your hands off her and do it right now."

"No," Lucas seethes, the single word dripping with anger.

"Now," Greg commands, firing a shot into the ceiling of the old building. "That was a warning, Lucas. The next one is for you and I *promise* I will not miss."

"You bastard," Lucas screams, suddenly turning from the girl on the bed and lunging toward Greg with such agility that he sees nothing but a blur in the dim light. "You ruined everything," the man-boy snarls. "You can't have her back. I won't let her go."

"Lucas," Greg warns, standing firm near the door, his feet anchored on the hard ground floor and spread slightly apart, his arms stretched out straight, elbows locked in place and weapon at the ready. "Stop. If you take one more step toward me, I will fire."

"Bastard," the emaciated man-boy screams as he sprints toward the police officer wielding what appears to be a knife that he must have hidden somewhere on his body.

"I'm sorry, Lucas," Greg whispers as he squeezes the trigger. "But you give me no choice."

Greg watches as the bullet finds its mark in the young man's chest. He's an excellent marksman, so he knows he hit his heart. He watches as the child abductor and killer, staggers toward him and then falls to the dirt floor near his feet like a limp ragdoll. He watches as his body spasms several times and then goes still.

He knows Lucas McCarthy is dead and while he thinks he should have some remorse for just having taken another man's life, he has no regrets. He feels no sympathy for the man who became a monster largely because of his environment and because of circumstances beyond his control.

Lowering his pistol, he sprints toward the bed where his daughter is squirming. He can hear her muffled sobs from under the duct tape.

"Lucy," he cries, reaching the bed. Bending and taking hold of the duct tape, he slowly peels it off his daughter's mouth. "I'm here, baby. . . . It's Daddy. I'm here. You're safe now. . . . I've got you."

"Daddy." She cries as Greg quickly kisses her on the forehead.

"Lay still, honey," he says as he moves to untie her feet and then her hands.

"Daddy," she says through her deep sobs. "The bad man hurt me."

"I know, honey," he whispers "I'm so sorry," he says, losing the battle to hold back his tears. "The bad man hurt a lot of people, but he's gone now. He can't hurt you anymore. . . . I promise he can't hurt you anymore." Picking her up and hugging her tightly in his arms, Greg says, "Let's get you out of here. Mommy will be very happy to see you."

"Greg," Cliff calls from outside the building.

"In here," he yells back.

"Are you okay," Cliff asks as he enters the windowless building and immediately sees the dead boy's body sprawled on the dirt floor. In the subdued light from the battery-powered lantern, he also sees the knife resting not far from his right hand. Kicking the weapon out of reach, he adds, "I heard gun shots and I was afraid you had been hurt."

"I'm good," Greg tells him, as the tears roll down his cheeks. "I'm good now."

"Uncle Cliff," Lucy says, as Greg rushes to get his daughter out of the death house. "The bad man is gone now."

"Yes, honey," Cliff bends and checks the young man's pulse. "The bad man is gone now and it's time to take you home."

Chapter 35

It has been eight days since the investigation into the abducted and murdered young girls came to a head with the events at the once celebrated Haddon House. As Greg sits behind the commander's desk for the last time, he sighs in relief.

I need a break, he thinks, scanning the piles of paper work in front him. The tower of reports seem daunting to him.

He knows it's time to consider everything that has happened since he brought his family here last year and that includes trying to figure out what he wants to do with the rest of his career. He was relieved when Division told him Cliff was cleared to return to work anytime he feels he's ready, which Greg hopes will be very soon. He has no regrets about turning the reigns of command for the thirteen-member detachment back over to his best friend.

In fact, he thinks, as he slips several eight-and-a-half-inch sheets of paper into a red folder, if they hadn't cleared Cliff to return to duty, he might have actually been ready to step down and turn the detachment over to someone else.

This case has taken its toll, both on his family and on his mental health. He fears he may have lost the edge that made him one of the best forensic investigators in the country. Before this case, he was able to look at the evidence and disconnect with the human side of the story, but now he fears he can longer do that. He knows something has changed in how he functions as an investigator. He's lost his edge and he's not sure he'll be able to get it back. A rest is what he needs and now that he has earned the extra time, he plans to take several months to do nothing but unwind and plan for his family's future. He's positive he'll continue to remain in law enforcement, because it's what he knows and loves, but in what capacity and where he'll do it, he's just not sure. All he knows right now is that he needs a change. And as long as it includes his family, he is fine with whatever life throws his way.

Now, as he awaits Cliff's arrival this morning, he dreads telling his friend that he and his family are leaving Liverpool as soon as all the paper work is wrapped up. He likes the town and the people he's met here the past few months, and he enjoys being close to the man who has been more like a brother to him over the past twenty-five years than his own biological brothers, but he can't, in all good conscious, stay any longer. Too many things have happened to his family since they moved here and he can't risk their safety any longer. Since last November, Lucy has almost drowned, she's been stabbed with a pair of scissors and was hospitalized for over a week, and then to top it off, she was abducted by a crazed madman who almost killed her.

Enough, he thinks.

A few more seconds, he shudders, and he's certain Lucy would have died, terrified and alone, in that dilapidated slaughterhouse. Something evil that he cannot explain or understand has taken hold of this town and, in turn, it has gotten hold of his daughter. She is his number one priority now—Lucy, his wife, Andrea, and their unborn child.

He knows he can't risk losing any of them, so once this transition of power is complete, over the next few days, he and Andrea will pack up the house and leave Liverpool—forever. They'll first move back to Ottawa where he can still work for the force if he chooses, but at this point, he's not sure where they'll finally end up.

"But," he sighs, "It can't be here."

"Sorry?" Cliff says, as he strolls into his office and places an extra-large black coffee on the cluttered desk in front of his friend. "Did you say something?"

"Huh?" Greg replies as he looks up from the papers he's scanning and smiles.

He's amazed and impressed at how good Cliff looks. Only a few months earlier, he was a middle-aged man poised precariously on the brink of self-destruction, death an imminent outcome, but now, after a near-fatal heart attack that led to several months of dieting, steady exercise and self-discovery, Greg thinks his friend literally looks like a new man.

"I asked what you said," Cliff replies, taking the chair in front of the desk and across from Greg as Constable Emily Murphy follows him in and sits in a second chair beside him.

"Nothing." Greg smiles at him. "I didn't say anything. . . . Thanks for the coffee."

"Okay." Cliff shrugs, staring at his friend. "Are you okay, Greg?"

"Yup."

"You're sure?"

"I am." Greg nods.

"And Lucy," Cliff asks. "How's the little angel doing?"

"She's still having nightmares."

"I'm sure she is."

"Physically, the doctors say there are no scars, but you and I both know what kind of lasting mental and emotional impact this sort of thing can have, especially on someone so young."

"I'm sure she'll be fine," Cliff offers with a reassuring smile. "She's a smart kid and she's got great parents who know how to get her through this."

"I hope so," Greg says. "I hope so."

"Should we begin," Cliff asks, glancing at Greg and Constable Murphy. "Are we all ready to digest what we know about this case?"

"Let's do it," Greg says and nods.

"Yes, Sirs," Emily answers. "I'm ready."

"Okay then," Greg says as he looks to Cliff. "Let's go right back to the beginning. Take us through it, friend."

"This is what we know," Cliff begins.

*****

Cliff takes a deep breath and reviews the facts.

It started last fall when the McCarthy family moved to town. They bought the Haddon House, a world-class bed and breakfast business that had a reputation as one of the finest tourist accommodations in the province. . . . At one time, it was also reputed to be haunted, but that's another story.

Right from the start, everyone thought the McCarthy family was a strange bunch, especially the father, Murdock, who outwardly appeared to dominate his family and to those who noticed such things, it was clear he ruled the household with an iron fist. It was like the kids were terrified of him and in turn, they acted as though they were afraid to be around other people. They didn't talk and hardly smiled. They remained sheltered and hidden away. And they didn't easily make friends.

There were three children in the family. The girls were Emma, aged eight, and Sophie, who was two years older. They were darling kids and seemed like sweethearts but it was difficult to know for sure because they mostly kept to themselves.

Then there was Lucas, the eldest. Physically, he looked like a boy who could pass for fifteen or sixteen, but in truth, he was twenty-three. He was the more vocal of the three McCarthy kids, often speaking for his sisters and appearing overly protective of them, but it was clear from the beginning that he was aloof and flighty. Outwardly, though, it was difficult to pinpoint exactly what his story was.

It was clear the McCarthy family was shrouded in mystery. Eventually, it was discovered the children never went to school anywhere and there are no official records for any children born in Manitoba with the names Emma, Sophie or Lucas McCarthy. In short, they did not exist and that's because they do not. They aren't real.

It was discovered that Murdock McCarthy was actually Ronald Silver and with his wife, Wanda Demings, it now appears the couple prowled the western provinces, trolling for children and are believed to be responsible for the abductions and disappearance of several dozen young boys and girls over a twenty-year period. It's believed that DNA tests will confirm that Lucas McCarthy was actually Robbie Finch who went missing from his home in Lethbridge, Alberta, when he was four years old. The parents never saw him again and it was believed the boy was long dead. It was a poster hanging in the Liverpool detachment that included a computerized rendition of what Robbie might look like today that finally led police to the boy. Silver and Demings had raised the boy as their own son, giving him a new identity and keeping him hidden from prying eyes.

Whatever happened to the other children that it's believed the couple may have abducted remains a mystery for now. However, once spring arrives and the ground thaws, Winnipeg police will be undertaking an excavation of the property where the couple's home once stood. It was levelled by fire several years ago, but police now suspect that many of those missing children are buried somewhere on that property.

As for the two young McCarthy girls, Emma and Sophie, it is now believed they were actually abducted by Lucas and taken into the home. However, their real identities are not yet known, but it's hoped DNA will help us locate their real parents. It's believed that once he became assimilated into the Silver-Demings family, Lucas—or Robbie—suffered a psychotic break and subsequently began emulating his "parents'" behaviour. In short, he believed it was normal to take children from their parents because that is exactly what had happened to him.

It's believed that Silver, a.k.a. McCarthy, may have moved to Nova Scotia to actually protect his "son" and to intervene in perhaps a misguided effort to prevent the boy from straying too far. Why Silver would suddenly think to prevent his son from following in the family footsteps remains a mystery, but it's clear that when the "family" unit imploded, we believe Silver had most likely discovered what the young man had been doing here and attempted to intervene. As a result, Silver ended up dead, the victim of a brutal axe attack by the boy.

As the pressure mounted, and Lucas felt the authorities were closing in on him, he methodically planned his escape and that included eliminating his "siblings," who by this time had become excess baggage. Before police could reach him, Lucas had already killed Sophie and it's believed he would have eventually killed the younger one as well. If he was going to survive the perceived threat the police presented, he decided he had to make a clean break and flee the house to go God knows where. The RCMP thwarted his efforts to escape before he could harm the young girl he had abducted, the young

Lucy Paris, who is the four-year-old stepdaughter of RCMP Sergeant Greg Paris. The boy was shot and killed in the ensuing investigation. That shooting is still under investigation but should be concluded very shortly and Sergeant Paris is expected to be cleared.

Regrettably, however, Lucas McCarthy has left a trail of heartbreak in the southwestern region of Nova Scotia that started with the abduction and eventual murder of five-year-old Holly Conrad and included victims Hillary Lawrence, aged seven, and Ruby Smith who was eight. Why he chose those girls still partially remains a mystery, but something attracted him to them, be it their physical appearance, the fact that they were isolated children and he may have believed they were lonely, or it could have been that he related to them on an intellectual level and had come in contact with them in the days leading up to their abduction. But whatever it was that brought these girls to his attention, died with him.

The investigation into these crimes following the young man's death revealed that after moving to Liverpool last fall, Lucas McCarthy had successfully acquired a part-time job for a regional courier service that operated in the southwestern region of the province. The company's records confirm that Lucas, who acted as an on-call driver and filled in for the full-time employees, had frequented Windsor, Yarmouth and Bridgewater in the weeks and days leading up to the subsequent disappearance of the victims, giving him ample opportunity to stalk the girls and then to steal them away when the opportunity presented itself.

While witnesses now confirm sightings of a white van in the neighbourhoods where the missing girls lived and went to school, at first, it was wrongly assumed that vehicle was the one owned by Murdock. In fact, it is now known the courier service operates with white vans. Two of the courier vans used by Lucas have been taken into custody and are currently being processed for forensic evidence. The courier company is fully cooperating in this process.

The boy's ritual of "cleansing" the remains and presenting the body with a silver cross—a token of his affection and appreciation—is most likely connected to some sort of activity performed by his father or mother or both, but again, those secrets died with Lucas.

*****

Glancing at Greg and then Constable Murphy, Cliff adds, "That's it."

"Thanks, Cliff," Greg says. "I think that just about sums things up." Glancing to Constable Emily, he adds, "Anything to add, Constable?"

"No, Sir," she answers. "I think the Corporal has covered everything that we know so far. Except for a few loose ends, I think we've wrapped it up."

"Not quite," Greg shakes his head. "Listen, Constable Murphy— Emily— you should know that both Corporal Graham and I recognize the valuable role you played in bringing this investigation to a successful conclusion."

"I was just doing my job, Sir," she shrugs.

"Indeed," Greg replies. "But seriously, we appreciate the extra effort and time you put into the case. You stuck with it from the beginning and there's no way we would have found our way to McCarthy as quickly as we had without your efforts that subsequently took you down the road to finding the man's true identity. We may have gotten there eventually, but God knows how long that would have taken or how many more children would have died before then."

"Thank you, Sir," she nods. "I appreciate the fact that you acknowledge that, but I was just following the clues."

"Being a good detective is not only about recognizing the clues but also knowing what to do with them," Cliff adds. "You exhibited those skills during this investigation and as a result, Sergeant Paris and I would like to recommend you for the Undercover Division in Halifax. Are you interested in that, Constable?"

"Yes, Sir," she says, her face beaming. "I am. Very much, Sir."

"Great," Cliff says. "Consider it done. We'll start the paper work right away. It will take a while to complete everything, but we'll get the ball rolling."

"As well," Greg jumps in. "I will place a letter of citation in your permanent file so the record shows your achievements. It will reflect on your future promotions."

"Thank you, Sirs," she answers, smiling with obvious pride that these two experienced and respected officers would recognize something special about her. "I don't know what to say."

"You don't have to say anything." Cliff smiles at her.

"Just go out there and catch those bad guys," Greg adds.

"You can count on it," she says and nods.

"Very well," Greg says. "I think we're done here for now. You're excused, Constable."

"Great," Cliff says, rising from his chair as Emily stands and extends her hand to Greg. "I've got a lot to do today. It's my last day of freedom."

"Just a second, Cliff," Greg says, waiting for Constable Murphy to leave the room. "I need to talk to you about something else. I've got one more thing I need your help with. I need some answers."

"Answers about what?" Cliff asks, studying his best friend's body language for any clues as to what he's talking about.

"You're going to think I'm crazy, but I need to go back and talk with Clara Underwood," Greg says. "I just can't stop thinking about her role in all of this. Will you go with me?"

"Sure . . . I guess," Cliff nods. "But I gotta say that I was more than a little freaked out after our last visit with the old lady. I'll admit she spooked me out with all that talk about the crows and what they were trying to tell us. . . . And all those personal things she knew about us, well, let's just say it left me wondering about her."

"Me too," Greg nods and smiles at his friend. "But that's precisely why I need to talk to her. It just feels like I've got some unfinished business with her. So what do you say? Want to go have a talk with her?"

"Sure," Cliff agrees and turns toward the office door. "Let's go get it done."

Epilogue

"Maybe we should have called ahead," Cliff suggests as Greg guides the RCMP cruiser down the narrow gravel road. The modest homes are built far apart, showcasing what will be beautiful gardens shortly, when spring arrives.

Greg thinks the area looks a lot different today than it did a few weeks ago, following what both men hope was the last major blizzard of the season. In two weeks, the snow has all but melted and the bare, muddy ground is now exposed. Spring is still officially a month away, but the temperatures have been steadily rising and most weather forecasters agree the winter season is finally over.

"I've already seen crocuses blooming all over town," Cliff says, changing the subject, "And they say that when the crocuses bloom this early, it means an early spring."

"Who the hell is *they*?" Greg says.

"I don't know," Cliff quickly answers. He shrugs. "It's *they*. As in 'they say.'"

"You and your old wives' tales," Greg laughs as he makes a right turn down a long and rough driveway, obviously not built for vehicles.

"Hey, mister," Cliff fires back. "Don't make light of the things you don't understand. Haven't you learned anything from what you've just gone through?"

"Yes," Greg answers while glancing at his friend. "As a matter of fact, I have, and I've been meaning to talk to you about that."

"Oh, oh." Cliff forces an exaggerated sigh. "That doesn't sound good. What's up?"

"Well," Greg begins, holding the steering wheel loosely and letting the tires follow the deep ruts in the mud. "Here's the thing. After you get settled back down in your job and I'm free, Andrea and I are leaving town."

"What? Why?"

"Seriously, Cliff?" The statement is more of a question. Greg keeps his eyes glued to the almost non-existent driveway that winds through thick stands of pine and fir trees. It leads back to an isolated property, far removed from the nearest neighbour. He quickly turns to his friend, trying to keep his anxiety tightly secured, as he has done ever since arriving in this small town. "There's no way we can stay here after everything that's happened to us."

Cliff pauses and then shakes his head.

"No, I guess you're right," he reluctantly agrees. "After everything that's gone down, it would be difficult on Andrea and Lucy."

"I can't expect them to stay here and, honestly, I don't want to stay," Greg says as he finally pulls up in front of the small neglected house. Its weather-beaten shingles cry out for a coat of paint.

"It looks deserted," Cliff observes, his well-trained eyes quickly scanning the property. "See, I told you we should have called ahead before coming all the way out here. Maybe she's away."

"I doubt she'd expect us to call," Greg says, putting the transmission in park and turning off the ignition. Glancing around the yard, through the mud-covered windshield, he whispers as though someone, or something, is listening, "Something doesn't feel right."

"I'm suddenly thinking the same thing," Cliff answers, opening the passenger side door and swinging his long legs out of the car. His boots immediately sink into the deep mud that now covers his ankles. "It's like a freaking sauna out here," he says to Greg who has also gotten out of the car. "Why is it so hot here?"

"I don't know." He barely has the words out when a loud thud pierces the muggy air. Both men jump and turn to the car's hood where the lifeless body of a large black crow is sprawled across the now bloodied paint, one of its wings tucked under it and its beady eyes clouded over with a thin milky film.

"Holy shit?" Cliff says, inching forward to get a better look. "Where the hell did that come from?"

"Don't know." Greg shrugs and glances around the large yard. "But look." He points to a corner off to the side of the house. "Jesus, there's dozens of them. Are they all dead? He squints and shades his eyes from the glaring sun. "It's like it snowed dead black birds."

"What the hell," Cliff says, pulling off his coat, tossing it onto the front seat and closing the door. Should we call someone?"

"I think we should check on the old woman first," Greg says, pulling his right foot from the mud and stepping forward.

Cliff scans the yard. "I don't see any other birds? Just crows. That doesn't make sense. Why the hell is it just crows?"

"You're asking me?" Greg says. He jumps back as another crow falls from the sky, nearly missing him. He looks up to see the sun is now all but blocked from view by a thick, dense haze that has crept over the property, coving it like a dome. The air is still and the quietness envelops them. The only sound they hear is the sickening thud made by the bodies of the large black crows as they smack the ground.

"This is crazy," Cliff says, wiping the beads of sweat from his forehead. "I know it's warm, but there's no way it should be this freakin' hot. Was it this hot when we left town?"

Reaching the rotting steps that lead up to the door, Greg says, "No, but if there's one thing I've learned, it's that nothing that happens in this town ever makes sense."

"True. Especially as far as the crows go," Cliff adds ignoring the familiar chill that now races up his spine. He knocks on the paint-chipped door. He waits a few seconds before he knocks again and calls out, "Mrs. Underwood? . . . It's the police. Can you please open the door?"

"That's odd," Greg says. "She always knows when someone's here. Last time she even opened the door before we had chance to knock. There's no way she didn't hear the car. Like I said, something doesn't feel right."

"I agree," Cliff nods, grasping the door latch and pushing it inward. It easily swings open.

Poking his head through the door, Greg glances around the small but immaculately cleaned kitchen. There's no sign of the elderly woman.

"Clara," he calls out. He pauses and then calls again. "Clara Underwood? Are you in here? It's the police. Do you remember us?"

"I don't like this," Cliff says, following his friend into the kitchen. Clara Underwood is the town's oldest resident and apparent keeper of all secrets related to the mystical crows that inhabit the community.

"Neither do I," Greg nods, stepping into the centre of the kitchen where they had last talked with her. He eyeballs the room and notices all the pictures are gone. "That's not right," he whispers, glancing at the empty spots where the photos had been secured. "There is no way the old woman would take down her pictures. They're all she talked about—they're all she basically has left."

"Agreed," Cliff says, noting that a door just off the kitchen that leads to a small bedroom is open a crack. The icy chill now makes him shudder. "Let's check in there," he says, taking a step toward the door.

"Easy," Greg cautions, following closely behind his friend. "You don't know what's behind that door."

"You don't have to tell me twice," Cliff whispers as he reaches the room. Slowly pushing the door open, he peeks inside. His breath catches in his throat. "Jesus!"

"What?" Greg joins him in the doorway. "What did you find?"

"Clara," Cliff answers, stepping aside the room to give his friend a better view of the elderly woman who is laid out on her bed. She's dressed in a long white gown and her hands are folded purposely across her chest. It looks as though she was going to a formal dance or dinner, or maybe even a wedding, but it's clear she's dead.

Studying her body, Greg says, "She's been dead for a few days. I don't see any signs of foul play though. It looks like she just lied down and died. She looks very peaceful . . . and content."

"Okay, friend," Cliff adds. "I don't know about you, but this just went from being freaky to over-the-top creepy."

"It's definitely unusual," Greg nods as he approaches the bed that's in the centre of the small and cluttered bedroom. "This just feels off to me. I can't explain it."

"What do you mean?"

"I don't really know," Greg admits as he pulls a pair of rubber gloves from his back pocket. As a forensic investigator he always makes sure he has a pair of gloves on him wherever he goes. He learned early in his career that he should always be prepared. Pulling them over his large hands, he bends and takes hold of a large, black-leather bound *Bible* the deceased woman is clutching to her chest as if she is holding it close to her heart. He can tell from its appearance that it's very old.

"What is it?"

"It's a *bible*," Greg replies, flipping through the pages. "And it's got a whole bunch of names and dates written all over the front pages. There's lots of them and some go back a few hundred years."

"Some people write important family dates and events in their *bibles*," Cliff replies. "My grandmother used to do that. Whenever someone was born or died in the family, or when they got married, she'd write it in the front of the *bible*."

"Hmmm." Greg continues to scan the pages that contain the entries made in various handwriting styles and what seems to be a variety of inks. "This is interesting. Clearly, this has been going on for a long time. These entries go way back."

Cliff notices a piece of paper fall from the *bible*. "Look," he says as the paper floats to the dusty floor.

"Looks like a note of some sort," Greg says, bending to retrieve the paper. "It was stuffed inside the *bible*." Unfolding the faded paper, he adds, "It looks like she left a message of some kind."

"So what does it say?"

"You won't believe this, but it looks like it's been left for someone named Alex, whoever that is."

"Alex," Cliff shrugs. "Can't think of anyone named Alex right off the top of my head."

"Are you sure?" Greg asks.

Cliff pauses and then finally says. "We'll, actually, I do know of an Alex, but he's just a baby."

"Whose baby," Greg asks.

"Lily Pittmann's," Cliff answers.

"Isn't she Clara's great-granddaughter?" Greg asks.

"That's right," Cliff nods. Pausing, he then asks, "What does the message say?"

Reviewing the paper, Greg answers, "It simply says, 'Six crows gold . . .'"

Coming soon ...

Six Crows Gold

When the nightfall comes, the lonely crows call. Their mournful cackling fills the night skies and spreads their message of despair, telling all who inhabit this small town that the powerful and majestic black birds are searching. They are looking for the one who will make their world complete.

Tradition dictates they find the new keeper, for the keeper is their reason for life. The old woman was with them for a long time. She gave them their purpose, but it's been over two years since she died. In that time, they've been lost, without a guardian to guide them and to show them the way.

When the old woman died, a part of them died with her, but they know there is another one somewhere in this town. There must be. There always is.

It is their mission to find the one. Since the time of the old woman's death, the six crows have wandered the countryside searching and waiting for the one who will rise up and take her place.

They know he or she will soon make their presence known to them, for that is the reason for their existence.

They sense the time is near and it is the duty of the black six to find the golden one. They will keep looking. It is their destiny to find and, no matter the cost, it is their duty to protect the keeper.